BENE

A Tale of Obsession

In memory of Len Johnson,
a good friend and fellow digger.

BENEATH

A Tale of Obsession

JOHN AUBIN

Published by John Aubin Books

A CIP catalogue record for this book is available from the British Library.

ISBN 978-1-7396959-8-9 (Paperback)
ISBN 978-1-7396959-9-6 (ePub)

Typeset by Clare Brayshaw

Manufacturer: York Publishing Services Ltd
64 Hallfield Road, Layerthorpe, York YO31 7ZQ
Tel: 01904 431213 | Email: enquiries@yps-publishing.co.uk
Website: www.yps-publishing.co.uk

Represented by: Authorised Rep Compliance Ltd.
Ground Floor, 71 Lower Baggot Street, Dublin D02 P593, Ireland
www.arccompliance.com

1

The café stood at a meeting of alleyways, or *calli*, as the Venetians know them. It had a broad, plate-glass window with a door to one side, and inside was an open room set with tables and benches and a serving bar along one wall. It was an old building with a ceiling framed by narrow beams of black oak that ran from front to rear, positioned so close together that the white plaster between them was no more than a foot or so wide. The effect was to darken the room, even though it was lit by the large front window. Opposite, the window was overshadowed by high tenement buildings with blank, shuttered windows.

Beneath the café window ran a broad, wooden ledge before which a number of high stools were placed. At the end of the ledge by the door lay a tattered heap of newspapers intended to be picked up by customers to read with the *caffè* and the *panini* that the establishment served. To sit on one of these stools and stare out through the window gave an uninterrupted view down the narrow, stone-paved *calle* that made a junction here. It was the perfect place to watch people passing by – locals and students (for university buildings were not far away), and occasional tourists, maps and guidebooks in hand, who had penetrated here from St. Mark's over the Accademia Bridge.

This day a stranger sat here and looked out. The winter afternoon was dark with rain, swirled by the wind between the high roofs and walls of the enclosing buildings, spattering on the grey stone of the *calli* so that they ran bright with water. Few people passed. Those that did were muffled against the wind and rain, heads down, baskets or satchels clasped under arms, coat tails flying. No tourists were amongst them, not in this weather, not at this time of year. Which made the presence of the stranger unusual, so much so that the proprietor and his assistant kept looking across at the figure sat on one of the stools at the window ledge, staring outwards, always outwards, looking down the *calle* that ran like a pointing finger towards the café, as if waiting for someone. But that person did not come. At last the stranger rose, paid at the bar for a *caffè macchiato*, largely undrunk, and left. The doorbell jangled behind.

2

He stood up and stepped back, and saw that the line of stones he had revealed made an arc that continued into the side of the trench. He looked at his watch. Two hours ago this had been a patch of hummocky grass covered with cow parsley and trailing brambles, and now it was laid bare – a neat, straight-sided hole, seven feet by four feet, dug down two feet or so, and the dark earth piled up in a compact mound beside. Anthony thought: I may be more than sixty, and feeling it a bit now, but I can still dig!

He climbed from the hole and stood on its edge, looking down. Yes, the limestone was definitely making a curve, and the earth between it and the end of the trench was much more clayey than the darker earth within the angle of the curve. Here also, there were far more stones with pieces of red Roman tile amongst them than on the far side of the limestone. Anthony felt a stir of excitement after the labour of digging. He seemed to have found something structural – just possibly the curving wall of a building, or perhaps even....the word 'well' came into his mind, but he pushed it aside: it was far too early for such speculation.

He pulled his sweat-soaked shirt from his back and straightened himself. Warm sunlight played on his face and neck and bare forearms, his fair skin already reddening with the sun. It was always the same after the long, dark days of winter. An hour in the sun and his face would begin to glow like a red bulb. The Easter holiday had been unseasonably hot this year.

Alongside his trench, a hedgerow separating him from the rest of the archaeological site was already in full leaf. As he watched, a white butterfly floated amongst the heads of cow parsley protruding through the pile of earth he had dumped. Birds sang and fussed within the hedgerow, and insects hummed about his ears, some settling on his damp flesh so he had to slap them away. Beyond, a broad field rising to a distant crest was already coloured by a growing crop, as if it was a picture that a child had at first painted brown, and then later added splashes of green.

A sudden harsh clanging split the air. It was the call, rung out on an old cracked bell, for the morning tea break. Anthony made his way stiffly – really this heavy work did not help his joints these days! – on a narrow path that passed through the hedgerow and emerged onto the main part of the site, where the walls and surfaces of a Roman villa, exposed in previous years, were being freshly cleaned by diggers on this first day of the yearly excavation work.

There seemed to be a fair number of volunteers this year, Anthony thought, as he approached the old static caravan, with a large, green-canvas tent erected beside it, which made up the site base. Some young people, probably students, were collecting polystyrene beakers of tea from an urn inside the tent.

Anthony spotted the site director emerging from the caravan and went up to him. 'I've got something that looks interesting, Brian.'

The director – a tall, big-bellied man of about the same age as Anthony, wearing a tee shirt and shorts – raised his eyebrows questioningly.

'It's early days, but it could be a drainage sump.' He would not mention the possibility of a well yet. He would only look foolish if all he was left with was a muddy, irregular pit.

'Ah! A sump would make sense. The ditch would discharge into it then. You might have some good finds. I'll come and have a look after tea.'

The reason Anthony had been asked to dig his trench at that particular spot had been hopefully to locate an early ditch that bordered the main villa house, the course of which was known up to a point some ten feet from the hedgerow. This ditch, when sections had been cut across it in earlier seasons of work, had been very prolific in finds, which showed it predated the stone-walled villa by possibly two hundred years.

'Oh, by the way,' Brian called out, as Anthony turned away to get his tea, 'You'll need help there now. I'll send someone over.'

Anthony groaned inwardly. He was one of the old stalwarts on the site, and preferred to dig by himself, or, if he must, with one or two regulars whom he knew well, but who weren't present this Easter. Really, Brian, for whom he'd dug for many years, should know better and not give him a newcomer like this.

Anthony felt morose and tired after some taxing months of late. This was to be his relaxation – and how he needed to be able to relax again! He had even arrived early and got under way before most of the others were on site. The last thing he wanted now was some bright-eyed beginner jabbering away at him, who would need to be instructed in what to do and how to do it, taking away all the enjoyment that he found in this activity. It was far more than a mere hobby to him. It was an interest – almost an obsession at times – that provided him with both intellectual and physical satisfaction.

To pare away the soil, to reveal what had been lost for so many centuries and to expose it to the light again; to bring the past to the present, making it fuse once more with the living day, these were the things that Anthony most enjoyed – and for their contemplation he needed solitariness and silence. But, even as he thought this, he knew what a miserable old codger he was becoming. Really, he told himself, you're turning quite cranky. Why are you so dismissive of other people? And why are you so frightened of youth? Is it because, as your joints begin to creak and the spring sap fails to rise so high within you, you are envious of young people? Is that the true reason why you are always complaining about them today?

Anthony obtained a beaker of tea, swapping some banter with one of the regulars he knew, and, sipping his tea, stood aside from the others, reflecting on the site – this small patch of countryside that he had known now for more than twenty years. The Roman villa here was a research excavation, a great luxury in the modern world where most excavation work these days was carried out by professional archaeology units ahead of the destruction of whole landscapes through development needs, and under great time pressures too. The day of the open-area excavation spread over many leisurely years, led perhaps by an academic with particular research objectives, and making use of amateur volunteer labour, lay largely in the past. So here at Glastington in Somerset, it was a rarity to find an excavation, run by an amateur group, going on year after year, slowly building up a picture of a complete Roman house and its accompanying farming estate.

Anthony remembered when he had first come to the site, on a hot August day in the early 2000s, driving the long, bumpy track from the village, treacherous in wet weather, and pitching his tent close to that same hedgerow where he now dug. In that first year, only the main block of the third century villa house had been known, but subsequently two wings had been traced and excavated, then various outbuildings that were set around a central courtyard. As layers had been peeled away, earlier phases in the villa's life were revealed, in particular the first small, timbered house from which the later stone villa had developed.

Many excavation seasons had passed, springs and autumns (even the winters of some years), with satisfaction from much hard work done, and at times bursts of excitement as discoveries were made; many passing friendships formed, some more permanent than others – for a year, two years, three years, and more – then disappearing as the course of life took other directions. Anthony was now about the last of the old brigade he had known from all those years back who still came regularly; apart from Brian Radleigh, the site director, of course, who had started it all off, and he seemed set to go on forever. And yet each year the site still filled with new diggers and fresh enthusiasm. Who of these people, thought Anthony looking around, would return for the main August excavation this year?

Anthony finished his tea and returned to his trench. A black beetle had fallen into the deepest part of the hole, and he rescued it from its plight, holding the scaly shape cupped in his hands, antennae and legs moving frantically against his flesh. He deposited it carefully on a patch of bare earth beneath the hedgerow, and returned to work.

He decided both to lengthen and widen the trench, so as to see more of the curving line of limestone. This meant working from the top again, opening a trench parallel with the one he had already dug, leaving just a thin baulk of earth between the two which he could knock out later. He was busy working at this, wielding a mattock against the hard soil, compressed over the centuries by innumerable plough teams turning here on the field's headland, when he heard a rustling of the grass behind him. Lowering the mattock, and swinging round, his face wet with sweat, he saw Brian approaching, his weighty body uncertain on the uneven ground, and behind him a woman – a tall, graceful, youthful woman, his first impression.

The sweat was running in his eyes, and he brushed it away with the back of his hand, relaxing his features into a welcoming smile.

'Let's see what you have then.' Brian tottered over the newly dug earth to the edge of the trench and looked down. 'Oh, yes, I see what you mean.'

With some difficulty, he lowered his bulk into the hole and stabbed at the earth with a trowel taken from the back pocket of his shorts. A shower of stone and fragments of tile shot away from the point. Almost at once, Brian's free hand closed over something on the ground, and he held it up. 'Pot. A nice rim. I'd say 3rd century.'

The woman was bending forward to look and he placed the pottery sherd in her hands. She turned it over, wiping earth away from the curvature of the rim.

'Very nice.' Her voice was throaty and accented. Anthony noticed this at the same time as a flash of irritation filled him at not being handed the piece of pot first. He reached across and took the fragment from her, examined it briefly, and then dropped it into a plastic finds tray at his feet.

'It looks like what you've got is the upper fill of a feature,' Brian said. 'It could just be a pit, with a lot of stone at the edge, or it could be deliberately stone-lined. If it's the latter, we might have more than a sump – we could even have a well here. There must have been one somewhere, very likely more than one over the life of the villa. We should know more when you've done the extension and cleaned up.'

So Brian's mentioned a well, Anthony thought. I didn't dare to. Again, he was filled with irritation – at himself mainly for not having the confidence to put forward the idea first.

Brian was hauling himself out of the trench and Anthony held out a hand to help him. Once back on the surface, Brian made the introductions.

'Anthony, this is Giuditta. She's dug before in Italy. Giuditta, Anthony will look after you.' And with that very summary statement, he had turned and was stumbling away.

'I'm sorry I didn't catch your name.' Anthony looked at the young woman anxiously. In fact, he had heard the name – or at least the sound of it – but it was not one he knew and he did not dare try to repeat it. He didn't want to look foolish in front of her.

'Giuditta'. She said it slowly, emphasising the syllables. 'It's like your Judith, with an 'a' instead of the 'h' at the end.'

'And you are Italian?'

'Yes, all Italian.' She smiled at him.

She wore a yellow tee-shirt and grey trousers. He tried to keep his eyes on her face, but could not help noting her breasts – small but sharp against her tee-shirt. Her dark brown hair was swept back and tied in a pony tail. Her face had a hawk-like profile, with a large nose and widely-spaced eyes. She was not the greatest beauty, perhaps, but certainly a most attractive woman. When she gazed directly at him, her features appeared to merge and soften, so that when she smiled he seemed drawn into that smile, and found himself smiling too.

How old was she? She was young – at least to him, she was – but there was a certain maturity about her face that told Anthony she was probably in her thirties – her mid-thirties, very likely. All these things Anthony absorbed in those first few moments of meeting her.

'So you've dug before?' he said.

'Yes, back in Italy. But some years back now.'

'What's brought you here then, if I may ask?'

'I wanted to get involved in archaeology again.' She was hesitant for the briefest of moments over some of her words, enough to show she was speaking in a second language, although fluent in the main. Her voice was quite deep, but her accent made it rise in places, so that to Anthony's fancy the sound was a little like the swelling motion of the sea

I mustn't ask her too many questions, he thought, feeling oddly uncertain of this woman who had been thrust upon him. Let's get under way. We can talk as we work. Aware of her cool eyes on him, he felt suddenly awkward in his sweat-stained clothes, knowing she was waiting for him to tell her what to do. He wondered how extensive her archaeological experience had been.

'What's your shovelling like? It'll be hard work. I'll cut and you shovel. Once we've cleared down to there' – he pointed at the existing trench – 'it'll be easier. Then we'll need to trowel up the surface.'

She nodded, and picked up a shovel from the tools lying on the grass. Her long fingers wrapped themselves around the handle. Was she used to heavy work? Anthony did not want those fine hands to be blistered.

But she proved strong, stepping down into the growing new hole to shovel away the clods of earth that Anthony loosened with the mattock and then pulled back behind him with the flat of the blade. She pitched the soil onto the spoil heap with all the efficiency of a fit man, but, in that particular feminine way Anthony had observed before that made use of the whole strength of the body rather than just that of the arms, so that the back was hunched and the length of the throw shortened. Here, because the spoil heap was close to the trench, it did not matter.

'Here, you take a turn,' Anthony said, handing her the mattock. He was proud of his skill using this tool, but did not want to monopolise it, perhaps giving her the impression that he considered it 'men's work' only.

And she was adept at that too, swinging the mattock with considerable force against the leading edge of uncut earth so that it splintered into clods. Standing behind her, Anthony saw dark stains of sweat begin to spread across her back, and, when she turned, her face was flushed, with loosened strands of hair plastered to her forehead. He thought how appealing that looked.

Seeing his eyes on her, she attacked the earth face again, knocking down the clods and then fragmenting them with the blade. She seemed to be working now with extra force, and Anthony thought this woman's trying to show that, whatever I can do, she can do as well. It's best I say nothing. And so he shovelled away the loose soil she had created without comment, and then called for a break.

They sat for a few minutes side by side on the edge of the trench while Anthony told her more about the site and the discoveries that had been made there, and what the current programme of work was about. Occasionally, she would ask him a question, but for the most part she sat in silence, so that he felt almost obliged to keep on talking, thinking at the same time that perhaps she would like him simply to be quiet. He hadn't had much experience of late in dealing with young women, and, as ever it seemed now, he lacked confidence in himself. At times she seemed to be lost in her own thoughts, as if all this – and he too – were a background to her real interests, which lay without and beyond anything at present she was prepared to talk about.

A walker, following the edge of the field with a dog, passed them and paused to see what they were doing. Giuditta hugged the dog to her chest as it leapt up to lick at her face. It was an Irish setter, with a lolling tongue, and its owner tried to pull it away, but Giuditta clearly loved the dog and spoke some words of Italian to it. Anthony thought what a charming little scene it made.

They went to work again, and by lunchtime had almost completed clearing the new trench to the desired depth. The curve of limestone was now much clearer and substantial. Would it indeed prove to make a circle?

'After lunch, I'll break down the baulk and we can trowel up the whole area,' Anthony said. 'That'll help your hands as well.'

As he had feared, her right palm had blistered. He had seen her winding a handkerchief around it, so he knew she had a problem.

'They'll give you a plaster at the caravan. You may be able to borrow some gloves.'

'It's nothing.' Her manner was suddenly abrupt. She was clearly a woman who did not like to be fussed over. Another lesson learnt, thought Anthony, as the lunch bell sounded across the site. Women! How very difficult they can be to understand!

Lunch at Glastington Roman villa during the Easter dig was very much a matter of the diggers bringing their own food. Later, during the main summer excavation, hot food would be provided on site. Anthony sat in his car to eat his sandwiches and read the newspaper, disdaining to join the group gathered around the site caravan. Afterwards he would go over to fetch a beaker of tea and exchange a word or two with acquaintances, so as not appear too anti-social. For the moment, however, he just wanted to relax, without the need for the constant trivial conversation that some people seemed to find essential to the enjoyment of their day.

He was tired also. He had slept badly last night at the bed and breakfast place where he always stayed while on the dig. In fact, he could not remember a really good night's sleep for many months, ever since Pamela had suddenly announced to him that she wanted their relationship to end. For the last couple of years it had been struggling on, largely through his own determination – desperately, obstinately, ignoring all the clear signals that something was badly wrong. But then it had been she – and not him – who had made the final decision. They had split up, and he had left her house and gone back to living in his Bromley flat on the southern fringes of London, which very fortunately he had not sold, although that had been the earlier intention.

The shock of the final break, and all the months of misery, suspicion, and name-calling that had gone before, had dented him badly. His self-esteem and confidence had slowly been pared from him, a bit like the soil he liked to scrape away here, layer by layer, removing his sense of well being and the very structure and meaning of his life – or so it had seemed to him in the darker moments. No wonder sleep now came only fitfully to him.

When he eventually wandered over to the caravan, it was to find quite an animated group, Giuditta amongst them, seated in a circle on canvas chairs.

'Ah, Anthony, there you are,' said Brian, his face full of a massive sandwich of cold sausage. 'Giuditta's been saying you're making good progress.'

'Yes, we have.' He looked across at her, but she was gazing absently away, as if now disinterested. She was taking small bites with perfect white teeth from a sandwich, cut neatly into squares, brought from a plastic container on her lap. She had loosened her hair from the tie at the back, and it hung now to her shoulders, framing her face and hiding the angularity of her profile with its beaked nose and high cheek bones. Her dark brown hair caught the sun, bringing out reddish tints that glowed as she moved her head.

'Have you got a well then?' one stout lady in the circle asked. He knew her by sight, but not her name, although she had been coming to the dig for years.

'Perhaps.' Someone's been talking already, Anthony thought. Probably Giuditta has said something, or even Brian himself. He added the usual caution, heard frequently in archaeology: 'But it's much too early to tell.'

He turned away to fetch himself some tea from the urn in the tent, hearing a trill of 'How exciting!' behind him. Really, these people, they had no idea about the work involved. It was not all about finding exciting things.

Yet a well – if there was indeed a well – might contain an enormous array of finds, including possibly, if it should turn out still to be water-logged, artefacts of wood or leather. By any measure that would be exciting. But he too was getting carried away now.

Anthony gulped back his tea. He looked around the group in their chairs, hearing them deep in conversation about some trashy television programme, and decided not to waste any more time. He returned to his newly expanded trench.

He had knocked away the baulk that had been left, and with the mattock was lightly reducing the surface to the level of the limestone slabs revealed in the first trench when he heard Giuditta returning.

'You begin without me?' Just occasionally her English was imperfectly phrased.

Anthony found himself grinning. 'I'm afraid so. I couldn't wait.'

She was tying her hair back again, twisting it through the tie held in her fingers. Without thinking, he paused and stood watching her. With the tie snapped into place, she brushed out the pony tail with her fingers.

'You've stopped? Why is that?'

Anthony had no answer. She climbed into the trench and began to shovel away the loose earth he had left. After a while he said, 'You know, I think we can work separately now. You take that half and I'll do this.'

He indicated the two sections of the trench. 'It's mainly a trowelling job. See if you can pick up the limestone over there.' He traced with his trowel how he thought the curving stone might cross the far corner of the extended trench.

So now they both knelt, with buckets and hand shovels beside them, cutting the earth with their trowels and dragging the soil towards them, then shaving the surface smooth again. Giuditta was more talkative now. She told him how in Italy, at a place called Aquileia – 'it was once the fourth largest Roman town in Italy' – she had been the first to locate a mosaic floor.

'There were just some loose red cubes at first, and then I could see there were more, these white and still together. I trowelled further and suddenly there was a black bird's head looking up at me….'

She squealed. Anthony thought this was to emphasise her story, but when he looked at her he saw she was holding up a round, green object.

'You've got a coin. Brilliant. Well done!'

There was recording work to be completed now, measuring in the exact find spot and writing a description of its context in the 'small finds book'. He let Giuditta take the coin to the finds hut (actually, just part of the site caravan), and soon she returned with Brian.

'It's a *dupondius* of the Emperor Hadrian,' Brian said, spitting on the coin and cleaning it with the ball of his thumb. 'See, how clear his head is.'

Anthony had found many coins in his time, but it was still fascinating to see the detail on them emerging from the soil. They made such a definite statement of the past; not of that misty, imagined half-world of yesteryear, ill understood, beloved of romanticists, but of a most certain real time, as defined and sure in all its details as our own age. The emperor's head, looking out from this coin across nearly two thousand years, seemed still to carry his authority, together with the structure and discipline of the society he ruled, into a world that would have been inconceivable to him, yet one that inevitably will vanish in its own turn as the further centuries pass.

'Since the coin comes from the top layer of our feature, that surely makes the date it was filled in early,' said Brian. 'And where there's one coin, there might be others.'

But there weren't that day. They did make very good progress, however, revealing the continuing curve of the limestone. In Giuditta's section of the trench, in particular, it was very clear. She had done an excellent job in picking out the stones, and Anthony was impressed by her work. By the end of the day, they had more than half a circle revealed, which, if projected to a full circle, would give a diameter of just over five feet.

It had been a long afternoon, divided by a further tea break. This time Anthony had remained with the group about the tea urn, and overheard Giuditta telling some other diggers that she would be staying for the two further days of the dig and going home on the Monday evening. She had not told him this herself, but then he had not asked her. Why was that? Perhaps, because he had grown happy in her company and had not wanted to hear of it ending. Ridiculous, he thought. What a sentimental old fool I'm becoming.

As five o'clock approached and they began to put their tools away, gathering their finds trays together to take up to the caravan, he asked her where she was staying.

'At a – how do you say? – bed and breakfast that Brian booked for me.'

'Ah, yes, of course.'

Anthony knew Brian had an arrangement with local villagers to provide accommodation for those of his diggers who did not wish to camp on the site. The place where Anthony stayed, expensive as it was but much more pleasant and spacious than the B&Bs Brian generally organised, was on a farm three miles away.

'Well, I'll see you tomorrow.' They had dumped their trays on a wooden bench by the caravan. The finds had been sparse – other than the coin, only a few further pieces of pot and some bone, including part of the jaw of a goat or sheep.

She had a smear of dirt on her cheek, and he reached across as if to rub it away. She stepped back sharply.

'*Ma che ca!* What the hell are you doing?' Her voice was sharp.

'You've got some dirt there.' He was embarrassed. Had anyone overheard?

She spat on a handkerchief and rubbed at her cheek. 'Has it gone?'

'Yes.'

'I'm sorry.'

'No, it's me.' Suddenly she was smiling again.

Anthony turned and left her. She's strange, he thought. As highly strung and scratchy as a cat. But then all women are odd. It's best not to get too involved with them.

And yet, he reflected as he drove away: She's lovely and she's intelligent. Would that I were more her age.

3

Anthony had a meal that evening at the pub – the Red Cow – in Glastington village. He didn't feel all that hungry, but still ordered a steak, which he knew would arrive with the usual piles of chips and onion rings. Not feeling sociable, and wishing to avoid conversation with the few locals in the bar, he raised his newspaper in front of him and depressed himself with the various reports that filled the paper of Britain's collapsing economy.

Anthony had retired early from his civil service job some years back, after receiving a substantial inheritance on the death of his father. Now this money, carefully invested, had lost twenty percent of its value thanks to major falls on the stock market, and, to make matters much worse, the interest on his savings accounts had dwindled to next to nothing. Whereas he had once faced his twilight years with equanimity, now he was becoming increasingly worried that his money would 'see him through'. It was typical of the inverted values of contemporary society, he thought, turning the pages of the newspaper viciously, that the ne'er do well, the spendthrifts, and the idle speculators should gain the government's attention and be encouraged to borrow and spend more and more, while those who had worked hard, and been prudent saving their money, were amongst those worst hit by the recession. How he hated modern Britain!

Lowering the paper, he raised his pint glass to his lips and took a swig of the local ale – deep, smooth, and dark, a fine drink. His mood improving, he thought back on the day and the new woman's part in it. He wondered what she was doing now. Where would she go for an evening meal? He felt almost guilty about her. It was difficult for a woman on her own to do simple things, such as eating out. Then, he thought: shall I ask her to join me after the dig tomorrow? The idea was momentarily attractive. It even sent something of a tingle of anticipation through him. He had enjoyed her company. She was vastly younger than him – could be his daughter, indeed – but she made him feel good. He found himself smiling at the memory of his day with her, all but for that sudden reaction when he had tried – innocently enough – to touch her face. That had been his fault. He mustn't do anything so silly again.

He had asked her a fair number of questions about herself. He racked his memory to recall her answers. She had first come to England some twelve years ago – he thought he had got that right – to practice her English. He was confused by her education. She seemed to have completed a couple of degrees back in Italy – one in languages (he remembered that, but not where she had studied) and another at a university in Venice, the subject of which he didn't think she had told him. She appeared well versed in European history, so perhaps that had been her subject. Her archaeological interests seemed to have been pursued only as a hobby while she was living in Venice. Aquileia, where she'd dug, was not all that far away, she'd told him. He must look the place up on the internet.

What he didn't know, he realised, was what work she did in England, and where she lived. It was strange, but it had not occurred to him to ask those questions. Perhaps he had thought they were too personal, too immediately intrusive.

He went to the bar and topped his pint up with a further half. No more, or I'm in danger of being over the limit. I must be careful. He had lost his licence for drink driving many years back when he had worked in the publishing game. He had been entertaining a book wholesaler from South Africa in company with his sales director, and he had foolishly agreed to be the driver for the evening. After a boozy lunch in Winchester, which had lasted most of the afternoon, he had driven into a pedestrianised street by mistake, almost running over the boots of a passing policeman. The subsequent year's driving ban had cost him his job; not many publishers wanted a sales manager who was unable to drive. After a period of unemployment, he had been fortunate to find a job in the civil service with such a blot on his record.

That was not something he would tell.......What was her name now? Surely he hadn't forgotten it already. He recalled it with an effort – of course: Giuditta. He repeated the name in his mind, feeling a certain frisson at the sound – irrational as he knew that to be. He didn't understand why the name should excite him. Silly fool, he was. Old lecher as well.

He thought: I asked her quite a bit about herself, but did she ever ask one question about me? He didn't think she had. That showed then the extent of her interest in *him*. In any event, he felt there was little about him to be interested in. At sixty-four, he was still in good trim, six feet tall, and unbent, with a broad chest, relatively flat stomach, and a good head of hair. He was well muscled too. Much hard digging over the years – at other sites than Glastington, at a time when there had been a lot of archaeological work available to volunteers – had seen to that. But he was sure none of that would impress an attractive woman in her thirties. Young women were only drawn to older men by success, power, and money, and he was pretty sure he would measure up poorly in all those departments.

Would she be interested in the archaeology he had done since retirement? Or perhaps in his writing? As a man of leisure now, he had pursued his hobbies – travel and archaeology – and he had written a novel, which he thought was quite good. It had always been his ambition to write fiction. Although he had made many submissions to publishers and literary agents, the breakthrough to getting the novel published had not come – a cause of great frustration to him.

A young waitress brought him, as he had anticipated, a great plate of food. He folded his paper and strove to create a space on the small, circular table top.

'Any sauces or mustard?'

'No, thanks. I'm fine.'

'Well, enjoy.'

Always that awful expression these days. Enjoy. Enjoy what? Why should he have to enjoy anything? What a miserable, old fart he was turning into. He admitted that!

This misery and desire for isolation from other people had only come fairly recently. He knew it had much to do with the loss of Pamela. When he had met her – how long ago was it now? ten years at least – things had been very good. She had been happy. Her body, in fact, had glowed with happiness. And her body had been good – slim with good hips and breasts. Yes, she had been beautiful then – and a wonderful, sympathetic companion. Yet after a while – two years, three years? – the criticisms had begun.

'We're always doing your things,' she had complained. 'Never mine.'

'Well, what do you want to do?' he had asked, tetchily. But she had never said, apart from some vague generalisations about the need for lightness and life, and not always the past and the dead.

He admitted that perhaps he had overdone the history and archaeology at times, but once she had really enjoyed those things which they had seen and done together. There was no doubt of that: the many visits to places of historic or literary interest they had made, and her own participation at Glastington. How she had loved the digging, taking to it naturally and learning quickly. For a few seasons, indeed, she had been one of the mainstays of the site. But later it seemed she wanted to beat him over the head with it all, complaining that he was far too sombre, too melancholy – indeed, far too much stuck in the past. This criticism, he felt, was unfair. Or was it? Perhaps there was some truth in it. Shouldn't he have made a greater effort to understand her? But, God knows, how he had tried!

With the meal beneath his belt – literally, for he had to loosen the belt by a notch – he left the pub, and drove back through the black night to the farm where he was staying. As he arrived in the gravelled area that served as a car park, he noted there were now three other cars there. He groaned, for this would undoubtedly mean others at the communal breakfast table in the morning. On previous stays he had sometimes had interesting conversations over the toast and marmalade, but normally – even at the best of times and certainly now – all he wanted was his own company at breakfast without the need to gabble on to strangers. Yes, he had indeed turned into a most anti-social and disagreeable man!

This night he did sleep well. It must have been all the exercise that helped plunge him into deep slumber, for he woke at six with the bed scarcely disturbed and with his brain so full of sleep that it was a few moments before he realised where he was. He had been dreaming, and they had been most satisfying dreams, of an erotic nature even, sensations long vanished from his life.

Who had been the subject of the dreams? Had it been Pamela? He didn't think so. It had been some time since he had last viewed Pamela in such a light. She had put on a great deal of weight, and their physical relationship had slowly dwindled to a virtual nothingness. He would readily admit that this was not her fault alone. His own libido – if he must use such a dreadful world – had also become much suppressed, that's if it had ever been particularly lively! It was not a subject that he wished to dwell too much on.

So had last night's dreams then been of earlier days, earlier fantasies, or had they…- a sudden suspicion came to him – had they perhaps been of Giuditta? If so, that was odd too, for he had not really thought of her in such a light. But now he remembered that when she had been trowelling beside him, and reaching forward, he had seen her tee shirt slide up revealing the bare flesh of her mid-riff, and he had had the thought – he had to admit to it – of how nice it would be to touch that flesh But that had been a very fleeting, passing thing, nothing to trouble him for too long. No, it was absurd. He could be Giuditta's father. He had no reason – no need – to lust after the impossible. That was what stupid old men did, and he would not like to be regarded as such.

He showered and dressed, and went into breakfast. He was pleased to find he had the dining room to himself.

'It's not good weather for you,' said Mrs Reynolds, the landlady, as she took his order for scrambled egg and bacon.

'What do you mean?' Anthony had not looked outside yet.

'It's been raining. They say it'll clear up, though.'

Mrs Reynolds padded away, and Anthony got up from the table to push aside the net curtains and view the prospect without. He could see from the puddles on the garden terrace that the rain was still falling. Blast!

He had no sooner re-seated himself than the door opened and a middle-aged couple, wearing identical yellow jumpers emblazoned with the words 'Go Zero', came into the room. He exchanged morning greetings with them. After Mrs.

Reynolds had taken their orders, he was pleased to see the two were content to chat together. They seemed pleasant enough, quietly-spoken people, not like some of the loudmouths he had had to share breakfast with in the past.

When he heard the doorknob rattling again, however, and the sound of feet on the bare-boarded floor, his heart sank further. What would *these* people be like? They would have to sit close to him, since the far end of the table was now occupied by the other couple. He looked up, and was astonished to see Giuditta looking down at him. She had changed her yellow tee-shirt for a green one, and had a white cardigan draped loosely over her shoulders.

'I didn't realise you were staying here!' he exclaimed, aware of the eyes of the 'Go Zero' couple on them.

She was smiling. Her hair was freshly brushed; strands were still charged with static electricity, for he could see the individual hairs curling upwards. She sat down opposite him.

'Did Brian book you in here?' Anthony asked.

'Yes, he said the people I was due to stay with had had to go away suddenly. So he made a phone call and gave me directions to this place. I had a meal at his house before I drove here. He said you'd probably take me with you to the site today. I think I might get lost going the other way. Is that okay?

'Of course. He might have warned me, though. I could have left by now and missed you. He's got my mobile number.'

'I think he tried, but got no answer.'

'I must have been flat out.'

Her brow furrowed. 'Flat out, what is that?'

'Asleep. Unconscious.'

She laughed, dipping her head charmingly. 'Flat out.' She tested the words. 'I must remember that.'

How lovely she is, he thought, fresh and bright-eyed. He had not looked at her so closely face to face before.

With the arrival of a further couple at the table, they eat largely in silence.

'It's still raining,' Anthony said, as he squeezed a final cup of coffee from his pot. 'We can't dig in the rain. So there's little point in going to the site until it stops.'

'That's what I thought when I heard the rain on my window this morning. Oh well, I'll sit and read.'

Apart from her accent, and just the occasional hesitation, her English was generally faultless. It was easy to forget she was Italian; but then, looking at her dark hair and her high domed forehead, her wide brown eyes and the generous curve of her mouth, his impression – based probably on Italian actresses he had seen on film – was: could she be anything else? He didn't think he had ever spoken to an Italian woman before – German, yes, Spanish, French, and even Polish, but not Italian.

They got up from the table and went into the hallway outside that led to the bedrooms. Anthony had a sudden idea. He would ask her to come out on a trip with him, just somewhere nearby until the weather improved. But he felt shy of suggesting it. There was time yet for courage to come to him, for Giuditta was lingering, opening the front door and looking out. The rain was still pattering down out of a leaden grey sky, yet it was far from heavy. They could perhaps go into the local town and have an early lunch. By then, if Mrs. Reynolds' forecast was right, the rain might have stopped. Taking the plunge, Anthony suggested this.

He thought he had made a mistake when he saw her hesitate. Of course, she wouldn't want to be shut in a car with a man she scarcely knew. No sensible woman would put herself in that position. But he was wrong. Her hesitation was not about going with him, but their destination.

'That would be good, but I don't want to go to a town, Anthony.' It was the first time she had said his name. She emphasised the second syllable in a way an English person never would. 'I love the country. I love the rain. I want to be – how do you say? – outdoors.'

'It'll be wet.' What a silly comment that was to make. Of course, it would be wet. It was raining.

'We have boots. We have mackintoshes.' That word had clearly been learnt from a dictionary.

'Right. That's fine with me. Where shall we go then?'

He fetched a map from his room, and opened it over a table in the hallway, they standing close together while the 'Go Zero' couple left the dining room and pressed past them.

'Have a nice day.'

'Yes, you too.'

'What does Go Zero mean?' Giuditta asked when they had gone.

'Don't you know? Haven't you got something similar in Italy? It means they are very keen to save the planet; cut carbon emissions, that sort of thing.'

'Very keen? *Come un pazzo* – like a madman?'

'That's a bit unfair. We're all mad really. I mean to be in the state we are.'

For some reason, she giggled. He joined in her laughter. He felt suddenly bold and light-hearted. When she laughed, she bent her whole body forward, as if the act of standing was too much to contain the laughter. He could see, and almost feel, the vibrations of her body. He found himself longing to hold her, to let the laughter ripple over his hands. She made him laugh. It was a good medicine. But at all costs he mustn't make a fool of himself.

He decided to head for the fortified hill of South Cadbury, which lay only some five miles away as the crow flew, rather longer by the winding lanes. Anthony had dug there many years ago when he was young. He told Giuditta about this, pointing the place out on the map. She was immediately enthusiastic.

'When you were young, Anthony? When was that? Long before I was born?'

'Yes, I'm sure. It was the late 1970s. I had only just left school. You wouldn't have even been thought of then.'

Was that a sudden shadow that fell across her face, a tightening of her mouth? It would have been the chance to tell him her age, but she said nothing. They went to their rooms to prepare for the day.

4

Anthony's car was an ex-army Land Rover, which he had bought as a second car at a time before diesel fuel prices had rocketed and the 'Go Zero' admonitions of his breakfast table companions had become the approved, unchallengeable consensus of the day. His first service bill of well over £500 had also come as a shock. For those reasons, Anthony now used it rarely, but kept it taxed and tucked away in his garage, into which it just fitted like a hand in a snug glove. Evidence of its former military role was restricted to swirling dark green and black camouflage on the bodywork, a cluster of mysterious bolts and other fittings at front and rear, and some silver lettering stencilled on the inside of a door post, the import of which was meaningless to him.

Giuditta loved it when she saw it. 'Oh, I saw this on the site. I didn't know it was yours.' Wearing a yellow waterproof, she circled the vehicle and bent to look at the wheels, kicking at their knobbly treads with a booted foot.

'Can I drive?' She was suddenly like a small girl requesting a favour from her father.

'No, I'm sorry. It's not insured for you.'

Her mouth turned down and she looked sulky, but she brightened up when he opened the door for her and she clambered up into the front passenger seat.

'It's so high up! Do you have a dog, Anthony? It could sit here beside you and look out.'

'No, I'm afraid not. But I know what you mean. Like a farmer perhaps.'

'Yes, that's right. Like a farmer.'

'You're fond of dogs, aren't you?'

'I *love* dogs.'

The drive to South Cadbury was mainly along narrow, winding country lanes. Steep-sided hills overlooked flat valleys studded with well-tended farms, the fields stretching away grey in the splashing rain. The wiper blades slapped against the windscreen, sounding over the deep growl of the engine. The height of the Land Rover enabled Giuditta to see above the roadside hedgerows, and, when a darker mass of a hill, ringed on its lower slopes by trees, hove into view like a blunt fist raised against the sky, she commented on it excitedly.

'There! There! That's the hill I want to climb.'

'Well, that's fortunate,' said Anthony dryly, 'for it's where we're heading. You're looking at South Cadbury hillfort, the legendary Camelot, fortress of King Arthur.'

They parked by a pub in the village called The Camelot. The rain had almost stopped.

'When I dug here all those years ago,' Anthony said, 'I'm sure the pub was called something else. I can't remember what, though. We played skittles there and drank scrumpy.'

'What is scrumpy?'

'It's a type of rough cider. Very powerful.'

'Powerful?'

Anthony made a turning action with his hand in front of his head and Giuditta laughed.

'Ah, I understand. In Italy it is *cedro*. I don't like.'

'No?'

'We have Aperol though. It's my favourite drink. You

come to Venice and drink Aperol and you won't want your cider anymore.'

They fastened their rain-clothes against the continuing drizzle, and left the Land Rover, walking along the lane away from the village. Giuditta wore an olive green hat with a broad brim, beneath which she bundled up her hair; a few errant strands hung down at the back.

He felt elated in the company of this lovely woman, wanting others to look out from their houses and see them pass – to be amazed, to be jealous. How many times had he walked by himself of late, longing for such company. But the windows of the houses were dark and empty, and the village street silent except for the rainwater trickling in the gutters.

He began to tell her the story of South Cadbury; how legend made it one of the places frequented by King Arthur and his knights, and how the great king's wild night hunt was still said to be seen riding out from the gates. The hill was first fortified in the Iron Age when the summit plateau was encircled by parallel lines of ditches and ramparts.

'But when we dug here in the late 1970s,' he told her, 'we found evidence that the place had been refortified in the Dark Ages – the 5th and 6th centuries, that is – the very period associated with King Arthur, who may have been a local warlord leading resistance to the Saxon invaders.'

He was losing his inhibitions with her. He could see she was hanging on his words, and could not believe this was happening to him. How sudden and unexpected were the many twists and turns of life. Yet, he knew not to get too carried away, as, for sure, this would be just a short-lived episode, over almost as soon as it had begun. What else could he expect? It was best just to enjoy her company while he could.

He continued telling her about the hillfort, 'It was one of the big excavations of that time. There were many students taking part – and others too, volunteers like myself. We all stayed at a school nearby: it was their holiday time, you see.'

'You were young then. I bet you got up to many things.'

'Oh, a few. Nothing I regret too much, though.'

She laughed, 'You have some memories, Anthony, I'm sure. You must tell me some time.'

At least I'm not boring her, he thought. Not that there would be too much to tell.

Some vehicles passed them on the lane, splashing water against their legs. A tractor pulling a great yellow bowser forced them to press themselves against the hedge. The driver raised his hand in acknowledgement, and Giuditta waved cheerily back. At last they came to a trackway leading off on the right.

'This is the way up,' Anthony said. 'It leads to the eastern gateway.'

They stumbled up the track, which became increasingly steep, the stony surface cut deep by rivulets running with rain water.

'I drove a Land Rover up here during the dig.' Anthony was breathing fast as he struggled to keep up with Giuditta's pace.

'You did? You had one then too?'

'No, it belonged to the dig. I was one of the few insured to drive it. The students weren't allowed to.'

She stopped, and turned back to look at him. 'You weren't a student then?'

'No, I didn't go to university. I was working on a farm at that time.'

'Really!' She said that word with such an emphasis of curiosity that it spurred him on to further disclosures he might otherwise have thought twice about.

'I'd had enough of education. I wanted to get out into the

world. I didn't get on too well with my parents, you see, so I didn't want to be dependent on them anymore.'

'But couldn't you get a grant for university?'

'I'd fluffed my 'A' levels. They weren't good enough. I would have had to sit two of them again.'

'So you went to a farm. Were you learning farming?'

'No, I was just knocking about. Getting experience, I suppose. It was good fun.'

She gave him a keen look, then turned away, and continued up the track. He clomped along rather disconsolately in her wake, watching her long, trousered legs bite easily at the rising ground, her body in the waterproof yellow bright against the dark bushes to either side. He knew he had said far too much and given her a poor impression of himself. Now, why had he done that, when he could have told her anything? Something, at least, far more purposeful. What was wrong with him? It was unlike him to open up about himself in this way. He had not even told Pamela these things.

They came to the fort gateway. It had begun raining harder again. Away from the shelter of the trees where the bare hilltop began, they could see the rain slanting against a sky still grey with cloud.

'We'll get too wet,' said Anthony. 'Let's wait awhile.'

Giuditta seemed impatient to be out in the open, rain or no rain, but allowed herself to be led into the shelter of a high holly bush that grew out of the rampart bank close to the gateway.

'They excavated this gateway – it was some years after I was here – and found many skeletons, some with evidence of wounds on the bones. There seems to have been a massacre here, possibly when the Roman army stormed the fort.'

She didn't say anything at first. She was looking out at the rain-swept slope ahead.

'It's creepy here.'

'Yes, isn't it? A heavy atmosphere...'

'Come, Anthony. Let's go.'

She actually tugged at his hand as if to pull him away, and started out into the open. Anthony followed her rather reluctantly. The rain slashed at his waterproof jacket and against his face. His head was bare, and water began trickling from his hair into his eyes.

Giuditta was well ahead, climbing to the highest point of the hill, where the flat, grassy summit was surrounded on three sides by steep terracing. He caught up with her as she stood there, spinning her body around with her arms held out horizontally.

'I love the rain.' Her eyes shone bright beneath the rim of her hat.

'So do I. Normally, anyhow.'

He would have loved to clasp her to him, and press those wet lips to his. But he knew he would never dare. He could not forget how she had reacted when he had reached to wipe her cheek. And now she was away, running down one of the terraced slopes towards the edge of the hill.

He followed, thinking this woman is crazy. Why am I doing this? Why am I chasing after her? What sort of fantasy am I getting dragged into? It is absurd. I must not crave the unattainable.

All this, of course, passed through his head in a flash, so he may not even have been properly aware of it. By the time he caught up with her, he was in control of himself again, as if no crazed impulse had ever been. At least, he thought, I have not made a fool of myself.

He stood beside her as she looked out across the side of the hill into the distance, where a pattern of small, square fields spread towards the foot of a further high hill half a mile away.

The rain was easing To the south – the direction in which they were looking – the greyness of the sky was lighter.

'We dug a trench across the ramparts here,' Anthony told her. 'From the top, where we're standing, all the way to the bottom. The director called us his goats. Those that dug on the plateau – where we were just now – they were his sheep. The ditches were deep – much deeper than you see them now – and the faces of the ramparts bare rock. It was this upper rampart we're standing on that was rebuilt in the Dark Ages.' – he kicked with a foot at the turf beneath him – 'and a post-built hall was built on that high plateau. Then, whoever was here at that time – whether King Arthur or not; more likely 'not" – he laughed at his own little joke – 'they left, and the hill's been unoccupied ever since. It makes you think, doesn't it, all those lives lived out here, and now just the grass and the wind and the sky.'

'It's a good place,' she said quietly. 'Thank you for bringing me.'

He felt such simple pleasure at those words. 'Let's get a coffee and a bun,' he said. 'And think about getting to Glastington. It looks like the weather's improving.'

The rain had stopped by the time they reached the bottom of the hill, and they shed their wet outer clothes in the back of the Land Rover and crossed the road to the pub. They took off their muddied boots at the door. There were no memories for Anthony inside; the interior looked as if it had been greatly changed in recent years. He had a recollection of a skittle alley at the side of the pub with rusty bicycles propped up against it. Everything looked far posher than it had been in the 1970s.

They had their coffee, and then, on checking his watch and seeing that the time was fast approaching noon, Anthony ordered cheese rolls by way of an early lunch. Giuditta tried to pay, but he insisted she put her money away. When at last they left, he was surprised to see the sky had cleared and the sun was shining.

They arrived at Glastington an hour later. Anthony had tried a short cut through the tangle of lanes, but had got lost. The Land Rover had no SatNav and Giuditta had proved of little use at map reading. So Anthony was in a rather flustered state when he eventually drove up the track, now slippery with mud and wet grass, to the villa site. To his surprise, tinged with something like alarm, he found the diggers already hard at work. He felt absurdly self-conscious as he emerged from the Land Rover with Giuditta beside him. He saw Brian looking across at him; nothing was said but Anthony wondered what he might be thinking.

The Glastington site was noted for drying extremely quickly, even after heavy rain. Once back in his trench, all Anthony had to do was soak up a few puddles with sponges and the surface was ready to dig again. However, care was needed, as the still damp soil tended to stick to boots and make something of a mess if trodden onto trowelled surfaces.

He set Giuditta to work, first scraping off the newly sponged earth with a hand-shovel, warning her to keep a sharp lookout for any finds. It was just as well he did, for within five minutes she let out a cry and held up a green metal object in her fingers which she had plucked from the shovel face. Anthony, who had been busy with paperwork, took it from her and saw she had found a pair of bronze tweezers, with inturned ends to the flexible blades and a decorated terminal at the top.

Having recorded its position, this time he took the find himself up to the caravan where he met Brian, who was examining some pieces of cow bone.

'You'll like this.'

Brian held out his hands expectantly and Anthony placed the tweezers in them.

'Ah, yes. Very fine. Unusual with the terminal. I haven't seen one as good for some time. Where was it?'

'Close to the position of the Hadrianic coin, as far as I can judge. I'm afraid it came up on the shovel with a lot of mud.'

'It could be much the same date. Keep your eyes peeled. There may be more.'

'Oh, by the way,' Brian called out as Anthony was turning away, 'where did you get to this morning?'

Anthony hesitated. What business was it of Brian's? But perhaps Brian was simply curious, nothing more.

'I took Giuditta over to South Cadbury. We got very wet.'

'South Cadbury, eh? A wonderful place.' And then he said quietly in Anthony's ear. 'Be careful with her. This is in confidence, you understand. She's recovering from something of a breakdown. Has she told you?'

'No, nothing.' Anthony was both surprised and concerned. 'She seemed happy enough this morning.'

Brian didn't respond to that. Instead, he continued, 'Yes, she told me in her application she'd been through a rough patch. She's been ill and off work and was worried about coming here. The dig's to help her get back to normal – the first thing she's done on her own for a little while, it seems. I thought you should be aware of that, particularly as you're staying at the same place. I'm sure you'll help her if she needs it. But don't let her know I've told you. She wanted it kept quiet.'

'Of course not.'

'And, Anthony. We've known each other for a long time – haven't we? – so forgive me saying this. I'm not sure if you're wise to be taking her out with you, as you have done, however well-intentioned you undoubtedly are. It might seem odd to some – the age difference and all that. Think about it. I'm sure you'll understand.'

Anthony's face closed down like a trap. How dare Brian say that? What business was it of his? What was he suggesting? He felt his heart thumping. Giuditta was a mature woman, not an adolescent girl being pursued by some dirty old man. He looked at Brian, but didn't reply. He felt too angry for that – but was it just anger or was there, in fact, a feeling of guilt as well? He remembered those desires he had felt, although quickly suppressed.

He turned on his heel and walked away without saying anything. Half way back to his trench, he realised that his reaction had not been the most sensible. Brian must have noted it and very probably felt there was some substance to his suspicions.

All the pleasure for Anthony in the work he had been doing with Giuditta seemed suddenly to have evaporated. He even spoke sharply to her, telling her to be more careful searching the wet earth that she was clearing up. She had missed part of a bronze buckle that he had later picked out of the spoil heap. She must have been bewildered by the sudden change in him. Would he be able to find a way later to explain and apologise? He was full of despair, for he had so enjoyed her company.

Giuditta, confronted by this strange, new Anthony, was very likely more than pleased when Brian arrived later to inspect the trench and to tell her he was going to move her. He justified the move by saying there had been a change in site priorities.

'I'd like you to join the main group trowelling,' he told Giuditta. 'The rain's set us back a bit. I need as many hands as possible there for the moment to get the area clean. You can manage for the moment by yourself, Anthony, can't you?'

'Oh yes, of course.' Anthony forced a smile. He didn't want Brian to know how annoyed he was. It would all pass. There had been occasions before when they had fallen out –

but never for long. Perhaps Brian would send Giuditta back to him tomorrow.

However, without Giuditta beside him, Anthony fumed for the rest of the afternoon. Perhaps she had seen the expression on his face and wondered at what was wrong. But he hoped she had no suspicion that he knew more about her than he should.

Anthony tried to get his mind off Giuditta and concentrate on reducing the level of his now extended trench, exposing more of the curving wall – for wall, it did seem certain to be, although whether of a well or something else was less certain. While working on what would be the interior fill of whatever structure it was, he made a number of further finds – a bone pin that had likely kept a woman's hair in place and a long, thin bronze object, decorated with an engraved spiral, that might have been the shaft of a stylus for writing in wax.. An increasing amount of pottery was also coming up, including the top of a flagon and a piece of what looked like the handle of an amphora.

Taking his finds trays up to the caravan at the end of the day, he met Giuditta there.

'How have you been getting on?' he asked.

'Not too bad, but boring compared with your trench. Just cleaning up a surface.'

'I'll be leaving in ten minutes. Is that okay for you?'

'*Sì*, fine.'

Some people were still digging as he set off with Giuditta down the track. He didn't want to get a reputation for working short hours. But that was quite ridiculous! For years he had been one of the most hard-working diggers on the site. But Brian had upset him, and he had had enough for today. That was all. Tomorrow, he would feel better. Tomorrow would also be the last day of the short Easter dig.

'Would you like a meal with me tonight?' he asked.

'You know, I'm not really hungry.'

'But you've got to eat something. You've only had that cheese roll.'

'Well, perhaps. When will you be going?'

'Let's see, about 7.00.'

'If I'm in the hall then, I'll be coming. If not, I won't be. I feel really tired.'

He glanced quickly at her as he drove, and saw there were dark rings around her eyes. Yet she had seemed so fresh and rested this morning.

'Don't knock on my door. I might be asleep,' she added.

'No, of course not. Well, I hope you feel better. I do enjoy your company, you know. I'm sorry if I was snappy earlier.'

'Snappy?'

'Like a crocodile,' and he made a movement with his fingers to indicate a crocodile's jaws.

She smiled, but he could sense she was strangely subdued. Perhaps it was the illness Brian had spoken about that explained her sudden tiredness.

In fact, there was no sign of Giuditta when he left his room at 7.00. He felt a keen sense of disappointment, and paced the passageway for a while, whistling and jangling his keys in his pocket so that she might hear him. Then other people staying there came by and looked at him strangely, so he decided that there was nothing to do but leave by himself.

When he returned, fully fed, he saw that her car – he assumed it was her car, it was a battered Ford Focus with faded red paintwork – was still in the car park. In the light of an outside lamp, he peered through the windows and saw a jumble of clothes on the back seat and a couple of crumpled Tesco's shopping bags. Inside the house, there was no sign of her. She must still be sleeping or watching television. She had told him not to knock on her door, so, although he was tempted to do so, he resisted the urge. He felt anxious about her, though, sorry that a day which had started so well had ended so disappointingly.

At breakfast the next morning, he felt rather bleary, for he had slept poorly. His mind had been racing over yesterday's events, in particular Brian's criticism. He thought, when I see Giuditta, I shall feel much better. She will make me smile again. I hope she's thrown off the tiredness that sent her to bed so early last night. One thing is certain – she must be very hungry by now.

So he felt increasingly perturbed as he sat at the breakfast table, forced to engage in conversation with other people, and Giuditta did not appear. Although now left to himself, he could not linger any longer, and he went outside into the hallway where Giuditta and he had spread out the map the day before. There was still no sign of her. He would have to leave for the site soon, and he did not want to do that without knowing how she was. He had been expecting her to travel with him. It was the last day of the dig. He would be driving home from the site afterwards. So, emboldened by necessity, he went to her door and knocked. There was no answer. He rapped with his knuckles once more. At last a thin voice came from within.

'Who is it?'

'It's Anthony. How are you?'

'I thought I told you not to knock!'

'That was yesterday.'

'*Merda!* Leave me alone, can't you.'

Anthony was shocked, mortified. He went to his room to pack and found his hands were shaking. What on earth had happened to her? It was ridiculous. They had been so happy together yesterday. Hadn't they? At least, he had been happy.

He thought she had been too. Was she ill then? Was this the illness Brian had referred to? The poor girl. He wanted to help her, but he knew there was no way he could.

He paid Mrs. Reynolds and took his cases to the Land Rover. Before leaving, he walked around the house, and peered at the windows of the extension that contained the guest bedrooms. That must be Giuditta's room where the curtains were drawn. She was probably still in bed. There was nothing he could do. What a shame it was. It was unlikely now that she would come to the site, and he would not see her again. This was like so many other things in his life, he thought bitterly. It had been a strange interlude, and that was all – just another thing that had gone wrong for which he didn't understand the reason.

Once on the site, he dug vigorously to try and rid his mind of Giuditta, or at least the worry of her. How was she feeling? Was she now up and about, perhaps leaving on her journey home? He realised he did not even know where that was; he never would now.

His task was to extend the trench even further so that he could hope to include the full extent of the stone-lined feature within it, hoping it would prove a full circle. This meant bringing one edge closer to the field under crop than he would have liked, in particular as a footpath ran through here too. There were safety considerations to consider, but Brian had readily given his permission.

'We'll put some hazard tape up. You need to get the complete circumference before thinking of going any deeper.' Brian seemed to have made up his mind already that a well had been found. He sounded friendly and made no reference to the conversation he had had with Anthony yesterday. Giuditta was not mentioned.

It was hard work. At least the weather was clear today, the sun shining out of a pale blue sky, warming the fields and the hedgerows after the rain. Anthony could sense the new growth all around him, shoots thrusting upwards, leaves unfolding. By morning tea break, he had spaded out the shape of the extension to the trench and lifted off the thickly-set turf. Next he must attack the soil once more with the mattock. This is where Giuditta's help would have been invaluable.

He still had hopes that she might come up to the site. He checked just to make sure her car was not in the parking area and she was on site somewhere else, and, when that proved negative, he scanned the trackway to see if a battered Focus was not even now lurching towards him over the ruts, but to no avail. He did not like to ask Brian if he knew anything more. After yesterday, it seemed to be a good idea for him to play down any interest in Giuditta.

By lunch break, he had cleared the new area to a depth where he could begin more careful work to try and see if the limestone walling made a full circuit. A first trial with a light pick showed that there was a mass of stone beneath. He must now work with a trowel to outline individual stones. The interpretation of a well was looking increasingly probable.

He retired to his car for lunch and to read the newspaper he had bought with his sandwiches at a shop in the village that morning. On joining the main group of diggers later to pour himself a beaker of tea, he overheard a conversation between two ladies who worked with the finds.

'She didn't look well, did she?'

'No. It's best not to struggle on when you feel bad.'

'Who are you talking about?' Anthony asked, his heart beginning to pump.

'Why, the Italian girl.'

'You mean Giuditta. Has she been here today then?'

'Yes. Not all that long ago. Brian wanted her to work with us, but she said she wasn't feeling very well, so he sent her away. He was worried about her driving, but she said she'd be alright.'

Anthony felt hurt. So she had been at the site after all and he had missed her. Why hadn't she come over to see him? She may have been feeling poorly, but surely she could have managed that.

He sought Brian out. He was fussing around the boot of his car which was filled with trays of pottery, including some vessels taped together in various states of reassembly.

'Ah, Anthony. Glad you came over. I've got something for you.'

He held out a piece of folded paper and Anthony's heart leapt. He had no idea what it would say, but he knew it was from Giuditta.

'Giuditta wanted me to give this to you, so I'm passing it on.'

His eyes met Anthony's. Although they were of a similar age, Anthony always considered Brian by far the senior. This may have had much to do with his position as site director, but Anthony also felt his own inadequacy, perhaps even immaturity. He had never married, he had never had children, he had never experienced the cares of fatherhood, of raising a family, of looking after a wife. Brian had done all those things. He might be overweight and unfit, and his appearance at times a little ridiculous, but he nonetheless had a gravitas and a command about him that Anthony felt he, himself, lacked and instinctively deferred to.

'I've told you what I think. I shan't mention it again,' Brian said in a flat tone. 'After all, it has nothing to do with me.'

Anthony looked at the ground and bit his lip. He refused to be roused. It would be absurdly undignified.

'How was she?' he asked.

'Just out of sorts, I think, rather than unwell as such.

Women's problems, probably. She just wanted to get home, but didn't like to go without telling me.'

'A shame,' said Anthony. 'I liked her.'

Brian stared at him for a long moment, then smiled and clapped him on the shoulder.

'We've covered a lot of ground together over the years, haven't we? Literally. Good luck to you. I know you've had a bad time yourself recently.'

'Do you know what this says?' Anthony held up the piece of paper.

'Of course not. As I've said, it's not my business – certainly not when away from my site.'

No. It's not! Anthony said to himself. He felt uneasy. The whole thing was ridiculous and in danger of getting out of hand.

Anthony did not open the piece of paper until he was back by his trench. Then, seated on the edge, he unfolded it.

'Antony,' he read – of course, being Italian she would use the wrong spelling – 'I'm sorry if I seemed rude this morning. I haven't felt well and had a terrible night, not fit for you to see. So I haven't come to find you. Thanks for the lovely day you shared with me yesterday. I really <u>loved</u> it. I hope the trench is good. Perhaps I'll be back in August to see it. If you'd like to keep in touch, here is my phone number and my email address.'

Anthony's heart, so recently cast down, was raised up again So, she hadn't rejected him. And she clearly liked him or she would never have given him her contact details.

A robin which had hopped onto the handle of his spade looked at him with its bright eye. Was the bird an omen of good fortune or of disaster to come? Anthony was reluctant to get to his feet, for he knew he would scare the bird away. He just wanted this moment to linger on.

He knew that he had to see her again. She had brought some joy – brief, as it was – back into his life, and he wanted it to go on. He suspected he was being foolish, but he didn't care. There is nothing, he thought, I would not do for that girl.

5

As soon as he had returned home after his Easter digging break, Anthony sent Giuditta an email. The address she had given him – giuditta@ponti.co.uk – sounded alluringly exotic, and brought back tantalising memories of her that he spent hours sifting through in his mind. So Ponti was likely to be her surname, although it might equally be a place in Italy where she had lived, or perhaps the name of the company she worked for. He even carried out a Google search of 'giuditta' and 'ponti', but could not come up with anything that made any sense.

He tried to think what work she might do – a fashion designer, a magazine editor, a translator, a civil servant with the Foreign Office? Or did she perhaps work with the Italian embassy in London, or a top travel company that did tours to Italy? Was she employed by an Italian airline – a flight attendant possibly, or in some office capacity? – and then he remembered the degrees she had said she had, and how she loved life out of doors, and could not imagine her doing anything routine or mundane, however superficially glamorous. He was astonished with himself now – and more than a little irritated – that he had not asked her these questions while he had had the chance.

His email had been direct and brisk enough; simply to make contact and for her to reply when she had the time. He had written –

'Hello Giuditta. Brian gave me your note at lunchtime yesterday. I must have just missed you. I hope you are feeling better now. No, I didn't think you were rude, so please don't worry about that. I was just concerned about you. Yes, I'd love to keep in touch. You'll get my email address from this message, and my phone number is below. Hear from you soon. By the way, it is a well for sure! All the best. Anthony.'

Would she answer? Would she really want to hear from him now that she had returned to her normal life away from the unreal world of Glastington? When she got better from the exhaustion and the depression that clearly had beset her, she would probably soon forget the man – who had been old enough to be her father – with whom she had worked to uncover a Roman well.

For, as he had written to her, it *was* a well. He had proved that later on that last afternoon. Having gained a complete circle of stone some five feet across, he had taken down the interior soil some six to nine inches all over revealing the upper two courses of a well-constructed shaft made of unmortared limestone blocks. There was only one point on the circumference where the shaft wall was not clearly defined, and here for several feet there was a greater spread of stone, so that it looked as if that part of the shaft had tumbled in – or been robbed away – at some distant time. Anthony hoped, however, that this damaged section would not go very deep.

There was no answer to his email. One day, two, then three days went by. Anthony waited expectantly as he worked on his computer, but there was no satisfying ping in his inbox that would bring a reply from her. First thing each morning, he rushed to switch on the watching eye of the machine, but, no – not among the drifts of spam offering him replica watches, golden investment opportunities, or supplies of potency drugs, was there the email he sought.

On the fourth day, he decided to phone. The number she had given was that of a mobile phone, so he couldn't tell from it the area where she lived. He phoned three times that day, but there was no answer and the call went through to the Voicemail service. On the third occasion, he plucked up the courage to leave a message –

'Hello, Giuditta. It's Anthony – you remember, from the Glastington villa. I've been trying to contact you, as you suggested in the note you left for me. Please email me or phone me. You'll get my number from this call, or it's on the email I sent you. Hope you're okay. Speak to you soon.'

It was late in the evening of the fifth day – a Friday – that the phone rang. He had been on the toilet, and he almost did not make it to the phone in his living room before it stopped ringing.

'Hello. Anthony Winters here.'

'Hello, Anthony. It's Giuditta.' Of course, he recognised that deep, accented voice. His heart leapt.

'Oh, wonderful. At last! How are you?'

'I'm fine. I've been away for a few days. That's why I haven't answered your messages.'

'I thought it must have been something like that.'

Anthony found his throat was dry, and he was almost gabbling in his anxiety to respond to what she said. He felt suddenly guilty at having chased her. He didn't like to ask her where she had been, just in case it had something to do with that illness of hers he was not meant to know about.

But she told him anyhow. 'I've been staying for a few days with a friend in Birmingham.'

'Birmingham!'

'Yes, she's a nurse working at a hospital there. An old friend from my first days in England.'

Anthony found himself relieved to hear it was a 'she' and not a 'he', although he knew such a reaction was absurd. He had no claims on her.

'Where do you live?' he asked. 'You never told me.'

'Didn't I? You couldn't have asked me then. In Cambridge.'

She must be feeling better, he thought, for the bold, slightly cheeky Giuditta he had glimpsed before had clearly returned.

'Cambridge! Do you work at the university then?'

She laughed. He could see her, bent forward giggling as she held the phone.

'No, not at the university.'

'What do you do then?'

'Oh, Anthony, so many questions.'

His heart sank. He was putting too much pressure on her. He had cautioned himself against that. He must try to be more relaxed and natural, and not concern her with his questions.

'What *I* wanted to ask you,' she continued, 'is, do you ever go into London? I remember you said you live quite close.'

He couldn't recall now what he had told her about himself. He must have rambled on about once having worked in London.

'Yes, I do. Why are you planning to come to London some time?'

'I want to go to an exhibition on Pompeii and Herculaneum that's being held at the Italian Institute.'

'Sounds interesting. I haven't read about it.'

'It's only a small affair. A reception really. Cultural exchange, that sort of thing. It's by invitation only. But I've got two tickets.'

'When is it?'

'In May, I think.' He could hear her rustling some papers. '26th May.'

'Almost certainly fine with me. If it's not, I'll make it so.'

'Well, okay. Look, I've got to go just now. The friend I share with has just told me dinner's ready. I'll send you an email about the exhibition.'

'That's great. Thanks.' He had barely got the words out when the line went dead.

How abrupt she could be, he thought. And how mysterious were some of the things she said. Who was the friend she lived with? Was it a man? He considered that unlikely. If she had a man in her life, surely she would not be phoning him – especially an old man like himself. And then, despite these worries, a wave of pleasure swept over him at the thought he would be seeing her again. Her manner might be a bit offhand at times, but she must have enjoyed his company or she would never have suggested this. Was there just a chance it might lead on to something even better?

When Giuditta's promised email arrived it was very brief and to the point. It read:

'Put the 26th May in your diary, as we discussed. Reception at 7.30pm at the Italian Cultural Institute, Belgrave Square. We'll discuss the details nearer the time. Best wishes. Giuditta.'

On reading this, Anthony thought: That is five weeks away. I wonder if she'd agree to meet me before then if I went up to Cambridge. I wouldn't mind a trip to Cambridge anyhow, as it's been a long time since I was last there. I'd like to visit the Fitzwilliam Museum again. So he put the suggestion to her in an email, only to receive a swift response that said:

'Busy at the moment. Let's leave it until after London, and see how we're fixed then.'

He was disappointed. He had no idea what might be making her so busy, and indeed had little knowledge of her life at all. He was aware she was becoming something of an obsession for him, out of all proportion to the reality. But he knew what he would like from her – hoped for, anyhow – which was really just friendship. Shared interests, archaeological or otherwise, and some companionship on trips out, as at South Cadbury – that would be about it. Realistically, he could not hope for anything further. Their age difference was just too great for that.

However, despite this reasoning, he realised already he could be setting himself up for an emotional fall. He even tried to pour metaphorical cold water over himself by repeating the line: 'There's no fool like an old fool.' But, however hard he tried, he found he could not stop the fantasy – the dream journey – of what could be.

He was rescued from such self-indulgent reflections, which came during a particularly dull period for him when whole days would pass with scarcely any human contact at all, by a phone call one weekday evening – it was at the end of April – from Brian Radleigh.

'I want to push on with the well,' he said. 'so we can have a hope of bottoming it out during the August dig. That's assuming the depth's not too great, of course: I don't think it will be, as the water table here is pretty high. Can you come up for another weekend? I'm asking Miles and Stan as well so we can get up a good team.'

Miles and Stan were two of the regulars – they had not been at the Easter dig – whom Anthony felt comfortable working with. They generally knew what they were doing, got on with it, and were good fun to dig with. Over the years they had shared many a joke together. The prospect was welcome, and he agreed straightaway.

'Can you make this coming weekend?' Brian asked. 'It's the May Day bank holiday next Monday. How about the Sunday and the Monday?'

'Okay. I'm sure I can do that. I'll get myself booked in at the B&B.'

'I'll confirm by email,' Brian said. 'The others I'm pretty sure can make it. Let's hope the weather's good.'

Brian's confirmation came through less than half an hour later. Anthony was pleased to have the date in his diary. It was something to look forward to. Then it occurred to him that Giuditta might be interested in coming along also. She could stay at the B&B with him again. He was sure Brian would not mind her presence. The more helpers there were, the better it was for the major digging job the well would likely prove.

Dare he phone and ask her, or should he email? She had said she was busy, but perhaps she could find the time for some exciting archaeological work. As it would be a long journey for her just for a weekend, he might even suggest that she come down by train from Cambridge to Bromley – the nearest station to him – and they could then drive to Glastington together.

Excited by this prospect, he made a quick decision and phoned her. A woman's voice answered – quite a harsh voice, which was certainly not Giuditta's.

'Hello. Is Giuditta there?'

'Just a moment.' Then a pause. 'Who's calling?'

'Anthony. Anthony Winters.'

A longer pause, and then Giuditta came on.

'How did you get this number?' She was sharp and accusatory, with no greeting at all. With a sinking heart, Anthony realised he had made a bad mistake.

'From the time you last phoned me. My handset showed the number.'

'I didn't want you phoning me here. If you must phone, use my mobile number. What do you want, anyhow?'

'It's about Glastington. Brian's digging the well this weekend. I wondered if you were interested in coming.'

There was a sigh of exasperation. 'But I told you I was busy, didn't I? Don't you ever listen? Yes, it would be lovely to come to Glastington and dig holes, but unfortunately I've got much more important things to do – like earning my fucking living.'

Anthony was shocked – both by what she said and the way she said it, in particular the swear word. For some reason, the obscenity seemed to sound more direct and personal delivered with a foreign accent. His dream world was suddenly shattered.

'I'm sorry.'

There was silence, and Anthony was aware of her gathering herself at the other end of the phone.

'No, it's me. I shouldn't have said that. But I couldn't come even if I wanted to. You have a good time though.'

'I'm so sorry.' Anthony was vastly relieved that she was still talking to him, that there was the chance of recovery from his error of judgement. Any annoyance he felt was wiped out by his fear of losing her entirely.

'Please don't say you're sorry again. I can't stand that. I'll see you in London next month, as we've arranged.'

Anthony tried to add something more, attempting to conjure up words that were confident and optimistic, instead of whining and grovelling, when he heard the phone put down. Oh God, he groaned. How I messed that one up. He felt shattered. Was it really fair that she should rail at him like that when he was only trying to be nice? He was so upset by the whole thing that it occupied his mind for ages.

He felt a little better when an email arrived from Giuditta the next morning –

'I probably overreacted. It's been a difficult time for me of late. Sorry. Let me know how you get on at Glastington.'

It was alright then for her to say sorry, but not him! It would be best to draw a veil over the whole matter, and forget it. He was pleased he still had the London trip to look forward to. Until that time, he must try to get her out of his mind.

6

Anthony left very early on the Sunday morning in the Land Rover so that he would reach Glastington by the 10 o'clock starting time that Brian had decided on. It was a fine morning, with the sun rising behind him as he drove out of the London suburbs and onto the M25, heading towards its junction with the M3. A light mist clung to the wooded upper slopes of the North Downs as he passed them to his right, and to his left there were glimpses of the great, dark heartland of the Weald, which in this uncertain light seemed to Anthony to retain a sense of the primeval forest it had once been.

He made very good progress to the M3, and stopped briefly at the Fleet Services to have a quick mug of coffee and to buy sandwiches and other snacks for the weekend. He seldom did more than a steady sixty in the Land Rover, but he soon reached the junction of the M3 with the dual-carriageway A303. There was more traffic about now, but no hold ups, and, after a further half hour or so, he came within sight of Stonehenge, cresting a hill and seeing the stones below him like a giant's box of building blocks dumped onto the green plain. He stopped near here in a layby to take a bite out of a sandwich, his only breakfast before leaving home having been a slice of cold toast.

Back on the road, the miles sped easily away until he was entering Somerset, and, once beyond Wincanton, branched onto a side road that soon placed him amongst the winding lanes that would lead him eventually to Glastington. It was here that he began to think of Giuditta again: he had been successful in shutting off thoughts of her over the few days since her last email. It was these lanes that they had driven together on the way to South Cadbury that brought back the memories – her lovely dark hair radiant with undertones of coppery-red, the broad-brimmed hat at an angle on her head, her face turned to him, puzzled at first by what he said, and then dissolving into child-like laughter. Was that really the same Giuditta who had sworn at him over the phone?

As he came into Glastington village, he glanced at the clock on the dashboard and saw that it was a quarter of an hour before 10.00. He had made excellent time. The village seemed still to be asleep. Apart from one car he passed, there was no one about. The place slumbered in the bright morning sunlight, the grey stone church with its battlemented tower topped by a golden weather vane. There were no worshippers about the church; perhaps they had already been and gone.

On the far side of the village, past the Red Cow pub, the lane became the rough track that led to the Roman villa site. The hedgerows hung white with hawthorn, and the fields, spread out beneath the sun, were dark green with growing crops. Ahead of him he could see cars standing in the square area of rough grass that bordered the villa, and he knew the others had arrived ahead of him.

As he swung the Land Rover to a halt beside the cars, Miles approached with his hand held out. He was lean and wiry, in his mid 50s. He lived close to Bristol.

'Good to see you, Anthony. The drive not too bad?'

'So, so. Pretty clear.' Seeing a tent pitched on the far side of the cars, he asked, 'Are you camping?'

'Yes, that's my tent.'

'Haven't you still got your caravan?'

'Yes, but I didn't want the hassle of bringing it just for one night. I'll have it here in August, though.'

Brian appeared from the site caravan with Stan. The latter was older than Anthony, a little into his 70s. After the death of his wife, he had moved recently to Yeovil to be close to his daughter. Yeovil was only a short distance from Glastington, so he would be going home at night.

'What's this about a well?' said Stan with a chuckle. 'Who's going to be the mug digging that out?'

Anthony hoped Stan was still as strong and fit as he had been in previous years, despite his advancing years. They had dug much together – ditches, pits, even a deep sump, but never a well before. Miles was much newer to the site, and had only joined them as part of their 'oldies' digging team a couple of years back.

'We don't know what we're facing,' Brian said. 'But if it proves a deep well – below head height, that is – we'll have to proceed with the greatest care: helmets on all the time, lads, please.'

Brian was wearing his vast shorts again, with a dark-blue tee-shirt adorned with the logo of the Glastington Archaeological Society – a couple of Roman flagons standing side by side. The acronym GAS underneath was a standing joke in the society.

It was Brian who had found the site some twenty-five years ago while field walking the area as an amateur archaeological enthusiast. At that time, he had only recently moved to the Glastington area, and had asked the farmer for permission to walk his fields in the autumn after the crop was harvested. The results had been immediate and clear – a great amount of Roman tile and pottery spread over two fields defining the site of what had seemed likely from the very beginning – a large

Roman villa. Brian had got a group together – the origins of GAS – and slowly, methodically and diligently, the villa had been uncovered. As the layers were stripped off, an earlier settlement, had also been revealed underlying the Roman buildings – the round huts of late-Iron Age forbears.

They began the work by lugging tools through the gap in the hedgerow to the trench Anthony had dug. It already seemed to him a long time since he had been here with Giuditta, hacking with the mattock, shovelling away the loose earth, chopping down the edges of the trench with the spade so as to make the sides vertical. During the weeks that had passed, the vegetation had reasserted itself. There were patches of weeds growing on the surfaces that he had left neatly trowelled, and the long grass at the sides of the trench was now trailing untidily over the edges. Brambles within the hedgerow, now fully in leaf, had curled outwards like barbed wire to catch their flesh and clothing. The first thing Anthony did was to attack them with shears, cutting them back into the hedge.

They prepared the trench for the work that was to come. Although eager to begin, Anthony felt some regret – pathetic as this might seem – that they were also stamping out Giuditta's earlier presence here, his most sensitive memories of how the two of them had knelt side by side trowelling, and the bursts of laughter they had shared and the excitement at their finds. Now it was three men in clumping boots, with iron tools and buckets and trays, and Brian as well balanced at the edge of the trench watching the preparations.

Bran was having a close look at the limestone walling, over a foot thick, that Anthony had exposed. The complete circle of stone stood proud of the earth, but had been excavated deeper within, as Anthony had left it, the fill here much darker than that on the outer side of the circle. Blades of grass had already established themselves amongst the crevices of the newly-exposed stones.

'I reckon you'll have only a foot or two more of that walling, and then the well may have had a timber lining – that will have long-decayed, of course. Unless, that is, the bedrock here proves very high, in which case the well won't be very deep. I wouldn't have thought they would have bored too far into natural rock.'

He cast his eye beyond the stone circle. 'We'll concentrate on the shaft first, but later we'll need to have a look at the areas around it. There could be post holes for a well head building, and perhaps a paved working surface.'

When they got under way, the excavation proved slow work. Any hopes they might have had of digging quickly through a capping of earth were soon dispelled by the quantity of Roman building material that came up. Anthony was using a light mattock to cut the soil, with Miles shovelling it into a wheel barrow, where Stan sorted the spoil with his trowel. Almost straightaway Stan's hand began closing over pieces of Roman tile.

'You'll need to go a bit slower,' he called out.

He was finding decorated flue tile, with a criss-cross pattern that had been scored with a knife before firing. The pieces went into a finds tray that was already filling rapidly.

'It looks like there could have been a bath house near by,' Anthony observed. The flue tile was normally associated with a heating system of some sort.

Other finds were of small red brick *tesserae* from a tiled floor, roofing tile with its distinctive flanged edges, and lumps of a crumbly pink-coloured concrete known as *opus signinum*, the presence of which was also indicative of a heated building. There was very little pottery, or organic material such as bone.

The careful extraction of this dump of demolition rubble took them most of the morning. Brian, who had left to attend to other matters at the site caravan, now returned to examine what had been discovered.

'It looks like the well may have been filled in with debris from the first house when it was demolished,' he said. 'It must have been quite a high status building then, even though it was probably timber-framed above its foundations. It seems it was heated and had tiled floors. If that's true the well must be quite early, so there's likely a second one around somewhere too.'

'Well, we ain't looking for that today!' said Stan.

Shortly before they were due to break for lunch, Anthony, who had been watching Stan bent over the barrow sorting, saw his hand dart into the earth and pull out an object. It was a large coin.

'Blimey,' said Miles, who had been shovelling. 'How did I miss that?'

'A *sestertius*,' Brian pronounced, taking it from Stan. 'Early commemorative issue, by the look of it.' He bore it away triumphantly to the caravan for further examination.

After the necessary recording, Anthony, flushed with the excitement of discovery, looked around him. Stan – old soldier that he was – with gaiters above his boots, his head, sparse of hair, bent over the recently dumped spoil, double-checking that nothing else had been missed; Miles, in red-checked shirt and blue jeans, leaning momentarily on his shovel while watching the flight of a kestrel hovering above the fields; and himself, with reddened face and forearms, holding the mattock before him like a miner at a coal face – all this in earnest pursuit of the past. Why, he wondered? Why this fascination for what has gone by – for kings and emperors, soldiers and peasants, for all the living and the breathing and the dying of our forbears? Is it because their lives seem more fascinating, more eventful, than our own? No, that cannot be the reason. For, by any consideration, most people's lives had been humdrum, hard-working, and short, interspersed by brief bursts of joy, then silenced in pain and grief.

There has to be another reason. Perhaps it is the quest for knowledge, for discovery, for evidence that will illuminate darkness. Or is it that we explore these things simply because they are there, rather as a climber has to set himself against a mountain? There is companionship as well, of course, and working as a team in a common pursuit, and all the good social activity which results from that. At that last thought, Anthony wondered at his own hypocrisy, he who had so often wanted to dig by himself!

Now it was lunchtime. They stacked the tools neatly, emptied the barrows, and entered up the written record. The trench was left ready for the afternoon's work to come.

They sat around the site caravan eating their sandwiches in companionable silence. Then Miles began putting some questions about the finding of the well, and Brian told of Anthony's work with Giuditta that had first revealed the curving line of stone. As Anthony had feared, mention of a new woman on the site was like a dose of viagra to his fellow diggers.

'Ah! You sly old bugger,' Miles exclaimed. 'You kept that quiet. Good was she?

'Yes,' Anthony said levelly. 'She worked very well. She enjoyed it.'

'I bet she did!' Miles was one of those men for whom the sexually suggestive lay in wait at every possible turn. Anthony liked him, and had had similar risqué repartee with him in the past, but didn't feel like joining in today.

'Is she coming back?' asked Stan.

'I'm not sure,' Anthony said. 'I did ask her this weekend but she couldn't make it.'

'A pity. She sounds a winner. How would you rate her out of ten then?'

Despite himself, Anthony felt compelled to join in with this laddish humour. 'Oh, ten, of course. For her archaeological skill, I mean. I wouldn't know about anything else.'

As Miles chortled in disbelief, Anthony looked across at Brian, and saw him looking back with something like pity on his face – pity mixed with scorn – or at least that's how he interpreted the expression. All the pleasure at the mention of Giuditta went from him like air from a punctured balloon.

Brian changed the subject by referring to the coin that had been found that morning. 'It's very worn, but I think it's of the Emperor Claudius – so, very early indeed in the Roman conquest period. It may have been over-stamped to keep it in circulation; they sometimes did that with worn coins. Perhaps lost mid to late 1st century. I'll look at it under a glass tonight.'

As Anthony took in this information, he looked across at Miles to find him still gazing at him with an amused smile, and, as their eyes met, he winked.

'Good on yer,' that wink seemed to say. 'You do what you want, mate.'

Below the mass of building debris was a fill of darker earth containing large quantities of pottery, and with organic materials as well, such as bone and oyster shell. Having dispensed with the mattock for the time being, Anthony was able to spade much of this out, lifting it to Miles to search on the surface behind him, and then for Miles to pitch up into Stan's barrow for further scrutiny.

As the surface level of the well shaft was slowly lowered, Anthony – or Miles, when it was his turn – would scrape down the limestone walling with their trowels, revealing more of the small rectangular blocks that made up the curving wall. The only place where this could not be done was the segment of the wall which had been damaged in antiquity; here there was only a jumble of blocks that had formed the back of the wall, most of these clearly askew and surrounded by others that were entirely loose and may have been thrown back in soon after the damage was done.

By mid-afternoon, when Brian came to pay them a further visit, they had cleared the well to a depth of nearly three feet – careful, methodical work that could only proceed at the speed of sorting and soil disposal.

Brian examined the trays of finds. 'The pottery all looks pretty early,' he said 'The well may have been filled in by the early second century…' – he stood to one side considering – '….although perhaps a little later. That would tie in with the date range we're getting for the first house.'

Spotting something, he called down to Miles who was standing in the well. 'What's that in the wall by your feet?'

Miles bent to see what he was looking at. 'Do you mean the hole there? I thought that was simply where a stone had come out.'

Close to the excavated surface, on the opposite side from the collapsed section, was a square-shaped inset into the wall. Anthony, who had done the digging there, had partly cleared it of earth with his trowel.

'That could be a purpose-made step,' Brian said, 'one of a number at different heights to climb in and out of the well. They're known elsewhere.'

'Or it could be a niche for a dedication,' said Stan, grinning broadly. 'A ritual deposit to all the young virgins who were chucked down here.'

'Sometimes, Stan, you talk like an idiot,' retorted Brian, who was not noted for his sense of humour when it came to archaeology.

As Brian's rotund form disappeared, clutching finds trays in both hands, the three of them collapsed in giggles, like schoolboys who had been ragging their teacher. Anthony thought: this is what I need – good humour and some belly laughs. He realised that for an hour or two Giuditta had vanished completely from his mind, and, when she eventually reappeared with his returning consciousness of her, her presence seemed much more distant, further to the background and in better context with his life, a pleasing diversion, largely irrelevant, certainly not an obsession. It was not good to take anything too seriously.

When they finished for the day, they had gone down a further ten inches or so, which revealed fully the base of the step in the wall, wide and deep enough to have taken a Roman foot scrambling out of the well, if that person had also been able to cling to something with his hands – perhaps, Anthony speculated, a hand-hold fixed to whatever apparatus there was at the top to raise the water.

Before leaving the well, they gathered around it to look at the fruits of their labours. A bank of cloud was filling the sky to the west, not rain-bearing cloud but a drifting, billowing mass of cumulus, through which the sinking sun shone in rays so bright that they seemed the work of some master painter, an allegory of light battling darkness. They all watched the sky spell-bound, seeing the rays striking at the ground so that the fields seemed crossed by bars of gold shining against the green of the crops. The well was in shadow, and stood within the trampled earth of the trench like a dark mouth re-opened after the many centuries of blackness to this revelation of new light. Anthony thought: archaeology reveals the past to us in the present, but the converse is also true. He shivered. He noted that his companions were strangely silent as they trudged together back to the site caravan.

They went directly from the site to the Red Cow in the village – except Brian, that was, who had stayed at the caravan to do some further work with the finds. They bought pints of the local beer, and Anthony felt its effects smoothing away his cares and apprehensions, washing away strains and tensions – those strange, disordered workings of his nervous system that had plagued him throughout his life.

Stan soon left to drive home, but Miles – who had a night alone on the site ahead of him – and Anthony ordered a meal to be served after 6.30 when the kitchen opened. After another half pint of the beer, Anthony had to content himself with soft drinks, as he would have to drive to his B&B at the farm a little later. Miles, however, who had travelled with Anthony, ordered further pints with considerable thirst.

They played darts, and the beer seemed to add to Miles's skill, for his arrows flew with an accuracy that left Anthony hopelessly beaten in game after game. Some locals were now arriving, and, as 6.30 approached, they retired from the stone-paved bar to a table in the small, carpeted restaurant beyond.

'Now tell me more about this Giuditta,' said Miles, with a beery smile on his crinkly-lined, moustached face.

Miles's disposition was generally most amiable, and Anthony knew that, unlike Brian, there was nothing judgemental in his questioning, just simple curiosity. Miles was popular with everyone on the site during the summer excavation, particularly with the students, who would gather round his caravan and drink with him in the evenings. When he returned home to Bristol – as he sometimes needed to do in the course of his stay – he would take his car but leave the caravan behind, allowing some of his new young friends to use it in his absence. Anthony had been a little shocked by this at first, because he knew what it was likely to be used for by some – so much more comfortable and convenient than the narrow groundsheet of a small tent. Miles liked to pretend sometimes that his caravan served a similar purpose for himself, but Anthony refused to believe that. Middle aged men often made extravagant boasts about their sexual prowess.

'There's nothing to tell.' Anthony was on the defensive about Giuditta.

'Is she a looker?'

'An attractive woman, yes.'

'How old is she?'

'I don't know for sure – perhaps mid-thirties.'

Miles's arm came round to clasp Anthony on the arm and to gaze with pretended wide eyes into his face. 'The perfect age. You lucky bugger!'

'What are you talking about, Miles?' Anthony didn't mind a joke, but this was getting ridiculous. 'I only dug with her for a day or so. Nothing more. Old fattie, Brian, moved her from me, anyhow.'

Miles laughed. 'He must have thought you were getting too close. He told me you'd been out with her.'

'Oh, did he?' Anthony was growing cross now. 'Well, he shouldn't have done. I didn't take her out, anyhow, only filled in a morning with her when it was raining. When did he tell you that?'

'When he phoned me about this weekend. He said you'd arrived late on site when everyone else had been back at work for hours. You dirty dog, what did you do with her?'

Anthony knew it would be silly getting too annoyed with Miles, whom he realised was only teasing him. He was much more angry with Brian for his sanctimonious hypocrisy in betraying a confidence and spreading gossip.

'Miles, she's a lovely woman. But that's all. There're lots of lovely women. We can't have them all – or any of them, for that matter! In particular, you. You're a married man. I'm not.'

'Methinks, he doth protest too much. We'll see, mate. Good luck to you, anyway.'

And Anthony was left thinking: What on earth's he think I'm up to? And then: What *am* I up to? What he did know was that he was looking forward to seeing Giuditta in a few weeks in London. He hadn't told anyone about that, nor would he. Let them joke as much as they liked. There was just the chance – the smallest, slimmest chance – that something might indeed happen between himself and Giuditta. The thought shone within him like a flame, giving him a feeling of – what exactly? Hope? Fantasy? Adventure? – something good for the future, at least. He needed it to raise himself out of the humdrum of his present life.

After their meal, Anthony drove Miles back to the site. It was dark now and the headlights stabbed the blackness along the track, shining on the hedgerows, so that their white light seemed frozen like snow. Brian had long since gone, and Miles's tent sat solitary on the ground next to the site caravan.

'Rather you than me,' said Anthony. 'Don't you ever worry about the ghosts here?'

'Bollocks to ghosts.' The alcohol was still flowing strongly in Miles's veins. 'I wish there were some. I could ask them some questions. How deep's our well, for instance?'

'I don't know why you don't use a B&B when you haven't got your caravan.'

'Just more convenient really, and much cheaper.'

'See you tomorrow then.'

'Yes. Sweet dreams. Not too sweet, though.'

And, as Anthony gunned up the engine, he could hear him still laughing maniacally out in the night. Laugh on, my friend. You've got more courage than I have – or at least less imagination. For some reason he found himself shuddering, thinking of the black, half-opened mouth of the well so close by.

7

When Anthony returned home from Glastington after his second day on the site – it had proved an exciting one – it was with good feelings of a most interesting job well done. The dreary routines of his life seemed far less noticeable now: they had fallen back into their correct place as a necessary but undemanding background to his real life, to which a new focus had been added – the well and the work on it to come, and – dare he think this still? – his hopes with Giuditta, whom he would see again soon. The well gave him excitement, Giuditta pleasure, although, as he tried to gain clarity on his thoughts, the two were not necessarily mutually exclusive, and might, with a little luck, be interchangeable. And so, he realised, his growing obsession with her was still there despite the fresh perspective gained at the weekend, although now edged with a greater realism.

On checking his emails as soon as he got in – it was after nine in the evening: the journey back through the May Day holiday traffic had been tortuous and slow – he found there was one from Giuditta. As he clicked on to it, he was filled with tension. Despite her apology, would she still be disapproving of what he had asked her before? Had she now decided to cancel the agreed date in London? But no, her email was friendly, full of interest, and tinged with a regret that sent hope rushing like hot blood into his veins –

'Hi Antony. I've been thinking of you at the villa, and wishing I had been there with you. Thanks for asking me to go. I'm sorry I snapped at you. Difficult times. I'll tell you about them one day. What did you find? Anything really good? Is the well still going down? Please let me know when you get back. It's pretty boring here at present. Boring, you see, like to bore the well. A joke in English! *Noioso* we say in Italian – but that does not also mean to dig. Giuditta.'

Although he still had his coat on, and had not unloaded the Land Rover, Anthony rushed to send an answer:

'Hello Giuditta. Great to hear from you. I've just got back. You would really have enjoyed it. A bucketful of silver coins on the second day (today! – it already seems an age back). There were twenty-three of them all together about four feet down. Miles – one of the guys I was digging with – found them in a great clod of earth which I'd heaved up to him. We think they would have been deliberately placed in the well, perhaps for safety, when it was already mostly filled in. They would probably have been in a leather or fabric purse, which, of course, has rotted away. Otherwise, we had one or two other coins, and a lot of pottery, including some early Samian – the glossy red stuff, *terra sigillata*. I'm sure you're familiar with it.'

'So we've excavated to something over six feet, with fine stone walling still going vertically down except the bit that's damaged and we think we may have found the extent of that now. Brian thought the shaft might have been lined with timber below the well-head, but he's been proved wrong and the stone's still going down and there's no sign yet of the bottom. We'll probably be going back for another weekend (perhaps in June), so let me know if you want to come.'

'Looking forward to seeing you in London soon. We need to discuss the arrangements. Perhaps you can phone me for that. All the very best. Anthony.'

That second day had indeed been most exciting. The coin hoard had come up in the morning.

'Well, bugger me!' Miles had exclaimed inelegantly when the compact mass of blue-grey corroded coins had first been revealed as he stabbed with his trowel at the lump of earth in the bucket. After photography by Brian, they had spent the next hour freeing all the coins, and checking the digging surface to see none had been missed.

By mid-afternoon they had had to fetch a short length of ladder, stored under the caravan, in order to get in and out of the shaft. A second niche, below the first and offset from it by a short distance, was revealed, strengthening the theory that these had been used to get in and out of the well. Anthony had suggested that perhaps a weighted rope had been let down into the shaft to serve as a hand support, and Brian had been impressed by this idea.

Brian gave them a preliminary assessment of the coins – all silver *denarii* of the early second century, some of Trajan, but most of Hadrian, who had made a visit to Britain and ordered his wall in the north to be built.

'I wonder why someone should have wanted to hide that money,' Brian had pondered. 'It's a large amount – someone's pay for a year, at least.'

He had been leaning on a stick at the edge of the trench as he stood over Anthony and Miles side by side in the shaft. 'If the well was filled in around 150 AD' – he mused – 'that was during a period of stability. You wouldn't have thought people were hiding stashes of money then. That sort of thing happened later, perhaps from the mid third century when the province was much more unstable. No, the concealment must have been because of some local issue we can't even guess at now.'

'Probably Marius's money for a 6-pack of vino that his missus didn't want him to spend,' said Stan, idiotically.

While the others had chuckled, Brian turned to look at him with a sorrowful shake of his head. Then at last the rubbery mask of his face cracked, and he laughed too – surprising, unexpected: Anthony had been anticipating some sarcastic retort.

'Your theory's as good as any other, Stan.' Brian was still chuckling as he stumbled away, weaving between hummocks of grass, prodding the ground with his stick.

Later they fetched plastic builders' hardhats from the caravan, and wore them all the time when in the shaft. It was an elementary precaution against stones, or anything else, falling upon them while bent over digging. When they had finished for the day, Anthony had clambered out last and pulled up the ladder after him. Placing covering boards over it, with plastic sheeting pegged down on top, they left the excavated shaft at a depth of nearly ten feet, which was close on three metres in the metric measurements used to record the site. Being old-fashioned in temperament and inclination, Anthony still thought in terms of feet. Ten feet was deep. Three metres meant little to him.

'Next time, we're going to have to set up a system to get the spoil out,' he had said. 'It's too deep now simply to toss up.'

That comment, of course, had sent Miles into convulsions of laughter.

'Well you're a tosser, mate. You should know.' He had given Anthony a friendly punch. 'Only joking.'

Anthony, comfortably back at home and elated that Giuditta had written to him, sounding so friendly, remembered these things with a grin on his face, In fact, in the course of the next few days, he found himself breaking into a smile often for no particular reason, even when shopping in the local supermarket or doing some other mundane task.

Time passed slowly for him as the days ticked away towards the 26th May. He grew ever more impatient for that day to come, so that he could be with Giuditta again – just to see her once more and to walk beside her and to look into her face. He found he had to draw together his memories of her and force himself to remember what she looked like. At times, he had only an outline of her in his mind, like a cartoonist's black and white drawing, still to be filled in with all its coloured detail. If he could not conjure up her face, then he thought of her hair – that dark hair framing her face and falling to her shoulders, filled with the colour of chestnut.

With only a week to go, she had still not contacted him with the details of how they would meet. He did not want to email her about this – or least of all phone her – in case she should be irritated by his prompting. He realised by now she got irritated easily, in particular, it seemed, if under stress, and he felt it was wise to hold off until she was in touch with him herself. Despite the occasional doubt, he felt sure that she would not let him down.

To give himself something purposeful to do, he decided to plan another novel. The first he had written – the one he could not get published – had been set in England during the Second World War, about the love of a young man for an older woman; ironic this, as his situation now was the other way around. He had presented the story through the eyes of the woman. He had found it difficult to write, in particular as he had had such a series of disasters himself with women and had often been accused by them of being unsympathetic and misunderstanding. Pamela had been but his latest and greatest failure.

However, as the plot he had devised demanded it and he did not want to have to rethink the format, he persisted with the woman as his central character, and in the end was relatively satisfied with the result. None of the literary agents who rejected the book had commented on any lack of conviction in his approach, but then, since most of their rejections seemed to be based on his synopsis only – if even that – and not the sample chapters he had submitted, he knew that that probably counted for little.

He wondered if he dared ask Giuditta to look at the book. He would appreciate her female viewpoint. She might be able to suggest things – terminology, language, imagery, feelings, sexuality – to which he had not given a plausible feminine emphasis, and which he should alter. And that would give him something tangible through which to maintain contact and friendship with her. It was just possible, of course, that she might actually be impressed by his writing, which could give him the sort of kudos in her eyes he was seeking. Greater, of course, would be publication. The successful novelist! If he could achieve that, then she might well want more to do with him. Or so he thought amongst the many fantasies that wove through his brain during this anxious period of waiting.

He had been much affected by the visit he had made with Giuditta to South Cadbury Hill, which had brought back into his mind the associations of that place with the myths of King Arthur. He began to think of a new story he might write that would take an Arthurian romance and give it a setting today, with the fate of the characters known already as they played out modern versions of the original legends. The fantasies, the romances, the adventures, would all be lived anew and carried through to their bitter ends in the present world. He thought there was 'mileage' – he used that awful term reluctantly – in the idea.

Again, could he hope to discuss this with Giuditta? It was something that might interest her, because she had now been to South Cadbury and knew of the Arthurian stories. Would she be attracted to a story of romance? Or would she be put off if it turned into a black tragedy? He knew so little about her and what her likes and dislikes were. He did so want Giuditta to become part of his life. If he could not offer her youth or riches, he had to find a role, a purpose, an involvement with her that raised him in her eyes from the ordinary to the exceptional – or at least, he considered, the different.

Two days before the date of their meeting, just when Anthony was beginning to despair, an email came from Giuditta. It was brief and to the point –

'The 26th. I've got the afternoon off. I'm coming down by train. Can you meet me at King's Cross at the end of platform 7 at 3.00?'

Greatly relieved, he emailed back –

'Yes. Great. I'll be there. I assume you don't mean the far (front of the train) end of the platform! Anthony.'

The last sentence he put in as a joke, just for something to extend his message, a little quip to make her smile, the sort of thing you might say to someone when they were with you. He was dismayed to learn by return that he had made another mistake:

'What are you talking about? Why would I go to the wrong end of the platform? Do you think I'm stupid? Or perhaps it's you that's stupid.'

He did not know what to make of this unpleasant reply, but decided – wisely, he felt – not to try and defend himself. However, the abrupt words left a knot of misery in his stomach. He didn't want to be spoken to in that way. He wanted to make Giuditta laugh, not irritate her. He was becoming increasingly worried about stepping on one of the landmines she seemed to scatter about herself. Hidden and unexpected, as they were, he was losing confidence as to how and where he should tread. He would have to be more careful in future about what exactly he said and wrote. He didn't like her to be upset, particularly when there was no reason for it.

The next day he began jotting down some further ideas for his proposed novel. He wanted to have something rather more definite of structure and storyline to present to Giuditta than the admittedly hazy ideas – as misty and insubstantial as the Arthurian landscapes he wished to use as a backdrop – he had gathered together so far. He thought this time the story should be of a younger woman who is in love with an older man; or is it the man who at first is pressing his attentions on the woman, and she is indifferent? There would be an irony in the latter scenario out of his own present circumstances. Could he write a story based on his own experiences, his own emotional drives, his desires for fair, young flesh? Would Giuditta recognise this? Would she respond to the story, or would she be put off, even repelled?

He thought: what about a central character who is a powerful man – a soldier, or a politician, or a 'captain of industry', perhaps even a media celebrity – who has never, for whatever reason, settled down to have a family, and seeks now a last chance for a child of his own? He courts a much younger woman who might yet provide him with what he desires so desperately – his immortality by the perpetuation of his genes through a son – for, Anthony thought, the child must be a boy rather than a daughter. So the woman surrenders to him and marries him because he has position, power, and money, but she never loves him and, it turns out, cannot give him, anyhow, what he desires most.

The reason for that, Anthony had yet to decide – it might be his declining potency or her inability to conceive, or a combination of both (each believing that the other is at fault) – but the effect on her is more catastrophic than on him. While he obtains release for his frustrations elsewhere, her life is closeted and unfulfilled, and she is shut away from all the things she might have had, but which will not now be. Until, that is, a much younger man comes suddenly into her life. And that will lead to a terrible tragedy when the husband discovers her secret.

What that tragedy would be exactly, again Anthony had not yet determined. He knew, however, that it must arise naturally out of the Arthurian parallel he would introduce. The story he would use would be that of the Lady of Shalott – the version told by Tennyson in one of his best-known poems. The woman had been shut away in a tower by a river outside Camelot, until the wonderful knight Sir Launcelot hove into sight and broke the curse that bound her. The tragedy, therefore, must be her death, borne away on the water towards a modern Camelot, where her faithless lover is allowed one last look at her beautiful face.

Anthony did not know if he could write such a story – his confidence rose and fell with his changing moods – but the thought of it filled his mind with ideas and colours, and he felt the emotion of the story washing over him, so that tears came to his eyes. Silly fool, he thought of himself. As I get older, I seem to want to weep more and more. Is that a stage of life's journey towards the senility and death awaiting us – the vale of tears through which we all must pass, out of brief sunlight into darkness? If I could only put over some of these ideas to Giuditta, what would she think of them? Would she understand what I am trying to express? Would she be in sympathy?

He could not imagine that she would be – he had to confess that – and began to feel the planned novel was all contrived nonsense out of his own present sad inadequacies, striving to be something he was not, to do things that were now beyond him. He went to bed that night with his head in a whirl, with thoughts jumping out of his brain onto the pillow so that he twisted and turned for much of the night and obtained only a few hours of poor sleep, which was a pity for the next day was to bring his long awaited time in London with Giuditta and he wanted it to be relaxed and happy.

8

Anthony left home at midday to make sure he would be at King's Cross Station in plenty of time for the 3 o'clock meeting with Giuditta. It was a warm, sunny day, and he wore a blue jacket, a red tie (for there would be a formal occasion involved), and fawn-coloured trousers, carrying in a backpack a rolled up pullover in case it grew chillier later on.

Because he was tired, he was nervous. Lack of sleep always affected him like that. Still he bore up against it, forcing himself to feel positive and assertive and not allowing himself to surrender to the tiredness.

He had brought a sandwich in his pack, and he took it out on the train, much to the evident disgust of the elderly lady opposite, who clearly disliked the idea of anyone eating in a public place. He eat quickly, ignoring the woman's glances, and stuffed the wrapping back into his pack. She had seemed particularly intent on what he would do with that. Throw it out of the window, perhaps? Did he really look to her the sort of person likely to chuck litter about? He tried to smile reassuringly at her, but she looked abruptly away. These days all values were inverted, he reflected, and no one trusted anyone now, for the unthinkable could come anywhere, at any moment.

The train drew into Victoria at a few minutes past 1 o'clock, and Anthony took the tube for King's Cross straightaway. He wanted to be there in position in very good time. Although it was a working day, it was not busy on the underground. The workers were in their shops and offices, and the main hordes of summer tourists had yet to leave their home shores, so Anthony was able to settle back into a seat and stare out at his fellow travellers ranged about him.

He hated coming to London, not only for its usual crowds, its dirt, and its unwholesome torrent of noise, but because so many of the people – in their dress and general appearance – seemed alien to him now. If they weren't dressed like comic book clowns, with faces and bodies pierced and tattooed, then they wore shiny city-slicker suits, their heads topped with gelled-up crests of hair, and bore arrays of shiny instruments which they usually kept glued to their eyes and ears. And when they spoke, long gone were the days of self-conscious introspection, for they yelled into these machines with the outgoing confidence of a drill sergeant on the parade ground, and in language often as caustic and uncouth.

Yet, amongst such examples of what he considered modern vulgarity, Anthony had to admit there were many beautiful women. Look at that one there, opposite him to his left, in her smart charcoal-grey jacket and skirt, with her fine crossed legs as if turned on a master craftsman's lathe, and her bust swelling beneath an embroidered white blouse, with all the promise of a nude painted by Titian or Botticelli. Her hair was particularly beautiful, he thought, long, sleek and black, gleaming in the light of the flickering, rumbling compartment. At the next stop she got off, and those wonderful legs uncrossed themselves and resumed their purpose of walking, which – he concluded – they performed most admirably. He wondered fleetingly what Giuditta's legs looked like. He had only ever seen her in trousers.

At King's Cross Station, he had well over an hour to fill in. Firstly, he checked the position of Platform 7, and established where amongst the throngs of people – here it *was* busy – he should stand to meet Giuditta. He could understand now her irritation at his silly comment about which end of the platform he should meet her. Seeing it curving away into the distance beyond the barrier, he realised he might as well have said, about meeting her, for example, at Westminster Abbey: 'Do you mean at the door or on the roof?' It would have been an equally stupid remark. Why was he such a fool at times?

He found a coffee bar outside the station on the far side of the Euston Road, where he bought himself an expensive Americano with a Danish pastry, and tried to relax enough to read the paper. However, he found his thoughts wandering, and the print to his tired eyes kept jumping up and down like so many small, errant children. He went to the toilet, a tiny room into which, carrying his pack, he scarcely fitted, and splashed cold water onto his face, wiping it off with a paper towel. This revived him considerably, and brought back his resolution to ignore the tiredness and not to be so stupid. He was about to meet a beautiful young woman, that was all. He was not due to have a job interview or face a court hearing or….He could not think of any other event that would give equal cause to set his nervous system trembling. Relax! How many times had he told himself that over the years. He had always been a martyr to fears and anxieties about which other people, he suspected, never gave a thought.

What would she be thinking, he wondered, as she sat in her train speeding down from Cambridge? Now, that was a point! He hadn't checked yet when her train should come in. Or had she, like him, arrived early and was perhaps already waiting for him?

He raced back over the busy Euston Road to the station, looking at his watch and tut-tutting as he was held up by the pedestrian crossing lights. There was still half an hour to the appointed time of 3.00, but it would be as well to be in place early. The arrivals board said there were two Cambridge trains arriving around half past two, and then none until about 3.20, so – he checked his watch again – was she arriving even now?

Rather than go to the platforms where the trains were due, both at some distance, he stayed put at platform 7 – why had she chosen this platform he wondered? – scanning the crowds who swirled past him, singly, in couples, in groups, stopping close to where he stood so his view was blocked, then moving on, brushing against him, with drinks in hands, cases trundling close to his feet. He found it very annoying having to stand still waiting like this, apparently invisible to others.

The minutes clicked by, and he could see no sign of her. He peered amongst the throng, seeking that tall, willowy figure with the long dark hair and the smile that lit her face when she chose to bestow it, or perhaps she would be showing her look of absorbed preoccupation, busy with what she had to do, in control and unfazed; not like him, with his worry all the time about what other people were thinking of him.

And then the hands of his wristwatch reached 3.00, and still she had not come, and he began to be concerned. Five more minutes passed – six, then seven – and at last he caught sight of her. She was deep in the concourse close to the front of W. H. Smith's, and she was talking to a man – a man in a jacket and tie, and with a beard, of much the same age as himself: just for a moment the man looked towards Anthony, and then back to Giuditta, laughing and taking her hand, and then walking away, turning back briefly to call something over his shoulder.

The first reaction in Anthony was as if someone had punched him in the stomach. And then desperately he tried to force that feeling from himself, fixing his tired, strained features into a welcoming smile, for now she was walking straight towards him. He must not spoil anything by appearing sulky.

He saw first she was wearing trousers that were dark blue, and above them some type of beige-coloured, woollen jacket, with around her neck a pink scarf threaded through a loop beneath her throat. A handbag was slung across her body. The ends of the scarf swung as she walked. Her head was bare, her hair hanging free, curling up on her shoulders.

'Hi.' She was standing before him at last, after all those weeks of waiting, and he felt as if struck dumb, the shock at seeing the other man still crazy upon him. 'Been waiting long?'

She did not seek to take his hand, and he did not like to offer it. He had no familiarity with her, as she clearly had with that other man.

'Hello. There you are. No, only a few minutes.'

She was smiling. 'I'm sorry. I'm a little late. I came down with a friend a bit earlier. We had lunch together.'

'Oh, so you won't want to eat now?'

No, not a meal. Unless you want to eat.'

'No. I'm fine.

He found they were walking across the station concourse and he did not know where they were heading.

'Where are we going?' He tried to make his voice light, to enjoy being with her, to be positive, not to suggest puzzlement or complaint.

'Oh, I thought you knew. You're the London expert.'

'No, I'm not. I never told you that. Not this part of London, anyhow.'

She swung round, looking into his face a little perplexed, as he had feared, perhaps detecting something in his tone.

'What's wrong, Anthony?' There was that lovely accent, as he remembered it, making play with his name, and here she was beside him, and he was complaining. He sought inspiration.

'Nothing's wrong. Of course not. Let's have a quick coffee and we'll have a think.'

Before she could reply, he turned and led her on, sensing that she was stepping close behind. He knew now where he would take her, just up the Euston Road, past St. Pancras, to the British Library. It had a restaurant and a coffee shop, not like that chain place where he had just been, with its battered sofas and grimy tables, but something different in a unique environment she would like. He wondered where Mr. Gentleman Friend had taken her for lunch.

Once on the pavement, he slowed so he could walk beside her. 'I used to come here when I was researching my novel. The one set during the last war. I told you about it.'

He was pleased to hear her giggle, her wonderful rippling laughter that told him he was forgiven ….It didn't matter for what or whose fault it had been. Whatever had been wrong was now over, for she appeared in a good mood, swinging along beside him. He relaxed a little.

'You used to do research here. What in the road?' It was the challenging, mocking Giuditta he had known at Glastington. She never seemed to take him too seriously.

He turned towards her and placed his hand lightly on her shoulder as they walked side by side. 'No, at the British Library. That's where we're going for coffee.'

It proved an inspired choice. She was intrigued by the buildings of the Library as they approached them and entered – the blunt, brick walls, the Lego-like clock tower, the glass panels in the entrance way, the sculptured, decorated interior with the flights of steps upwards, and the escalator which they took to the first landing. Here she gave an audible intake of breath as the first book stacks came into view, ranged against the glass walls as if they were an enormous line of outsize pictures. They came into the cafeteria, with its square columns rising high to a lamp-lit ceiling, and overlooked by row after row of ancient books that towered above through several floors.

'Where are the reading rooms?' Giuditta asked.

'Off the various landings. You can only enter them with a reader's ticket.'

They collected a cafetiere of coffee and two large pieces of chocolate cake from the servery and took them to a table, where Giuditta unslung her handbag, then unwound her scarf from her neck, draping it on the chair beside her.

'I had a sore throat this morning. It feels a bit better now.'

She looked lovely. Anthony was so proud to be with her, feeling as he had before that others were looking at them, absorbing this beautiful woman and the man who was accompanying her. He felt fine now. He seemed to have shrugged off his tiredness, which he knew had been made much worse by his nervous tension. Suddenly, indeed, he felt wonderfully relaxed.

'You know, I don't even know your surname for sure,' he said. 'Is it Ponti?'

She looked surprised. 'Yes. I thought I told you that.'

'No. I had to guess from your email address.'

'Well, you guessed right.' She was a little short with him, a little sarcastic in tone – but that seemed to be her way at times. He didn't let it detract from his new sense of confidence with her.

'Who was the man you were with?' he asked after a pause. It felt natural to put this question to her now. It would be strange, in fact, if he did not ask. Whatever the answer, it did not matter; nothing could matter at this moment. He was with her again and time hung still for them. There was nothing that could intrude on the pleasure he felt.

Giuditta, however, must play her games. 'My lover, of course. Who do you imagine he is?'

'I don't know, that's why I ask.'

He felt confident, amused by her, not worried now. Whatever she said in answer, whatever type of look she gave him, it would only make him laugh. He felt the chuckles rising within him even as he saw her pondering her reply. She placed a piece of cake between her lips, biting down on it with teeth that were very white against the pink lipstick she wore, and then dabbing at her lips delicately with a napkin.

She evidently decided his question was reasonable for she answered, 'I work with him. I came down on the train with him and we had lunch together. He's off to meet his daughter. She's a cellist playing at the Festival Hall tonight.'

'What is the work you do, Giuditta? You've never told me.'

For a moment he thought she looked a little furtive, as if she did not want to answer. She fiddled with her cup and he poured her some more coffee

'I teach in an English language school in Cambridge. The man I was with – Robin – he's the principal.'

'Who do you teach? Children, adolescents?'

'Foreign students, in the main. Late teens, early twenties, most of them.' She had become a little impatient, a little snappy.

'What Italians learning English?'

'Yes, some. But many other nationalities as well. Africans and Asians and Eastern Europeans.'

'It must be difficult. Exhausting. Particularly teaching what is a second language for you.'

'Yes, it is.' She said the words flatly and didn't seem inclined to expand. Then, she brightened, 'But it's not all the year. I only take a couple of terms.'

'What do you do for the rest of the time then?'

'I travel. I enjoy myself.'

'Yes, I'm sure. But don't you have to do other work?'

'I do translations. Written work. Oral work. I'm on the books of an agency.'

She lapsed into silence, looking down at her plate, picking up cake crumbs by wetting her index finger. Anthony watched the movement of finger to mouth, seeing the tip of her tongue flick the crumb from the finger, finding this irresistible, erotic – fool that he was! He had to look away.

He guessed she did not enjoy her work. He knew she loved the outdoors. She would want to be out and about, gaining new experiences, seeing new places, mixing in the colourful, changing hurly-burly of the world. At least that is what he thought. He did not know for sure. He realised he did not know much about her at all. She had had a period of darkness which had made her ill – Brian Radleigh had told him that. Had it been the stress of her work that had caused it? He knew he could not ask her, for he was not meant to know.

'Where do you like to travel to?' he asked instead.

The quest for travel, he was thinking, was normally fulfilled when you were young, or perhaps much later in life after retirement. In middle age – and that's where she was, or nearly so, for sure, despite seeming so youthful compared with him – you were normally settled down, pursuing a career, having babies, and up to your neck in mortgage and other debts All these things, as far as he could determine, did not seem to apply to her.

'I go back to Italy quite a bit. And to Germany where I've got friends.' She hesitated just for a moment. 'Last year I stayed with someone in California – on a ranch he owns.'

'Oh, my! You can't beat that, can you?' He said those words out loud, without thinking, in sudden shock. He probably didn't even know he had spoken them, for he then continued politely and evenly, 'Where did you meet this friend?'

His world was beginning to shelve away again. He clung on to it desperately, refusing to let his feelings of inadequacy and jealousy triumph, that fear of the unknown in other people's lives, their present and past, when what he wished most for was for there to be nothing but his own present, his own sad, unfulfilled life, just to see her smile and laugh with him, to share interest in his book, his archaeology, his excavation of the well. California indeed! A ranch. She might just as well have spoken of the far side of the moon.

Giuditta did not seem to have noticed any change in him. She was raising her coffee cup to her mouth. 'Oh, I've known him for a very long time.' He noted she said this in something of a rush, not meeting his eyes. 'I may go out again later this year. If I do go, it's likely to be in August and would clash with Glastington.'

'I see.' Anthony's misery was complete. He was no longer relaxed. The tired nerves were rising again to grip his body, bringing tension into his limbs and through his eyes. She was rising to her feet.

'I must go to the ladies.' She picked up her handbag and wound her scarf around her neck.

'I'll see you at the head of the stairs,' he said.

He went to the toilets as well, trailing behind Giuditta, thinking how good she looked in her tight-fitting trousers, but with a heavy sense of despondency deep within him now that only cold water, dashed violently onto his face, might dispel. The water did its trick again, and brought back some perspective.

For the moment. Live for the moment. For we all dwell within thin bubbles of sunlight that can be burst at any time. Never mind Mr. Ranchman amidst his Californian acres. She is here with you now, and that is all that matters.

So he smiled at her as he came up to her, leaning against the tubular steel handrail of the main staircase. Lovely. So lovely. She was a vision of loveliness. The sunlight shone through the upper windows and was in her hair. How he longed to hold that hair, to pour it through his fingers, to twist it into ropes with his hands, pulling her head towards him, meeting her lips with his.

9

They walked together along the Euston Road to the top of Gower Street. Anthony had wanted to hail a taxi, but Giuditta said she preferred to walk.

The plan Anthony outlined was now to go to the British Museum, and then perhaps a light meal somewhere before moving on to the Pompeii reception. The Italian Institute, where this was to take place, he had checked, was in Belgrave Square, close to Hyde Park Corner, a much lengthier and more complicated journey, so it would be best to take a taxi there. Giuditta had not demurred at that. She did not seem to know London well, although she said she had been to the British Museum several times.

'I always like going there,' were her words, and Anthony felt a raising of his spirits that what he had suggested would give her pleasure. He had been half fearful that she would expect an expensive restaurant – or perhaps even some other exotic venue, although he could not really imagine what that might be – but he had been reassured by her smile when she accepted his ideas.

She seemed happy to be beside him, apparently unaware of any tensions that she might have induced in him. They passed the buildings of London University, and Anthony told her he had done an archaeology diploma there at Birkbeck College, which he had only completed a couple of years back.

'Really,' she said with her usual contrived sarcasm. 'I didn't know you were so clever.'

He did not mind the sarcasm, knowing that at least he meant something to her if she was bothered to address him like that. What he dreaded was the return of her moodiness, and the abruptness and the rudeness that had punctuated some of her emails.

They came to Bedford Square, and, not far beyond, turned left into Great Russell Street, with the railings of the British Museum on their left. The pavement was crowded now, and Anthony led on, weaving amongst parties of Japanese and American tourists. Having queued to pass through the security check, they stood at last before the great colonnaded front of the Museum, then climbed the flights of steps where tourists swayed and turned, taking photographs of each other, and where a party of schoolchildren shrieked in their play.

Once within the Museum, they entered the recently-constructed Central Court, and Anthony took Giuditta to show her the original circular reading room of the British Library before its move to the new St. Pancras building that they had just seen.

'I once read here,' he said. 'It was way back in the mid-80s'. I can't even recall what I was doing then exactly. It was probably some sort of topographical study, for which I couldn't get the books locally. I remember a friend who was an academic wrote a letter supporting my application for a reader's ticket. Now anyone can get a ticket apparently – even students who could easily study elsewhere.'

'Ah, those students,' said Giuditta with some feeling. By the manner in which she had pushed through some of the groups of chattering young people who were barring their passage in the walkways, Anthony gained the impression that she did not have the greatest of patience with them – not the best attribute for a teacher, perhaps.

Leaving the Central Court, they wandered at random through some of the ground-floor galleries, passing great sculptured Assyrian bulls and reliefs of ranked warriors, each man with an identical spade-like beard, then through rooms of strange, squat Egyptian gods and cases full of brightly-coloured jewellery taken from tombs, and on to groups of Hellenistic sculpture, set around the reconstructed façade of a temple. Close by, a Roman wall painting was displayed that Anthony always enjoyed viewing. It had long been in this position, even in earlier times when the layout of the galleries was different. In those days, there had been a mosaic here, he remembered, and a trickling fountain, and even a small café as well – now all long since removed. Yet the wall painting was still there.

He pointed it out to Giuditta. It showed dancers – men and women – at a Bacchanalia, in a place beneath trees, with musicians playing, and the dancers, caught by the artist, in movement that seemed contorted and powerfully sexual. The central dancer was naked with a large, dangling penis.

'That seems a bit exaggerated,' he mouthed to her, surprised at his own boldness. To his embarrassment, she looked long at the painting, then laughed so loudly that he had to say 'Shhh!' for others were turning to look. He felt himself reddening as he walked away.

She looked sideways at him, but did not say anything, and he felt too embarrassed now to do anything but chuckle himself and say, 'I wish I hadn't shown you that.' And all she replied, as if puzzled, was, 'Why do you say that?', and he knew he was out of his depth with her.

They left the Museum as it closed at 5.30, and he took her along Great Russell Street to a small Italian café he knew. Here she spoke in Italian to the proprietor and his waitress, and he forgot his early confusion and was pleased by the conversation and the laughter around him.

'What were they saying?' he asked in a lull in the chatter.

'Oh, nothing much. He was asking if I'd like to work for him. His family own restaurants in Naples as well.'

'And what did you say?'

'Oh yes, that's a job with a future.'

'He's probably a millionaire.'

'It's not money I want.'

He looked at her, and thought it was best to say nothing further. There were some subjects she shut up about, abruptly and tightly. He had learnt by now how easily she could be irritated and, studying her sudden closed face, he didn't want to risk that.

He talked about himself instead. She had seldom asked him anything about his life, so he thought he would be on safer ground if he gave her some inconsequential detail about his recent activities. She seemed a little distant now, picking at the toasted sandwich with its side garnish of salad that the waitress had brought her, but she listened attentively enough. He moved onto the safest subject of all, their shared experience at Glastington. He gave her more details of their weekend excavation of the well than he had been able to put into his emails.

'It sounds tremendous,' she said. 'What discoveries there must be to come.'

Something about her tone of voice, and her lack of eye contact, worried him. She was *pretending* interest. That was strange. She had been so full of the dig when she was there with him and in her email enquiry since. What an odd woman of fluctuating moods she was.

'Do you think you could get there for a weekend – or a day at least – next month?' he persisted.

'I don't know. I'm not sure. I'd like to but I've got a lot on.' She had pulled out a diary from her handbag and was consulting it. 'Just possibly at the end of June. Yes, that would be good.' Now, surely, this was the real Giuditta re-emerging, with a smile and a hint, at least, of returning enthusiasm. How he wanted to see and hear those things, how worried he was when they disappeared. It was like the sun sliding across a sky of scudding cloud. He never knew when shadows would come or brightness return.

'Well, let me know as soon as you can. Brian hasn't fixed an exact date yet. If you can say when you can make it, we'll see if the others can too.'

'Okay. Okay. Of course.'

Sensing irritation again, he desperately sought a more benign subject and began to talk to her about his writing. He described the novel he had written, the love story with the background of England during the last war; how the story was told by his principal character, a beautiful woman who seduces a young Home Guard soldier – but apart from a few inconsequential remarks she did not really respond. So, plunging on rather desperately, he told her about his current idea of a modern retelling of the story of the Lady of Shalott, describing the tower she was imprisoned in and the road and the river beneath that led to Camelot.

To his dismay, she seemed not to be interested in this either. Perhaps it was the stories he was setting out that did not hold her attention, or perhaps it was her current distraction: she seemed to be coming and going from him as if he was seeing her through a mist. One moment she was in focus and intent on him, the next it was as if she were some person he did not know whose only concern was for him to be quiet. As he talked now, she was not looking at him but fiddling with her table napkin, tearing small strips from it, then pressing them together and rolling them into a ball with her palms. She had picked out the meat from her sandwich, but most of the toast and the salad remained on her plate.

'I'm sorry. I can see you're not listening. Are you alright?'

'Yes, of course, I'm alright. Why shouldn't I be?'

'You seem distant.'

'No, not at all. It must be you that's distant.' She added a word in Italian.

'What's that?'

'Oh nothing.' She heaved her body upright in her chair, making a clear effort. She fixed her eyes on his face. 'Now what were you saying?'

He paused, looking at her, just for a moment too long.

'Forget it! she snapped. 'Come on. Let's get going. Let's get this fucking thing over. It was a mistake.'

He was horrified. He didn't know what she meant. He was still half way through his plate of spaghetti bolognese. She was standing up now. What should he do? He took a couple of quick bites of the food, with the spaghetti trailing out of his mouth so that he had to suck it in like so many wriggling worms, and hastened after her.

She was saying something to the proprietor in Italian, proffering £20 notes. She waved her hands.

'*Grazie. Grazie, signorina.*'

Anthony caught a quick glimpse of the proprietor's face, amused, contemptuous, and then he was outside on the pavement. She had her back to him, looking along the road.

'Let's get a taxi.'

He looked desperately to right and left, and, as if in a dream where miracles can happen, saw a black cab in the distance, with its 'For Hire' sign lit up, just now turning into Great Russell Street from Tottenham Court Road. He positioned himself in the road waving at it, causing a cyclist in a red helmet to swerve and curse at him, and only stepped back on the pavement when he saw the taxi begin to indicate that it was pulling in.

He let Giuditta enter first, then hauled himself in behind. He looked at his watch. It was only a quarter past six.

'Do you want to go straight there?'

She didn't answer. She had settled back across the far corner of the seat as if unconcerned. The cab driver had his head turned expectantly towards them.

'Belgrave Square,' Anthony said. 'The Italian Institute. Number 39, I think.'

They pulled away, turning right into Bloomsbury Street. Then the evening London traffic enveloped and held them.

There was silence in the cab. It hung upon Anthony like a weight. He could not bring himself even to look at Giuditta.

'Don't you *ever* ask if I'm alright again.' The words were suddenly spat out at him.

'Well, okay. I won't. What not ever?'

'No!'

There was another pause, and through his shock and his unhappiness he felt a bubble of laughter rising – or perhaps it was simply hysteria. He didn't know why, but, despite the sharpness of her words and her evident fury, he felt that laughter was not far from her too. She couldn't really be angry with him. He hadn't done anything. There had to be a misunderstanding and she would realise it soon. She was so evidently a woman of moods, of sudden, scarcely-controlled passion. He had just set off one of those mines again. When the dust settled, she and he might still be there and laughing once more – just possibly.

'I was concerned about you,' he said rather plaintively.

'Well, don't be. I can look after myself.'

Silence again. The taxi dived, turned, and twisted through back streets until at last, emerging onto a much broader road, Anthony recognised the area of Victoria.

'I'm sorry.' While he gazed unhappily out of the window, her voice came to him, soft and low. 'I'm too harsh on you.'

'That's alright. I can take it. But what did I do?'

'You irritated me.'

'I was eating and telling you about my book.'

They were passing Victoria Station and about to turn into Grosvenor Place when Giuditta suddenly bent forward and rapped on the driver's partition glass.

'Could you stop here, please.'

What's the problem now? thought Anthony, fear returning to bite at his stomach.

'We've got almost an hour,' Giuditta said. 'I've been here before. We're only a short distance from the Institute. We can walk the rest of the way.' Now she did begin to laugh. 'Come, let me buy you something else to eat. I dragged you away from the last place with your mouth full of spaghetti.'

He joined in her laughter, albeit largely pretending, both in their merriment unable to leave the cab for the moment to the mystification of the driver, who must witness many strange things in the course of his job.

Anthony eventually paid him, and followed Giuditta, who was already pushing open the door of a pub that stood a few yards further down the pavement. The street was busy here, and Anthony collided with a couple of men walking past with fingers inter-twined – 'Sorry. Sorry' – before reaching the door too. Inside, the bar was crowded, but Giuditta had already pressed her way up to it and caught the young barman's attention.

'Do you serve food?'

'Just hot pies.'

'Two of them then.'

'Chips or beans?'

'Both.'

Anthony was intrigued to see how the men at the bar fell back and turned to watch her. And she was certainly worth watching, he thought – poised, confident, reaching out across the bar, one leg raised, her knee resting on a stool vacated hurriedly by somebody so she could look across to the menu chalked on a board, her dangling pink scarf supplying colour like a rose amongst the drab greys and browns around, her jacket hanging open showing the small mounds of her breasts. Had he really been arguing with this woman a short time ago? – she, raising him up, then dashing him down again as if he were a toy – he who could be her father and who might well give her a slap and put her to bed.

He tried to push some money into her hand from his position behind her, but she refused it, taking out her own wallet from her bag and paying. They ordered drinks as well – two glasses of white wine – which, as all the tables were taken, they took to a shelf surrounding a pillar. Giuditta found one stool which she offered to him, but he waved to her to sit. Seeing one or two faces still turned towards them, he wondered if people would be thinking he was her father. In his tie and jacket, amongst all the tee-shirts and denim in the bar, he felt he must look like that – the father taking his daughter out for an evening in London.

The pies came very quickly, and Giuditta eat hers hungrily, looking now the exact opposite of that withdrawn figure of half an hour ago who had been picking at her food.

'I was famished,' she said. 'I think that was the trouble.'

'Just let me know in future,' Anthony said. 'Then I won't antagonise you.'

But what was she to let him know, she who had said he must never ask her if she was alright? Anyhow, if she had been so hungry, why hadn't she ordered something she *did like* at the Italian café?

'I will,' she said, and she giggled like a naughty girl.

Relieved as he was that Giuditta was back with him, her happiness returned, Anthony couldn't help reflecting: this is a moody bitch; she's likely to drive me mad.

It was a longer walk to the Italian Cultural Institute than Anthony had anticipated, not helped by Giuditta taking one or two wrong turns, and when they found Belgrave Square at last they were some ten minutes late. As others were evidently still arriving by taxi, their lateness did not seem to matter. Anthony had not known what to expect, for the simple reason, he realised, that Giuditta had told him virtually nothing.

They went up a flight of steps and through a columned porch into the Institute, where they were met by a man in a dark suit, who looked at the tickets which Giuditta produced from her handbag. She spoke to him in Italian, and he waved them through open doors into a broad reception area, with a patterned stone floor, from one side of which a stairway with elaborate wrought-iron balustrades rose to the upper floors.

Guests were mingling here amongst potted ferns, so that the effect for Anthony was rather like standing in the palm court of a grand hotel many years ago. Everyone was dressed smartly, the men mostly in suits and some women even in long gowns. Anthony felt immediately awkward. If only Giuditta had told him what to expect. Thank heavens, he had at least put on a jacket and tie that morning. A young man approached and took his backpack from him, and Giuditta also gave up her scarf, and then a waitress sidled up with a tray of glasses charged with white wine, and another came with a tray of canapés.

'What's all this in aid of?' he hissed at Giuditta, seeing her looking around, holding her glass by its stem. He was suddenly terrified she would recognise someone and leave him isolated and solitary amongst strangers babbling incomprehensible Italian. For he could hear much Italian being spoken all about, interspersed by some conversations in exaggeratedly cultivated English – 'Oh, my dear, you should see what they have found at Terrafino. The frescos are out of this world, simply divine. Are they not, Charles….?'

'What do you mean?' she mouthed at him. He saw to his alarm that she had indeed spotted someone across the room and was waving to her.

'I thought this was an exhibition, not a cocktail party. Where are the exhibits?'

'It's a *reception*. They must have things on show next door.'

She gestured towards open doors at the far end of the room through which some couples were already wandering.

'You go and have a look. I want to talk to someone I know.'

It was as he feared. But before either of them could move there came a loud clapping of hands and calls for silence. A small, dark man was climbing onto a low podium positioned beside the staircase.

'*Buona sera, signore e signori. Vi do il benvenuto al Instituto Italiano.*'

Oh God, groaned Anthony inwardly.

The rest of this smiling individual's short speech, however, was in faultless, if heavily accented, English. Anthony learnt now that the reception was to launch an exhibition of recent discoveries made at Pompeii and Herculaneum – destroyed by the eruption of Vesuvius in 79AD – which would be going on tour around Britain during the summer. It was organised by the Italian Ministry of Cultural Activities, in collaboration with the British Council and the British School at Rome.

Anthony heard all this in something of a whirl. He had picked up a second glass of wine from a passing tray, and was sipping the cool Frascati appreciatively. The effect of the alcohol was beginning to work its deceptive ease upon him. Life was good. What did the Italians call it? *La bella vita.*

When the speech was over, the assembled throng broke up, their conversation rising like a droning cloud of massive bees, and Giuditta, with the lightest of touches on his arm – he was grateful for that recognition, at least – left him to join her friend. He drifted with a crowd that was going through the doors to the second room. On the journey, he located a third glass of wine and bore it before him like a small trophy. This room had clearly once been – and perhaps still was – a grand reception room, for its ceiling was painted and gilded and the walls hung with paintings. A blue rope, suspended from portable posts, discouraged the visitors from approaching the paintings too closely.

Brightly-lit display cases were set up in a line at the centre of the room, with some placed at the corners as well, and around these groups of people were beginning to gather. Some large objects stood by the windows, unprotected by glass – a massive mill wheel of volcanic grit was one, with, close by, a number of paving stones from a street with wheel ruts grooved deeply across them, then a couple of amphorae standing upright, and, beside the latter, set on a low stand, the white plaster cast of a contorted human figure, one of the victims of Vesuvius whose decayed body space had been located in the excavations.

Seeing it was impossible at present to view the display cases without joining a competing scrum, Anthony made his solitary way to the mill stone and examined it closely. Then, content that it was indeed a mill stone and had once ground the Pompeiians' daily bread, he turned his back on it, balancing his wine glass briefly on its upper surface. Almost at once, a uniformed figure appeared, picking the glass up and placing it back in his hand.

'Not on the artefacts, sir,' he said, faultlessly correct in tone and phrase.

Anthony was highly embarrassed. That he of all people should be guilty of such a solecism, he who had done so much digging and knew so much about the practices and principles of archaeology. He hoped no one else had noticed. No, the groups were all still ranged around the cases, and more people were filtering in, their gaze lifting to the decorated ceiling. But, oh dear, one lady, apparently by herself – and that was unusual in this gathering – was looking directly at him. She was standing in a corner close to the door, and now she was coming forward.

'Easily done,' she said. She was English then. Close up, she looked quite elderly. Her face was lined, but it was a finely-sculptured face with shrewd, intelligent eyes. Her hair, cut straight to the nape of her neck, was exquisitely groomed, honey-blonde. Small silver earrings glittered through the hair. She was wearing a long, dark, sleeveless dress, high-waisted, with a white wrap draped over her arms and chest.

'Excuse me? Anthony was not sure what she meant, or whether indeed he wanted to converse with her.

'Placing your glass there. You couldn't do any damage if you threw your glass at it.'

'Yes, true. But it was crass of me at an event like this. I deserved to be told off.'

'Oh, I'm sure not. Are you an archaeologist?'

'Just an amateur dabbler.'

She laughed.

'And you?'

'No. It's just an interest. I read about it and I watch television.'

'How did you happen to come here?' Now he did want to talk to this woman. She wouldn't be rude to him and throw a tantrum at every shifting moment.

'Oh, my husband works here for the Institute. He has a cold tonight, so I came by myself.'

'Is he Italian?'

'Yes, he's Italian.' She laughed. 'My name's Juliana, by the way.'

'Mine's, Anthony. Anthony Winters.'

'Well, Anthony, it's nice to meet you. Shall we look at the exhibits? There's some space around the cases now.'

With a sense of unreality at this sudden change of female companion, Anthony first drained his glass, then moved to stand alongside her as she peered into a case of jewellery – fine gold bracelets and necklaces, and rings so small they must have been worn by children, yet others large, set with heavy stones, the largest one of gold with a great red intaglio at its centre.

'That must have belonged to someone of the senatorial class,' said Juliana, pointing at the intaglio. 'As I'm sure you'll know, only senators were allowed to wear gold signet rings like that.'

Standing beside her, he could smell her perfume – subtle, delicate, hinting rather than stating, enticing rather than overwhelming. Ridiculous, thought Anthony, that I should have such thoughts. Is my fantasy now to make a conquest of this woman? But he did feel an attraction to her and knew he was being lured on despite himself, although he could not believe there was any such intention on her part. Yet, it had been her who had come up to speak to him. If her husband worked here, did she not know others who were present?

They viewed the other cases together – silver items, dishes, bowls, plates, bronze statuettes and figurines, then ceramics, a pile of *terra sigillata* dishes fused together by heat, and a large earthenware flagon decorated with a rampant winged phallus. He could see Juliana looking at the latter carefully, with her head on one side, but she made no comment on it.

They walked over to the plaster cast and examined it. The man whose form was preserved here had been wearing a tunic that was rucked up at the back – the folds could be seen in the plaster. He lay on his side, with his head buried beneath his arms. His facial features were mercifully hidden.

Anthony was wondering where Giuditta was. She must surely want to see these displays as well.

Perhaps sensing his thoughts, Juliana said, 'I have monopolised you for far too long. It's been lovely to meet you, and thank you so much for accompanying me around the displays.'

'Not at all. The pleasure's been mine.'

He thought, then said quickly, 'You know, if you want to see a Roman site being dug in England, you could come to the one we're digging at present at Glastington. The main dig this year will be in August.'

'Oh really. Where is that?'

He told her. She looked interested.

'Perhaps my husband and I could make it. In August, you say? Not to dig, though.' She smiled. She had a lovely smile, he thought. The smile seemed to take the lines from her face.

'Look at our web site,' he said. 'Just Google 'Glastington Roman villa' and you'll find it. My email address is on there as well, if I can help at all. Just look under 'Members." In fact, he had asked Brian recently to take his details down, but it hadn't been done yet.

'Oh, I'm not very good at all that. I'll tell my husband, though. Thank you again, Mr. Winters.' She walked slowly away back into the main reception area.

That formal conclusion using his surname, ended the matter, he felt sure. He doubted whether Juliana would ever come to Glastington. Juliana. What a lovely name! He said it over to himself, savouring the sound.

He looked around, and with a start spotted Giuditta peering into one of the display cases, her hair falling forward about her face. Why had she not come over to him? She must have looked for him, surely. He went up to her, having to push past a large, plump lady before he could get to her side.

'There you are.' Giuditta was smiling which was a good sign.

'I'll go around the cases with you,' he said.

She moved across to the case holding the silver dishes, and he followed her.

'I saw you were occupied.'

'Oh yes, a lady who spoke to me. Her husband works here.'

'Indeed.' Giuditta was not cross, nor pleased either, just passive. Why should she be anything else? It was tedious how he had to worry all the time about her mood.

He didn't want to say any more for there were other people close to them, so he followed her from case to case until they too finished by the plaster cast.

'Sad,' she said.

'Yes, one man's moment of death captured for people to stare at.'

'No, it's you who's sad.'

'What! What on earth do you mean?'

'You seem to spend all your time running after women. Why don't I get her address for you. I'm sure I probably could through my friend who works here and got us the tickets.'

Suddenly Anthony's world was collapsing again. Giuditta was the very trickiest – the most difficult – of women. There did not seem to be anything he could do with her – or say – that was right. His faults, in outline or detail, outrageously assumed, were liable to fly at him from all directions, unexpected, totally unjustified. He couldn't go on like that. No one could She clearly had no respect for him at all. Sad? Indeed, it was. But she was looking at him now, seeing the hurt on his face, and she was smiling.

'Joke!' she said. 'I'm teasing you. I really don't mind you sniffing after other women. She's much more your age, anyhow.'

Even in her jokes then there came the sarcasm and the cruelty. He tried to smile back, but his heart was heavy.

Taxis were lining up at the corner of Belgrave Square to take the guests away, and Giuditta and Anthony joined the queue waiting outside. Anthony had almost forgotten his backpack, and only been reminded by Giuditta's collection of her scarf from the cloakroom. It was dark now, and the air much cooler. Giuditta pulled her jacket across her body, and snuggled her chin into her scarf. A few places ahead of them stood Juliana, now wearing a coat, who turned and saw them, raising a hand in acknowledgement. As they approached the head of the queue, Anthony insisted on accompanying Giuditta to King's Cross, whereas Victoria Station was only a short distance away and he could easily have walked. She didn't say anything, but simply looked at him. Was there any gratitude in her expression? He couldn't say for sure.

In the taxi, she sat close to him. She looked at her watch. It was approaching 9.30.

'Robin's said he'd be on the 11.00 train. Would you wait with me until nearer that time.'

'Of course, I will.' He was so pleased he had made the right decision and she was now asking for his company. It would make him very late home, but, providing he didn't miss his last train, that hardly mattered. He was not sure he wanted to meet Robin, though. Perhaps he wouldn't need to.

They found a bar in the station concourse that connected with St. Pancras, and Anthony bought her a gin and tonic. He felt drained with tiredness, and by all the ups and downs of the day, and ordered a pint of Stella lager for himself. They found a quiet corner away from the noisier customers and from the flickering plasma screen radiating eternal football.

'It's been good. I've enjoyed it,' he said, as if to convince himself.

'So have I.' She was nice and quiet and normal now, not challenging, scathing or critical. How he would have loved to snuggle up to her, to take her hand and hold it. But he knew he was as far from such things as he had ever been.

'I'm sorry,' she said.

'What for?'

'For making things so difficult for you.'

'I haven't noticed.'

'Yes you have. I know you have.'

'I think you get tired, he said. 'Perhaps a bit depressed.' This was dangerous territory, he realised, for it was very personal and suggested criticism, something she clearly did not welcome. But this time she did not react.

'Yes, I do. I get terrible headaches at times.' She placed her hand to her head. 'It's just clearing now.'

'You poor darling.' The words were out before he could stop them. Again there was no reaction. Perhaps she had not heard.

'Let me come up to Cambridge to see you,' he said in a rush. 'It'll be much calmer there. There are many things I'd like to see and share with you.'

'Alright,' she said with only the slightest hesitation. 'Yes, I'd like that. Perhaps a little later in the summer.'

'Not too long, please. I shall miss you.'

She smiled. 'Always the trier. I'll give you that.'

He was a little deflated by those last words, but his spirits nonetheless soared high. He would see her again! They'd sort out a date by email. And next time everything would be fine.

They sat comfortably together, talking about small things – no more questioning for now, although there was still so much he did not know about her, and nothing expressed either about his plans and hopes, or about his writing, nothing even about Glastington – until Giuditta looked at her watch.

'It's a quarter to 11.00. My train goes at 11.15. I'd better be on the platform so Robin can find me.'

He rose reluctantly. Outside, the evening air struck a chill into him. He took out his crumpled pullover from his backpack and pulled it over his head hurriedly while she watched him. She was so patient with him now, he thought. All that pent up nervous energy and its accompanying irritation seemed to have quite dissipated.

'Well, goodbye,' he said, 'and thanks.'

He was about to strike out for the underground entrance, when she leant forward quickly and brushed her lips against his cheek. He wanted to kiss her back, but she had already pulled away. She turned once, smiling, her dark hair swinging, and then she was gone, treading determinedly along the concourse mall.

Anthony, of course, was in seventh heaven. He floated onto the tube, and to Victoria, catching his last train with only a few minutes to spare. He did not even mind the late night noise that filled it, and the obscenities from a group of youths and their shrieking 'babes' in the adjacent seats. He was thinking all the way home of Giuditta, feeling sure now he had a chance with her.

Perhaps, he thought, her intention had been to test him and to find out how he reacted. Perhaps she had simply needed to get anxieties and tensions he might arouse in her out of her system. That was part of the process of getting to know someone. After all, it could not have been easy for her – away from the prescribed, artificial environment at Glastington – to share the intimate company of a man so much older than herself. He would need to play his cards right, but, yes, there was just a chance – a slim chance – and he was determined to make the most of it.

How he adored her! She may have problems, but he would help her overcome them. This was to be his new mission in life. The rewards could be almost too wonderful to contemplate. And within the golden mists that swirled in his mind he had quite lost sight for the moment of Mr. Ranchman of California. When that memory returned in the early hours, racked in his narrow bed, he turned over and buried his head deep in the pillows.

10

About a week later – it was early June – there was an email from Brian. Could Anthony make a single day on the well this coming Sunday? Stan would be able to come, but not Miles. Brian wanted to press on as soon as possible, since he would have to be away for much of June and probably the first part of July as well. After that, there were only a few short weeks until the start of the main summer dig at the beginning of August.

Blast! thought Anthony. Giuditta had told him that late June was the time she might be able to get to Glastington, but unlikely so now at the beginning of the month. He phoned Brian, however, saying he would be there.

'I've got someone else coming,' Brian said. 'A big lad – Olaf. A German. He's doing a PhD at Cardiff on the Roman army. He's worked on the German frontier defences; a good, strong digger – just what we want.'

Anthony, who had carried out such a massive amount of digging for Brian over the years and was still proud of his strength and endurance, was a little piqued by this. It would be someone else new to work with, this time without the companionship of Miles. Still, Stan would be present to share a joke and do the sorting. Stan was an inveterate chatterbox. He would soon sort Olaf out. Anthony didn't want this much younger, fitter man grabbing all the exciting cutting work in the shaft. They would share and share about. He would see to that.

Anthony, who was still unsure of how best to communicate with Giuditta, decided to phone her on her mobile, and this time got an answer straightaway.

'Where are you?' he asked. The line was bad and it sounded as if she was in some remote place.

'I'm at work. What can I do for you?'

'I'm sorry to disturb you. I've just been on the phone to Brian. He's digging the well this weekend. Is there any outside chance you could make it? I know it's a long shot and you talked of coming at the end of the month, but he needs as many as possible. I'm sure he'd put you up if you came on the Saturday.'

There was a silence. Anthony could sense her trying to control her response. There was a long pause on the crackling line. By now he understood the sudden irritations that could fill her when she was put under stress. Whatever she said, it would not hurt him. He would understand.

When she spoke, however, Giuditta was measured and polite. 'Oh, I can't make it Anthony. It's a shame. I'll be busy here with the students on Saturday, and I'll need my rest on Sunday. It's my one day off. It's not as if Glastington is just down the road from me, either.'

'Of course, of course…' He was anxious to reassure her that he understood.

'As I told you. I could probably do some date later in June or July.'

'Brian will be away then. That's why he's brought the date right forward.'

'That's a pity.'

'When can I come and see you in Cambridge then?'

'Oh, Anthony. Now's not a good time to discuss that. I'll give you a ring about it later.'

He rang off, feeling fairly pleased with the way the conversation had gone. Although he felt a thousand miles from her now, he could still feel the brush of her lips on his cheek. She was still there, the dream continued, and he would be seeing her again sometime – sooner or later.

However, she did not phone as she had promised, and, not daring to contact her again, he drove to Glastington early on the Sunday morning, feeling very unsettled. It was probably for the best, in fact, that Giuditta hadn't been able to come. The journey there and back was indeed too much for one day, and Giuditta's journey would have been even further, and she as well in a car that had clearly known better days. He should really have booked in with Mrs. Reynolds and made plans to spend the Monday in Somerset as well. If he had thought, he might have suggested that to Giuditta, but then she wasn't a retired person of leisure as he was and likely had to work on the Monday.

Perhaps on another occasion – in the school holidays – he could suggest such a weekend to Giuditta. It would be nice to show her some of the other Arthurian sites in the area – Glastonbury, for instance, or the fair Isle of Avilion to which the mortally wounded King Arthur had been taken – 'where falls not hail, or rain, or any snow, nor ever wind blows loudly.'

Olaf turned out to be tall, lean and strong. With his blond hair curling about his ears, and a stubbly beard, he looked to Anthony a typical representative of the former master race transported to the new frontierless Europe of the 21st century. Not that Anthony disliked Germans; just the opposite, in fact. Those he had worked with had been conscientious and reliable, if perhaps a little dull. He couldn't help thinking, however – much as he usually abhorred such long-outdated Second World War fixations – that Olaf looked like the archetype U-Boat commander. He could see him striding ashore, binoculars dangling around his neck, on some palm-fringed beach, with the bows of the ships he had sunk still jutting from the waters of the bay beyond.

Olaf didn't say much, although his English was good. It wasn't that he was shy, Anthony deduced; he was simply quiet and self-contained, working away skilfully and competently without the need for supervision. In fact, he was the very sort of person that Anthony had always admired, not susceptible – as he knew to be true of himself – to neurotic self-doubting and the constant need to prove himself. No, Olaf would surely move quietly and assuredly forward in his studies and his career, and Anthony was certain that in time he would hear his name in connection with a major research project somewhere in the archaeological world.

Looking at Olaf's honey-bronzed face, arms, and legs (for it was a sunny day warm enough for shorts), Anthony wondered why it was that people who were naturally blond tanned so well, whereas he, fair-skinned and red-haired (at least, that had been his hair colour when much younger) simply burnt and went red like scalded lobsters.

It irritated him to see the perfection of Olaf's skin. At his age – and Olaf must have been only 20 or 21 – Anthony would have had a mass of blotches, freckles, burns, and scrapes running across his white, seldom-exposed flesh. And his digging clothes then would have been clear cast-offs from their former days as smart wear – baggy and torn, bunched at the waist and slipping from the shoulders, not worn so easily and casually as were Olaf's grey tee-shirt and tight-fitting shorts. Anthony had to confess he was full of admiration for Olaf's appearance and style.

Stan – to Anthony's growing annoyance and embarrassment – showed from the start that he had no compunctions about making references to the last war in his conversation. Not for him Basil Fawlty's admonition – 'Don't mention the war!'

'Your lot were prisoners in a camp down the lane from our house,' he told Olaf, as if the latter had been personally involved. 'My father used to tell us they marched to work on the farms singing.'

'Good soldiers, my Dad said they were too,' he added, perhaps thinking Olaf would appreciate this recognition of the martial skills of his countrymen eighty years ago. Stan had served in the Territorial Army, and in the echoing chambers of his mind he clearly intended to extend soldierly friendship across the troubled history of the two nations.

'Is that so?' Olaf said, stooping to pull off the plastic sheeting placed over the boards covering the well shaft. The area next to the footpath was now strung around with hazard tape affixed to posts, and with a sign stating, 'Danger. Keep Out.' That was more likely to attract the village louts, thought Anthony, rather than deter them. However, nothing appeared to have been touched.

Brian came up, hobbling with his stick, also in his shorts but with his upper body wrapped in a voluminous, floral shirt that looked as if it might have been used once as curtaining. Feeling hot and sticky already, Anthony regretted not bringing his own shorts. He would wear them for Giuditta's benefit in August, he thought, feeling at first a rush of blood at the idea, which subsided quickly with the certain realisation that blotchy, age-wearied legs were less appealing to a young woman than the smooth, muscled thighs of an Olaf.

When the boards were removed, they all stood around peering into the shaft revealed,

'You must wear hardhats at all times down there, Brian said. 'The shaft looks solid enough, although I don't like that collapsed section. He looked at Anthony. 'Do you think it goes much deeper?'

'Another two or three feet, perhaps.' He really had no idea. There had been no change in the type of filling of the well. Last time, they had still been pulling out building debris. What would you chuck in first, anyhow, to fill up a well?

'How are you going to work?'

'With buckets on ropes. One cutting, one hauling up, one sorting. I'll change with Olaf periodically. Stan's happy with the sorting, aren't you Stan?'

'Right on.'

Stan looked a little like an elderly, nut-brown gnome, thought Anthony. He too wore shorts, showing sinewy legs and sharp knees, and with his short, stumpy body only needed a red coat and a pointed hat, with perhaps a fishing rod in his hands, for him to be added to the rockery of some well-tended bungalow garden. He was stumping away now to fetch a barrow – 'Hi ho. Hi ho. It's off to work we go.'

'I suppose there was no indication of the water level when you were down there last?' Brian said.

'No, everything was dry enough,' Anthony replied.

'I don't think now you'll hit water until you're much lower. I've got a pump on hire in case it's needed.'

'Brian, you think the shaft safe?' Olaf asked. He was peering at the curving stone lining and in particular the collapsed section.

'Yes.' Brian said abruptly. 'Any danger would be in dropping something down with someone below. So keep your wits about you and be very careful when hauling up buckets. Check the handles and the ropes all the time.'

He left them to get started. Anthony worked with Olaf, selecting three of the stoutest rubber buckets with strong steel handles, tying lengths of nylon rope to them and pulling the knots tight.

'I think Brian's right. The shaft does look safe,' Anthony

told Olaf. He was excited about the digging to come. He didn't want anything to hold it up, or, worst of all, prevent it.

Olaf made no answer. Anthony thought he didn't look convinced, which did worry him a little. He wondered if Olaf had had experience of digging wells in Germany. He was about to ask when Stan returned with the clatter of a barrow weighed down with tools, and with finds trays and hardhats perched on top.

All three of them went next to fetch the main length of aluminium ladder that was kept on site under the caravan. They bore it back to the well, with Olaf at the front leading the way and with Anthony at the rear with Stan.

'Big bugger, ain't he?' said Stan, indicating Olaf. He put a forefinger under his nose and flung out his right arm, jerking his legs up and down. Olaf chose that moment to swing round to check the route they should take.

'Stan!' hissed Anthony, red with embarrassment, after waving Olaf towards the correct gap in the hedge. There had been no flicker of expression on Olaf's face. 'Pack it in and grow up. We've got to work as a team. I don't want him to have you shot.'

But Stan, ageing child that he was, unfortunately found that as funny as anything else.

When the excavation got under way, straightaway they came upon a compressed mass of stone wedged into the well shaft. Anthony thought this stone must have come from a building, for many of the blocks were shaped with right-angled corners. Brian was surprised by the presence of these blocks as, by his interpretation, there had been no stone building on the site dating from the early period when it appeared the well had been filled in. It was also unusual for building stone of such quality to be dumped, as it would have been most valuable for reuse.

'It just goes to show,' he said on one of his tours of inspection, 'that you can never assume anything in archaeology. There's always a surprise.'

The blocks were difficult and dangerous to raise, placed one by one in buckets and pulled up by their attached ropes, the puller taking the full weight with his arms until he could reach forward to grab the handle of the bucket as it appeared from the shaft. The danger lay in the chance of a stone tipping from a tilted bucket, or of a handle breaking or a knot slipping.

Anthony noted that Olaf, when in the well, was not happy as the bucket rose above his head, and kept his arms raised in anticipation of shielding himself in the event of an accident. Anthony, in the same situation, however, felt much more confident, even perhaps relishing the slight danger. It seemed to provide an edge to the otherwise dull routines of his life. He did not believe for one second that anything bad would happen.

The tumbled section of the shaft lining was by now clearly defined. It ran from the top for a width of some three to four feet, reaching a depth of nearly seven feet, at which point the securely laid courses of stones recommenced. At some points amongst the collapsed area, the stones had almost all disappeared, revealing the original earthen cut behind against which they had once been set. In all other places, however, as the digging went deeper, and more and more of the shaft was revealed, the curving stone walls were complete and looked secure. Anthony felt confident the whole structure was stable.

After lunch, they reached the bottom of the fill of stone blocks. Their removal had lowered the shaft by a further three feet. There was no indication yet of the bottom. The well indeed was looking increasingly forbidding, a black cylindrical hole descending into the bowels of the earth, with the niches in the wall continuing down, one below the other, offset from each other and so regularly spaced that Anthony and Olaf knew when the next would appear. They outlined the positions of the niches first, then dug them out later of the earth and chips of stone that filled them. In one, a single bronze coin was found, the emperor's head being too eroded to be identified. Brian said he thought it was an early issue.

'Someone had that stuck to the soles of his *caligae* – the last one out of the well,' said Stan with a grin. Anthony thought that for once Stan's little joke might have been close to the truth.

During their lunch break Olaf had been largely silent, but, pressed by Brian, with whom he appeared to have a good relationship, he revealed that he had dug on the German *limes* – the Roman frontier defence systems in that part of the empire.

'There was very good recovery of artefacts,' he said. 'Many wet deposits. Much leather, for instance. Boots, shoes, pieces of tents, shield covers.'

'Like the Vindolanda excavations near Hadrian's Wall,' Anthony suggested. 'Have you been there?'

'No, but I hope to go one day.'

'A wonderful place to visit. You've heard of the writing tablets found there?'

'Ah yes, of course.' Olaf was animated now, his face alight. 'Such a – in English, how do you say? – window on the past. So much learnt about Roman army.'

'Perhaps we'll find some tablets in the well,' Stan said. And, as Brian's head turned towards him, knowing Stan's propensity to make foolish comments, he hastened to defend his statement. 'Well, it would be the right conditions for them to survive.'

'A Roman estate archive dumped in a well,' said Brian, his face wistful. 'Now that would be a find to set the archaeological world on fire.'

Brian, it was clear, lived to make a name for himself from his excavations – the sensational discovery, the media attention, the visit of one or other of the well-known television archaeologists; all these things were the stuff of life to him. Indeed, the spotlight had shone on him on a number of occasions over the years, but not often enough to satiate his craving for the attentions of his peers and betters. Yes, Brian would very much like to discover the Glastington Tablets in his well.

When they got back to work, it was to find that beneath the layer of cut stones, there was a band of sterile soil extending over much of the shaft – sterile, that was, in its almost total absence of finds. In one small area, however, below the tumbled part of the well lining, a lighter patch of soil, almost like sand, was revealed. When Anthony, taking over from Olaf in the shaft, poked at this with his trowel, he realised straightaway what it was – a dump of Roman wall plaster, face down in the soil. He began turning over individual broken fragments, and found that the painted side was predominantly a deep red, but that some pieces had additional bands of colour on them – blue, brown, and green stripes. This plaster had once decorated the walls of a room, and then at some time been stripped off and dumped with other rubbish in the well.

The fragments had to be placed carefully into finds trays and raised from the shaft. Olaf came back into the well to help do this, both he and Anthony kneeling side by side in the shaft – a tight fit – while Stan and Brian hung over them watching. At last seven trays of plaster were lifted out, and Brian bore them away for further examination. Anthony followed Olaf up the ladder into the sunlight and collapsed onto the grass at the edge of the field. It was surely time for another break.

Stan and Olaf had left to fetch tea and Anthony lay by himself beside the well. Full summer was opening over the site.

The field was now high with green wheat and the hedgerows were thick with leaf. Poppies bloomed in scarlet clusters upon the spoil heaps. Even the heap created since the well had been found at Easter bore a plume of poppies on its crest.

The ground was warm and firm, bearing Anthony up. He wanted to relax against the earth, feeling it wrapping its dusty arms around him. He felt suddenly very tired, and he closed his eyes, feeling the ground swaying beneath him. Hell! How exhausted he was! He should really take things a little easier at his age, yet hated to accept he was growing old. It had been an exceptionally early start for him that morning.

A sense of unease began to steal over him. He opened his eyes and looked towards the well where blades of grass moved across his vision. Despite the warm sun, his flesh felt cold. His nerves seemed to be crawling beneath the surface of his skin like a trail of ants scurrying through his veins, foraging along his sinews, seeking an escape out of his extremities – from his toes, from his fingertips, through the jelly of his eyes. At the mouth of the well he thought he could see a pale stirring of the air, like breath issuing from deep within the earth. Was that cold air trapped in the shaft condensing in the warmth above? Or was it….?

He scrambled to his feet, shaking himself,, rubbing his forearms with his hands to try and rid himself of the awful chill. He stepped away from the well, then looked back. The sun was warm on him again and the circle of grey-white limestone shone against the dark earth behind. All was as it should be.

With a thud of boots Stan and Olaf returned bearing beakers of tea.

'What's wrong?' said Stan, seeing Anthony's distracted face. 'You look as if you've seen a ghost.'

'No, nothing like that,' Anthony answered hastily with a shrug and a grin. 'I'm just tired. That's all. The tea's just what I need.'

But the bad feelings stayed with him, so much so that he asked Olaf to do most of the remaining work in the shaft that day. Olaf seemed a little surprised, but did not comment. Looking down the shaft, seeing Olaf kneeling on the working surface with his helmeted head bent forward as he freed some pottery sherds from the earth fill, Anthony was impressed by its depth now. They were about thirteen feet down – perhaps a foot more in some parts of the circuit – but the depth looked even greater from his standing position. The soil that was being brought up now was wetter than before. It contained more organic materials – heavy, yellow cattle bones, jaw bones also, and a large number of oyster shells scattered in white patches amongst the dark, clinging earth.

Olaf worked hard, saying very little, standing on the lower rungs of the ladder to raise up the heavy buckets over his head, so that by kneeling on the shaft edge and reaching down Anthony was able to catch hold of the handles without the need to use the ropes. There was a muscular rhythm to Olaf's work that was not only impressive to watch but also strangely relaxing. Anthony thought, once I could have done that too, but not really now, indeed not now at all. Already his joints were creaking and aching, and he was coming to the end of his strength for the day.

Olaf was spading the wet earth directly into the buckets. The contents of these buckets, handed on by Anthony to Stan to be tipped out into his barrow, had only been quickly looked at in the shaft. Anything might be contained within the damp, clinging earth cut out by the spade. Stan's sorting was thus doubly important to ensure nothing was missed.

Anthony had handed a bucket to Stan, and was watching him as he decanted its contents into the barrow when he saw his shoulders stiffen and a hand shoot out.

'There's something here!' Stan shouted.

Anthony went over to him, while even Olaf, deep in the well, stopped and stood up, peering upwards as if hoping to see from his dark pit what had been found.

'It's a figurine,' Stan said, scraping away earth with his fingers. A white human shape was emerging from the dirt.

'A pipeclay figurine,' said Anthony. 'A first for Glastington, I think.' He tried to take it from Stan, who was clearly reluctant to release it but continued to remove its coating of earth.

'It's a female,' Stan said. 'Little boobies and all.'

Now Anthony had the find in his hands, having had almost to tug it from Stan's grasp. He was determined that such an important discovery was not going to be treated with such idiot disrespect.

'We've got a figurine of Venus,' Anthony called down to Olaf, showing the German the head protruding from his enclosing hands. Now Olaf's boots were on the ladder rungs and he was coming up.

Anthony placed the figurine in a finds tray and insisted no one touch it further until Brian had seen it. 'It needs to be washed carefully,' he said. 'These figures were likely painted and there could be traces of the paint remaining. We could rub that away with the dirt if we're not careful.'

Stan didn't look at all abashed. 'I found it,' he said. 'It's got my name on it.'

'What, 'Stanius Idiotus?' Anthony said. He was cross with Stan. His jocular crudity – stupidity might be a better word – and constant desire to be at the centre of attention might be funny at times, but at others were a source of great irritation.

Olaf bent his big blond head over the tray and touched the figurine with his finger tips. 'Lovely,' he said, clearly struggling to find an appropriate English word. 'One like I never find before.'

'*I* found it,' said Stan again, childlike. 'You're lucky you didn't chop it in two with your spade.'

'Ah, but Stan' – Olaf's face for once had relaxed into a smile – 'if I did not dig it out for you, you would have been *sehr lange* – for a long time finding it.'

'A long time finding what?' Brian's flowery shirt had suddenly appeared beside them. He had an uncanny knack of materialising silently and unexpectedly when something interesting had just come up.

Anthony was now further irritated to see Brian pick up the figurine and continue to rub off the dirt. He didn't like to repeat his cautions. Brian after all was the director and could do as he wished. Stan, puffed out and expectant, was poised beside him. What did Stan want? Anthony wondered. A reward? Really the annoyances of working here were sometimes almost too much!

'Look at her little titties,' Stan drooled.

With his thin legs and round upper trunk, Stan was not only like a gnome, Anthony thought, but one of those priapic herms the Romans had set up in their gardens, appropriate indeed for Stan who seemed to keep his brain in that part of his body much of the time. And this from a man in his seventies, whose lusts should have withered away years ago. Anthony felt a sudden dislike for Stan, hoping Brian would put him in his place. But Brian didn't. He probably hadn't even heard Stan's comments. He was absorbed by the figurine.

'It's in the standard pose,' he said. 'Venus arising from the waves, one hand raised wringing out her hair, the other holding a robe which she's about to wrap around herself. The Romans loved Venus. Perhaps she was worshipped here. One of the *lares* possibly – the household gods.'

'Or it might have been placed in a niche to protect the well,' Anthony suggested.

'Yes, indeed. That's quite possible.'

Brian replaced Venus in the finds tray and prepared to bear her off. 'I'll get it washed,' he said. 'You'll be finishing soon, won't you? You'll see it when you come up to the caravan. I've sponged some of the plaster pieces, by the way, bringing the colours up. They really are worth looking at.'

Anthony's morale was now somewhat restored. He watched Stan retreating for a further sift of his barrow spoil, while Olaf clumped back down the ladder into the shaft. What an ill-matched team they were!

They worked for another half hour, giving Olaf time to check over the area from which the figurine had come, making sure there was no other immediate find to be removed. He then shovelled the remaining loose earth into buckets. The soil was very wet and heavy now: they must be close to the water table. As the final act of the digging day, Anthony dropped a tape measure into the shaft. The depth they had excavated was now a shade over fifteen feet.

It had been a long, rewarding day, only spoilt for Anthony by his irritation at Stan, and by those sudden strange feelings he had experienced while lying by the well. He was sure it had all been on account of his tiredness. And now he had to face a long drive home. He was suddenly anxious to get away. A picture of Giuditta came into his mind – he had not thought of her for several hours – and he brushed it impatiently away. She would have enjoyed the digging if she could only have come. But she had not even bothered to phone him, as she had said she would. He was fed up with people who didn't do what they promised.

The wall plaster, dabbed carefully with a damp cloth, had been placed face up in a series of finds trays on a table top outside the caravan. The colours now glowed with much of their original brightness. There were deep reds, greens, blues, and oranges, and some fragments with clearly delineated stripes and swirls that might – Brian suggested – have once depicted some form of architectural fantasy, with columns and arches and possibly hanging swags of vegetation. The building the plaster had come from must have been of a high status.

The cleaned pipeclay figurine was also face up in a tray, the face full and round with a somewhat pensive expression, the hair braided, the body slim and waisted with good hips, the breasts – as Stan had already appreciated – small but prominent, the *mons pubis* raised and defined.

'What shall we call her?' asked Stan.

'What else but Venus?' Anthony said lightly, wanting to say farewell to Stan with a grin, and not a snarl. They had dug together for so many years. He should have learnt how to handle him by now.

'She looks like a Sandra to me,' Stan said. 'I knew a Sandra once who had a figure just like that.'

Oh, ever the idiot, thought Anthony. He never learns. Stan was now turning the figurine over to inspect her rounded backside. It seemed to be up to Sandra standards for he placed it back satisfied.

'You English,' said Olaf suddenly. He was touching an index finger to his head. 'You are like children. You are crazy.' He was smiling, yet there was a hard edge to what he said.

Anthony felt instantly ashamed, but Brian, who was still sponging pieces of plaster, did not appear to hear. Stan missed the thrust of the comment entirely. He must have thought Olaf wanted to rival his choice of name.

'What would you suggest then?' he said. 'Greta, or Helga? I know. How about Eva? Eva Braun?' He burst into laughter at this as if he had said something really funny, but the others shook their heads in frozen horror. Even Olaf's affable smile faded.

Brian looked up. 'Have you not got a home to go to, Stan?' was all he commented.

Anthony was angry with Stan – his absurd posturings, his crude fixations, his ignorant pretences – and this anger lasted for a considerable part of his dreary drive home, to the extent that he didn't seem to notice long sections of the journey at all. And then the tensions within him began to ease, and he thought back on the pleasure Glastington had given him and the excitement of the excavation. When would they next be able to work on the well? Brian was going to be away for several weeks soon, so it was unlikely that they could continue until the beginning of the main August dig. He hoped Giuditta could be present then. He had forgotten for the moment that she had said she might be in California at that time, and when he remembered that all his pleasure evaporated from him like water draining from a bowl. It was a long time before he reached the outer suburbs of London, and by then night lay heavily over his world.

11

Anthony slept late the morning after his return from Glastington, grateful that he did not have to tackle a labouring day with the masses who commuted daily from Bromley to London. Once he was fully awake, however, he staggered to his computer and switched it on, hoping there would be an email from Giuditta – but there wasn't.

After a round of chores, and a chat with a neighbour, he sat at his desk before the bright watching screen of the computer and pulled a piece of blank white paper before him. He would make some further notes for his planned novel. He would do these in longhand rather than on the screen. It meant he could write and cross out, add and alter, in a way that gave him greater contact with his thoughts than the cold impersonality of the screen with its pulsing cursor. That cursor seemed to him like the heartbeat of an alien life-form beyond his capacity to understand. He found he could not think because of it. He would stare at the screen and the cursor would take his attention, absorbing his thoughts, threatening to precipitate him into a cyber sub-existence he did not wish.

The computer was invaluable for setting up his text, however. Here the process was more mechanical – the choice of the words, the rhythm and balance of the sentences, the arrangement of the paragraphs, the growth and flow of the narrative. He would do all this directly onto the computer, which he felt he could control for these functions. As with any piece of machinery, it was then his to command. The thinking, the creation of ideas and characters, however, could only be expressed on paper.

Computer screen or writing paper, the ideas would not come. He thought of a name for the woman who would play the central role in the story, then crossed it through and inserted another. He wanted a name that was dreamy and mystical, that might be used in both the fantasy world of the Arthurian romances he imagined and the stark reality of the modern day about him.

Then he had an idea: the Pre-Raphaelites had painted scenes out of the Arthurian legends, hadn't they? He returned to the computer and made a Google search, and found image after image of the most magnificent paintings, not only of scenes from the stories of King Arthur but out of other great literary works as well. Amongst the women's names that appeared were Ophelia, Vivien, Guinevere, Psyche, Juliette, Undine, Isabella, Elaine. None of these had quite the romantic ring that Anthony required. And then he began to find several references amongst the paintings to a name that he felt was just right – Rosalind. It seemed to have been a made-up, poetic confection some centuries ago – used by the Great Bard himself – meaning 'beautiful rose'. The sound, the images it inspired,, were exactly what he wanted, so he decided to name his heroine that.

The leading male character's name was not quite so critical, but it must also have an 'old English' ring to it. He selected Richard. Rosalind and Richard – these two were now destined to live out the tragedy he would set for them.

It was lunch time. Pleased he had made at least a little progress, Anthony put his notes away for the time being, and made himself a sandwich of processed chicken and cheese. He must get out to the supermarket this afternoon. His supplies were growing low. There came the sudden ping from the computer of an email arriving in his inbox. Was it from Giuditta? No, but from the Premium Bonds people. He had had a win! Excitedly, he checked for how much? Good God, for £1000!

He danced around his lounge, setting his computer shaking on the desk, the pens and pencils in their plastic container rattling. In the kitchen he poured himself a glass of Pinot Grigio to celebrate. Oh, Giuditta, if you could be with me now! Suddenly he felt compelled to tell her of his good fortune.

He sent her an email –

'Hi. Back from an exciting day at Glastington. Will tell you more soon. I've just had some good news – a win on the Premium Bonds! Don't come rushing down, though! Please contact me. You said you would. Anthony.'

He read this through carefully before he sent it to make sure there was nothing in it she could possibly object to. No, it was fine. She'd be curious about the Glastington discoveries and also about his win. Perhaps he could persuade her to go away for a few days with him – separate rooms, of course. No, she'd never agree to that; not yet. Still, his Cambridge visit she *had* agreed to. That surely was the time when his relationship with her would be able to develop.

In the afternoon he set out his notes again, and tried to work up a plot within which Rosalind and Richard would move inexorably to the tragedy that awaited them – the imprisoned Lady of Shalott and her lover in a contemporary setting. The background to the story he decided to make the publishing business; it was something he could write of from direct experience. Richard, silver-haired and in his mid fifties, a sales director, would set his sights on young Rosalind, still in her twenties, perhaps an editor working in the paperback division of a large publishing house. That would give them the right sort of age difference he required, similar, he reflected, to that between himself and Giuditta.

Now, how would the story develop? What exact conclusion did he seek for his ill-starred lovers? He sat and chewed the end of his pencil. It was hard to get ideas today. The sun was glaring through the windows making the room very hot. He had all but closed the Venetian blinds to keep the shafts of yellow light from striking across his desk.

The sun seemed to be warming his libido as well, making it very hard to imagine stories of sexual desire when that was what he would most like to fulfil – here now, at this very moment – with a willing partner. It was not only the pleasure he would gain, but the escape from tension, bringing his thoughts back into focus, allowing the ideas to flow once more.

Oh God! Without release he could not write – not now, not thinking of Giuditta, hoping she would contact him. He knew he was growing crazed with the sheer frustration of wanting her. His inbox suddenly pinged once more. Ah, another email had arrived And this one *was* from Giuditta! His own email to her had clearly stimulated a reply. She must have been too busy to contact him earlier.

The email was headed, 'Congratulations!' She must be referring to his Premium Bond win, he thought He read the email eagerly, then felt his heated blood turning to ice.

'I must congratulate you on your great good fortune. I hope the money you have won makes you very happy. I can assure you, however, that I shall not be rushing to your side seeking a share of it. How dare you suggest such a thing! What sort of person do you think I am? Whatever money I have, I work hard for. I can assure I don't want an old man's money, anyhow. If I did, I would be rich by now. Never, never tell me of your pecuniary affairs again!!'

Anthony read this through – once, twice, three times – in a type of daze. Then he groaned aloud. Why, oh why, had he mentioned that wretched win? He had only intended it as a joke; something good that had happened to him to tell her about. When he had written of her 'not rushing down', he had not meant to imply that she would do so literally. Of course not. Just the opposite, in fact. His intention had been to say, 'It's not such a big win that you – or anyone – should get too excited about it.' And, as if for a moment he thought she'd be after a share of the loot, that was absurd. Surely she could not think he saw her in such a light?

He sent a reply straightaway, typing so fast he made many mistakes and had to go back over the message to edit them out –

'You've got it all wrong. My fault, I'm sure. It was a joke, that's all. I only meant to tell you that something nice had happened to me. *It's not worth rushing down for* was not meant literally. What I intended to say was that my win is only very modest, not worth a fuss. Please let me know that you forgive me. Sorry again. Anthony'.

He couldn't work any more. He lay down on his bed and closed his eyes, feeling the surges and turns within his brain almost like a physical force, as if blasts of a strong wind were buffeting the inside of his skull. His mind was dead of everything – all ideas, all hopes, all equilibrium – by this great upset of Giuditta's violent, sneering reaction to his wretched email. How could she have written what she did? What contempt for him it showed. He had done nothing to deserve such a response. Surely she could understand that it was all a mistake – some ill-chosen words only, which she had misinterpreted – and no more? What a great pity it was.

Despite earlier misunderstandings, they had been getting on very well. He had been so happy after the London trip. If only he could see her and speak to her. Should he phone? He didn't dare to.

After a time he rose and went to his computer again. He composed a second email,

'You know I think a lot of the problem is cultural. You have a brilliant command of English, but you miss the occasional idiomatic phrase. 'Don't rush over' – or whatever it was I said exactly – only meant don't get too excited. Why should you get excited? I hear you say. Only because it's nice surely for someone you know to be lucky for once. Never for one fraction of a moment did I think you would be interested in my money, as such. The idea that I was writing to tell you not to expect a share of it is so much the opposite of my intention as to be absurd. Sorry, can you understand that? I can't express myself anymore, I'm really so upset, so sorry.'

He went back to his bed, and, stripping off his clothes, pulled the covers over his head, as if this action would shield him from the distress raging inside him. Like this, he actually slept for an hour or so – troubled, disturbed sleep perhaps but at least some form of the blessed unconsciousness that he craved.

He was woken by the phone ringing, and tumbled out of bed, falling to his knees naked on the floor. Still on his knees, he made it to the phone in his small hallway on the sixth ring, barely awake as he answered – 'Hello.'

It was not Giuditta, but some wretched cold-calling from 'a design company in your area: your post code has been selected for a special promotion.....' He slammed the handset down with such force that it rebounded from the cradle.

He felt dirty and unwashed, thirsty and hungry. He realised he was now standing nude in his lounge with the blinds only half-closed, and hastened to pull the slats tightly together. Then he dressed, and, opening the blinds again, peered down at the street below from his position on the upper floor of his apartment block.

The block was part of 'flatland', set amongst tree-lined streets midway between Bromley and Beckenham. He could see mums with pushchairs on the pavements passing by on their way from the nearby infants' school. The weather was hot enough now for the lightest summer wear, and he watched as the strong, brown legs propelled the pushchairs up the hill towards him. The heads of long hair – yellow, brown, red – floated briefly beneath him. There was no consolation for him in the sight of other people's lives going on, so desirable, so lustful, so unreachable. Oh Giuditta! Why have you done this to me? He was in an agony of pain and frustration. Oh, the wretched girl! How stupid he had been ever to think that he and she could get together and be intimate. What an absurd fantasy it was for an old man to have such thoughts.

It could not go on! He was growing angry now, both with Giuditta for being so senselessly cruel to him and with himself for allowing himself to get trapped into such an absurd position where he was in her power. He could sense her reading his efforts to explain, and giggling to herself over them – perhaps showing them to her friends – while she, and they, laughed at the old fool who thought he could make it with a young woman.

But she was not so young, that was the point. He had never learnt her true age, but she must at least be in her thirties, or even a little older. She was therefore a mature woman. If only she would behave more like one. A gap – he calculated quickly –of some twenty-five years, or perhaps a few more, was just about bridgeable. It had been a reasonable expectation.

So – he told himself – he had not been foolish after all. They had been thrown together on the dig and had got on well. It was not as if he had pursued her hopelessly from the outset. No, it was she – not him – who had behaved badly, apparently happy to be with him at one moment, then the next, twisting and turning and criticising, so he never knew where he was with her, as if he could absorb any amount of verbal attack and continue as if nothing had happened. Well, he couldn't – and he wouldn't!

He checked his email. There was nothing further from her. He would give her another two hours, and then he would make a decision. He was already composing in his mind what he would really like to say to her. After these days of pandering to her every whim, he wanted to tell her to get lost, to get out of his life, once and for all. It was not as if he would be unable to live without her!

But he would far rather say something clever to her, something that suggested he was a little amused, as if he was aware he had been dealing with a woman who reacted like an errant child, and now he had to admit failure. Whatever he wrote, it had to be final. There would be no going back once he had clicked on that 'Send' button.

By now it was late afternoon. He decided to drive to the supermarket, as he had originally planned. He had nothing in the flat to cook, except a packet of rather green looking bacon, some tins of soup and a can of stewed steak. He took his elderly Toyota Yaris, his Land Rover being now locked up in his garage. The Yaris, which he kept parked in a bay at the back of the flats, was much more practical and economical for urban driving. He had bought it when Pamela and he had split up almost a year ago. She had retained the Volvo that they had bought together in happier years and which he had loved almost as much as his Land Rover.

The Yaris was utilitarian, functional, efficient. It served him faithfully on the supermarket run and returned him to his flat with bulging carrier bags and a depleted wallet. As he unpacked the goods in his kitchen, his anger with Giuditta returned, filling his head. He checked his phone and his computer once more. There was no fresh message from her. He decided he would cook a meal and see how he felt after he had eaten. Perhaps, with food inside him, his view would alter. Possibly he would become more understanding, less condemnatory.

He enjoyed a bottle of strong cider with his food, and then opened another and –what the hell! – a third. Giuditta, in the role of adored person, was now diminishing to a flicker at the back of his brain. Giuditta – the yo-yoing complainer, the impossible critic, the exploding firebrand, the inconsistent mad woman – was falling away. He felt liberated from her. Mad! Yes, she had been mad – perhaps the problem Brian had told him about. He felt sorry for her. And for himself. It was all, in fact, a great sadness. But he had to be rid of her. There was no time left to wait for an apology. He must get this thing over and done with now.

He went to his computer, opened a new email, clicked on her address, and began to write –

'You have not answered. It may be that you have been out. I don't know. But you must have expected me to reply to your most unpleasant email, and the fact that you cannot be bothered to respond further shows me the profound contempt you hold for me. Perhaps, however, I was simply a cause of amusement to you.

Well, I don't want any more of it. This is what *I* have decided, not you. I had only wanted to share some pleasant things with you. You made me laugh and brought me some brief happiness. For that I thank you. But I can't tolerate anymore of the other side of you. So, with sadness, I have to say goodbye. Goodbye, my Giuditta, whom I have liked so very much.'

Before he had even read through what he had written, with his alcohol-flooded blood singing in his ears, he pressed the 'Send' button and the message had gone. The deed was done. He did not feel sorry. He knew it had been the right decision. He felt proud of himself for having been so strong and decisive; and for not having returned her insults either. Only a little later, as he lay on top of his bed, with the washing up still undone, he felt a flash of panic. Too late! Too late! What would she think? Would she even care? And to his shame he found he had tears in his eyes at all his hopes lost, his fantasies, now scattered like dying flowers alongside the pathways he had hoped to follow with her.

He went back into his lounge, switched on his television, and lost himself in the inanities of some evening comedy show. He fell asleep in front of the screen, another half-emptied bottle of cider beside him.

The phone rang sharply just before 11.00, precipitating him from his chair, the cider bottle toppling – he caught it with one hand just before it fell. Before he reached the receiver, he knew for sure who was calling.

'It's Giuditta. I've only just got in and received your messages.'

'Oh yes?' He cringed, awaiting some furious reaction.

'I understand you want to finish with me.'

'I thought it would be for the best – for both of us.' He slurred the words. They could not really be his.

'I'm sorry. I've read through what you wrote. I understand now.'

He was breathing deeply, his heart thudding. 'You know, I hoped you would phone. In fact, I felt sure you would.'

'You did?'

'I'm sorry too. Perhaps I overreacted. I didn't mean what I wrote, in particular…..'

'So we're still friends?' She sounded small and plaintive, like a little girl appealing to her father. A lump came to his throat.

'Yes, very much so. If you still want to be.'

'Good. I wasn't sure. I think you're right. It was cultural. About language. I didn't understand you…..'

'I thought that could be the reason ….' He was talking over her, rushing to get out what he had to say, just in case she rang off.

'Let me finish. Please.'

'Of course. I'm sorry.'

'And when I said 'old man', I meant like you say, 'Yes, old man. Old chap.' You see?'

'Of course, of course.'

But amongst the relief flooding through him, he knew that last point, at least, was nonsense. Of course, she had intended to be abusive, and she was now trying to deny it. Oh, hell, what did it matter? He had no wish to challenge her again.

"Let's put all this behind us,' he said. 'When can I come to Cambridge to see you?'

'Yes, Yes. Of course. That sounds good.'

From despair to sudden joy in the space of a few moments. His world was taking shape again, turning from bleak defeat into a new hope that was bright with colour.

'How about the weekend 27th/28th at the end of the month?' she said.

'Yes. Perfect. That'll be great.' He hadn't checked his diary, but he knew nothing would keep him from Cambridge that weekend.

'We'll firm up the details later.'

'We certainly will.'

'Well, goodnight then.'

'Goodnight. Oh, Giuditta…'

'Yes?'

'I'm sorry for what I wrote.'

'Get some rest, Anthony. And don't worry.'

He lay unable to sleep for a long time after that. *She was back with him.* It was too wonderful to sleep. And it was *she* who had returned to him, not the other way around. He was going to see her again in Cambridge in only a few weeks. Perhaps she really did want to be with him after all.

At last he fell into a deep sleep. He could not say he dreamt of her, but he had a sense all night that she was by his side, turning to him, staring into his eyes in the darkness.

12

It had been several years since Anthony had last been to Cambridge. A Saturday morning was probably not the best time to be driving into the city. Still, he had precise directions from Giuditta as to where to go, and a definite time to meet her, and he was feeling relaxed and happy as he drove, although perhaps a little tired – a state which seemed to be always with him these days.. He had had to get up early in order to leave Bromley before the morning traffic began in earnest.

He had been under way by 7.30, taking the Yaris, as the Land Rover was unlikely to fit into the Cambridge multi-storey car park where Giuditta had said they should meet. That was set for 10.00, so there was plenty of time, Anthony knew, as he directed the dimunitive Yaris with its round-sloping bonnet towards the M25 motorway. He passed through the Dartford Tunnel toll barriers and under the Thames, emerging into Essex – an unfamiliar land to him. The dull, concrete strips of the motorway stretched ahead of him, through a landscape of industrial units crossed by lines of pylons, like so many marching metal monsters from some SciFi tale. After a while, the landscape 'greened', with fields beginning to appear amongst the lingering tendrils of urbanisation.

With the sun rising to his right out of a sky studded with trailing puffs of pink cloud, Anthony felt the joy of escaping from London and setting out on a journey of discovery, keen with the zest for new experience, happy in the fresh hope of Giuditta's company, now that they understood each other so much better.

It seemed it was no time at all before he was taking the exit for the M11, the motorway that would lead him into Cambridgeshire, heading for the university city of Cambridge itself, passing signposts that announced other places distant amongst the fastnesses of East Anglia. The little Yaris purred ever further north, keeping mainly to the inside lane, passing the occasional lumbering HGV or caravan. Close to Stansted Airport, where sleek aircraft shone in the morning sun as they climbed grandly into the sky, Anthony stopped at a service station where he bought a newspaper and had a beaker of coffee.

It was a little after 8.30. Now for the last lap into Cambridge; he should be there well ahead of the appointed time. He followed Giuditta's directions – the Yaris had no SatNav – and, leaving the motorway that was continuing on towards the west, he took a road which came into Cambridge directly from the south. He passed over the hill at Wandlebury – there was an Iron Age fort here that was on his list of sites to see – and beyond saw a flat plain with the city spread upon it like a vast planners' model gleaming in the sunlight. Beyond Addenbrooke's Hospital, he came into heavy traffic, and it was stop and start and creeping past temporary lights, until at last Anthony could see he was close to the city centre. Hurriedly consulting a notepad, where he had written out the directions, he turned right at a busy junction, avoiding a phalanx of cyclists who seemed intent on suicide, and found himself in crawling traffic beside a wide expanse of green grass to his left.

Ah! he thought. That must be Parker's Piece – an open recreation ground – which Giuditta told me about. Somewhere close by is the building where she works.

The parking garage she had identified for him stood only a short distance further on to the right, and he swung the Yaris gratefully into its approach lane and, after obtaining a ticket, found a space alongside a concrete pillar on an upper floor. He switched off the engine and looked at his watch. It was only 9.30. He had half an hour to wait.

He got out of the car, unstuck his shirt from the sweat on his back, looked in a wing mirror and combed out his hair with his fingers – now much more grey than its original ginger – and pulled on his white calico summer jacket. The day was already warm, and the weatherman on the car radio had given a forecast of hot sun all day.

He descended by a stairwell and found himself at street level close to the car park's main entrance. Giuditta had said she would meet him at the paved area beside the adjacent swimming baths. He looked across to find the place she meant, and to his delight there she was already, fifteen minutes early: most impressive! She saw him, then appeared to hesitate a moment as if not sure she recognised him. He waved, and she waved back. Half-running, he went to meet her.

She greeted him with a kiss – the merest whisper of a kiss on his right cheek, but a kiss indeed. How beautiful she was! Was he not a lucky man to have an assignation like this with such a lovely woman? Despite the arrangements made, he had probably thought it would never happen. And, if it did, would she not be tired and complaining, regretting her agreement to meet with him at all, let alone to spend the weekend with him? Now everything seemed too marvellous to be true. He expected her to disappear like a mirage in front of his gaze. Was she not just part of the imagining – a fantasy of his overwrought brain?

But, no, she was real! The butterfly brush of her lips was real. The delicate scent of her perfume was real. She stood before him smiling, with her long, dark, gorgeous hair curling from her shoulders, a necklace of white beads about her throat, and small, silver stars at her ears. She wore a dress, patterned grey and white, with a skirt that floated over bare, bronzed legs. A small handbag hung by its leather strap from her shoulder.

He had never seen her legs before. He wanted to ogle them, to run his eyes over her, taking in and appreciating every curve of her body, but he could only sweep his glance quickly over her as he received her kiss.

'Hello Giuditta.'

'Hello Anthony. How nice to see you again.'

Was this really the same woman as the one who had snarled and sneered at him in her emails, who had led him by the nose in London, who had shouted and sworn at him down the phone – the one whom he had so recently said he wished nothing more to do with? Strain and tiredness, he realised, had been heavy upon her at such times. Now, she was welcoming and friendly, and looked so wonderfully relaxed. Anthony felt he should shake his head to make sure this dream did not evaporate.

She took his hand. The dream was continuing. Her fingers curled into his palm. 'Come. I will show you where I work.'

Together they crossed the road, and then, releasing his hand, she walked ahead, steering him towards a gap in the railings bordering Parker's Piece. She set a course across the grass, heading towards distant trees with houses beyond, moving at such a fast pace that Anthony found himself struggling to keep up. The fine brown legs scythed over the grass, the handbag swung, the skirt swirled deliciously, with Anthony now almost trotting behind. They rounded one or two groups of young people sprawled on the ground, dodged a frisbee thrown by a youth with spiked, pink hair, and reached the trees. Here a long-haired terrier was playing with its owner, and Giuditta bent forward to take the dog's head in her hands while it sniffed at her, at first suspiciously and then with delight, its tail wagging vigorously.

'Good dog. Good dog'.

'Gerry, come here! Careful. He'll jump up at you.' The owner, a pale-faced, middle-aged woman with short black hair, was stepping forward anxiously to catch hold of her dog by its collar. 'Pity to get dirt on that lovely dress.'

Giuditta skipped away from the dog, which was watching her as if entranced, its mouth open and smiling, perhaps sensing that something special had entered its canine world. She said to Anthony, who was standing by, watching, 'I love dogs. We had many when I was young. I wish I could have one now.'

'I know – you told me that at Glastington. Why don't you get one then?'

'Because I couldn't look after it. I share a house, you see. It's only a small place.' It was the first time she had mentioned where she lived.

Saying farewell to the dog and its owner, she stepped over the railing bordering the trees, standing for a moment astride it, the rail bunching up her dress at front and rear.

'Come on, we're almost there.'

Anthony followed her over the rail. He walked beside her as they trod a narrow service road running between Parker's Piece and the houses overlooking it. They stepped around parked cars while cyclists swished by close to them, and then Giuditta halted in front of what had clearly once been a fine town house, with a flight of steps leading up to its front door. It now bore a sign across its façade – 'Henderson's Language School.' Through one broad, uncurtained window at the front, Anthony could make out tables and chairs and a whiteboard with papers affixed to it, and in the background some figures moving about.

'This is it – this is where I work.' Giuditta said, looking expectantly at Anthony, as if to gauge his reaction. His first impression was, the place is small and rather shabby.

'Henderson is Robin. My boss. The man you saw at King's Cross.'

'It all looks very good,' Anthony said. He could not speak his thoughts. 'The school's open today then?'

'Yes, but only for private study. We do normally have classes on three saturdays a month, but that's followed by a saturday when pupils can come in and make use of the facilities themselves, if they wish, without supervision. That's what's going on at present.'

She waved a hand at the window, from which two pupils – dark-skinned males – were peering. One flourished a hand in return. 'They're two of mine – from Pakistan. Pleasant lads. They learn well.'

Anthony was still lost in amazement at the change in her. At Glastington, she had been temperamental, difficult, her moods flickering like shadows. And now here she was with him – calm and controlled, and beautiful.

'Do you teach here every day?' he asked.

'Of course. In term time.'

'When do you do your translation work then?'

'Well any time really. In the evenings mostly, at home.'

'You live here in Cambridge?'

'Yes, but to the north of the city. At a place called Chesterton. It's a little way.'

'How do you travel in then?'

'By bus. Sometimes I cycle: when the weather's good. Everyone in Cambridge cycles.'

'I'd like to see that.'

'Why, Anthony? I wear trousers. You would not see my legs.'

'No, I didn't mean that.' She was smiling, and he realised she was teasing him. He felt himself blushing.

'Is that your classroom?' he asked to cover his embarrassment, pointing at the ground floor front window.

'I do teach there sometimes. But normally upstairs.' She flung out an arm indicating the two floors of upper windows.

'Amazing. I'd like to hear you teaching.'

'It's boring really. Very boring.' The smile had left her face.

'You like to be outside in the open, don't you?

'Yes, I do. Anthony. It's good you understand me so well.'

They walked on towards the centre of Cambridge while Anthony reflected on her last comment. Was he becoming a father figure to her then, someone she felt she could trust and lean upon? He hoped so. He would like to fulfil that role – any role, in fact, as long as he could be with her.

They had come into busy St. Andrew's Street. Buses were disgorging hordes of determined shoppers. It was here the shopping malls began.

'Would you like to go to the Fitzwilliam?' Giuditta asked.

'I'd love to. Anywhere but the shops.'

Anthony hated the crowds, the shuffling steps and twisting body necessary to survive on choked pavements. He was hot now. The sun was rising to its noon time height. Giuditta by his side still looked delightfully fresh. He had seen more than one male head turn to follow her as she passed. That made him feel good – very good!

At a busy junction, they turned into Downing Street, now passing the stone walls of college buildings running on either side. Reaching broad Trumpington Street, they soon came to the Fitzwilliam Museum, with its huge classical façade looming over the street. Once inside, however, the glories offered by the museum succumbed for the moment to a more pressing need – felt particularly by Anthony – for refreshment of coffee and cake. They found the café in a new part of the building. Sunlight streamed in through a high-glassed roof, but it was air-conditioned here and much cooler. At the counter, Giuditta made to open her bag to pay, but Anthony shushed her away.

'No. No. This is on me. And the rest of the weekend's expenses as well.'

'But you have great costs. I must share them.'

'No. Please, my dear, the pleasure's mine.'

Bearing their tray, she found a table and subsided into a chair. He could not tell if she was pleased or peeved. Some young women today, he knew, did not like to be over-dependent on a man; but he could not allow her to pay. Not yet, anyhow. Perhaps later – tomorrow maybe – he would let her buy a coffee for him. The 'my dear' had come out without thinking. Had she been offended by it? Perhaps it had made him sound a little old, a touch too paternal. He would have liked to have said 'my love', but it was far too early to be using sentiments like that. He must make her feel easy with him.

It was all going far better than he could have imagined. Who would have thought she would have been so happy at meeting him, so smiling, so full of energy and joy. It was almost as if she were acting a part. A slight worry began to tinge his mind that all this enthusiasm, this apparent carefree happiness, indeed was exactly that, and it might suddenly change, as she had changed before.

But for now, she sat beside him enjoying the chocolate cake he had bought for her, slicing it with her fork, placing portions into her mouth, licking her lips with that darting pink tongue of hers. Why should this ever cease? Time – as he was used to reflecting – was like a bubble of sunlight. We dwelt within it, taking the most from it, knowing that at any moment it must surely end, but for the immediate moment all is well, all is eternal.

'Do you come here often?' he asked, forgetting what a hackneyed line that was.

She laughed, although he did not understand why, but was pleased to see her still happy. 'Not as much as I'd like. A fair number of times, though. I love the art galleries best.'

'Do you come by yourself?'

'Oh, Anthony. You want to know so much.'

A shadow of worry fell over the table. Fool that he was to ask her so many personal questions. But, to his relief, her smile returned. 'Sometimes. Sometimes not. I have friends in Cambridge. The girl I share my house with – Lika – she and I do many things together.'

'Lika. That's an unusual name.'

'She's Croatian. Lika is the place she comes from, so I call her that. Her real name's much longer than even I can get my tongue around.' She took a sip from her coffee, the demolition of her cake complete. 'She's a bit older than me, but we get on well.'

'How old are you, Giuditta? Do you mind me asking?'

'No, I don't mind. I'm 36, coming up for 37.'

'When's your birthday?'

'Ah, that's a secret.'

'If you don't tell me, I can't send you a card. Or buy you a present.'

'I wouldn't want that, Anthony. The card perhaps. Not the present, though.' The shadow had flickered across her again, but she brightened straightaway. 'Unless it was something I really desired, of course – like fabulous diamonds.'

'It'd be diamonds then.'

She laid her hand on his arm. 'Why, Anthony, do you wish to be my sugar-daddy?'

He felt himself blushing – awkward and embarrassed now because she was continuing what had only been intended as a light-hearted joke, making fun of him. 'No. No. Of course not.'

'What *do* you want, Anthony?'

'Just your friendship. Your company.'

Her eyes were on his face, her cup half-raised to her lips. 'We are friends, I hope. But I have many friends, Anthony, men and women. Do not get too *geloso* for you do not own me.'

'Of course I don't!' Anthony was quite shocked. This conversation had not gone as he wished.

'How old are you, Anthony?'

'Sixty-four.' That was not true. He had just turned sixty-five. Pamela had remembered and sent him a card.

'Really. You don't look it.' If she was worried by his age, she did not say so, but rose to her feet, brushing crumbs from her dress.

'Come. Let's see the paintings.'

He gulped down the last of his coffee, filled his mouth with cake, and stumbled to his feet, following blindly.

13

They spent two hours touring the Fitzwilliam first floor galleries, emerging at last onto the landing above the main flight of stairs where many still-life studies of flowers and fruit hung from the dark-panelled walls. The galleries had been a joy. Giuditta had roamed ahead, darting from side to side of the rooms, enjoying the paintings, at times enraptured by them. Occasionally, she would take Anthony's arm and pull him to her side so that he might look at a picture with her – a Dutch winter scene or an English landscape or a portrait of an old man, and one particular strange, small painting, hung low so that they both had to bend to see it, of a country lane bordered by a high wall and shadowed by a great tree, while the lane itself was filled with yellow sunlight. This picture Giuditta appeared to find particularly absorbing. Anthony thought he could understand her preoccupation with it. There was something haunting about the shadows, the way mystery and danger seemed to lurk in the darkness to one side of the picture, while the other was so clear and full of light.

The last painting they had looked at together before emerging onto the landing had been a view of Venice by Canaletto. Giuditta had poised herself before it, coming so close to the canvas with her pointing finger that Anthony was aware of the growing concern of the room custodian nearby.

'That's the Grand Canal, and there's the church of Santa Maria della Salute. Canaletto's jumbled some things up to get a good composition. He used to do that, you know; move Venice around to suit the view he wanted.'

'You went to university in Venice, didn't you?'

'Yes. I did.'

'How long ago was that?'

'Oh, about twelve years. It was a marvellous place to study. Another world entirely.'

'What were you studying?'

'Art – painting, literature; some history: that sort of thing.'

It all sounded rather vague. Anthony refrained from pressing her for more details.

'I lived in a little room in a house overlooking a narrow canal, with shutters and a window box full of red geraniums.' Giuditta's eyes were alight with the memories. It had clearly been a happy time in her life.

They descended the great staircase to the ground floor, from which flights of steps continued down to rooms filled with antiquities from the classical world. Anthony would have liked to see these; indeed, if he hadn't been with Giuditta, he would have made them his first port of call. However, he was becoming tired now and was glad when she dragged at his arm. He was growing used to being pulled around by her, like some sort of inanimate toy – a great, cuddly bear of a toy, he suspected. He liked the feeling it gave him.

'Let's go to Brown's for lunch,' she said. 'Just over the road. You'll love it there.'

And so they left the Fitzwilliam by the front steps below the great portico, crossed busy Trumpington Street, dodging cars and swooping cyclists, and entered the column-fronted terrace of a restaurant a short distance away.

'This building was once part of the old Addenbrooke's

hospital,' Giuditta said, pushing with her shoulder at brown-stained swing doors.

They came into a broad, bare-boarded space set with tables, some of the tables positioned on raised platforms running on two sides of the room. Waiters and waitresses in green aprons and bearing round, silver trays bustled about the room. The restaurant was busy, but they were ushered to a table that had just fallen vacant in a corner of one of the platforms.

'Perfect,' said Giuditta, unhooking her bag from her shoulder and placing it on a padded bench-seat before shuffling her bottom along behind the table, a delightful movement to Anthony's eyes.. He seated himself on a wooden chair opposite her.

They ordered drinks – sparkling water only – from a waiter, who then took their food order. Giuditta asked for a Caesar salad, but with a side serving of chips as well, and Anthony a dish of lamb cutlets in an onion sauce. The service was excellent. The food arrived quickly.

'Tell me about when you first came to England,' Anthony said, helping himself to a side-salad. Giuditta's own salad on its foundation of chicken pieces was piled high on her plate. She had yet to start upon it, but was picking out chips from a bowl beside her.

'What do you want to know?'

'When you came here and why?'

'In 2012, I think it was, perhaps early 2013. I had my 22nd birthday in London, I know that. I had a degree in English and wanted to practice the language. I came and I stayed.'

'Just like that?'

'Just like that. What else?'

She sounded a little defensive. Was there something she did not want to admit to, Anthony wondered? But what on earth would she have to hide?

'What did you do at first?' Anthony wanted her to talk openly, to describe her life at that time. He did not want to have to ask a series of questions. He knew that in the end they would only irritate her – the last thing he wanted.

'I did some study at a college in Kent for a time, and then I came up here to Cambridgeshire.'

'What to work at the school you've just shown me?'

'No – not at first. I've only been there for around three years.'

She was not going to tell him. She was looking away from him, still putting the chips in her mouth one by one. He decided it might be wise to change the subject. Not for the first time, he noted, she did not ask him anything about his own life.

They eat in silence for a while. Anthony was pleased to see Giuditta begin on her salad, attacking it hungrily. He did not know why this woman created such tension in him. He was never sure what she was going to say or do from minute to minute. Hanging over him always was the fear that she would descend into one of her sudden tempers. And yet everything today– or almost everything – had so far been sunshine and light.

So when she spoke again, what she said came as a sudden bombshell. 'I was ill for a while.' With a start, he remembered now what Brian had told him at Glastington.

'You were ill?' All he could do was repeat the words stupidly.

'Yes! I was ill. That's what I'm telling you.'

'What was wrong? May I ask you?'

'Nothing much really. I think I was a bit tired and depressed. My mother had just died. I loved my mother. When I returned to England after her funeral, I found I didn't want to do anything much at all.'

He realised it was not her recent illness she was talking about – the one Brian had mentioned to him – but another earlier one. 'You poor girl', he said, laying his hand briefly over hers on the table top.

'Yes, perhaps. I was a bit of a mess at that time.'

'What about your father. Is he still alive?'

'Yes, he is. But he and I don't get on!'

She said this with some emphasis, and Anthony did not like to ask anything more. Had her recent illness then been similar to her previous suffering? If so, it might explain those sudden swings of mood and irritations that he had experienced with her.

Her voice was a little higher pitched now, a little less self-contained. Anthony was concerned. It had been a perfect day up to now. He wanted to hear no more about illness when she had been so relaxed and happy with him – at least he thought she had. He would steer the conversation onto more neutral ground. He watched her as she concentrated on her food, trying not to appear in any way affected by what she had told him, although he knew he was. When she looked up at him to speak again, he made sure his face bore an understanding and comforting look.

'The clinic in Sussex where they sent me to get better was – how shall I say? – high class and expensive. My father paid. It was one thing he did for me. It was a quite a place, a remarkable experience.'

'In what way?'

Anthony found it impossible not to ask this last question, despite his earlier determination just to let her talk. If he didn't, it might look as if he was indifferent to what she was telling him, and that might upset her. It must take a lot of courage for her to tell him these things. How could this wonderful girl have had such an illness? Why did she dislike her father so?

'What a collection of misfits we were,' she said, 'yet there were some nice people amongst them. Alcoholics and drug users, obsessives, self-harmers, even some perverts. And those who had simply given up on life for a while, like me. We were a strange bunch. So you see, Anthony, your lovely girl is not so lovely really.'

He reached forward to stroke her arm. 'Don't be silly. None of that makes a jot of difference to what I think of you. I think you're wonderful – that's all that matters to me.'

She didn't answer, but looked down at her plate. The salad was nearly finished; a few chips remained. 'My father wanted me to go back home to him in Italy, as I'd finished my studies here. I suppose he thought he'd paid out enough money on my behalf, and I should look after him next. Never mind my studies or what I wanted to do with my life. That was not important to him.'

'But you didn't go? You stayed on here.'

'I went back to Italy for a brief while. Then I returned to England – to Cambridgeshire. It was a big decision. It upset my father a lot. I had a friend, you see, whom I'd met at Roffey – that was the name of the clinic where they'd put me. He was a farm worker. He'd worked last on a mushroom farm in Sussex, not far from Roffey, in fact; but that was just a coincidence. When he got better – actually they kicked him out because he wouldn't – how do you say in English? – play ball with them: he was quite a character, loved his drink – he got a job as a tractor driver at a place called Tipps End in the middle of the Fens, an appropriate name, he would joke, for there was nothing there but a ramshackle farm, a few houses, and endless, flat expanses of fen, as level as a billiard table. He kept in touch with me by letter, and, when I was discharged, I went and joined him there.'

Anthony was astonished by this story. 'What did you do?'

'I worked on the land – like you told me you did after you left school: I thought that was a strange coincidence. I picked out the sugar beet and lifted the cabbages. There was lots of work, with two crops a year. And there were many of us to do it, most from overseas – Poles, Lithuanians, Ukrainians, even some Africans. Long lines of us used to be spread out across the fields. For a while we lived in portakabins on the farm. It was hard work, but quite good fun. And, if we worked all the hours of the day and in the evening, the pay was not too bad.'

The astonishment Anthony felt at this narrative must have showed in his face. 'You should understand,' she went on, 'I was picking myself up again, getting back into the land of the living. Working in the fields – in the fresh air – was what I needed, away from the study, the reading, the writing, the assembly of facts, the seminars, the professors with their dry seriousness. What lechers, though, some of them were.'

'Surely not?'

'Oh, Anthony. You know nothing. I cannot tell you. You older men. How you want the young girls.'

And now Anthony felt crushed, shamed, but with some annoyance flickering inside him at being lumped together in Giuditta's mind with whatever elderly academic sex pests – surely only one or two – she had been unfortunate enough to come into contact with. And here he was thinking that she was enjoying his company, while perhaps all the while she had been regarding him as another equivalent threat. But that didn't make sense. If it were the case, why had she agreed to spend time with him? And why tell him her intimate life story and the reduced state she had been brought to? She must trust him, then. All these revelations, however, were so unexpected, it was hard for him to think clearly.

'What happened to the farm worker you mentioned?' he asked. 'The one who was a friend.'

'He was sacked for being drunk one morning. His name was Dominic. I liked him. It was sad.'

'Did you leave with him?'

'No, I stayed on for a while. I was even offered a permanent job as a type of bailiff, supervising, making up the rotas, doing some of the accounts – that sort of thing. I thought about it for a while, but turned it down in the end because I knew it would be a dead-end. What tempted me briefly, you see, was the land – those broad green fields with the great sky above, the dykes and the long straight roads on causeways. I loved it. It was so similar to the Po Valley where I had been brought up, and where my father had farmed.'

'Ah!' said Anthony. 'Now I understand.'

Some pieces were falling into place. Her background was beginning to make a little more sense, and yet…..There were many gaps, many things, she had not explained. He looked at her across the table, so alive when she talked, her brown eyes bright – growing misty at times with reflection – her mouth, smiling, bent upwards into a bow, her lips…How suddenly he wanted to touch her lips, if not with his own, then with his little finger, for the lips to part, and the white teeth to open to take his bony flesh between them.

'Dominic's kept in touch all these years,' she said. 'I still get the occasional email from him. He seems to have straightened himself out. He's on a farm in Wiltshire now, and has met a girl. They run a smallholding. He's asked me down, but I've never been.'

Good old Dominic, thought Anthony, trying to get the last of the meat from his lamb chops and wishing he was at home so he could pick them up and chew them. By himself, he might have done that even here, but not with Giuditta opposite him. Then the fleeting thought came into his mind, of Giuditta and Dominic together in their portakabin, sending the metal frame rocking and rattling with the rhythm of their coupling, while outside the sun pierced the steaming landscape with the whitest of lights.

'When did your teaching start?' he asked.

'I got a place in a training college in Cambridge first. Graduated after a year. Then, after a break back in Venice, I began with Robin three – perhaps nearer four – years ago. I lose track of time.'

'So do I. It goes far too fast for me.'

Their plates were whisked away by a waitress, and a desserts menu appeared equally quickly. The service was fast but a little rough and ready, Anthony considered. Yet he preferred it that way. It seemed to suit the bare floorboards, the brown wood partitions, and the elevated platforms, where once patients had queued to have their ailments attended to.

They ordered sweets – Giuditta a fresh fruit salad but Anthony a confection that promised delight at high-calorific cost. He was still enjoying it when their coffee arrived, together with the bill. The latter he snatched up, just in case Giuditta should try to appropriate it.

They lingered over their coffee. Anthony would have liked to have asked Giuditta more questions – about her Italian background, her childhood on her father's farm, her education, the universities she had attended. And about the recurrence of her illness that she had confided in Brian about. How serious had it been and what had brought it on? She would have to tell him about that herself, however, because he was not meant to know anything about it. It was enough of questioning for the present, however. He knew that any further probing might provoke a reaction.

Giuditta did not put up any resistance to Anthony's settlement of the bill. She seemed to have accepted his position as provider this day – which pleased him. All he wanted was a 'thank you', and she gave him that most charmingly as they rose from their places and made to leave. Once again, Anthony was aware of heads – women as well as men – on other tables turning to look at her. In her linen dress, with its cool colours of grey and white, with the sun from a high skylight behind her, shining through her hair, she was most certainly worth their stares.

If she was aware of them, however, she showed supreme indifference, but shouldered her bag and stepped with great poise between the tables. Once they were in an open gangway, it was Anthony's great pleasure to take her by the arm and steer her towards the swing doors at the front of the restaurant. What colour, what shape, what fine definition, what pleasure – he thought – does the company of a beautiful woman give a man.

Outside, on the pavement, the sounds and colours of Cambridge struck at him as if he were locked inside some noisy, turning kaleidoscope. A passer-by brushed hard against his shoulder, tempting him for one mad moment to shove back– but restraining clasps of sanity stopped him doing so. Giuditta – he was sure – would not have been impressed by anything like that. He stood with her beside a stone wall with the portico of the Fitzwilliam rising over them like some vast temple of ancient Rome – or so his fancy told him at that moment. He was sure the real Rome would have been far noisier, dirtier, and more brutal and dangerous than anything around him here in 21st century Cambridge, sunny and busy as it was, with the black lines of shadows harsh against the heated stones where they stood.

They had decided to go to see King's College Chapel – that wonderful vision of late Gothic glory, with its great, coloured windows laced together by thin bars of masonry as if, suspended in thin air, floating in light, and with its vaults high overhead spread in intricate fans of stone carving. They had to push through crowds of tourists to reach these wonders, an ill-natured journey with Anthony increasingly irritated by the photographers whose lines of sight he must step around or his image be preserved forever on some distant memory stick. He could see that Giuditta's step was not as lively as it had been earlier, and he ushered her as quickly as he could into the necessary queue, where the hot sun bore down upon them, until at last they were within the cool interior of the Chapel.

It was her first visit here, Giuditta told him, and he watched her as she gazed about her, and then raised her face to the vaulting – her countenance serene after the heat and jostling of the queue. She was beautiful. Oh, she was beautiful indeed! How she stood out amongst the throngs of visitors in their vulgar shorts and their tawdry shirts, obsessed with the bright viewing screens of their various devices while she simply moved in quiet loveliness, looking and seeing, taking in everything, without the need for constant comment and exclamation. He did not want to interrupt her contemplation himself, but, after a while, touched her arm and whispered, 'Are you done?', and they came out once more into the sunlight.

'Magnificent,' she said. 'Worth all the effort. I shall come again one day when it's much quieter.'

'I hope I can return as well,' Anthony said. 'The winter months are probably the best time to see Cambridge before the tourists come.'

She did not reply, but they wandered together into the main shopping streets where the crowds of shoppers pressed upon them once more.

When they reached Sidney Street, where the pavements were perhaps at their busiest, she took him by the hand and pulled him into the shelter of a shop doorway.

'I think I must get home now, Anthony. I'm feeling tired.'

'Of course. Of course.'

'You need to check into your hotel. And I'm sure you'll want a rest yourself.'

Anthony looked at his watch. It was only half past three. The hotel he had booked at Giuditta's suggestion faced Parker's Piece, a short distance from the parking garage.

'Can I give you a lift home. If you can wait somewhere obvious, I can get the car and pick you up.'

'Oh, no, Anthony. That would be too much trouble. I'll be alright getting the bus. I'm used to it.'

'Are you sure? It's no trouble for me.' He felt anxious for her now.

'Quite sure. I shall be home in no time at all.'

'Did you come by bus then this morning?'

'Yes, as I always do going to work. It gets me into town very quickly, and no parking to pay.'

'What about this evening?' Anthony asked.

'What do you mean?'

'Aren't I going to see you later? For dinner perhaps.'

'Oh, Anthony. I couldn't eat another thing.' She placed a hand on his arm. 'I don't want to disappoint you, but do you think we could have a break until tomorrow? We'll do some more lovely things then. You can show me some of those places in the Fens I know you want to see.'

He *was* disappointed. He had imagined Giuditta perhaps coming to his hotel and dining with him. It would have been no trouble to pick her up in the Yaris. He didn't want to be by himself in a hotel bedroom with the long hours of a Saturday evening slowly ticking by.

'That's fine,' he forced himself to say, but he knew the disappointment must show on his face. Was she only tolerating him for a while? She could stand a few hours of his company – but then, was that enough?

'I'll have an early night,' he said, forcing himself to sound bright and positive. 'And then we'll have a really good day out and about tomorrow.'

And, as she continued to look into his face with a troubled expression, he added, 'Don't worry. It's quite alright – and probably the best thing as I *am* tired. It's been a wonderful day, and it's been a joy to be with you. More to come tomorrow!'

He was happy to see her smile again, and knew it was always best to go along with her wishes, however arbitrary and quick-changing they might be at times.

'I've enjoyed today as well,' she said simply.

'Can I pick you up tomorrow then?'

'Yes.'

'What time? Ten?'

'Yes. That sounds about right.'

'You'll have to give me your address.'

'Of course. How silly of me. It's 78, Elmfield Road, Chesterton.'

'I'll find it. I've got a street map in the car.' He scrawled a quick note of the address on a page of his pocket diary.

'You've got my phone number?' she asked.

'Yes, two of them!'

'Goodbye for now then.'

'Goodbye.'

He kissed her briefly on the cheek and turned away. He didn't want to leave her like that, amongst those crowds, for her to travel alone. Surely, with more thought, more planning, he could have organised something better. But there was nothing he could do now. After a few yards, he turned back, looking for the shop entrance where they had stood, but she had gone. She was lovely, but how strange she could be. He remembered what she had told him about her illness and he wondered how much of that stayed with her still.

That evening, after he had moved the Yaris to the car park of the hotel and checked in there, he had only the lightest of meals, eating early in a room off the bar. He had decided to drive out to the Wandlebury ridge that he had crossed coming into Cambridge. He was oppressed by the noise and heat of Cambridge, and longed to be in the open air again.

Wandlebury was a place he had read about and wanted to visit. On the chalk heights there, known as the Gog Magog Hills – high for Cambridgeshire, that was, rising some 200ft above the plain upon which Cambridge city was set – was a circular Iron Age hillfort. Excavations within the fort in recent years had found evidence of ancient assault, with bodies buried in the outer ditch. Anthony wondered if the mythical Gog Magog battling giants, famous in folklore, might preserve a distant memory of a battle acted out here long ago.

He found the hillfort with little difficulty. He left the Yaris in a car park, its gates open on this summer's evening, with the air still warm after the long heat of the day, and entered the bordering woods. He soon came upon the great outer ditch of the fort, and descended into it by a narrow path, following the circuit of the defences. The centre of the fort had been landscaped two hundred years ago for the building of a great house, much of which had since been pulled down.

The evening air seemed heavy upon him. Anthony stood still and listened. There was no bird song. The trees that overhung the ditch were thick with summer leaf, but no breeze stirred them. The light filtering through the leaves was grey with the approaching dusk, so that he blinked his eyes to try and sharpen his sight – leaves and branches and trunks were fusing together, and the bottom of the ditch, deep with last year's leaf, was darkening, so that its line made a black curve through the silent, watching woods.

He found the place oppressive – not comforting or relaxing, or simply melancholic and thought-inducing, as he had hoped to experience. Anthony was used to going to ancient places – usually by himself at a time when they were empty of others – for that reason. His visits helped clear his head of the modern world, allowing his mind to seek out and dwell within the past, a journey of thought which usually brought him considerable satisfaction. Such communion with the past, he suspected – for he understood himself well – was his attempt to escape from everyday realities. But he liked to believe there was also a shade of mysticism about it – that he could indeed touch upon the past and understand things that others, without his insight, could never achieve.

Here now, however, there was no ease, only a sense of growing disorder, so he hastened his step within the ditch, and rounded the circle of the fort, coming at last to the arch of a bridge that crossed above, where he scrambled up the bank and stepped onto a narrow road. He found he was sweating and a little out of breath – strange, for the air was now cooling rapidly with the onset of night.

He came to an area beyond the hill fort where there was a stretch of rough, open grass, and he thought for a moment that he saw a dark figure standing there some yards distant – a figure which had its back to him, then began to turn slowly towards him...He blinked his eyes in sudden alarm, and the figure was no longer there. It was only the empty grass now that stretched away to a line of trees, and in the distance he could hear the sound of the traffic on the main road.

Back at his car, he found his hands were trembling as he placed them on the steering wheel. He gathered himself to drive, telling himself not to be so stupid for he had seen nothing but the product of a tired brain. He felt much better as the Yaris slid into the traffic stream approaching Cambridge for the revelry of a Saturday night.

That revelry disturbed Anthony as he lay in bed in his stuffy room, not daring to open his window more than a crack for the sound of a city at play – loud voices outside, or within the hotel – he was not sure which – giggles and shrieks, drunken shouting, and above all occasionally the high- pitched wail of police cars and ambulances.

As he lay sleepless, he thought of Wandlebury again, and shuddered at the idea of that place now black beneath the stars. He would not go there again. There was something wrong about it, something evil he had sensed, something he could not understand.

So he thought of Giuditta instead, hoping she was sleeping in her narrow bed, and not….Not what? He did not know. He tried to place his mind in a black box into which no anxiety or fear or absurd longing could ever intrude.

14

It was after seven when Anthony awoke. The morning was perfectly quiet. Splashes of sunlight danced upon the walls. The air in the room was cool, stirring the curtains at the open window.

He had slept after all. He retained a sense of deep sleep lasting a few short hours, with coloured dreams that had floated distantly in his mind, so he could not remember them exactly, but he knew they had been refreshing, dispersing last night's fear – which he did recall, but any lingering unease seemed ridiculous now.

At some point in the night he must have got up and opened the window. He had no recollection of doing this, but he did recall the hellish noise that had earlier kept him awake. It had all vanished now, probably ending in the early hours, the ugliness washed away by the dew of a new day. He thought: the world is perpetually renewing itself, bringing hope once more with the rising sun.

He would be seeing Giuditta again! The pleasure of that thought brought a smile to his face as he lay in bed. And he would be adding to the picture he was building up of her, for he would be going to her home and meeting her housemate. And, after that, they would have the day ahead of them, making for a place that so far he had only read about and had long wished to visit.

It was known as Stonea, and lay a lengthy journey north of Cambridge in the centre of the Fens, on one of the low gravel islands that had once risen a few feet above the watery waste about. Here peoples had lived throughout the many centuries, until the surrounding marshlands, with their twisting water courses and open lagoons bordered by thick reed beds, had been drained in the modern era. Way back in the 2nd century AD, the Roman occupiers had carried out their own reclamation work around Stonea, digging canals both for drainage and transport, and laying roads to other islands across the marsh. Stonea was undoubtedly their most important settlement site in the Fens.

So Anthony ran through what he had read while sipping a cup of tea in bed that morning. He hoped Giuditta would like the place. He suspected its location would be remote. On another hot, sunny day – as the weatherman on the television foretold – it would be good just to rest quietly on the grass and think about the sights and sounds that had once been lived out there.

Nothing of the Roman site remained above ground now – it had all been backfilled long since – but he had a map that would show him exactly where their settlement lay. And adjacent as well – and this was the main thing you could actually see today – were the ramparts of an extensive Iron Age fortification. Unlike Wandlebury, however, this one was not constructed on some high point – that did not exist in the Fens – but had been laid out to cut off a peninsula of the Stonea island so that it would have been bordered on three sides by marshland and open water.

Anthony threw off his pyjamas and stood naked before the looking glass, pushing a fist against the palm of the other hand so that his biceps and his pectorals were accentuated. Yes indeed, he was still in good condition. He clawed at his waist filling his hands with flesh. A little overweight, perhaps, but nothing a sensible diet and more rigorous exercise could not sort out. After Glastington this August, and all the work in the well to come, he should be back in trim, as fit as he had ever been.

He thought of Giuditta. Would she ever look upon his naked body, and he hers? Unlikely, perhaps – but you never knew Anything was possible with her. She was a strange one indeed – tantalising and contradictory. Life with her must be lived on the edge.

And then he felt ashamed of such thoughts, remembering how beautiful she had looked yesterday, her almost childlike delight at the paintings in the Fitzwilliam and her silent, watching wonder of the ethereal beauty of King's College Chapel. No, he was her mentor, her confidant, her father figure. He could not hope to become her lover. To continue in that expectation was too gross. It would most certainly destroy his friendship with her.

When he was dressed, he went down to breakfast, taking his Cambridge street atlas with him. He found Elmfield Road in the index, and then over his coffee busied himself working out the route to get there. He did not know the Cambridge suburbs, but the road did not seem too hard to find.

Having paid his bill, he was away shortly after 9.30, finding there was little traffic. However, he was glad he had left plenty of time because – perhaps inevitably – he took a wrong turn, and found himself beginning to head out of Cambridge towards the north – the route, in fact, he was planning to take after picking up Giuditta. He managed to turn round and work his way back, entering a network of residential roads lined by mean-looking houses, until, thankfully, he located Elmfield Road. Many of the properties here were bungalows, set back behind a small space of grass or – in many cases – asphalt, with cars parked right up to their front doors. Anthony's heart sank. Surely Giuditta did not live in one of these?

When he found no.78 at last, he saw that it was a somewhat larger bungalow than most, occupying a corner plot with a side gate and short driveway where he could see Giuditta's small red car parked. There was a front lawn as well and some beds of straggling flowers. He drew the Yaris up outside, seeing the curtain twitch at a front window. It was exactly 10.00 o'clock. He was pleased by that. He prided himself on his punctuality.

Giuditta opened the door as he got out of the car. She was dressed in a cream-coloured pair of trousers and a yellow blouse, her hair pulled back and fastened by a tie behind. She waved briefly, then disappeared, so that Anthony came to the door not knowing whether to enter or not. He stepped into a musty-smelling hall with a floor of red linoleum tiles and a hideous wooden hat-stand with a mirror set into it, on which a grey-green trilby with a feather was perched like some bedraggled parrot.

'Come in.' Giuditta's voice was calling, and he could see movement through a far door, so he trod across the hallway and entered a kitchen. With Giuditta was a stout, black-haired woman of indeterminate age in a tee-shirt and pyjama bottoms, who looked as if she had just got up – as Anthony thought she probably had.

'Lika, this is Anthony.'

He shook her hand, feeling the chubby fingers sliding damply against his. She had a lovely smile, though. The pasty, white face with its double chin came immediately alive.

'Lika is my very good friend,' said Giuditta.

Anthony smiled, feeling awkward and struggling to make some suitable inconsequential remark.

'And Giuditta is the one I look after,' said Lika. 'Now do you have everything, darling? Don't you need a cardigan for later in case it gets cooler? And what about some food and drink? Would you like to take some fruit?' Her hand hovered over a bowl on a shelf by the sink.

'We'll be eating out,' said Anthony. But he saw Giuditta take a couple of apples and place them in a carrier bag on the countertop. For a moment – and it was a matter quite beyond his capacity to assess – he wondered at the nature of their relationship.

Lika's accent was very much heavier than Giuditta's, and her English not nearly so good. She must know much about her companion and her problems. Had she helped her through her illness recently? She was like a mother, he thought, seeing her daughter off for the day. Lika, the mother; he, the father. What sort of oddball family had Giuditta gathered about her!

Lika actually came to the door to wave them off, giving Giuditta a peck on the cheek. 'Have a lovely day. The weather will be nice – no?' The latter was directed at Anthony.

'They say so,' he said as cheerily as he could, wanting to get away from this woman, so he could relax with Giuditta, to whom as yet he had scarcely spoken a word. About her only comment to him so far, on getting into the Yaris, had been to say, 'I prefer your Land Rover.'

As he weaved the car out of the housing estates back onto the main road, he was pleased to find that she seemed relaxed and rested.

'What did you do last night?' she asked.

'Oh, just a little food and a short trip out?'

'What to a night club?'

'You're joking! No, to Wandlebury to see the hill fort there.'

'And did you like it?'

'Most impressive.' Anthony did not tell her of his strange experience. He was not sure of it, anyhow.

'And you?' he asked. 'What did you do?'

'A little television. Then, after Lika came in, I went to bed. I was tired.'

'Did you sleep okay?'

'Like a baby.'

They were out of Cambridge by now and heading between open fields towards Newmarket. Giuditta asked, 'Where are we going?'

'To Stonea. Not far from March. We can walk there.' He had told her something about the place yesterday.

'I won't need boots, will I? I haven't brought any.'

'Your shoes will be fine, I'm sure. It hasn't been wet for a long time.'

'Good.' She settled back and watched the countryside going by. Then suddenly she started forward. 'We could go to Tipps End – where I used to work. It can't be far away from this Stonea. I'd like to see it again.'

'Sure. Of course. Anything, you like.'

Anthony brought the car to a halt in the gateway to a field, and spread his map out, making use of Giuditta's trousered lap. He was disappointed she was not wearing a skirt today. Yet trousers – he had to admit – were much more practical for walking.

'Where was your Tipps End exactly?'

'Let's see. Welney was the closest place. We used to get a bus there and then walk.'

'I've got it.' Anthony pointed at the map. 'That's fine. We can pass through there on the way to Stonea. It's not out of our way at all. What a coincidence.'

He looked at her and grinned broadly. How he would love to stroke her cheek, or at least take her hand; make some sort of physical contact with her. The agony of this closeness, but still the great gulf of separation, was hard to bear. He put the Yaris into gear and moved on.

They came into the Fens by the road that led from Newmarket to Ely. This was Anthony's first visit since childhood to the Fens, and he did not really know what to expect. When they had passed over a low ridge, Ely Cathedral, with its tall tower and long, crowned nave, could be seen etched against the blue horizon, dominating the flat countryside around. The main road was raised several feet above the fields, which were separated one from the other by deep ditches. Occasionally a narrow track would run away at right angles to the road, like a raised seam crossing the land, heading for a distant farm huddled behind a dark mass of protective trees. Only a few wind-blasted trees bordered the road itself, and there were no copses or leafy hedgerows beside it. The whole landscape was taken up with growing crops.

'*Bellissimo*. Every time I see that view it catches my breath,' said Giuditta, gazing at the Cathedral which was sailing ever closer to them like a grey ship on a green sea.

'You know Ely?'

'I only went there once – briefly – with Dominic. We were looking for somewhere to eat. I had no more than a peek in the Cathedral.'

'Perhaps we can go this afternoon,' said Anthony. He did not want to know any more of what Dominic and Giuditta had done together.

'I'm pretty sure I know the way now,' Giuditta said. She had picked up Anthony's map and scanned it briefly.

They rounded Ely by its bypass and were heading north towards the western outreaches of Norfolk. After a few miles, at a roundabout, Giuditta directed Anthony to the left where they followed a road running straight towards a high bank that cut across their view ahead. When they reached it, the road bent to the right to run parallel with the bank.

'That's one of the great cuts made to drain the land,' Giuditta told him, pointing out of her side window at the bank. 'It's much higher than the road now, and the roads are higher than the fields. They say the peat shrinks with the draining. The ground surface today is much lower than it used to be. So, if you could see your Romans today, they would be marching in thin air.'

Anthony was impressed, both by what she told him and the evocative way she did so. More evidence of the drainage engineering he saw a little later when they turned to cross the channel they had been following. Broad, with raised banks on either side to hold in the water, it ran as straight as an arrow into the far distance.

'This countryside is similar to the Po delta where I grew up,' Giuditta told him. 'Only much of the land there hasn't been drained, unlike here, so it still looks like it would have done long ago – lagoons and winding rivers and great areas of marshland flats where the seabirds come. You should go and see it one day.'

'You must take me.'

Giuditta laughed. 'Yes, that'll be the day.'

Anthony felt a little hurt at this dismissive comment, but he thought she probably didn't mean it quite like that – perhaps something more like 'that would take a bit to organise'. Why shouldn't he think of accompanying Giuditta back to her homeland? They were doing things together in his country, so why not hers?

Perhaps Giuditta realised she had bruised him a little, for she added a few minutes later, 'You'd love the city of Ferrara at the head of the Po delta. In some ways, I suppose, it is like Ely. And you should visit the great Abbey of Pomposa further towards the sea. The monks drained the land there and farmed it, as I suspect the monks did around Ely too.'

The idea was growing quickly in Anthony's mind. Yes, he could suggest a trip to the Ferrara area with her. He would pay. After all, the costs for two were proportionately not much greater than for one, particularly if they shared a room: twin beds, perhaps. He would like to see some of the other places she had mentioned earlier as well. What was the name of the Roman site where she had told him she had dug – Aquila? No, Aquileia, that was it. It sounded a wonderful place for a visit. And, of course, there was Venice as well. Magnificent, beautiful Venice, where she had studied. He had always wanted to go there. She could show him the sights she knew so well. Yes, he was excited by the idea. He would discuss it with her at a time when she was more relaxed and mellow – perhaps later in the year, after the Glastington dig.

They came into the small village of Welney with its tree-lined main street, and then Giuditta's finger stabbed towards the left. 'You turn there! That's the way we used to walk.'

Anthony swung the Yaris onto a narrow road, then through a series of right-angled bends, so that they were zig-zagging across the fenland, which looked ever more open and remote. Giuditta was tense now, her face close to the windscreen. 'Go more slowly, Anthony.'

'There a van right behind me...... Oh, it's okay, he's overtaking.'

'That house.' Giuditta pointed at a square, brick-built building set back from the road by a short drive: it was surrounded by a cocoon of trees and thick shrubs. 'We asked for a drink there once. It was a really hot day. There were about ten of us walking to the farm from the bus. The woman took pity on us and gave us lemonade, but the man didn't want her to. He stood in the background with a shotgun over his arm.'

'Invaders, eh?'

'I don't think they like outsiders here,' said Giuditta. 'Let alone foreigners. It would be the same in Italy, I suppose.'

Further on, the lane passed between trees, and some houses

began to appear on either side, set widely apart, with the open fen seen between them. It stretched away to a flat blue-green horizon, interrupted by only the dark hump of an occasional farm, the lattice-work trail of distant electricity pylons, or a cluster of wind turbines with their turning sails.

'This is it. Tipps End.' Anthony saw the name on a board, half-obscured by mud flung up by passing vehicles.

'It doesn't seem to have changed. But – My God! – it has. They're building there. That's where the farm was.'

At a sharp corner of the road, three houses were under construction, one of them immense, built like a barn, with great plate-glass front windows.

'Stop, Anthony. Stop!'

Anthony pulled onto the verge close to the builders' entrance to the houses, allowing an approaching tractor to squeeze past him and continue along the lane, clods of mud flung up from its great wheels.

'There used to be sheds here and a house where we got our meals and a yard in front where our portakabins were. It's all gone.'

'The farmer must have sold up,' said Anthony.

'Yes. He was a miserable man. I can't see him sunning himself in the Maldives, though.'

'Where was the land you used to work on?'

'Oh, just a few hundred yards up the lane. On both sides. He owned hundreds of acres.'

Anthony pulled away, and crawled slowly forward.

'Yes, yes. That's where I worked. You see where the turnips are growing. I did hour after hour in that field.'

Anthony would not have known the green crop was turnips, but he didn't say so. He looked across the open expanse of the fields wondering at the scene when Giuditta had been one of a line of workers here, in rain, hail, or sun, picking, lifting, sorting, packing.

'There! That hut was a base for us.' Giuditta jabbed the windscreen, indicating a small, square brick building with a red corrugated-iron roof at the edge of a field. 'We had our breaks there and there were portable loos. God. They stank! He didn't get them changed often enough.'

'Oh, my poor girl,' said Anthony. 'What on earth were you thinking then?'

She didn't seem to hear him, but continued looking out enraptured over the fields as the car crept on. Seeing a heavy lorry coming up behind him, he indicated and pulled as far in to his left as he could, allowing the lorry, with a blast of its klaxon horn, to overtake.

'We'll have to move on,' he said, 'unless I find parking somewhere and we walk back.'

'No. No. It's enough. I've seen what I want.'

Her voice was lower, duller, and, looking across at her, he saw her eyes were moist. Such pity – such love – he felt for her in that moment. He put his arm around her shoulders and she did not shrug him off.

'Don't cry. It's all over. You're well now. You're happy.'

For a few short minutes they sat there together, he with his arm still around her, she with her head forward. Then she raised her shoulders suddenly as if wondering at the weight upon them. She looked up at him, his face hovering anxiously close to hers. He was worried for her now, her dark eyes filled with shadows against the whiteness of her face.

'Let's get going, Anthony.'

'Are you sure you're alright?'

'Yes.'

There was a hint of irritation in her tone, and he quickly removed his arm and placed it on the gear lever, reaching to start the engine, then realising just in time that it was still running. I'm out of control again, he thought. I can't even drive my car now. Let me get back to things I understand and not try to force something which is probably not wanted. If Giuditta wishes more than simple companionship, then *she* must indicate that to me. I should not try to touch her again.

But it's hard, so very hard – he told himself – for I truly love that girl.

15

They drove first to the small Fenland market town of March before setting out to find the site of Stonea. Anthony's map was a detailed Ordnance Survey sheet. However, the route to Stonea was not clear. A number of pathways ran close to the site, but he was not sure which you could follow by car.

The diversion to March had been Anthony's idea in order to buy some bits and pieces for a picnic. Giuditta, cheering up quickly after her tears at Tipps End, Anthony was pleased to see, had thought this a good plan.

'How lovely to have a picnic,' she had said, stretching her body luxuriously in her seat. 'I haven't had a picnic for ages.' Anthony thought: she is like a child at times, given to these sudden pleasures and fancies.

They had found a Sainsbury's in the centre of the town, and he had put Giuditta in charge of buying some bread, cheese, and cold meats, together with a bunch of grapes and some satsumas. When it came to selecting something to drink, he chose a bottle of an Italian white wine, as well as adding to his increasingly heavy basket some fruit juice and mineral water in case Giuditta would prefer those. In the domestic hardware section, he found a pack of cheap tumblers and some plastic cutlery, which, together with a pack of cardboard plates, he thought was all they needed for their picnic.

The wine will be warm, he thought, as they issued from the store, each bearing a weighty carrier bag, but we'll have to put up with that. I won't be able to drink much, anyhow.

It was another hot day, but Anthony knew it would be cooler once they were outside the town, for there was a fresh breeze strong enough to tug at their clothing as they walked back to the Yaris. It was the sort of breeze that might bring rain in later. Giuditta looked delightful in her slacks and shirt, he thought. Her tied-back hair made her appear almost tomboyish.

After a couple of wrong turnings, they found the way to Stonea. A narrow track, roughly tarred and full of potholes, ran off at right angles from the causewayed road they had been following south-east from March. There was a steep drop down for the Yaris to reach the side track. At the junction, a small sign – almost indecipherable unless close-up – stated 'To Stonea Camp Iron Age Fort'.

They passed through a farmyard, where a man standing beside a tractor looked at them curiously and a dog ran at the car barking, and then they were back on the track which continued straight on towards a line of trees. The fields stretched away flat and empty on all sides. From this distance there was no sign of the ancient fortification ahead. But when the track came to an end by the trees, Anthony saw they had reached a fenced-off parking place, empty of any other car, with an information board set beside it. Despite the unprepossessing approach, they had arrived at Stonea Camp.

The heat wrapped itself heavily around them as they left the car. Together they walked across the grass to the information board and stood side by side to read it. Stonea Camp had first been laid out in the 3rd century BC, it informed them. The ditches and ramparts that could be seen today had been constructed in differing phases. The latest phase had been just before the Roman invasion of 43AD. Since burials had been found from that date period, some with sharp cuts on their bones, it was thought that the camp might have been stormed by the Romans. The Roman historian, Tacitus, had described a rebellion of the Iceni tribe in the early invasion period that had been put down by a battle at a place with an earth rampart and a narrow entrance. These details – archaeologists appeared to agree – matched the Stonea site.

They went through a gate and entered the grassed enclosure of the fort, meeting at once with a complex of ditches and banks that ran off in different directions. They climbed to a high bank on which another information board was set. It was cooler here beneath trees that crowned the bank, meeting a breeze that stirred the thick leaves overhead, and swept the grass so that it seemed to shiver and change colour, from green to silver like the sea, across the great enclosure before them. Dotted over the grass were the plump, white, woolly shapes of sheep, some with their spring lambs, now half-grown, still butting at their mothers for milk.

Giuditta opened her arms wide like the wings of an aeroplane, and ran down the bank, looking back at Anthony like the child she was at heart to see if she was admired. He thought: How carefree she is now. Like she was at South Cadbury. How adorable. I'm in love with her, and there's nothing I can do about it.

'Let's go this way, Anthony.'

She strode ahead of him across the enclosure, heading for a bank that could be seen on the far side. He caught up with her by a group of sheep, who turned their heads to watch them but did not move away.

'Hello, sheep. Are you having a nice day?'

They reached the bank and climbed onto it, looking out over the level landscape, with fields of green and gold and yellow opening out to a flat horizon. In one or two places a church spire pierced the rim of the sky, the vast blue bowl of which, heated by the sun, spun round above them so that they felt like small black ants on the green turf beneath. To the north, where the buildings of March were hidden by trees, a row of white wind turbines stood against the sky, their sails turning in the breeze. Anthony felt utterly at peace here. The site was as remote as he had hoped. He and Giuditta were the only people here – for the present they and the sheep had it to themselves.

They followed the bank further to their right, and then saw there was another, higher bank that ran before them, its side dark with the shadow it cast. They crossed to it and climbed it too.

'We're on the outer bank at the north of the fort,' Anthony said, consulting a plan of the site he held. 'You have to imagine the other sides bordered by marshland and the southern part of the interior, where we first entered from the car park, covered by trees. At least that's what the environmental evidence from the excavations showed.'

'Where would the Romans have attacked?' asked Giuditta, leaning across him to see the map that was flapping in the wind. He saw the fine textured skin of her cheek close to his face, and he longed....oh, he longed... But, of course, he could not. He must not even try.

'On this side most likely,' he answered. 'They would have advanced over the dry land connecting with the rest of the island – over here.' He thrust his arm out indicating fields of corn in the mid-distance, with a farm and a row of cottages standing against a line of trees.

'I'm not sure where the main gateway of the fort was. Very likely' – he pointed – 'where the gap in the bank is now. I can't remember what I read about that in the excavation report. One of the problems is that there was a farm within the fort until quite recently. It's all been pulled down now, but – as you'd expect – the business of farming over the centuries caused damage to the banks and ditches. Some of the gaps we see now may have been made quite recently.'

'So that is where the Roman army would have been drawn up.' Giuditta said, looking out over the fields. The wind tugged at her hair, a loose lock flapping at her temple. She smoothed it back with her hand.

'Yes. It was quite a large force apparently. Infantry and cavalry. They would have made short work of these defences, I feel sure.'

'So here were burning huts and screaming people – women and children trying to flee, the survivors rounded up in groups with shackles on their wrists.'

'Yes, I'm afraid so. You paint a good picture. The Roman conquest was a brutal business. It doesn't pay to romanticise it.'

'I can feel their fear,' she said, her chin raised as if she was scenting the air. 'Come, let's get warm again in the sun.'

Anthony thought: But we are in the sun. In fact, he felt far too hot, despite the cooling breeze. He was almost tearful by what she had just spoken. This is what he had sought for so long – a mind in sympathy with his own. She was not only beautiful, but could become a true soul mate, sharing his feelings and his intuitions. It only needed a small shift of chance to keep her with him. Oh, please God, let it be so.

She was ahead of him again, making for another information board high on the outer bank. A climb up a short flight of steps to a wooden platform was necessary to reach it.

'This one's about the Roman town that stood close by,' said Anthony, glancing over the board and turning to look out across a field that was high with ripening wheat. It lay on the far side of a deep drainage channel that wound away like the sinuous back of a giant snake.

She read more of what the board described. 'It says there was a great tower here?' she said. 'Where would that have been?'

He consulted his plan. 'Over there.' With outthrust arm, he indicated the distant field under its waving crop. 'That's where the Roman settlement stood. The tower occupied just one of the eight *insulae* that were excavated. It was the only stone building amongst the others built of timber and clay. You have to imagine it rising some 60 feet – an immense square block, almost as wide as it was high. It would have been visible from miles away.'

'And it probably had some administrative purpose?' Giuditta was intent on understanding the site now. Her previous persona of a little girl playing on the banks and amongst the sheep had vanished.

'Yes. Tim Potter, the British Museum excavator here in the 1980s – he died tragically young – thought it might be the headquarters building of a great imperial estate spreading over the Fens. The Romans built roads and canals in the area, had large parts of the dry land – the islands in the marsh, that is – under crops, probably bred sheep and cattle on the fen margins, and extracted salt in those places where the flooding was tidal. All in all, it would have added up to a massive operation that would have had to be managed by someone – someone with an important base and headquarters building. Stonea, with its tower, is the most likely candidate. The Iron Age fort we're standing in had clearly been an important tribal centre of the Iceni people for a long time – they're the people led by Queen Boudica in the great rebellion when London and other towns were burnt down. A number of their roundhouses were excavated. Presumably they were all abandoned after the Romans came.'

It was hot standing directly in the sun on the wooden platform, and Anthony led Giuditta down the bank so that they were able to sit on its cooler, shaded side, carefully selecting tussocks of grass free from sheep droppings.

'This place has quite an atmosphere,' he said. 'You've felt it already, I think.'

She looked at him, perhaps a little surprised at his change of mood – from fact now to something much more fanciful. But she sat with her hands around her raised knees, her head on one side, attentive to what he was saying, like a pupil before her teacher. 'When I first read about the tower,' he said, 'and stated reflecting on this place – which I had yet to visit, as you know – I kept on getting a picture in my head of a man on the upper floor who was looking out through a half-shuttered window. It would come to me at night, but whether I was dreaming, or half-awake and just imagining, I'm not sure. It was a very strong image. The man would be watching something on the ground beneath the tower, and in the distance was the road coming onto the Stonea island across the surrounding marsh, and there were canals that crossed the landscape as well, with barges on them being hauled by horses alongside.'

'What did the man do?' Giuditta asked.

She was looking down at the grass and plucking a daisy which she held up before her face. Was her attention slipping, he wondered? Did she want to hear these strange, revelations from his subconscious, which he was almost too embarrassed to relate, but from the telling of which he knew he would gain relief?

'Nothing, as far as I remember. He simply looked out through the upper window. It had shutters, but one leaf was open and he stood there. I could see the upper half of his body. He wore a white tunic – or at least some sort of garment that covered the length of his body.'

'Very strange.' Giuditta's voice was flat. He was anxious now. Was she bored? Was her mood changing? She had been happy just now. So why was he inflicting his inner turmoil on her? Did he think it made him sound more interesting to her? Was that what he was trying to achieve?

'Yes, it was strange,' he said. And oddly, now I am here, I do not see those pictures in my head at all. That's what imagination can do to you, eh!'

He jumped to his feet. 'Come on. I'm getting hungry. Shall we find a spot to have our picnic?'

But she remained seated. 'You know,' she said slowly, 'your story of the tower reminds me of the other one you told me about – it was when we were in London, I think – of the lady shut up in a tower, and a road and a canal – or was it a river? – that ran by where she was imprisoned.'

Anthony was amazed. So she had been listening to him. And she had listened too that time in London when she had seemed so distracted, just before they had argued. And she had put the two sets of ideas together in a way he had not even thought of himself – of an equation between the Stonea tower and that of the Lady of Shalott. She was quite remarkable, utterly unpredictable.

He told her so, and her eyes were cast down still picking at the grass. 'I do hear. I do listen and understand what you say.' She looked up at him, her brown eyes on his. 'The only trouble is one tower has a woman and the other a man. Now, how do we explain that?'

And she began laughing in that way of hers – doubled-up in mirth, her head almost to the ground – and Anthony laughed with her, not sure if she was laughing at him, but vastly relieved that her happy mood had so evidently returned.

They selected a place for a picnic beneath trees on a grassy knoll beside a pond at the south-west corner of the site, where several ditches and ramparts made a junction. The water of the pond lay black and still in the shadow of the trees despite the hot day. Many hoof marks in the dried mud on the far side of the pond told that the sheep came down here to drink.

On returning to the car park to collect their food and drink, they found another car had arrived – a family with a dog, whom they saw in the distance on one of the outer banks, the dog on a lead because of the sheep. Giuditta was happy to see the dog: 'A labrador, I think,' she said, screwing up her eyes against the sun.

The picnic proved a great success. Giuditta set out the various items on the cardboard plates, while Anthony unscrewed the twist cap of the wine bottle, pouring into two plastic beakers. He sipped his. 'Drinkable enough,' he said, 'if a little too sun-warmed.' In fact, he thought the warm wine tasted execrable, but he did not want to say that in case it affected Giuditta's own pleasure in drinking it.

Anthony ate his veal and ham pie, and his sliced Wiltshire ham on fresh crusty bread, with relish, and followed this up by nibbling on a chunk of hard Cheddar. He could see Giuditta was enjoying her food as well. She half sat, half lay, on the side of the knoll away from him, with the picnic spread out on the grass in front of her. She had taken a few sips of the wine, then put her beaker down.

'I'll have some mineral water,' she said reaching across for the bottle. 'Wine will only give me a headache in this sun.'

But Anthony poured himself more wine, liking the hazy feeling it gave him although the taste was insipid against the dryness of his mouth.

Although they were partly in shade on their grassy bank, and the breeze would seek them out at times, ruffling the papers on which their food was spread and catching at loose strands of Giuditta's hair, it was very hot, as if they were roasting gently in some monster oven. He saw Giuditta pull occasionally at her yellow blouse to free it from the sweat on her back.

'It's hot, eh?' Anthony was undoing some of his shirt buttons. 'Let's hope Glastington is fine like this in August. Hot, sunny weather, though, is not the best for digging. Too exhausting, and everything gets very dry and dusty, so you can't see the colours in the earth.'

'That's what it was like in Italy,' Giuditta said. She was peeling a satsuma, laying the pieces of peel delicately beside her. 'We avoided the hottest weather, though. September was the preferred month at Aquileia. It was a little cooler then with the air from the mountains.'

'The mountains?' Anthony was helping himself to some grapes.

'Yes, the Dolomites – part of the Alps. You see them on the horizon from Aquileia, a line of white peaks where the snow never melts. Very beautiful. There's a town in the foothills you should go to – Cividale del Friuli, an amazing place built around a great river gorge. It was founded by Julius Caesar, as they will tell you there.'

'Julius Caesar! He got everywhere. Even here.'

'What here at Stonea?' She looked her surprise, checking to see from his face if he was joking, her eyes falling to his chest, now open to the sun. 'You'll get sunburnt.'

'Oh, I'll be okay. Well, perhaps great Julius didn't quite reach here, but he wasn't far to the south in his British campaigns.

'Really. I didn't know that.'

'There's a lot to tell you,' Anthony said, and then hoped that hadn't sounded too pompous. 'What are you planning for Glastington?' he asked.

'What do you mean?'

'You are planning to come, aren't you? To work on the well with us. It should be exciting.'

'Oh yes, I want to do that.'

Anthony felt a sense of relief. He remembered she had said to him in London that she might go out to California at that time. He had not dared to mention the matter since. He was growing desperate now for her company to continue.

'You'll have to book in with Brian. I'll be there from the first week in August. It would be good if you could be there at the same time.'

'Yes, I've already told him.'

'You have! You didn't tell me.'

'No. I'm sorry. I was going to. I only decided the other day. It depended on other things.'

Anthony felt sick now at this abrupt re-emergence of the worry he had thought gone. 'What? The man in California?'

'Yes, partly.'

'You're not going over there then?'

'No.'

'I'm pleased about that, my girl.' Anthony felt a further rush of relief. He sipped at his wine.

'He's coming here.'

'What! When?'

'In a couple of weeks.'

'To stay with you...?'

Giuditta looked coolly at Anthony. She did indeed seem cool now despite the heat, in her yellows and creams, with her neatly tied hair, the small orange pile of the Satsuma peel by her knee.

'He is a wealthy man, Anthony. He will stay in a hotel.'

And take you into his bed there, thought Anthony angrily – his day so suddenly wrecked. And then have room service of champagne and caviare, and do all those things that wealthy arseholes do with young women. How old is he, I wonder? As old as me, or some much younger man – a bronzed, steely-eyed, firm-jawed, denim-clad champion of his bucking, fucking broncos.....Anthony felt quite mad with it all, not helped by the wine that he took a further gulp of.

Seeing her eyes on his face, and the absence of any concern for him in her expression, told Anthony a great deal – most of which he did not wish to accept. He did know, however, that he must not rage and fume, or lose his dignity, but at all costs – even now – stay calm.

'Well, you and he will enjoy yourselves.' He tried to say this without bitterness, but knew he hadn't succeeded.

And now for the first time there was a sop of something resembling feeling for him, for she reached across and placed her hand on his – for just a moment, before withdrawing it. 'Don't let it worry you. It's not what you think. I look forward to your company at Glastington. At least I'll be able to do that now.'

'There's so much I don't understand about you,' he groaned.

'Well, what do you want to know?'

'Who this man is? That seems to be a good question to begin with.'

She didn't reply at first, but sat still, the water of the pond behind her beneath the shading trees shining darker even than her hair. As Anthony looked, bubbles would burst occasionally on the surface, from whatever moved, or decayed, beneath. Insects skimmed over the water, one with tiny wings that gleamed green for a fraction of a second, and was gone. Green, thought Anthony. Green for my jealousy. What does any of it really matter to me, anyhow?

And yet it did, and more so too when Giuditta at last gave her answer.

'He is my father.'

16

'Your father! Oh, I'm so sorry. I had no idea.'

'Why should you be sorry, Anthony? Because you thought he was my lover? You should have more confidence in yourself. Although I have had many male admirers, it is you I am with at the moment – as a friend, as a confidant; is that not enough for you?'

Anthony was embarrassed. He felt himself blushing, his body wanting to wriggle away from the bank where they sat, the sweat running upon him. Where he had opened the top buttons of his shirt, the sun was now scorching a red V-shape onto his white flesh.

'Do you want more than friendship then, Anthony? Do you want to possess me, perhaps? To add me to your harem?'

The latter was so plainly ridiculous that, despite his embarrassment, Anthony giggled, seeing Giuditta's hard gaze alter to one of puzzlement.

'Why do you laugh?'

'Because I don't have any harem. I'm separated from my long term partner and it's very unlikely we'll ever get back together again. Rather than having a bevy of women available to me, I don't even have one. Where on earth do you get such an idea?'

'You give me the impression of liking women.'

'Yes, but....'

'You are an attractive man. You must be used to women – how do you say? – dropping their knickers for you.'

She caught the look on his face, and then she began laughing too, until they were both helpless, beating the earth with their hands, and only a couple of surprised sheep to see them. As Anthony began to recover, there were several thoughts surfacing in his brain. One was, in fact, further vast relief that Mr. Ranchman had dematerialised as a threat to him, accompanied by a gloating, floating pleasure that Giuditta had told him she found him attractive. And, amongst these feelings, was an intense curiosity about this father of hers who apparently hailed now not from Italy but California.

The sound of voices and the swish of feet in the grass made him start, but Giuditta was already on her feet, as the party with the Labrador dog suddenly appeared, walking along one of the banks towards them. Anthony had forgotten about these people; presumably they had settled somewhere else on the site – he hoped well beyond earshot.

'Come, dog, come.' Giuditta joyfully greeted the bounding, black Labrador. The dog, sensing a human spirit sympathetic to its own world, stopped in its tracks, and sat close to her, eyes on her, mouth open, body panting.

'Bruce! Come here!' a woman called, but the dog ignored her.

'May I?' said Giuditta, holding up a piece of ham from her unfinished meal.

'He'll be your friend for life.'

Watching the dog take the meat from her open palm – gently, not snatching – Anthony thought that the friendship seemed in place already. How was it she had such an affinity with dogs? Did it extend to other animals as well? He did not know. There was so much he did not know about Giuditta

Ponti. As the family moved away, tugging the dog by its collar, he thought he would make a fresh start now by asking about her father.

Happily, Giuditta was in a mood to talk. Perhaps their laughter had released the tension between them that was usually not far away. Anthony was never sure what she was going to say, what swing of feeling or understanding would cause her to close up, or become depressed and suspicious, changing her to contempt and anger. But now she was as open as she had ever been with him – much as she had disclosed her illness to him as they sat in the Cambridge restaurant.

Her childhood on the family farm somewhere close to the city of Ferrara had not been happy, Anthony learnt. She had been the youngest of three siblings – the other two were boys, one who had gone on to run the farm (and who still did), and the other who had left home at fifteen and with whom all contact had since been lost. Giuditta feared he was dead. He had been a wild boy who had fought her father.

Francesco Ponti, the patriarch, had been autocratic and single-mindedly selfish. He had ruled the family with a rod of iron, and had a violent temper. Her mother – Maria – a gentle, patient woman – had kept the family together as long as she could, and protected her children from the worst of their father's tantrums. But – so Giuditta said – even she had not known some of the things Francesco was capable of: she did not specify what these had been.

It was Maria's influence – and the money of one of her unmarried sisters – that had enabled Giuditta to go away to university. Francesco's wish was for her to stay on the farm and act as an unpaid help to him, taking over increasingly from his wife who had already developed the long, wasting illness – pulmonary tuberculosis – that was eventually to kill her.

Because of all the problems at home, which had affected her local schooling, Giuditta was late in going to university – in Padua – where she had studied English. Once she had graduated, her aunt, wishing to keep the young, intellectually gifted girl away from her father's influence for as long as possible, offered her the money for a second course in Venice, where she studied the history of art. This had proved the most formative period of her life when she gathered the strength and the maturity to shake off her father's continuing influence at last.

And so, once she had graduated in Venice, she had determined to make a complete break by going to England, even though it involved the awful decision of leaving her mother, who by now was in a sanatorium for the terminally ill. Only, as Anthony had already learned, Giuditta herself had become ill, and her father had made a last bid to bring her home by paying for her treatment. Anthony could understand now how strong she had had to be to make that final break – the one that had brought her back to England to work on the land.

'And what about your father?' Anthony asked. 'How was it he went out to California?'

'After my mother died, he sold the farm to a consortium, of which my elder brother was a member. It was a wealthy farm: my father had been a good farmer. He treated his land better than he treated his family; he certainly got better rewards from it.'

She had remained seated on the bank while she spoke, and Anthony from time to time would rise to stretch his legs and stand before her, before sinking once more to the grass beside her. The sun still blazed out of a vault of deepest blue. Beside the pond the wind seemed to have dropped. The black waters shimmered invitingly cool, but beyond the shelter of the trees it felt hotter than ever.

'Then he went off to America. It was only – let's see – about eight years ago. A branch of the Ponti family from Ferrara had settled there back in the 1930s: my father had kept in contact with them. He got work, made a very good investment, and has become rich – all in a few years. He owns a ranch – I told you, I think – but it's only a small ranch, more of a large house and some surrounding land really. They use the term 'ranch' a lot out there, and people think of great estates spread across plains and mountain ranges. But it's nothing like that. I think my father's only regret is that he did not make the move years ago – but then I suppose he was tied to us and the farm, and he wouldn't leave my mother while she still lived. Despite the way he had treated her at times, he loved my mother. We all did.'

Tears were welling in Giuditta's eyes, and Anthony walked discretely away to stand at the edge of the pond looking over the water. Eventually she rose to her feet, brushing down her slacks, and joined him.

'And despite what your father did to you, you've kept in touch with him,' Anthony said. 'What *did* he do to you – if I can ask? Was he violent?'

'Yes. He would hit us all at times – even my mother. *Porco!* He was a pig.'

'And yet…You must still love him, or at least respect him, to keep in touch.'

'Oh, Anthony, he is an unhappy man today. For, you see, he is ill now as well. In fact, he should not travel, but he insists. He doesn't want me to go back out to California now, although I did once visit him there. Why I went, I'm not sure; out of respect for my mother, I think, who had just died and who loved us all equally. She would have wanted to see us all getting on. But he wasn't nice to me, even then. He argued with me – shouted at me – to try and get me to stay with him.

A couple of years later, I learnt he was unwell. Now, when he comes to England soon, he will go on to Italy, back to his old home. My brother will look after him there. I think he may never leave.'

'What's wrong with him?'

'He has a degenerative disease that's wasting away his body and his mind. He is finding it increasingly hard to remember things. He may not even recognise me now: the decline, I'm told, has been very sudden. He has recently gained a partner – an American woman half his age, whom I suspect has worked her way in with him since his confusion began. She helps him, though. She will probably get all his money. It's my fault, because if I'd stayed with him as he wished, none of that would have happened. It would be me caring for him – his own daughter, as he had a right to expect. So I only have myself to blame. She will be with him when he comes to Cambridge to see me. I don't look forward to that, because I have never met her, and I don't want to be put in such a position of hatred and guilt. It may destroy me entirely.'

She put her head down and Anthony suspected she was crying, although her body was still and her face hidden from him.

Standing by the water, with the heat weighing upon him, the alcohol he had drunk still drumming in his ears, he could feel the tenseness within her almost as if he held her in his arms. It must have been a considerable ordeal for her to tell him what she had. She must have confidence in him to have entrusted so much of her inner life to him. He felt such pity for her, and respect too for her courage, out of all the sadness she had endured. What she had described was surely what had made her ill so recently.

What he found so unspeakably difficult was that he had no way of communicating his feelings, other than for a quick touch of her hand or a squeeze of her shoulder – when what he most wanted to do was to pull her against him, to hug her to his chest, to kiss her, and tell her that he loved her and would look after her. All that, of course, was impossible – now and probably always. This girl – for he thought of her as a girl – had been unspeakably hurt. If he loved her, he must not be the cause of further pain.

Guiditta said, 'It's hard to love someone whom you have hated, but I have found in recent years that I still love my father. I have pity for him too, but I do love him.' She said this so quietly that he could scarcely hear her, but, when he was sure he had understood, he did now take her hand and press it.

'You are a beautiful person,' he said.

She smiled. 'Perhaps. Perhaps not. I am not nice at times, I know.'

'I think you're perfect.'

She was laughing now. How he loved to see her laugh. 'But you would think that, wouldn't you?'

He was not quite sure what she meant by that, but he didn't comment further. They cleared up the debris of the picnic and took it to the car. Anthony opened the doors to try and cool the interior, but he knew it would help but little until they got moving.

He looked across at Giuditta, and saw her standing a little apart from him close to the information board, a hand on her chin. He knew by now that at times like this she wanted to be by herself – perhaps just for a few moments to think her own thoughts, perhaps to gather herself for whatever was to come next. He hoped she didn't consider his company a 'task', and he was ever mindful of her swingeing moods that seemed to strike her with the sudden intensity of a whirlwind. This might be such a time, for her face, so recently full of laughter,

Anthony could see now was in-turned and reflective, a self-absorption that had brought a puckered frown to her brow.

Fearing the change, Anthony called across, 'Are you okay, Giuditta?'

She didn't seem to hear him, then started, made an effort at a smile, and said, 'Yes, of course. Why shouldn't I be?'

'No reason.' Anthony tried to keep his tone bright. Inside, a voice was telling him: Something is wrong. With her and about her, there is something I do not yet understand, and it keeps coming back to drive the sunlight out of our day.

She came over to the car, and looked at him – strangely and intensely, as if seeing him for the first time – so that for just one wild moment he thought she was going to hold him and let him kiss her, and he felt his body begin to rise in expectation, his blood racing. However, she seated herself carefully on the edge of the open boot, and looked up at him standing anxiously before her.

'I want to tell you something. I think it will help you understand me.' Her voice sounded flat and tense, her Italian accent strong – her accent that was always more pronounced when something was troubling her, as Anthony had learnt by now.

'Of course. I want to know everything.' He placed a rubbish bag on the rear bumper beside her, pushing it back into the boot.

'This is the very worst.'

'What do you mean? Are you quite sure you want to tell me?'

'Yes. At least, I think I do. I've told very few people, but you need to know now. I'll feel better when it's out in the open. It's been burdening me again of late. I know how difficult I can be at times, and this should give you some understanding of why –some sort of explanation at least. ...but I'm *not* looking for sympathy!'

Anthony was increasingly alarmed by the intensity of this development, so suddenly in the midst of their perfect day. His heart had begun to pump faster and there was a tingling and a tremor in his hands, which he always experienced at times of stress. He did not know what to say. He felt he must make some comment, if only to try and comfort her. What would the revelation be and why was she compelled to tell him now?

'Oh, my dear, what on earth is it? What has been done to you? You can tell me anything, you know. I'll do what I can to help.'

'I know you will. Thank you. But it's so hard. You won't believe it. And I'm disgusted by it – and the disgust comes back and will never disappear. That's why I get sad at times. But talking about it helps. It was so bad. I did not even tell my mother, and Lika only knows some of it. Why do I want to tell you then? Perhaps it's because you're an older man, a mature man. I trust you. I feel I can confide in you and you won't judge me or blame me.'

So that was it. He had been right. That was how she saw him. A father figure – sexless in his assumed paternity. She must be about to tell him of some embarrassing indiscretion, like a daughter might to her father, hoping he would understand and forgive her. But why? Why should she be so worried by what he thought of some distant incident from her past?

'Why should I blame you for anything? You're worrying me now.'

He realised, even as he said those last words, that he should not have uttered them. Her reaction was immediate.

'I certainly don't want to *worry you*,' she said, and rose to her feet, striding away from the car down a long green track that ran beside the fort.

He hastened after her. 'I didn't mean that. I meant I'm worried by what worries you. Don't you understand?'

She didn't answer.

'What was so bad? Tell me. Please tell me now.'

Crazily, he realised he had lost control of the situation and was begging her now.

'No. It was a mistake. We've had a lovely day. I don't want to spoil it. I'll tell you about other things instead – of Italy, of Venice, of the places where I grew up.'

She was chirrupy and smiling again, as suddenly and bewilderingly to Anthony as anything else he had experienced with her – a burst of sunlight piercing storm clouds that had now passed over her horizon as quickly as they had appeared. The trouble was that he *had* to know now what it was she had been about to divulge. He *needed* to know, otherwise it would bear upon him, troubling him, making him think fantastical things. Yet, he had learnt enough about Giuditta not to argue with her. His best course was to accept her sudden changes and take a path of least resistance. Perhaps the divulgement would come later.

He stopped her progress along the track. 'Let's drive to Ely. You can tell me about Venice and your other places as we go along.'

Although Giuditta's secret remained undisclosed, it was as if the very mention of it – the statement that it existed – had released some pressure within her, for, once back in the car, she was as friendly to him as she had been at any time that weekend. As she talked, she positively leant towards him, with her body turned fully in her seat. To emphasise the occasional point, she even placed a hand on his thigh – albeit fleetingly – and, while stopped at a level crossing, reached across him to do up a button of his shirt he had mistakenly left undone. This familiarity with him was new and seemed to be growing; from worry and near despair to fresh excitement and a hint of erotic promise. Was there no end to the ups and downs with this woman? There was, of course, the dark cloud of the revelation still to come. Would that prove the last obstacle to getting to know her properly?

As he drove, she told him more about her digging in Italy – at Aquileia, only a small place now, close to the coast some fifty miles north-east of Venice. Once it had been a great Roman city, the remains of which lay today under the village and its surrounding fields, the greater part unexcavated. Giuditta had dug for one excavation season on the site of what was probably the principal public baths.

'That is where I found my mosaic,' she said, tapping Anthony on his knee. 'It was so hot and so dusty; you have no idea. The scale of what we found – the objects themselves – were spectacular. The whole of your Glastington would fit into one corner of the site: it went on field after field, and, beyond the baths, there were streets of houses.'

'But, as an archaeologist once wrote,' Anthony said. 'In our country you can see what the Romans could do when they were *up against it*. They were carving their culture into an alien environment. It was much easier for them in Italy itself.'

'I don't know about that. I certainly found Aquileia hard work.'

'No. I didn't mean that…..'

'I know what you meant, Anthony.' Again there came the tap on his leg, this time a little higher up on a fleshy part of his thigh.

'Where did you stay when you were digging?' he asked.

'I was camping. There was a large camp site for the diggers. A few – the director and his hangers-on – stayed at a nearby hotel. We would go there in the evenings for a shower and to drink. It was good fun. We would sometimes walk through the ruins at night under the moon. There is a great basilica church there, with a campanile alongside, dating from the eleventh century, with Roman pavements beneath it; whole areas of ruins as well by the river where the docks were. And...' – once more her hand jabbed at Anthony's leg – '....there is a street of tombs in one corner of the village, which would have been outside the Roman walls: they were excavated after the war and are more perfect than anything found at Pompeii, just as they were built, with a cobbled road in front of them. They were a great sight by moonlight – very mysterious, *misterioso;* how do you say? – creepy even.'

Who did Giuditta do these things with, he wondered? He didn't care to ask. Despite her earlier account of her boyfriend Dominic in her farming days, he wanted to preserve in his mind an image of her innocence, of her freshness, of her modesty. He didn't like to think of her as part of a pack of copulating, hard-drinking youth, high on wine and sex, and worse, when their day's digging was over: he felt sure such things would have gone on in the camp site she had mentioned, or at night amongst those cold grey tombs she described.

They were now on the main road heading towards Ely. As they passed over the crest of a low rise, Anthony saw the shape of the Cathedral as a small grey-white block against the shimmering horizon. Giuditta seemed happy now, continuing to talk about her places. She had moved on to describe Venice, a city to which he had long wished to go. He remembered his previous idea; perhaps they could travel together to see the sights she was describing.

She told him about the Piazza San Marco with its two columns which you should not walk between, and the great Basilica and the Palazzo Ducale, and some of the magnificent museums and galleries, with their paintings by Tintoretto and Bellini and Titian which it would take many visits to see adequately. Then she described the Grand Canal, and the water bus (the *vaporetto),* and the Rialto Bridge – and how

Venice moves largely by water, and how smaller canals branch from the bigger canals, so that each district is approached by a network of canals, with walking streets (or *calli*) between them, crossed by many humped-back bridges.

'Venice is decaying,' she told him. 'Many people are moving out, as it is so expensive to live there and so many buildings need repair and refurbishment; the communities are going, and, even while I was at university living there, the butchers and the bakers and the fruiterers, and all the other small shops, were closing. Now it is the tourist industry that keeps Venice afloat.'

Anthony, concentrating on his driving, was entranced by what she said, and would like to have stopped so he could have listened better, but he drove on steadily towards that silhouette of Ely Cathedral flickering between the green fields and the sky.

'There was one particular place I really loved. It was a café at a junction of two narrow paved streets – alleys you would call them, walking ways only, for there are no cars or bicycles or electric scooters, or anything like that, in Venice. It was in the Dorsoduro district near the university library where I used to study and not far from the house where I lived.'

Her face was alight with memory. 'That house had pink walls of crumbling plaster bordering a tiny canal, only wide enough for the small boat moored there and perhaps one other. When I opened the shutters of the room, I looked out over the canal and the boat was always there. I never learnt who owned it, but we took it once when we went to a nearby bar – and brought it back safely although we were rather merry.'

She laughed, and he could see that in her mind she was not in the car at all but living now in that distant corner of Venice where she had been so happy. He wondered who had been accompanying her then.

'You mentioned a café. What was so special about it?' he asked.

'Ah, yes. I was telling you of my café. It was not far from the Campo San Barnaba – a small square with a most beautiful church. It was actually situated on a *rio tera* – that's a former canal, now filled in – at a point where an alley -a *calle* – once joined it. Students, like me, used the café, and the local people too, as well as some tourists in summer, although it was off the regular tourist trails. It had a large front window and I used to sit on a stool and look out along the *calle* seeing the people coming towards me, and occasionally they would not know they were approaching a junction and would almost bump into the glass. That made me laugh. I sometimes used to think that, if I sat on there, in time the whole world would pass me by: it was as if that joining *calle* went on for ever and the people would never stop coming down it; that if I waited long enough, anyone I was seeking would eventually come to me, and....' – she paused just for a moment, but long enough for Anthony to glance sideways at her, seeing her face lost in thought – '.....and, perhaps, if someone was looking for me, they would know they could always find me there.'

After this little speech, Giuditta was silent, while Anthony reflected on what she had said. How similar to his own were many of her thoughts. How he could empathise with them out of his own fixation on the past – that black corridor of long-lost light – with so little understanding of its innumerable unknowns, but with the hope (no, the belief) that one day – at one moment – he could find a meeting of its many ways, of past and present coming together as one, with all those mysteries out of time understood at last.

How strange she was, shifting always before him like a mirage; sometimes the happy, laughing child, then disgruntled and gloomy, so he did not know what she truly thought or what he might possibly have done to upset her, then clear in the open again with the dark mists rolled back and her intellect shining out in clear joy of life. She was a girl – a woman – with whom there was never a moment to be taken for granted, beautiful and demanding as she was, self-serving and selfish at times, but generous and giving as well. Happiness and despair in equal measure followed after her, but he knew – that whatever the pain and frustration – he must continue at her heels.

17

They came into the city of Ely in the late afternoon sunlight, shining hotly on the grey, sculptured walls of the Cathedral that rose from the green grass of the close in front of the high west tower. The interior was as cool as a refrigerator. Anthony was grateful to feel the sweat that had soaked his clothes chilling now that he was out of the sun. He screwed up his eyes in the gloom of the church so as to see better, his retinas still seared by the bright sunlight outside.

They walked along the nave and came to the great vault of the octagonal lantern, created out of the space left when the tower that had stood here fell in the early fourteenth century. They looked upwards at this triumph of construction, which seemed to float above them without apparent support, its sides decorated with painted panels. Close by, in the south transept they found a piece of modern sculpture showing Mary Magdalene coming face to face with the Christ, newly risen from the tomb. The forms were extended and thinned as if blasted by a great energy, and Anthony – who was otherwise not over fond of contemporary sculpture – found the piece most interesting and satisfying, moving his emotions in a way he found hard to express. Giuditta too looked at it for a long time, then lit a candle to join others flaring at its base.

'I am not a great religious person,' she said – perhaps muddling her words in the English, for Anthony was sure they would have sounded less clumsy in Italian – 'but I love this: it has such power. With the candle, I remember my mother.'

Anthony walked discretely away, for he could see her eyes were wet, and he felt in that moment a great compassion for her and would have liked to have hugged her in pure love. They came together again within the eastern apse beyond the choir, where stood a modern statue of St. Etheldreda, who had founded this church, again with a blaze of candles at her side.

'*Bellissima. Più belle.*'

They found the entrance to the Lady Chapel, and were astonished by its great vaulted size, and by the light that streamed in through windows of clear glass. Overlooking the chapel, set against the eastern window, stood a statue of the Virgin Mary clothed in a blue dress and with streaming red-blonde hair.

'I find that rather creepy,' Anthony said, mouthing the words close to Giuditta's ear, as there were other people near to them gazing at the statue.

'She is the mother of Christ. She is love and peace,' Giuditta said. 'How can she be creepy?'

'Perhaps it is the position she is placed in then. She dominates.'

'I think she is intended to, Anthony.'

Anthony walked away to examine some of the carvings around the chapel walls, many hacked off during the Reformation by iconoclast louts with hammers and axes. One head that had survived took his attention – that of a young man with tendrils of ivy growing from his mouth. He went to fetch Giuditta and pointed it out to her.

'A green man,' he told her. 'A pagan spirit of the fields and woods – an idea still strong in English folklore. There are even dances to propitiate the green men.'

Giuditta looked at him, her eyes widening. 'Yes? You're not joking, are you? Now that is *misterioso*.'

He could see she continued to be drawn to the Virgin Mary statue for she kept looking back at it, and finally seated herself on one of the carved stalls lining the walls where she could rest and gaze at it more directly. Anthony joined her.

'Squeeze up a bit.' And she moved a little to one side.

'Powerful,' she said. 'She enters me and tells me I must be truthful. I must confess. You cannot come before God without truth in your heart.'

'I thought you said you were not particularly religious.' Anthony spoke softly for he did not want to suggest he did not believe her. He was curious as to how the statue had come to impress itself upon her in this way.

Giuditta did not answer him directly. 'You can believe one minute, and then not the next. At the moment something – someone – speaks to me.'

'Do you wish to be alone?'

'No stay with me.' To his great pleasure she took and held his hand, so that they sat there like any two lovers, while people gave them sideways glances as they passed, perhaps wondering at this disparate couple whispering amongst the broken stone carving of the walls.

'Anthony…'

'Yes?'

'I must tell you now.'

'Tell me what?'

'What I was going to tell you at Stonea.'

'Oh, yes. Of course. If you want to.' The fear was upon him again. He felt his heart thumping. She must hear it too reverberating from the stone around them.

She drew a deep breath so that her shirt tightened over the points of her breasts and he could see the jut of her nipples. The other visitors were leaving, and for the moment they were alone in the chapel.

'My father...', she mouthed in his ear.

'Yes. I'm listening.' His fingers were trembling. He knew that what she would tell him, he did not wish to hear.

'My father used to abuse me.'

'You've already told me that. He would hit you.'

'No. He placed his hands on me. He would touch my body.'

Anthony felt the horror descending upon him like a black cloud. Was it now a cloak of darkness that hung over the shoulders of the Virgin Mary, watching them, or was it she who was keeping the blackness back? – just for a minute longer so Giuditta could stay in clear, unsullied light.

'But only with his finger, never with...' And just for a moment she placed her hand over his lap so that he felt its weight against his penis. She looked at him stricken. 'How could he do that?! To his little girl. *Il bastardo!*'

Anthony sat rigid. He did not know what to say. Desperately he sought words, to offer understanding, comfort. She was looking into his eyes, staring at him with an almost demonic intensity and he could offer her nothing but the sense of awfulness her words had given him.

Horror too rose for her out of this silence. '*Bastardo!*. You too. You are all the same. I shouldn't have told you. I thought you would understand.' She was choking, her back heaving, her mouth wide open desperately seeking air.

'I do. I do. I will help you. Please, Giuditta. Come back!'

But she was on her feet, and running from the chapel, brushing past a group of visitors who were just entering, so that they all looked across at him accusingly sitting by the wall, the clear cause of this young woman's disturbance and flight.

He caught up with her outside on the grass, leaning against the great black cannon that faced the cathedral's west front, a trophy from the Crimean War. He had been terrified as he sped after her along the nave, pushing past concerned stewards, that he would not be able to find her. Poor girl! What a state she was in. He saw it now. Much of her time she was keeping the darkness at bay. And now it had broken through. And he didn't know what to do. But he had to try and help her – she who had confessed to him, moved by the peace of the church.

He came up to her at the cannon slowly, not wanting her to break away from him again, and prepared to run after her if she did. She was no longer gasping for air. In fact, she looked quite normal, other than for her sudden fixation with the cannon. No one appeared to have noticed anything strange or was looking towards her.

He stood in silence beside her, tensed for her to speak or shout or slap at him. But she stayed perfectly quiet, staring down at her hands spread over the black gun metal. He saw how beautiful her nails were, each one carefully rounded, pared, and clean.

At last he said, 'Do you want to come back to the car? Or get a drink? Or do you want to talk here?'

She raised her eyes to him, and he saw how white her face was, and how dark again the circles around her eyes. 'I've never known anyone who talks so much in questions as you,' she said tonelessly. 'Why don't you, just for once, say what *you* want me to do.'

He was hurt by that. Had he not kept by her, and swayed to her changing moods, and tried to placate her and help her – and now he was blamed for that too. But, after what she had told him, could he not excuse her anything? His mind remained numbed by what she had said. He could still feel her quick touch on his groin, like a butterfly's wings: she was like a butterfly indeed that had been scorched in the sun.

He took her hand and led her back to the car, which was

parked nearby. The Yaris had been standing in the sun, so it was very hot inside, but Giuditta got in uncomplaining and slumped into her seat as if her body was filled with water. He slid onto the driver's seat beside her, but left the door open so a little of the cooling breeze could enter. In front of them, a high wall bordering the car park cascaded with crimson roses. Bees hovered amongst them in droning flight.

He felt suddenly terribly tired. He could sleep if he could only lay down his head – perhaps if Giuditta could cradle him, or he her, they could sleep together and when they awoke all this would be gone and the world would be pleasant once more, as it had been just a short hour ago. Such naivety of thought, he knew, for what had happened, what had been said, must be faced. Yet it would be nice to sleep, just for a brief while, with her hair against his face, and, waking, to press her breasts against his palms and kiss her lips. For, whatever had been done to her, he loved her – he knew – with all his strength.

'You think I'm mad, don't you? I saw it in your eyes.'

He was shocked by that. 'No. Not at all. You've had some terrible times. I want to understand. I would like to help.

'You can't do that now. You'll only add to my problems.'

That was even more hurtful to Anthony. The words sliced into him like a knife, a sudden thrust he had not expected out of a direction he had not anticipated, he who had been foolish enough to think he had the mastery, the maturity to comfort her. For one moment of silence in the cathedral – a stunned silence – he was now condemned.

'Take me home, Anthony. I'm sorry I made this mistake. I shouldn't have told you what I did. None of it is your fault. You've given me a wonderful couple of days.'

At least, the life was returning to her. She was sitting upright now, staring at the roses on the wall. 'Aren't those beautiful?'

'I'll pick you one.' He left the car and reached up at the wall, pulling down a bloom and catching his thumb on a thorn, then sawing at the stem with the edge of his car key to pull it free. He returned licking his thumb. 'For you. The most beautiful girl I've ever known.'

'Oh, Anthony. How foolish you are. Find yourself a proper woman to love. Not me. I'll only drive you crazy. As I've tried to tell you, I'm not nice. You must know that by now.' She took the rose from him and placed it on the dashboard in front of her. Already the petals were beginning to curl up.

'I love you,' he said simply. So that was out now, and there was no taking it back. And he went on, floating on a bubble of emotion, careless of his words, not thinking of her really but of his own needs. 'I so wish I could help you. You definitely need help.'

'What do you mean?' She had rounded on him, twisting sideways, her face suddenly savage. He did not see her at first, but plunged on, misunderstanding, like a man doomed to destroy himself.

'From what you've said, you need to get some sort of professional help. To try and lay some of those demons to rest…..'

Then, turning to her, he saw her face and realised his mistake.

'*Cazzo!* What the fuck! Who the hell do you think you are?' She spat the words out like a cobra, her face livid, hatred in her eyes. 'What do you think I've had? Where do you think I've been? What do you think they did to me? It *didn't work!* I can't rid myself of my past. It makes me ill over and over again. And recently too. I told you all about that. I spelt it out to you because you were pressing me so much. You wanted to know all about me and I've tried to tell you everything. But you never listen to me, you just ramble on about your own shit – your pathetic books, your miserable life. You're so fucking stupid, it's not real. Take me home. I don't want to see you anymore!'

The words lashed across Anthony so that he could not believe he was hearing them. This was not happening to him, his beautiful Giuditta, turned in an instance into a raging, foul-mouthed beast. He felt ill with the horror of it – a further layer piling upon the first, until he was choked and sick with it and had to escape out into the open air. He needed to leave the heated car, with its sickly perfume wafting from the roses, but he could not abandon Giuditta in that way; he would have to face her again.

'I'm so sorry…..' he began to say. 'I've got it wrong. I don't want to upset you like this…'

'Just drive me home, Anthony. Let's have no more of it. No more of your whining apologies. For Christ's sake, be a man!'

He didn't understand any of this. Be a man? How dare she!? A young woman talking to him like that! Should he reach across and slap her on the face? That would cut the hysteria, cut the crap. Her crap, not his!

Her head was down and she was crying now, silently but with heaving sobs. Anthony was frightened by this. He made to place a hand on her shoulder, but she twisted her body away from him. 'Don't touch me! You're always trying to touch me.'

That's rich, he thought, through the madness howling in his head. She's just laid her hand over my cock and she complains of me touching her.

He closed the car door – gently, quietly, so as not to attract any attention, for there were others in the car park going to their vehicles – and put the car into gear, easing it out of the cramped space where it had stood. Once on the main road and leaving the outskirts of the city behind, with the long, flat fields of green opening up around them, Giuditta turned once more to him. Her face was flushed and her eyes red from her crying. What a shame, what a shame, Anthony was thinking, for she had been so happy, and her eyes had been so bright, and she had been so lovely – and now this, once again, out of the clear blue sky. She was right. It had to finish. He could stand no more of it.

'Where are we going?'

'I'm taking you home. You asked me to.'

'Just like that?'

'What else? Isn't that what you want now?'

She didn't answer. Anthony concentrated on his driving. The road was busy, and the sinking sun slanted across his tired eyes, making him feel sick with all the horror filling him. He felt such fear of her. There was nothing he could say, for he was terrified of her reaction. What did she want of him? He could sense she was changing again, the explosion over, the dust settling – all the hideous words spoken, then forgotten as soon as said; and he was expected to forget them too, as if they had never been uttered. Well, he couldn't. He wouldn't. There had to be an end to this.

Yes, she was cajoling now, turned towards him, trying to smile. 'I'm sorry.'

Oh, yes, of course she was sorry. How many times had she told him that? Well, it wouldn't work again. It didn't matter what had happened to her, however badly she had been treated, whatever the abuse she had suffered at the hands of her perverted father, there was no excuse for the way she had behaved to him. Anger was growing in him. He grasped the wheel more firmly and set his jaw. He wouldn't turn to look at her again. He knew if he did, and saw that pretty, pleading face, he might forgive her. He had been right. She was mad. She needed help.

'Pull over somewhere, Anthony. Let's talk.'

There was no where he could stop, even if he had wanted to. The long straight road stretched ahead, with only a few dusty laybys and the traffic thundering past feet away – and he could not talk to her there. The road ran on and on like this until it reached the outskirts of Cambridge: there would be no place beside it where he – and she – could rest awhile and try to make sense out of what had happened. That's if he wished to do that, anyhow – and he didn't. He wanted no more discussion. Her words had been too hateful and too vile to be reasoned away.

And yet, he could sense her eyes on his face – those dark liquid eyes, now blurred with tears – and her body turned to him in the yellow blouse (how immaculately fresh she had looked this morning, the day being then so full of hope, now spoilt beyond recall), and he felt himself weakening; should they not at least try to end their friendship on a more dignified, happy note.

What had gone wrong, anyhow? He could not understand. All had been fine. Then a sudden, hideous revelation, and sharp shock filling both of them. That is what had caused the catastrophe. It was not Giuditta's fault: her past clearly controlled her, not the other way around. What she had told him was almost beyond belief. No wonder she was so traumatised, and no wonder she could not rid herself of the horror. She had contained these terrible things within herself for many long years. She could not give release to them without further pain, and perhaps – no, certainly – he had been insensitive, and had said the wrong thing. Could they not at least get these points agreed? And then indeed calmer reason might yet prevail. Perhaps this was the final exorcism that had been necessary. Afterwards, might there not be greater understanding and tolerance and peace? Oh peace, he thought; how I crave an end to this disturbance, an end to all the thought and mental turmoil, an end to the bodily lusting and the degradation that comes from it. How I wish my old life back. How much I want to be happy and still again.

As he drove on, he felt himself cleft in two. There was the half that wanted to help Giuditta – as he had said he would – and not abandon her, when she was so clearly appealing to him now for understanding, and there was the other half that was simply filled up with all the horror and could take no more of it, wanting to dump it by the wayside and continue as if he had never encountered it in the first place.

Why did her reactions to him have to be so extreme – so angry and laced with hatred? If she could only contain her annoyances – even if he was indeed the cause of them, and he was not sure that he was – then he would be much more able to cope with her. He did not want to lose her – of course, he didn't – and she had entrusted him with her big, awful secret, and he had let her down with the comments he had made. So was the fault not his then?

These thoughts – and much more – churned through his head as he drove those weary miles towards Cambridge, with the long, black channel of the road stretching ahead of him, looking neither to right or left, unaware of the landscape on either side, or of the sun, lower now in the sky, still shining its benison upon the earth. He could sense Giuditta casting glances at him, and, at the periphery of his vision if he turned his head a little, he could see her watching him, waiting for him to make some reply to her appeal. He saw her slim, bronzed hands in her hair, loosening the tie at the back, and shaking out the dark-brown locks with a toss of her head so that they tumbled to her shoulders. Was his resolve to be softened by her hair, by that wonderful brown-black sheen with its glimmers of red, that he had loved so much, and which at night in his imagination flowed over the pillows beside him?

He would have stopped if he could have – that he told himself later – but there was no place, no side road even to wander down to park by some copse of trees, to find the solitude needed for talk. There was only the ever busy road with its growing torrent of cars, the red and green and blue, white and gold, painted chariots of the hour, all moving under the sun's late afternoon brilliance, sweeping towards Cambridge and beyond. This fact made up his mind for him. It would be best now to get her home. They could talk another time. He would even drive back up to Cambridge to see her when she was calm once more – and he too. They would go over what had happened this day and reach some resolution. She would surely see the sense of that. For himself now, he was exhausted. He felt his finger tips shaking as he held them against the wheel.

He turned his head towards her. 'I'm getting you home. I think it's better we leave it all for now. I'm really sorry I upset you so much.'

She didn't protest. She didn't even reply, but sat staring fixedly forward, with one hand playing with the ends of her hair.

They were threading their way into the Cambridge traffic, with Anthony trying to remember the route back to Elmfield Road, not wanting to call across to Giuditta to help him. His mind was still dwelling on the secret she had told him; the sheer enormity of what she had said and its consequences for her life – her childhood, her young womanhood, right up to the present day – were only just becoming clear to him: the suddenness of her outbursts, and the shock to him, had frozen his comprehension until now.

'Up to the present day', he repeated to himself, and knew that the present now included himself, for he had become part of the story – and in his turn he was about to fail her too. Should they not seek out another place to talk? – beyond the city perhaps where there was somewhere quiet. He could surely find such a place. Even a walk in the city and a seat in a park might serve the purpose.

'I don't want to leave you like this,' he said.

She paused for several seconds before replying. 'It doesn't matter. We did some lovely things before it was all spoilt.'

He picked up a suggestion of bitterness in those words, and knew she was still angry with him.

'We could still talk somewhere. I won't need to leave straightaway.'

'No, you're right to get me home. At least you know all about me now.'

More bitterness, Anthony thought. How she must have steeled herself to reveal those things to him, moved by her emotions under the gaze of that wretched statue – and he had answered her so badly; she must have thought he was shoving her secret back at her as if he had not wished to hear it.

By the time the Yaris rounded the corner into Elmfield Road, Anthony had come to realise the mistake he was making. Any talk – even in the car as they drove – would have been better than a continuation of this condemning silence. And now it was too late.

As soon as the car had halted outside her house, Giuditta had pulled down the door handle and was stepping outside. He tried to stop her by getting out too and meeting her on the pavement, but she had already opened the gate and was going up the path. He half ran to catch up with her.

'I'm sorry, Giuditta. I wanted to discuss what's happened, but there seemed no chance. So I thought it best to drive you straight back. Can't we talk now, though? Please!'

She turned to him at the door. Her face was full of pain, and there was anger in her eyes. 'Anthony, you are a fool. All

I wanted was for you to reassure me and love me. 'And...' – she pushed her head forward, her face lit by a sardonic, contemptuous, smile – '...since you have desired me for so long, you might then have taken me All I wished was to be held and told I was not *unclean*.'

Anthony took a half pace back from her, his senses reeling, as the true extent of his mistake hit home at him. The front door opened and Lika appeared, her face troubled. Giuditta collapsed crying onto her breast, and Lika, with a quick look of hatred towards Anthony, slammed the door in his face.

It was a long journey for him back to the south-east of London. Later, he was to wonder how he ever made it, for he was in a state of shock. He remembered little but grim belts of snarling concrete, and rows of high buildings on either side with windows flashing in the evening sun, at every one of which shone the face of Giuditta. And, when he at last reached his apartment, he felt entirely drained of life, as if it were a river he had paddled in and the waters had now gone.

18

It rained for much of the next day, with fierce bursts of summer storm out of banks of rolling black cloud, washing the morning away, the streaming gutters choked with a detritus of leaves and twigs, torn by the flail of the wind and swept there by the lashing water. As Anthony watched from the windows of his flat, he wished the long minutes and hours of his misery could be washed away too and sent pouring with the other rubbish through the steel grills of the drains. He stirred little, seated in a stupor before a sea of paper notes of all the things he should attend to, but which now he could not face.

At noon he looked out again, and saw that the rainstorms had passed and the sky lightened, but that a steady, chill drizzle was still falling to the soaked earth. The people who passed in the street below were all wrapped in plastic and bore coloured umbrellas like huge moving flowers: they were anonymous to him, battling against nature's elements, no longer spread at ease in the sun – which pleased him, to see others struggling too.

In the early afternoon, he descended to the front of his apartment block, where he had left the Yaris parked, and opened up the car to retrieve various items from the trip. The inside was perfumed. He recognised Giuditta's fragrance, the clean, fresh scent she had worn when he had first met her in

Cambridge, overlain with that of the rose he had plucked, left by her in the car and now dying, a bruised, torn ball of deepest red. He swept it out angrily into the carrier bag he carried, and added to it the leftovers from the picnic, as well as his crumpled sheets of notes of timings and directions. Then he took the bag to the end door of the apartment block, behind which the communal rubbish bins were kept, and with a flick of his wrist spun the bag over the edge of the nearest bin.

Rubbing his hands as if to express satisfaction that the job was done, he returned up the flights of steps to his flat, and collapsed once more into an armchair. Perhaps it was her scent – or perhaps the sight of the rose – but he felt his tears coming, and he abandoned himself to them, his arms crossed over his chest and his head bowed.

He remained like this for a long while, rocking his body, calling out aloud from time to time, 'How did I get it wrong? It was going so well. You stupid fool. You fuck up everything for yourself – and, boy, did you fuck this one up.'

He was tortured by the realisation that she had turned to him for help; had chosen the cathedral – that most sacred place – to unburden herself to him, confident of his wisdom, his maturity, and seeking his support and understanding for all the terrible things that had so badly affected her life, and he had let her down utterly. And then – worse, far worse – he had not allowed her time to explain things – how many times had she asked him for that? – but got angry, childishly petulant, as if all this was about him, not her. Then he had virtually run away, stopping only at the last minute when his brain had at last re-engaged, to try and make things right again, by which time it was all far too late, obvious to anyone but a selfish dolt like himself. He had had the chance and he had blown it all away.

Anthony groaned out aloud as the memories came back and fresh realisations flooded into his mind. How happy she had been that weekend. How natural and charming she had looked. For once, she had been intent on him and his interests too, and shared his thoughts and his laughter, and come so very close to him. She had kissed him and held his hand. And yet at the very moment when she had wanted him most, when she had come to him trusting him, he had betrayed her.

Anthony thought back on what Giuditta had told him – her big secret, which he could see now she had felt compelled to tell him because their relationship was growing closer and closer. Fool that he was! Why hadn't he read those signs? If she had not felt close to him, and confident in him, she would never have revealed to him her inner turmoil. And what a turmoil it must have been, affecting her so badly over the years, causing her illness, wrecking her happiness, probably even making it impossible for her to enjoy a normal relationship with a man. Was that the real reason she had responded to his overtures – because he was an older man, and she wanted a father figure to take the place of her real parent? She had only ever mentioned one close male friend – Dominic – and he did not know how successful that relationship had been. They had split up, she had said, but whether by falling out or by differing circumstance, he did not know. Now, he realised glumly, it was impossible for him ever to know more.

He could see Giuditta again in the Ely chapel, with the white light pouring through the clear glass of the great windows, and the blue-clad statue of Mary high above them, her arms raised as if to strike them down – or at least that had been Anthony's impression when he had first seen the figure. But, of course, the sculptor's intention was to show Mary giving a blessing – Mary, mother of Christ: '*Ave Maria gratia plena.*' Whatever the evil that might surround her, Mary must never be viewed as anything but love.

Giuditta's words, 'but only with his finger' – at first he was only able to think of them by their shapes and their sounds, not by their direct meaning as she had spoken them – in time he forced himself to say out loud, and then released their full horror, so that he felt he was being choked by them. How truly terrible were those words that she had felt compelled to tell him. A father who had done such a thing should not have his daughter still attentive to him. At least vengeance was being exacted by the illness that now rotted away at him – divine justice indeed!

What had been her real purpose in telling him? Had she supplied the answer to that herself, in those last words to him in the car at the end of that terrible journey? – 'All I wished was to be told I was not unclean.' Was that it then? Without confession, there could be no absolution. Did she feel she had herself to be forgiven before she could get truly close to a man again?

It was impossible for him to judge the secret workings of her mind. Perhaps she had come to believe that what had happened to her had been her own fault, her own vileness, instead of that of her father. She said she still loved her father, so had she come to blame herself rather than him? Somewhere, at some time, these things must have been discussed with the professionals who had tried to help her. And yet, she had never been totally cured. She had kept on relapsing. It only needed an idiot like him to undo all the good work done, and bring the old wrongs screaming back into the present.

And yet, how could he possibly have known what to say and do? He might have been more confident, more assured, more loving perhaps, but even with those considerations he would still most certainly have said something wrong at some point or other. The fault, of course, was his, just for getting involved with her at all, and the true reason for that, which he had already admitted to himself, was lust – the lust of an ageing man for a younger woman. Not all his pretence about a meeting of minds, of a fusion of spirits, could alter that. What was so ironic was that, had he only been more understanding and patient, she might well have given herself to him – as indeed she had told him right at the very end. So, not only had he thrown away the friendship and the empathy that he had long wished for, but he had lost as well what he had desired most and fantasised about in his dreams – the physical joy of her.

He rose to his feet and started pacing his lounge, ten short feet forward and ten feet back again, with a side step to the window to check that the rain was still falling and the umbrellas of the Mums collecting their children from school were still passing beneath. What should he do? Should he try to contact her again? Or should he give up entirely, and try to forget the whole thing, hoping no one else would ever learn of his indiscretions. Who would know? Only those at Glastington. Would Brian spread the word of his foolishness, or would it all soon be forgotten? Thinking of Glastington made him realise that Giuditta was unlikely to go back there now. So he had thrown that away as well.

His phone rang sharply making him jump, hope surging briefly. It was not Giuditta, however, but Pamela. That was surprise enough by itself. He hadn't spoken to Pamela for a number of months. Despite their break up, they still kept in touch. Had he not received her email? she asked. She had sent him one that morning, but he hadn't replied. She had been waiting for an answer. She made absolutely no allowances, did Pamela. She never had. He might have been away. Or caught up in something else. As indeed he was.

What was your email about?' he asked. No message had been there when he had checked first thing, wretched with lack of sleep and scarcely able to concentrate on the screen.

'You read it and get back to me,' she said, and rang off. That was Pamela all over. Suddenly demanding, and peremptory, when she had absolutely no right to be. He owed her nothing now, he thought angrily – anger that soon subsided to renewed misery. However, he opened up his phone to find her mysterious message.

In fact, he had two messages: the second was even more unexpected than Pamela's. It was from Juliana, whom he had met at the Italian Cultural Institute. He remembered her clearly, her elegant figure, her conversation, her interest in the Glastington excavation. She had said she might visit with her husband while the August dig was on. He had told her to look up the site on the internet where she would find his email address too.

'I hope you don't mind me sending this to you' – she wrote – 'as our acquaintance back in May at the Pompeii displays was only brief, but I have found the Glastington excavation web pages you described, and I must say it all looks most interesting. I would love to see the dig underway. When do you suggest the best time to come would be? At the start of the dig, or perhaps later on when more discoveries have been made?! By chance, I shall be spending a large part of August at a friend's house in Sherborne (which I see is not all that far away), and shall be travelling down by train. As neither my friend or I drive, I would have to come to Glastington by taxi as I imagine public transport is non-existent. I must explain that my husband – with whom, of course, I would normally have travelled – has been seconded at short notice to the embassy in Rome, and will not return to England until late in September – long after the dig is over for the year, I suspect.....'

Anthony read all this in a type of daze. Did he really want to take on the trouble of dealing with this woman? Not now surely. It was the worst possible time to have asked him. She did not know that, of course, and he *had* offered to show her around. Courtesy demanded a quick, helpful answer. So he did so straightaway, before he had even opened Pamela's message. He knew that if he looked at the latter first he would most likely find that what Pamela had written would prove so disturbing he might well forget to respond to Juliana at all.

As he tapped out his reply, Glastington and its well seemed a long way away.

'How nice to hear from you. So pleased to hear you are going to come to Glastington. The last week in August would be the best time. By then we should have got the well finished. Did I tell you about the well? It's a major discovery made this year and will be well worth seeing (sorry about the pun!). You're right about the local bus service – about one a week! It'll be my pleasure to come and pick you up – and take you home again afterwards also. Really, no problem. The distances are quite short. The best thing will be for you to contact me nearer the time. I'll be there from the 7th August, so I'll put both my mobile and home numbers below.....'

After he had sent this off, with some trepidation he clicked on Pamela's message. As he had predicted, what she had written bowled him over. In essence, it was an appeal for them to get back together, to give it another try, to at least share some things together again, even if not their entire lives. Could she come and see him to discuss this?

He was astonished, for he thought she had found someone else – a younger man, he suspected, although he did not know for sure and had never asked. He was amazed as well that she – the one who had most determinedly sought their separation – should now be making such overtures to him, without any prior indication at all. Why? He could not imagine. No wonder she had phoned him to discover his reaction to her email.

Despite his tiredness and depression, he felt his blood beginning to course stronger. Might there be the chance of sex again with Pamela? He had to admit their sex had once been very good. He had missed the physical outlet for his lust while chasing the impossible, disguising his needs – he realised – in fantasy and pretence, in intellect washed out with sentiment. He knew the resulting frustration made up much of his present unhappiness. Giuditta had never excited him as Pamela always did. All that talk of mind and intellect and spiritual communion – it was bunkum, wasn't it? It was sex he needed.

He replied to Pamela by email – not wanting to phone her back yet as he was a little uncertain of his exact thoughts on her proposition – inviting her to come over to see him in a few days. She must have been hovering over her computer, for her further reply shot back straightaway: she'd call the day after tomorrow in the evening. Good, he thought, accepting this, it will give me a little more time to recover from Giuditta. He meant by that, to recover physically from the exhaustion and the lack of sleep, not from the loss of her itself. He had still to face up to that. He could not accept it yet, could not even get his mind around it properly, the sudden horror of it.

Having been shaken from his lethargy by these emails, he decided – against his better judgement – to send one to Giuditta, begging her to get in touch with him as they had to talk. He did not want to lose her friendship, he told her. His inbox pinged shortly afterwards, and he ran to the machine thinking the incoming email would be from her – but it was from Juliana again. She too must have been busy at her IPad, or whatever sort of device she might have.

Juliana thanked him for his 'very kind and generous offer' of giving her a lift, but felt she could not possibly accept such a 'time-consuming and expensive intervention' into his own work on the excavation. No, she had just wanted some advice on access: she would be embarrassed if he thought she had been looking to him for transport. It would be easy to arrange something, she said. If public transport was not possible, then she would simply take a taxi or hire a car for the day.

Well, sod you, thought Anthony, without grace in his peeved, exhausted state. Come how you like, you old bat – as if I care, anyhow. He must be much the same age as Juliana but he didn't want to be surrounded by older people. He wanted youth again. He wanted Giuditta. Even as he sent Juliana a conciliatory answer, the pain – distant for a while – surged back, sparking with probing needles behind his eyes, sending shocks of nausea through his bowels. Oh God, what had he done that this girl – the one whom he loved, and had told her so – had now gone from him in such an awful way? He had tried so hard with her, but in the end had got it wrong. Terribly wrong. Why didn't he just go to the window now and jump out? And serve him right too!

That evening, his tension over Giuditta had built up to such a degree that he could not rest or sit or eat without constant thought of her, going over and over again in his mind the circumstances by which they had come to this state, so that he felt he just had to do something further to try and contact her. He prepared the speech he would make to her – the apologies he would offer, the blaming of his own inadequacies and his own problems, which he did not expect her to want to listen to, but he hoped they would at least help her to understand he had not meant to hurt her. The pressure of everything had just got too much for him. That bit at least, he thought, was true.

He kept checking his emails. Giuditta had sent no reply. So at around eight o'clock he made a phone call to her home number. The phone rang and rang, and he was just about to give up on it when, through a series of clicks on the line, there came a voice that was not Giuditta's.

'Is that Lika?' He recognised the heavy accent.

'Yes?'

'It's Anthony. I met you the other day.'

'Yes.'

'Is Giuditta there?'

'She doesn't want to talk to you.'

'Can't she tell me that herself.'

'No. She says go away.' The phone was put down.

Anthony found he was shaking all over. He put his head in his hands to smother his tears. Then, through this intensification of his unhappiness, a spark of anger began to smoulder, bursting suddenly into flame. How dare that woman – Lika – dismiss him like that! It was little indeed that he had done wrong; very much he had done right. Was he now to be condemned and rubbished by someone whose business none of this was – someone to whom Giuditta herself had said she had not told her secret. What right had she to get involved?

He looked up the mobile number he had retained for Giuditta and dialled it. He wouldn't take no for an answer now. He *must* talk to her. Again the phone rang and rang, and went through to voicemail. He rang off and tried again, then a second time, then a third – possessed now, almost mad, by his frustration. The phone was suddenly answered.

'Hello? Giuditta?'

'No. It's Lika.'

'I want to speak to Giuditta.'

'She wants nothing to do with you. She says, you fuck off.' The obscenity, delivered in accented English by a foreigner, seemed the ultimate insult to poor, possessed Anthony, shaking him as he hunched over the phone.

The line went dead. He flung himself down on his bed fully clothed and tried to sleep. But he could not. How he longed for

Giuditta to be beside him, so he could love her, and give her his wisdom and his strength to help her, and make her laugh and be happy, as she had once laughed with him, doubled-up with fun. Now none of that was to be. He thought hell could not possibly hold anything worse for him than the way he was feeling now.

19

The period from the personal disaster that ended Anthony's Fenland visit at the end of June until the beginning of the August Glastington dig passed for him in something of a whirl – a whirl, which excluded Giuditta entirely, for, as he had feared on that terrible evening of his first day of loss, she made no attempt to contact him, and he knew he did not dare to do so again himself. Nor did he wish to ask Brian about her – whether she had confirmed or cancelled her place on the coming summer dig.

Brian was back now from his own break away, and had phoned Anthony about his plans for the further excavation of the well. He had done some work cutting back the trench wall on the side nearest the hedge and setting up a boarded platform by the shaft, which he thought would make it easier to conduct the excavation, in particular if it was wet underfoot. Olaf had helped him: he was camping on the site apparently while working on his thesis, and using the place as a base to explore the neighbouring countryside. He had a motorbike, Brian said, of impressive proportions, with a trail of village maidens whom he would take for rides and sometimes bring back to the site in the evenings. Anthony was not surprised that the U-boat commander was able to seduce poor, fickle English womanhood in this way.

Stan, who had worked on building sites at some point in his career, had also been present. Brian said he had helped place two Acrow bars across the top of the shaft. When Anthony queried what an Acrow bar was, Brian explained it was a stout steel rod that could be screwed into place to fit the well's diameter, thereby supporting its walls from any danger of collapse. It was used extensively in the building trade, Anthony learnt.

'And they look secure?' Anthony had asked. He had little confidence in anything Stan did.

Brian answered 'Oh, yes. Very much so. I've given them a good check. They're screwed tight against planks at four points on the upper walls. So the well will be absolutely safe to work in.'

Anthony thought his first action on getting to Glastington would be to inspect these bars. 'What about the ladder?' he asked.

'What do you mean?'

'Can you still lower it in the shaft with the bars there?'

'Yes. No problem really. It takes two of you to hold it up and slide it down vertically, though.'

'What about people getting in and out of the shaft?'

'You have to be a bit more careful on the upper rungs to work yourself through the bars, but it's quite possible.'

Not for you, mate, thought Anthony, knowing Brian's weight and lack of agility. It all sounded far from ideal.

'Do we really need these Acrow bars? The shaft always seemed stable to me.'

'Just an extra precaution. We can't be too careful.'

No we can't, thought Anthony. Brian's concern was commendable. But the biggest chance of an accident, he knew, would be caused by the inattention or stupidity of others – something accidentally dropped into the shaft, for instance.

In that regard he recognised that Stan, with his tendency to act a part, in particular if he had a female audience, could prove a liability. Perhaps he should try to persuade Brian to move him away from the working head of the shaft.

Anthony still thought about Giuditta constantly, but the pain was not now so immediate, and he had been able to pull himself together to get on with his daily life. Yet, occasionally he would still be overwhelmed by grief at what had happened – not only for himself but for her too, trapped within the trauma of her past: it must be the clear cause of her sharply-changing moods. Anthony felt sure he could not be the only one who had experienced these. What about the people she worked alongside?

He realised it was likely he would never hear from her again. Yet, at the back of his mind, there lingered the hope that, after enough time had passed, she might seek him out once more, for they had done some happy things together and he knew she had enjoyed being with him. Whatever she thought he had done, might it not be possible for her to forgive him and wish his friendship back? How he would love to enjoy her company again, with that earnestness and that energy, and that sense of beauty about her, he had found so beguiling. He would like at least to be able to think of her as a friend, without the accumulation of misery that had made him so unhappy – and her too, he was sure. Neither of them deserved that.

The major part of the whirl Anthony found himself caught up in, however, had been as a result of the visit of Pamela. She had arrived in the early evening two days after they had made their arrangement, and it seemed to Anthony that she had never been away. She had lost a great deal of weight and looked now much more like the Pamela he had known in the more distant, happy years. She was even wearing clothes he remembered – the blue dress, buttoned at the front, he had always liked, with the hem that flounced up when she walked.

If Pamela had wished to talk about their getting back together, and the reasons for her sudden change of heart, more dramatic even than a politician's U-turn, she gave no sign of wanting to begin. She simply sat and looked at Anthony, and sipped the tea he had made for her, while he gazed back at her. He thought she looked very good for her mid-fifties – her figure was now trim, her bust full, her legs slim. She had her hair in a new style – bleached blond and softly curled about her ears whereas before it had been reddish brown, short, and straight. It suited her, and he desired her, his blood beginning to race.

It did not take long. The tea was never finished. They had sex first on the carpet in the lounge, then on the bed. Pamela's need was as desperate as his. They tore at each other's clothes, and they kissed and they whispered breathy endearments to each other – 'Why did I ever leave you?' – 'Oh, I need you!' – accompanied by grunts, groans, screams, and pantings – until they were quite satiated. And if, during his long fast, Anthony had come to doubt his potency, he found to his great pleasure that he had nothing to fear. In fact, he felt quite the young stud again under Pamela's expert attention. Now would Giuditta ever have done that for him?

'Why don't you spend the night here,' he had whispered when they were done, before falling into the deep sleep of sexual release. When he awoke – How long had it been? Thirty minutes? An hour? – it was to find Pamela seated bare-breasted on the edge of the bed reading his diary (he kept a very full diary, written up as often as he could). She had been in the habit of checking up on him in the past, probing his cupboards and his drawers when he was not about, making sure he was not living a double life or simply – as she would explain as if in justification – 'trying to find out what makes you tick.' In consequence, he had had to keep his diary and other personal papers firmly under lock and key. Now, of course, he had dropped his guard. Who wouldn't have done so in their own home, thinking this woman had gone for good?

'You seem to have been having a fine time,' she said, seeing he was awake. She did not put the diary down, but held it up pretending to read from it. 'Gidite- is it?' – she could not make out his writing – 'and Julia, and probably others I haven't found yet. You've certainly been busy with *that*.'

She slid a hand under the sheet onto his penis, which rose again to her touch. She always had that immediate effect on him, however angry she made him. And her behaviour was unforgivable. Yet, once he had snatched the diary back, he did not have the heart to berate her.

They had sex again, and then Pamela said it was time for her to go. He did not know if she was angry, indeed what her mood and her intentions were at all.

'Why did you come here exactly?' he asked afterwards, pulling on a dressing gown while she reached for her underwear.

'What a question! Haven't you enjoyed it? Oh, I see what you mean. No, I thought in a mad moment we might get back together. But I see now nothing has changed with you and it would be a further disaster.'

She reached behind her to hook up her bra, then sat on the edge of the bed brushing out her hair. 'You'd soon get bored with me again. Obviously you want younger stuff. That's what you wrote. Half your age, isn't she – Judy or whoever?'

He didn't bother to correct the name. She had stepped into her dress and was now pulling it up, slipping her arms into the sleeves. Her body was hidden from him. Would he ever see it again?

'Promise me you won't make too much of a fool of yourself with those young women,' she said, buckling a shiny black belt about her waist. 'And, whatever you do, don't drone on and on about all that history. They won't want to hear it. They'll want parties and dancing and loud music. You'll find it hard to keep up. And I don't just mean that.' She prodded at his front with her hand.

She *was* still angry with him, he realised. But she kissed him on the cheek, then came back to give him a long, lingering kiss on the lips.

'Thanks,' she said. 'Good luck.' And then she was gone.

The rest of July passed quickly and relatively quietly for Anthony. The weather was hot and sunny, and he prayed the heat would break for the August dig. If it would only rain – say, in the last week before digging commenced – and then remain largely dry (some rain overnight, however, would be acceptable) then conditions would be perfect. But long days under blazing skies were too exhausting for him now, although he had done his share of them in the past.

In the well, however, he would not be so affected by heat, in particular if the water table was reached and he had to work with his feet in water, operating the suction head of a pump to keep the level down. He had not worked under such conditions before. He anticipated many experiments working out the best way to proceed.

Brian phoned not long afterwards to say that all was prepared: a pump, ladders, and an improved rope and bucket system were already stored on the site ready for the first day. He said he had examined the shaft with Olaf – he seemed almost perpetually on site now, rather to Anthony's irritation – and the water table had indeed risen because of the rains earlier in July. There were several inches of standing water in the shaft now, which might be still there in August, meaning they would have to pump from the start. Anthony wondered which of the two had gone down the shaft to check. He could not imagine it had been Brian, and for some reason he did not like the idea of Olaf descending the well without him also being present. The well shaft was his domain – his property!

When Brian had said the 'well team' for August would be as before – Anthony, Stan, Miles, and Olaf – Anthony had come close to asking him about Giuditta. Had she been in touch to cancel her participation in the dig, or would she still be present? But he had cut off the question just in time. It would be foolish to ask. He did not want his memories of her revived, particularly as they were at last slipping more into the background of his life.

In the last week before Glastington, he turned once more to his proposed novel, and read back the notes he had made so far. Somehow, the whole idea of his Arthurian romance in a modern setting seemed now trite and awkward. His characters of Rosalind and Richard, he felt were artificial, created for a purpose, rather than being 'real people' with whose lives it would be possible for his readers to empathise. Still, he did not want to give up entirely, so he forced himself to continue – or at least make another start – by getting something more down on paper, even if were just a succession of further notes.

He wrote, in his scrawling, jerky hand, across a white sheet of paper –

'Rosalind is cut off from the world. Because of her upbringing, she is emotionally dead. She might as well be locked up in a tower (like the good Lady of Shalott). She only sees the world through television, the internet, films, and magazines that show her the bright life she otherwise craves but can never be part of. She is a pretty, clever girl, however, and she holds down a good job, but her inner life is sterile. She longs to meet a man, and find fulfilment in love, and to have a child – but she is frightened of 'giving herself'.

Into her narrow world of work and home (her 'tower') comes Richard, who falls in love with her: he finds her beautiful, not only her physical appearance but her quiet and withdrawn personality, in such contrast with his brash, egocentric, extrovert wife. Rosalind in turn is greatly attracted to Richard and his lifestyle, but she feels he is so far from her in every way (including the fact he is married) that any chance of their being together is an impossible fantasy.'

Having reached this point in his notes, Anthony flung down his pencil, and left his flat to walk in the sun-warmed streets outside. Fantasy indeed! he thought. I'm trying to create a fantasy, but is it not my own life which is the fantasy? Once I had everything about me that I desired – an interesting job, a compliant woman, a fulfilling hobby, purpose, direction, meaning, and now it's all gone – except for the hobby, that is. So I live out a fantasy of younger women – a 'dream of fair women', as they have been described – and immerse myself in the past, thinking I can create a great novel out of it all. Truly, it is me who's in the tower and not my fair Rosalind. I'm hopeless. Quite hopeless. And probably going rapidly round the twist too.

He walked along the tree-lined avenues, gazing at the red-brick houses with their neat front gardens ablaze with flowers, and felt such a desire for the normality these houses represented to him. Really, he would give up all his pretensions for one day of normal life – to go to work, come home, see his wife, have breakfast, lunch, and dinner, spend an hour in the garden shed fiddling with plant pots, watch the late night news, and go to bed to lie with a woman, and hear her breathing beside him, and put an arm across her to know she was there. Then to wake up and start all over again.

All that would be wonderful: it would bring solidity, security, relaxation, peace. Why did he have to chase the unobtainable – to desire impossible women, to have impossible dreams? Why always the craving for something better, to be the best, to do something outstanding that others would notice? It was ridiculous. Why didn't he simply relax? Pamela had come back to him – but only for sex. He wanted sex. But he wished for far more than that – friendship, sympathy, awareness, empathy; or were they just words that buzzed in his brain? He thought Pamela would not return again. And Giuditta was a dream now that was finished. He did not know where to turn.

He returned to his flat, and took up a fresh sheet of white paper –

'Richard goes mad in pursuing his impossible dream. He slides into the water beneath the tower, thinking Rosalind floats beside him – but she has no flesh, no form; she is only moonlight shining on the black water.'

The man in the tower, he thought. I am haunted by that dream of the man in the tower. And he remembered as well the strange presence he had felt that evening at Wandlebury. Is it thought then which is eternal in the universe? Does thought transcend all material things? Everything that has ever been perhaps lingers within the power of thought, and can be recaptured by the conscious mind, the intelligence that can probe the hidden darkness of the past. Is this the true power of the past, out of history, out of myth, out of legend, that can be brought again into the present?

Anthony felt frightened. He knew he was at the edge of a great unknown, where everything that had ever lived or happened was still continuing. And whoever crossed its border would certainly go mad.

It would not be good to go mad, he thought.

20

The cars were arriving at the Glastington Roman villa, coming one after another along the dusty track to the site, now baking under a hot August sun. Soon the small, grassy compound that served as a car park was a sea of coloured, glittering metal, from which emerged tee-shirted, be-shorted youth – male and female – bearing various bundles of tenting and equipment. Now, the sharp hammering of metal, the rustle of unfolded nylon sheeting, with shouts and laughter, told of tents being erected across the slight slope of the hillside above the villa site, so that in no time at all the green grass was studded with low hillocks of green, yellow, and red. Amongst these, a few caravans and mobile homes manoeuvred, exhaust fumes rising briefly on the heated air until engines were thankfully shut off and the business of attaching awnings and water tanks began.

Close to the site caravan, large olive green tents were being put up, the stubborn canvas being hauled over metal poles, and guy ropes stretched out and fixed with much banging of mallets, by men of more senior years, one of whom – an ex-army officer – had gained the tents on loan from the MoD. Amongst these workers was Anthony Winters, who had arrived at Glastington in his Land Rover the evening before, and was now busy helping with the preparations for the main annual dig. He grunted and groaned amongst the band of perspiring men, bending, kneeling, tugging, fighting the recalcitrant tenting, hating having to take part in these preparatory duties, longing to be free to grapple with the archaeology once more.

As he squatted to bash a tent peg into place, he felt a pressure on his shoulder and heard a cheery voice in his year. 'Hello, you old bugger. How are you doing?'

Looking up, he confirmed the voice as that of Miles, his crinkly, lined face with its perpetual smile. How did Miles manage that eternal cheerfulness? he thought gloomily. Anthony did feel gloomy this morning – tired and harassed, and in some ways discontented at having had to leave the security and sanctity of home, to make the long journey to take part in this new maelstrom. Each year in recent times, he had felt the same, despite his otherwise pleasurable anticipation of the dig.

In a little while, things would settle down and the discipline of the excavation would replace the wild indiscipline at present surrounding him, and then he would be much happier. Anthony hated situations that were out of control, where people were free to express their personalities and – as Anthony thought – their stupidities, without restraint. How, at times, he would like to form them up as on an army parade ground, and set out rules and standards of behaviour to them. He loathed the modern freedoms of youth, their air of repressed rebellion, their boisterous self-confidence, their apparent lack of respect for all the things he – and by assumed extension, his generation – valued.

It was Brian, of course, who should address all the newcomers, setting out what was expected of them. But he never did. When the excavation started, it was left to the area supervisors to impose the correct discipline – and those supervisors varied between being very good (a few) to being downright incompetent (in Anthony's view, the majority). Sometimes, he almost felt tempted to take on the responsibility himself, but never did. He knew he did not really want to be bothered with advising and training others – unless, of course… unless they were like Giuditta.

He had not thought of her for a while, and now here was Miles pumping his hand, and he remembered their conversation before and knew Miles would soon be asking about her.

'Have you brought your caravan?' he said to Miles, forestalling any immediate questions.

'Yes, yes. Parked just there.' Miles swung out a hand indicating a small, white caravan backed up behind the main spoil heap, the slopes of which were red with poppies. 'It's a bit close to some of the tents but those buggers got there ahead of me.'

Anthony knew that those whom Miles called buggers today would tomorrow be his buddies. He had a habit of general matiness about the site, and – depressingly to Anthony –soon became Mr. Popular, everyone's friend. It would not be long before he would be sharing the copious bottles of alcohol he brought with him in the caravan with the camp fraternity at large. King of the Heap, he was, thought Anthony wearily. There was no way he could pretend to any such friendliness with that discordant rabble.

'Let's have a look at the well,' said Miles. 'I hear you've been making good progress.'

Anthony excused himself from his tent-erecting functions, leaving the ex-army man enveloped by a sudden collapse of green canvas, and accompanied Miles across the site – where a few newcomers were staring vaguely at the array of revealed walls and beaten surfaces they would soon be digging

– to the path through the hedge beyond which lay the well. Here Anthony was irritated to find Stan and Olaf already in attendance, with a couple of middle-aged women he had not seen before standing with them in the trench. Why are women interested in archaeology often so ugly? thought Anthony, looking at their bright tee-shirts and white shorts, with their comfy trainers on their big feet, and their goggling, hanging faces framed with large-lensed glasses. God! He felt depressed. Did he have to shush these away now? They shouldn't be close to the well like that, anyhow.

Stan was showing off to the women, as Anthony had known he would, leaning against the ladder that was already in position in the well and indicating features of the shaft as if he were the man in charge, the supreme excavator. As he spoke, Anthony could see Stan's body in casual pose becoming ever more suspended over thin air, and urgently called out to him.

'Watch what you're doing, Stan! It's dangerous there.'

Stan's reaction was to turn to Anthony with a cheeky grin on his red gnome-painted cheeks. He did, however, step back from the ladder. The two women looked surprised, then giggled at Anthony's intrusion, as if some crusty sergeant major had arrived, unbidden and unwanted, to spoil their fun.

'How can I help you ladies?' Anthony said.

'Stan's just showing us the well,' ventured one. She wore a yellow top that was copiously filled with undulating, unrestrained flesh, which clearly had provided Stan with the fillip to show off.

'You must be careful here. That's why the hazard tape's up. You should be outside it.' Anthony was looking around, seeing the tape trampled to the ground on one side. Olaf even now was gathering it up neatly to form a proper entrance to the well excavation.

'We must keep this under strict control,' Anthony said testily. He knew he had to assert himself if he was to be in charge here. 'This is an excavation site, not a picnic place.'

The women were growing annoyed now. Anthony could see a tightening of their jaws and a flush on their cheeks. 'Oh, I'm sorry, I'm sure,' said the second woman. 'We only wanted to see what was going on.'

'Of course.' Anthony tried desperately to be more pleasant. He didn't know who these women were. They might be friends of Brian. Any incident involving 'high-handedness and rudeness' was certain to be referred to the site director.

It was Miles, however, who now stepped forward with a placatory smile. 'Ladies. Ladies. Just stand the other side of the tape and we'll show you everything.'

The comment, of course, brought the expected chorus of pretended shock, accompanied by many giggles, and the tension was broken. The women soon trailed away with only a backward look at Anthony. He really didn't care. He couldn't work with people like that around him.

Anthony knew he was more depressed – more frustrated – than he had been for a very long time. He must get into the archaeology After all, it was the well he had come for, not Giuditta or any other woman.

Stan appeared unconcerned by his own role in this small affair. He seemed totally unaware that it was his behaviour that had created the situation antagonising Anthony. So no regret was expressed by him, only a grinning 'Well, you're a grumpy old sod today', followed by an explanation of the virtues of the Acrow bars he had positioned across the well shaft. Anthony, seeking to recover his composure, examined the two carefully, but was doubtful of their merits in preventing any possible collapse of the stone lining. Despite the planks they pressed against, all they did really was to support the small areas of stones immediately around them, undoubtedly holding these in place, but not necessarily the stones beside and below.

Indeed, the strength of the shaft relied upon the completeness of the stones laid in dry courses – so many concentric circles of stone, they were, descending layer by layer into the depths. The stones were held in place by their fellows either side, and were pressed against the earth wall behind, which also had a certain fixing quality. If you took one or more stones out, however, the whole wall in that immediate area might be weakened, as the solidity of the structure was thereby compromised.

Anthony ran his eye around the shaft away from Stan's Acrow bars. Clearly, it was the upper area of the stone lining, collapsed in antiquity, that presented the real danger – if danger there was – not the segments against which the Acrow bars pressed. Indeed to him, all those steel bars really achieved was to make access to the shaft more difficult.

Anthony thought they should be removed, but doubted if Brian would agree to that. They would probably have to muddle through with them in place, so Brian could say he had done everything he could to ensure the well was safe for further excavation. Not that Anthony really thought there was any chance of collapse. Even in the tumbled sections, the stones seemed solidly fixed. It would surely take a massive movement of the earth to disturb them, and earthquakes in Somerset were fortunately very rare!

No, the shaft was definitely safe for now, but Anthony would keep that opinion under review. The situation could alter if the well proved very much deeper. No, the principal dangers remained, as before – those of things dropped into the shaft, particularly from the buckets being hauled up, or of a missed footing on the ladder, or indeed a stumble on the boards of the new platform at the top of the open shaft, which would likely be slippery after rain. These were the areas where they had to keep their wits about them and take the greatest of care.

Olaf, who had been very quiet at the time of the conversations with the women and during the scrutiny of the well lining – he had been busy cleaning and tidying the trench about the shaft, a task which Brian presumably had set him to – now ventured a comment. Anthony had so far paid him little attention. Olaf seemed as controlled and organised as before, quietly getting on with his work. He was clean shaven now, making his face look thinner, but his blond hair was longer and gathered at the back in a clip, forming a short pigtail – an effeminate touch, thought Anthony, that was out of keeping with the masculinity that otherwise exuded from his lean, muscled body. He was wearing a sleeveless grey vest and shorts.

'The water gone down,' Olaf said looking up at Anthony. 'No need for pump now.'

Anthony was annoyed with himself. He had been so intent on dealing with the idiotic Stan and examining the well walling that he hadn't even thought about the bottom of the shaft and the all important question of the water table. The present depth of the well – some fifteen feet from the upper course of stones – was such that the working face at the bottom lay in deep shadow, and he had not yet looked to see if there was water lying there. Olaf's reassurance, therefore, was welcome, as having to use the pump early on would only make the digging operation more difficult.

'You want to do all digging, you welcome,' Olaf added, a longer statement than he was accustomed to deliver in his accented English.

'Don't you like it down there then?'

'Not too much. I have claustrophobia – a little.' He pronounced the 'claus' as the German 'klaus', making the word sound strange. Anthony was surprised. So the perfect Olaf had his flaws too. So he could never be that imagined U-boat commander. His nerve would not have allowed him to be shut up in a steel tube.

The situation was somewhat ironic because, when they had dug last, it had been Anthony who had not cared to be in the shaft, and had sent Olaf down. Now, recovered from the bad feelings he had experienced then, Anthony was secretly pleased by Olaf's unexpected timidity. Although the work at the bottom of the shaft would be hard, it was literally at the cutting edge and held all the glory that might be attended if further good finds were made.

'Who is down the well digging?' visitors would ask. And the answer would come back – 'Anthony, of course.' Anthony was the brave one, the fit one, the man capable of doing these things when everyone else was reluctant. Now he would not even have to share any of that fame. Stan and Olaf would remain working at the top, as would most probably Miles also. Although the latter had dug the shaft earlier on, Anthony thought it was unlikely he would want to dig at much greater depth. No, rather like Stan, Miles was a great talker and would prefer to be on the surface, spreading the story of what was going on below.

At this point in Anthony's thoughts, Brian appeared, stumbling up to the well. Anthony had scarcely spoken to him yet on this visit. He thought he might be displeased by his abandonment of the tent erection – Brian had been one of those he had left beneath the collapsed canvas – but, if so, he showed no sign of any ill feeling. He bore in a podgy hand a square of wood which Anthony saw was a painted sign. He held it up and Anthony read – 'Danger. Deep excavation. No entry without permission.' The lettering was well-formed, and the sign had clearly been made with care – red paint had been used for the word 'danger'.

'I made it last night,' Brian said in response to Anthony's query. 'We can't take any chances here. I heard you tell those women off. Quite right too. Do you understand, Stan and Miles? Don't let anyone into the immediate well area without Anthony's permission, or mine.'

As the two mumbled assent – Olaf was evidently trusted already in this regard -Anthony had to admit he was impressed. Brian's ideas on safety, he had thought, had been somewhat lax in the past, but now here he was on the ball and very much aware of the dangers. He had to be. He was the director of the site, and, in the event of any accident, the ultimate responsibility would be his.

Anthony took the sign from Brian, and twisted the wire that was attached to it around one of the posts holding the hazard tape.

'You must close up the entry gap each evening,' Brian said, 'and make sure the boards are pulled over the shaft. Weigh them down with sandbags at the corners as well to discourage any idiots wanting a peep.'

Anthony felt a sudden warmth towards Brian, who was so clearly supporting him as head of the well team. He had known him for many years, but their relationship had never been particularly easy. It had been severely tested by Brian's recent admonitions about Giuditta. But now, Anthony thought: He's not such a bad stick. He's got all this organised. None of it would ever have happened without him. It's because of him entirely that we have the chance to dig here – and to dig something that could turn out to be very exciting. So, as Anthony thought on these things and looked across at Brian, he felt something akin to affection for him – not an easy emotion to raise, as Brian had a difficult personality that could be at times domineering, often caustic in comment, and inclined to seek the credit for the ideas and hard work of others.

If the others had not been present, and despite Anthony's determinations to put the matter behind him – or at least keep it to himself – it was now he might have asked Brian if he had heard anything from Giuditta. Perhaps he might still take him to one side and then ask him – but, no, the moment was lost and Brian was stomping away to the main part of the site, where he would soon be engulfed by a multitude of activities demanding his attention. Anthony knew there would be no further chance of a quiet word that day – and unlikely on subsequent days either.

No, Giuditta was best put to the very back of his mind. Yet, he found he could not keep her there, and her face framed by her dark hair, as he had first seen it when she had dug to find the well with him, and her bright smile and her laughter, kept coming back to him, so that he was very glad of the others' presence to help keep the surge of returning misery at bay.

That evening the well team had a drink together at the Red Cow. The centre of attention was Olaf, who had arrived on his motor bike – a Teutonic machine, black with high chrome handlebars, on which he roared up the village street to the pub, bare-legged and without helmet. Holding their pint glasses, they gathered outside around the bike while Olaf fiddled with the engine. A gaggle of village girls, Anthony noted, stood at the corner of the street, watching. He wondered which ones Olaf had enjoyed: there was no acknowledgement from their master, who appeared entirely unselfconscious of any effect he might be creating.

At last – after a little talk on the well and the digging that would recommence tomorrow – they split up, Stan to return to his bungalow in Yeovil, Miles, to his caravan on the site, Anthony to his farm bed and breakfast, and Olaf to heaven only knows what. The girls were still waiting at the corner as Anthony drove his Land Rover away.

21

When Anthony began to dig the well the next morning, the first thing he noted was the dampness of the soil. The water level may have fallen but it must still be close to the present excavated surface. Water dripped from the first spadeful of earth that he placed in a bucket, and, knowing that the bucket would be heavy, he signalled for it be hauled up straightaway. Positioned on the boarded platform, Miles and Olaf were working on the ropes, and Stan had his usual sorting duty, with one of the other two to help him dump the raked-over earth onto the spoil heap.

Anthony knew they would have to proceed slowly. Nothing would be achieved by haste. Haste would only create problems and perhaps lead to potential discoveries being missed. The soil being lifted needed to be searched with the utmost of care, for in these conditions not only were the wet clumps more difficult to break up and sort, but all sorts of organic objects – of wood and leather, for instance – might survive within them.

He called up after the rising bucket. 'That's the first. Take your time.' In fact, a second bucket was already at his feet, and he spaded more of the wet earth into it, seeing one or two pieces of yellow bone amongst the soil and possibly a rim of pottery. 'Bone in this one,' he shouted upwards. 'And possibly some pot.' It would keep them all on the ball if they knew finds had already been noted.

As the buckets were hauled up in a steady procession, and Anthony leant on his spade awaiting the arrival of the next, trickles of water began to fall on him from the work of decanting the buckets above. It was damp and clammy in the shaft, and the hot sun and all the bright world of movement on the site above was restricted to the bright O of light some ten feet above his head; the distance to the well top, of course, being even greater when he was crouched over a bucket at the bottom. They worked steadily for an hour or so, in which time Anthony had removed a spit from across the complete circuit of the well. Sometimes, a shout from Len or Miles – occasionally, Olaf – would tell of pottery, of bone and oyster shell, and once a large nail, recovered.

The water was now oozing between Anthony's feet to create pools in those parts of the surface that had been dug a little deeper than the rest. He thought that the time had come to bring the pump to the shaft from the site caravan where it was stored, since clearly it would soon be needed. He decided they should do that next after a short break.

He shouted to Miles and Olaf to set the ladder at an angle in the shaft – it had been propped vertically against the wall to keep it as much out of the way of the digging operations as possible – and then climbed upwards towards the sunlight. As he climbed, he looked at the bands of limestone forming the walls, the individual stones now crisply delineated thanks to the cleaning work that Olaf had carried out earlier.

He also counted the niches offset one above the other that they had decided had formed a ladder for the Romans to get in and out of the well. Seven of these niches had now been revealed, positioned every two feet or so. Off to Anthony's right was the part of the walling that had collapsed – or been deliberately destroyed – at some time before the well was filled in. The ladder rose next to this area, so Anthony was able to inspect it closely as he reached the upper rim of the shaft. The damage spoilt the tidy symmetry of the shaft, but otherwise the section seemed solid and secure enough, now that they had removed the individual stones that had been lying loose there. Then, after circumventing Stan's wretched Acrow bars, Anthony knelt on the boards at the head of the shaft and gratefully took Miles's proffered hand to be hauled to his feet on the surface.

'God! You're a sight!' exclaimed Miles, discouragingly.

Anthony looked down at himself. There was mud and water on his shirt, and he suspected on his face also. He took off the white helmet he had been wearing, seeing that it too was covered with splodges of mud.

'Mr. Action Man,' said Miles, more kindly, and that pleased Anthony, for it was the sort of impression he sought to give out. He looked around. Olaf and Stan were still busy sorting the last two bucketfuls of earth, and, even as he watched, Stan held something up.

'Coin!'

It was a beautiful coin about the size of a modern 2p piece. Owing to the wetness of the earth it had lain in, it did not have the usual green patina of bronze coins found in dry earth, but was in its original bright condition, as perfect as the day it had been minted. It did not seem to be worn at all, for, when Anthony took it in his hand, he could see what seemed to be the wall of a fort or a city crisply defined, and on the other side the head of the emperor, bearded, instantly recognisable as that of Hadrian. Anthony could even pick out the letters making up 'Hadrianus'. It was the second coin of that emperor from the well, at greatly different depths, perhaps an indication that the infilling had been carried out all in one go.

'Well spotted, Stan.' Anthony felt a little praise was in order. Bronze coins that were properly bronze coloured were more difficult to see in the earth than those that had turned green. When searching, however, you were looking for defined shapes as much as colour. Amongst the many small stones and grit within the soil, the sharp, curving rim of a coin should stand out clearly to the practised eye. And Stan, despite his other faults, was skilled at sorting.

It was not necessary to tell him that, however. Even now he was strutting about pleased with himself, ready to bear off the find to show Brian and, if he got to him at the right place on the site, perhaps to a few admiring young women also who might happen to be gathered around. Stan lived for such moments of attention. I can't blame him, thought Anthony. Am I not just the same, whatever I might pretend?

After Stan had returned, the pump was brought from where it was stored in the site caravan. It was positioned on the boarded platform by the shaft. Miles – the most practically-minded of them – supervised its deployment, then fuelled and primed it ready to start. The polystyrene discharge hose was next unravelled until it reached a position where the water could jet out into the nearby ditch. When all was ready, Anthony carefully descended the ladder, bearing with him the suction piping with its head that was like the skull of some prehistoric lizard on a neck of coiled yellow.

At the foot of the ladder, Anthony found that there was now a pool of water some two inches deep across most of the shaft. The first task was to dig a sump into which the water could drain and in which the suction-head could be positioned. This took a few minutes to do, and the excavated soil raised in buckets to be sorted. When completed, Anthony had a sump about two feet square and a foot deep into which the water drained, leaving the rest of the shaft relatively dry. Now was the time to try out the pump.

He called up to Miles that he was ready. He heard the pump start up with a roar, the suction hose flexing and leaping like a frantic animal against the side of the well. He placed the head in the water, and it gurgled thirstily. It only took half a minute or so and then the sump was dry, the pump sucking at the underlying mud as if its thirst had scarcely begun to be satisfied.

'Switch off!'

'Switch off!'

Anthony heard his shout echoed by Miles on the surface, and the growl of the pump died away. Just then there came another yell, this time from the usually taciturn Olaf. For him to shout out was unusual; to do so in a high tone of excitement was exceptional – indeed previously unknown.

'Look, you guys!' He was struggling with his English, anxious to say the right thing in the way he thought Englishmen would. In this moment the words were found from somewhere (English or American, did it matter?), torn from him by what he saw before him. 'See this, dudes. Now. You must!'

Olaf had been prodding at the earth that had come from Anthony's digging of the sump. The earth was still contained within the bucket in which it had been raised. Olaf had run his trowel over its surface breaking down one or two lumps of the clayey soil. He had stopped suddenly at the glimpse of something that gleamed. With the fingers of one hand he had clawed back the dark earth at this spot, and a trail of further yellow brightness, with small shapes of green along its length, had emerged dramatically into the sunlight. It was a necklace – a most fine necklace of gold chain studded with green, cylindrically-shaped stones.

Olaf's cry had brought Anthony to his feet in the shaft, his head cocked sideways to pick up whatever else might follow.

When he heard Miles's excited call, 'Anthony come up and see this!', he was on the ladder in a trice and up onto the boarded platform without needing a helping hand at all.

They were all bent over the bucket – Stan and Miles, Olaf, and now Anthony – inspecting the wonder that protruded from the soil. It was Olaf who was continuing to pare at the earth with the point of his trowel, revealing more and more of the coiled gold chain, until at last its full length was revealed and lifted from the soil to be placed in a finds tray.

'I should tip the rest of the earth in the bucket out onto the boards,' he suggested. 'But slowly, slowly.'

As Olaf spilled the earth most carefully onto a clean area of the boards, Stan and Miles, now on their knees, poked at it with trowels and fingers, spreading it out and making sure there was nothing – not even the smallest link of chain – that might be hidden and thus lost. Anthony was content to watch, ready to offer advice when necessary. A final tip of the bucket and the eager search was rewarded by the finding of a detached piece of chain, a loose cylindrical stone, and incredibly a separate piece of jewellery – a complete earring – of dangling gold chain and green stone that clearly matched the necklace.

'Get Brian,' Anthony told Olaf. 'And some finds boxes. Don't worry, we won't do anything more until you come back.'

The latter seemed only fair. It had been Olaf's discovery. While he was away, Anthony and the others tidied up the board, removing the earth that had been already screened, and checking the film of soil still clinging to the sides of the bucket. They said little. The excitement was so intense that conversation seemed superfluous. Only Stan ventured the occasional comment. When he tried to run his fingers over the necklace, Anthony insisted he stop. Thwarted, Stan looked rather sulky, like a child separated from his sweets. But then the sound of footsteps in the grass told them that Olaf was returning. He had brought Brian with him, and, rather to Anthony's displeasure, a small knot of others from the site, who pressed beyond the hazard tape and stood around the trench watching them.

Brian's first comment was, 'Where exactly did this come from?' and, when told by Anthony, 'From the sump at the bottom', he said crisply, 'Is there anything more down there?', followed by, 'What about the pump. Was it working then?'

Olaf was sent away to look at the point where the pump had discharged water into the ditch, while Anthony descended again into the well to check the sump, already refilling with water. All this time, the onlookers hung over the well, making observations that Anthony found foolish and irritating. If it had been up to him, he would have sent them packing, but it was Brian's site and he didn't seem concerned at all by these idlers, who should have been busy elsewhere.

Using his hands and working by feel alone, Anthony scraped up earth from the sides and bottom of the sump, and then from around it, placing this in a bucket which Miles hauled to the surface. Stan searched it, but it proved empty of finds. Now back once more on the surface, Anthony watched Brian as he removed the last clinging earth from the necklace, and gathered it up in his hands before placing it on cotton wool within a plastic container.

'One of the clasps is missing,' Brian said. 'And probably some links lost. Possibly another stone as well. Keep looking. And there should be a second earring, I would have thought.'

A sudden shout from Olaf brought the amazing news that he had found the missing earring, complete and undamaged, lying within the slurry pumped from the well. He brought the jewel over cupped in his hands, the heads of the watchers swaying like trees in a breeze as he passed in front of them. The gold chain and green stone glittered in the light. So long in the soil, thought Anthony, then nearly washed away – lost once more, then found. How lucky we've been, for the pump could easily have destroyed it. The rest of the slurry would have to be searched minutely.

For now, however, Brian was satisfied. His new treasure was safe in the plastic containers. It was a treasure that would bring his site fresh attention. And there might be more to come. After directing a barrage of instructions to the well team, who were suitably drawn up before him as if on parade, he departed with his loot to the site caravan. The onlookers trailed behind him, like rats after the pied piper. Or so, thought Anthony, relieved to be left alone once more – alone that is except for Miles and Stan and Olaf, who were now discussing what had been found with much excited chatter. It was time for a short break. Then they must get on with the work again.

The finding of the jewellery was the talk of the site that day. For such a discovery to be made at the beginning of the annual dig was sensational. For some of the newcomers, for whom this was their first dig, it must have all seemed rather bewildering. Perhaps they thought that such items came up every day on archaeological sites. During the lunch break, however, Brian let the rarity of the find be known, and said that on no account should his diggers discuss it off the site. The last thing he wanted was for the locals to get wind of 'golden treasure' being found. It could bring all sorts of unwelcome attention, some perhaps in the form of aggressive individuals with metal detectors, the sort of thing that had plagued other sites in the recent past, resulting in great damage and much loss of valuable artefacts.

Before any work recommenced in the shaft, Anthony's team conducted a thorough search of the muddy slurry in the ditch in case it contained anything else that the pump had sucked up. They could find nothing, however. Then, visitors from elsewhere on the site started to appear, eager to see the well from which the wonderful necklace had come. Soon there was a steady flow of them. One of these was the woman to whom Stan had taken an earlier shine. Anthony still did not know her name or what her role was. He had just gone down the well when she arrived, and Stan had let her into the trench without seeking Anthony's approval. He hadn't the heart to complain, however, when he saw her bespectacled face peering down at him.

'Where was the find made?' she asked.

'Just here,' replied Anthony, indicating the water-filled sump with the toe of his boot.

'Oh! As deep as that. Why would a woman have been wearing jewellery in a well then?'

Anthony kept his patience. 'No. I don't think any woman was actually down here; particularly the type of high born lady who would have owned gold jewellery like that. The necklace and earrings were probably in a leather pouch or a small wooden box. Something happened and they were lost and never recovered. Then the well was filled in. We can only guess at the story. It's the sort of thing a novelist could recreate.'

'Are you going to do that? Someone said you write.'

I wonder who that was, thought Anthony, surprised but not deigning to answer. Instead, he spoke out his thoughts on something just occurring to him, 'I think the bottom of the well's not much deeper. What's coming up now is probably the primary fill – the first silting of the well when it was still in use. The jewellery was within that, so it's certainly early. The well seems never to have been cleaned out, otherwise what we've found would have been recovered by some other Roman later on.'

'What date's 'early' then?' She still hung there above him. Beyond her, he could just make out Stan's head moving from side to side against the light, trying to see what was going on.

'Perhaps the first part of the second century, the time of the first villa here. The necklace, from its style, I think belongs to that period as well.'

He was largely making up the last bit, as he had little knowledge of Roman jewellery and its dating. He had an idea, however, that heavier, more ornate jewellery was later in the Roman period, and less ornate styles, earlier. The items they had found had impressed him by their simplicity.

'I'd love to wear it,' said the goggling face above. 'Perhaps Brian would let me put it on.'

With that her mouth parted in a shrill giggle, which echoed down the shaft to strike against Anthony's startled nerves. No chance at all, he thought. He doubted if even Stan would be foolish enough to lay those beautiful strands of gold and green upon that heaving, white bosom.

They proceeded very slowly for the rest of the afternoon, removing fresh soil from the shaft sparingly and then only when everything on the surface was clear to receive it. Despite all this care, there were virtually no finds, only a few small sherds of pot. Occasionally, they would operate the pump when the water in the sump spilled over to cover the digging surface. The earth they were removing was becoming ever more stiff with clay, which Anthony thought might have been deliberately placed as a lining at the bottom of the well. In the side of the shaft by the sump, the layers of stones appeared to have finished; beneath them, bare rock was showing. Had the last few feet of the well, in fact, been hacked out of solid limestone?

About four o'clock, after a tea break, Anthony decided to call a halt for the day. There was a great deal of clearing up to do. The pump and ladder needed to be removed from the shaft, and the covering boards hauled into place over the top. Then the pump had to be carried to the site caravan. He also had notes to write up. And he was tired, tired….oh so tired.

He had slept poorly last night, as he so often did on a first night away from home. He wanted to get back to his digs for a bath and a change of clothing. And after that a meal and a drink or two, with or without companions. He didn't care. He suddenly felt he wanted to drink a lot. Perhaps he would buy a bottle of wine and take it to his room. Then there would be no problem with driving. But all he really wanted to do was to sleep and forget.

22

The well team were seated at their ease in Miles's caravan. It was lunchtime the next day. They had just viewed the Roman necklace and the two earrings at Brian's house in the village, having gone there at his invitation after the lunch bell had rung out over the site. Brian had displayed the jewellery on a flat board covered by a white cloth, itself resting on his kitchen table. He used this board for photographing some of the best finds, and had indeed just finished taking a large number of close up shots of the exquisite gold and green necklace and its matching earrings, now perfectly cleaned, so that, other than for the one broken end of the gold chain, they were ready to re-adorn whichever Roman lady had once owned them.

'The jewellery style definitely fits the Hadrianic period,' Brian had told them. 'I've emailed photographs to the BM and they confirm the date. They may even be interested in acquiring the items. There'll have to be a coroner's inquiry, of course, as it'll be treasure under the law. It'll go to the state under the recent Treasure Act, but we, as the finders, should get a good commercial value for it.'

'Who exactly will the money go to, Brian?' Miles asked.

'To the Society. To GAS. Not to me personally, of course. The landowner – old Farmer Coombs – will get a share. Half, I think. I made an agreement with him to that effect many years ago.'

'It'd be nice to keep it,' Anthony said. He was feeling rather fragile this day, having passed yet another night of restless sleep. The necklace had featured in his dreams, the face of a lady with coal black hair filling his inner vision: the gold and the green had glowed against her skin. She had seemed anxious. Her face had slid in and out of his sleeping until he had had to rouse himself fully to be rid of it. Even now, when he closed his tired eyes, the face reformed. The eyes had been dark and liquid, like…like – he realised suddenly – like Giuditta's eyes.

'It's possible we will be allowed to retain it,' Brian said. 'Or, if not the necklace, perhaps the earrings. What a miracle Olaf found that second one.'

And Olaf had looked down modestly at the table.

'Give him one of the earrings,' Stan said. 'It'll go with his bloody pigtail.'

Now they were catching up on their lunch in Miles' caravan, reclining on the padded bench seats, all except Olaf who had gone off somewhere on his motorbike. The caravan formed Miles's little command centre for the site. Here he entertained his many friends, here he dispensed cans and bottles from lockers overflowing with booze, here he slept, and here others, by invitation, sometimes slept too. The space was compact, but well laid out, with living and sleeping areas, and between them a small kitchen. Miles was away from wife and family, independent and organised. He obviously relished the periodic freedoms the caravan allowed him.

The harsh, flat sound of the cracked site bell rang out. 'Time to get back to work,' Anthony said.

Looking out of the caravan window, he could see there was little movement amongst the diggers sprawled across the grass. And little movement within the caravan either. By the second day of the dig, aching muscles and blistered hands had removed much of the initial enthusiasms. Some of the younger students present, so far book-read in archaeology only, might also have begun to rethink the subject of their degrees. Of course, the jewellery from the well had provided a tremendous boost for the morale of the site, but most diggers, confronted with the trowelling and brushing of great expanses of dusty, sun-baked soil, found it hard to imagine such a find coming from their own particular patches of ground.

The weather had changed also, the hot sun being hidden by an overcast of cloud that nonetheless left the day pleasantly warm. Much better for digging, thought Anthony, who disliked long periods of sun. He also was full of aches and pains. The digging in the shaft, with its need to bend and twist in a confined space, and then to climb the ladder, hauling himself between the Acrow bars, had been a test for his 65 years. He forced himself to his feet, groaning. 'Come on, lads. Look lively.'

As they crossed to the well, looking at the work that was being done on the main part of the site, where the attention of many trowels was crisply redefining the walls and features discovered last year, preparatory to further excavation, Anthony saw out of the corner of his eye a motorbike approaching along the track, leaving a cloud of rising dust in its wake. The unhelmeted rider told him it must be Olaf, but on the pillion was another figure, also without a helmet – a girl whose dark hair streamed out behind her. Good for Olaf! He must have brought one of his local conquests to the site, but probably not for the archaeology.

Prepared to allow Olaf some leeway in taking up his allotted place in the team, Anthony concentrated on the afternoon's work ahead. The morning's work had shown that the lining of the shaft had finished for sure and that it was now cut into the solid rock. As Anthony had spaded out a further spit of earth around the circumference of the well, it had proved impossible to keep the water at bay using the earlier sump method. Now he had to use the pump for steady periods, holding the suction-head like a vacuum cleaner, moving it about the floor of the shaft sucking up the water. Miles was sent to monitor the discharge hose, checking to see that no further finds had been sent hurtling through the pipes.

The finds, in fact, were few – disappointingly so, thought Anthony, for here in the primary fill of the shaft you might have expected to recover any number of objects that had perhaps fallen into the well during its early period of use. Other than for the very occasional piece of pot, the most significant discovery had been the complete sole of a shoe, the black leather still holding several of its hobnails. There were also some bone fragments and many oyster shells, the latter in such quantities that Anthony wondered if their placing in the well had been deliberate, perhaps even to act as some type of filter.

From its upper lip to the level where Anthony worked between the shelving walls of bare rock, the depth of the shaft was now slightly more than eighteen feet. Before breaking for lunch, Anthony had checked the depth with a tape measure dropped to him by Miles, one end pressed into the remaining silts below the water level and the other stretched taught above one of the Acrow bars. They had had to lengthen the ladder by attaching a further section to it, making it heavier and more cumbersome in the shaft.

Before climbing up, Anthony had inspected the rock below the stone lining, and run his hand across it. It was smooth and curved, but he thought he could see evidence of tool marks polished by the water over the ages. He could not be sure, however, for the light was not good. The bottom of the well was very close, he felt certain, as he could see that the walls were curving inwards, so that the bottom would probably have the shape of a rounded bowl cut out of the rock. As he stood there, the water rose steadily against his boots, and he stepped onto the first rung of the ladder which itself would soon be covered. He wondered if there was anything else to be found beneath the water.

Once back at the well after the break, it was the pumping that Anthony knew he must deal with first. A number of youthful diggers had arrived to view what was going on, standing respectfully behind the hazard tape, watching this group of older men getting ready for what must seem to the viewers – or so Anthony reflected – an exciting and even glamorous operation, with just a touch of danger. It was important that his team looked professional.

He glanced around. No one was letting them down. Even Stan was attending to his barrows and his buckets, cleaning them ready for the afternoon shift, without indulging in his usual banter. Miles was inspecting the ladder, making sure it was secure between the Acrow bars and the top edge of the shaft. Then he started coiling up the rope attached to one of the buckets, ready to drop it into the well once Anthony was in place below. Yes, they all looked very organised and in control. Only Olaf was missing. Perhaps he was still involved with the girl who had been on his bike.

Even as that last thought entered his mind, while it floated there innocuous and inert, just a reflection of interest, of amusement even, of good-looking Olaf and his girlfriends, something struck Anthony with force – not physically, of course, but actually far worse, deep within the very core of his being. No. No. Surely not. But, in that moment, he felt he knew for certain. There could be no doubt. Oh why hadn't he seen it before? That girl on the bike, with her floating dark hair. Incredible, ridiculous, as it seemed, he knew now who that girl was. It was Giuditta.

His heart was racing. His hands that were held forward in the act of seizing the top rung of the ladder were actually trembling. The shock was such that he felt he must sit down. But how could he do that with everyone watching him? – his team waiting for their leader to position himself, the youngsters observing every movement; what would they think if he collapsed in sudden jelly onto the boarded ground? No. No. He must carry on as if nothing had happened. But what in fact *had* happened? Was he wrong? If she were here, why in heaven's name had she been on the back of Olaf's bike?

He had to ask Olaf. Where was he? Was he even now with her in her tent? Ridiculous! Ridiculous! Get a grip. The truth would be nothing like he feared. But what *did* he fear? Get into the well. Get into the well now! Before you make a complete fool of yourself.

And so he descended the ladder, stepping off the bottom rung into water which covered his boots and trouser bottoms. Why, oh why, had he not thought to wear the wellingtons which he kept in the Land Rover? The water had risen much higher than he had anticipated during the extended lunch break. He could feel it trickling inside his boots and soaking his socks, and he squelched disconsolately about the dark hole moving the suction-head into position ready for the pump to be switched on. At last he heard it start above him, and the suction-head jumped in his hands like a snarling dog.

When the water had been reduced to a thin swirl moving over the dark, gritty soil, he called for the pump to be switched off. He did not wish to risk sucking up any of the mud. They had already had one near disaster by allowing that to happen.

A picture of Olaf holding out the recovered earring came into Anthony's mind, and he could see it too dangling from the ear of the woman who had been in his dream. Only now the woman was Giuditta: it hung from Giuditta's ear and her face was turned away from him. Crazy stuff! He was going quite mad. Soon Giuditta would explain things to him. Then all would be well. Well! He was in the well. Why were those words the same? He was well, as well as being in the well. 'Ding dong bell, pussy's in the well.' The crazy jingle was running through his head. 'Ding dong bell, Giuditta's in the well.' Get a grip! Get a grip! Whatever else you do, don't go mad!

He concentrated on the immediate task ahead of him. Seizing his short-handled spade, he scooped up some of the water-logged mud and placed the blade over the bucket by his feet so that the mud ran into it in a liquid stream. He did the same again, then once more, feeling that the bucket with its water content was now weighty enough to be hauled up. He noticed a dark lump in the mud on the surface, and pulled it out with his free hand. It appeared to be a rounded black stone, a curiosity perhaps but probably of no value. I'll look at it later, he thought, and pushed it into his pocket.

As the bucket swayed above him on its way to the surface, he thought he heard Olaf's voice. Yes, it must be Olaf, for Miles was saying cheerily, 'Where have you been, you crafty bugger?' and Stan made some comment in the background that he could not quite make out, followed by a throaty guffaw. The suspicions, the pain, returned to Anthony with a rush. He felt he would choke. If it was Giuditta they were laughing about, what was she doing here with Olaf?

The bucket was returned. He filled it again, and as he did so his spade struck against something hard beneath the mud. It was rock. He had reached the bottom of the shaft. Further buckets were filled, and then came another period of pumping, and, yes, he could trace now with his trowel through the seeping water a solid mass of rock across the full width of the now bowl-shaped shaft, of uneven depth as originally hacked out by the Roman slaves, now washed smooth by the action of the water over the many centuries.

He stood up. 'We've got the bottom!' A face moved across the opening of white light high above him, a face framed by dark hair that tumbled forwards. For a moment he feared – he knew not what he feared – but, as he blinked his eyes against the light, he saw it was Giuditta.

'Hello, Anthony,' she called down to him.

It rained that evening. After a meal by himself in the Red Cow, Anthony was in his room at the farm. He was watching the television news, then switched it off with an expression of irritation and went to the open window. The grey, rain-laden sky was darkening towards night. The rain drummed on the farmyard roofs and ran in rivulets between the stone cobbles to gurgle into the drains. Beneath his window, some hollyhocks bent beneath the rain, with bowed heads like mourners at a funeral. The dreary image came into Anthony's head, and he shut the window against it and against the grey air that seemed to hang upon his flesh like something unclean. What was happening to him?

He had been thrilled to see her again, of course, but she hadn't wanted to eat with him – to be alone with him – when he had asked.

'It's not a good idea,' she had said. 'In any event I have to get settled in here.'

What Giuditta meant was that she had to get her tent erected and her things organised for – unbelievably to Anthony – she was going to camp on the site. She had come by train to Yeovil station with rucksack and tent, and had taken a taxi to Brian's house in the village. The taxi-driver had not been prepared to drive up the rough track to the site. Brian, who was fortunately still at home, and in mobile phone contact with Olaf, had called him up to take her to the site on his bike. He hadn't been able to do so himself, being busy with a number of other commitments at that time. And he hadn't sent through a message for Anthony to help. Why not? What did Brian know about their relationship now? Surely, there was nothing he could know. It was later on that Brian returned to the site, delivering Giuditta's tent in his car.

Anthony had felt hurt and excluded as Giuditta explained all this to him. Her manner to him was quite normal, as if nothing had ever happened between them. He had not been able to say much to her with the others present, and Miles was already looking at him in a knowing way as if to gauge his reactions.

He had said to her as soon as he came up from the well, smothered in mud, 'I thought you said you weren't going to come here again.'

It was not a particularly welcoming remark. But his brain was in a whirl and he didn't know what he was saying – the words came without thought. He had never really expected to see her again. Now all that had happened between them came back with renewed force.

'Just try to stop me,' she had answered.

Was that in a mocking tone? She looked a little tense, but was polite with him – not particularly friendly, though, he realised with a sinking heart. She hadn't forgiven him then, but, thank God, there was no more hysteria. She must have recovered enough to want to come back to Glastington, when she knew he would be there.

The others had looked on, perhaps a little bemused by this interchange. Anthony had seen Stan staring at Giuditta speculatively: he must have been wondering how it was that Anthony already knew her. Stan for once, however, thankfully kept his mouth shut.

It was Olaf instead who annoyed Anthony. He seemed to have become something of a confidant to Giuditta already, standing quietly beside her, whispering in her ear when she turned to him.

'Olaf's going to help me put up my tent,' she had said. Anthony felt doubly hurt. Why couldn't she have asked him?

When Giuditta spoke to Olaf, it was in his own language, and Anthony realised that she was fluent in German too. Again, he felt his world – that domain of his imagination that for a short while had appeared to exist in reality – was being cut away from him. Giuditta and Olaf, he understood with sudden clarity, belonged to a different society entirely. Although they too were separated in age by many years, yet they both seemed to inhabit the same vibrant, modern way of living that he was divorced from entirely – which only existed now for him in his dreams of what might have been.

Recalling all this later, Anthony paced his room, up and down, up and down, over the threadbare rug, from the end of the bed to the bathroom door, and then back again. What was she thinking? She who had been so close to him. She who had stayed here. Was this not the room she had occupied when he had checked her drawn curtains outside in the yard that morning so many long weeks ago? So, in this very bed she had slept, her body laid out upon this mattress, her hair spread upon the pillows. Why was she not here with him now? What had he ever done to her other than to try and understand her and help her, only to make the smallest slip of the tongue that had so clearly offended her? Was she not concerned at all by how he felt? Could she not understand his puzzlement at why she was treating him like this, the pain that she must know she was inflicting?

He had driven away from the site in the Land Rover, in which she had once so loved to travel, and in his rear view mirror he had seen her standing with Olaf at the place where she was going to pitch her tent – next to Olaf's own, it seemed, and with Miles's caravan and car only a stone's throw away. It was Olaf who had been carrying the tent for her, good, old Olaf – no, good, young Olaf, fourteen years or so her junior – humping her tent upon his shoulder, soon to hump her too... Surely not! He must keep such wild imaginings under control or he would go quite barmy here pacing this stinking room.

Brian had said nothing to him, not even looked at him, although it was possible that he knew at least something of the story. Had Giuditta told him what had happened between them? Brian had been entrusted with the secret of her illness when she had first come to Glastington. Had she now confided in him further? Would he be looking out for her, seeing that mad, old Anthony did not trouble her further – he who thought he could woo a young woman and get her into his bed.

But it hadn't been like that, had it?! She had *wanted* to be with him. They had found pleasure in each other's company. She had been all sweetness and light when he came to Cambridge and they had gone to Stonea and to Ely...until... until *it had all gone wrong*! And what exactly had gone wrong? For the thousandth time he rehearsed in his mind that terrible conversation in the Cathedral.

And then another thought. By now her father would have visited her on his way to Italy. What had happened? Had it been the nightmare that she had anticipated, or had the two been reconciled? Had she truly forgiven him, that old, perverted bastard? If anyone deserved to be treated with hatred, with contempt, with cold indifference, it was he. But it is me instead – long-suffering Anthony – who now gets the blame; I, who only tried to share my world with her, to give her my thoughts, my most secret feelings and memories, and my hopes for writing some of this down one day; I, who tried to help her but made a mess of it – a total mess beyond all reason, beyond all forgiveness, it seems.

My writing, he thought. I was going to write such a book. I told her about it, about the lady in the tower and the silent water, and the man who came by who would take her away to a new life. It was to be a modern Lady of Shalott – the woman who lies down on the waters and is borne away because she cannot live in the present, because the secret world of her imagining must not die. I cannot write that story now, for I am not part of it any longer, but am one with that man – and that woman too – who look out at me from the tower and watch me in everything I do, even when I sleep? My God, thought Anthony. My God, I *am* going mad!

When he had returned from the site, and before going to the Red Cow, he had bathed and changed his clothes, flinging the mud-stained shirt and trousers to one side where he found them now, tidying up the room preparatory to going to bed. He wanted to lie in bed and close his mind to anything but the inanities of a TV comedy show, of grotesque strutting players passing before him on the flickering, crackling screen; out of tune, it was, like his own life, distorted with fuzzy double-images, so he didn't know for sure what anything was any more, or what was meant to be, or what people were saying.

He hung the trousers over the back of a chair. He would wear them tomorrow. It was not worth getting a second pair dirty when there was still work to do, cleaning out the very last of the well. After the shock of seeing Giuditta, he had done very little more that afternoon. They had all needed a rest. The clouds had been gathering too, and it had seemed a good idea to pack up early before rain came. How good it had been just to sit and be idle for a while, without the constant effort, without the constant need for thought. How much he wanted his mind to be still.

The others had avoided him, seeing he was preoccupied, although Miles had come over and clapped him on the shoulder, saying, 'Alright mate?'

He had answered. 'Yes, of course.' I am alright, he thought. I'm always alright. But thank you so much for asking.

As he now smoothed the trousers out against the back of the chair, he felt something hard against his hand, and he remembered the stone from the well he had found and placed in his pocket. He took the trousers up again and reached in the pocket, bringing out the stone, which was covered in mud. He took it into the bathroom and washed it, wiping it with a paper towel.

He inspected the stone. Now the mud was gone, he could see it was black – unusual for a stone from Glastington. Already the suspicions were beginning to grow in his mind. It must be a piece of jet. He knew the Romans had mined jet in the North-East of the country, and carved it for jewellery and pendants and items for the home. He had never found a piece of jet before. This one, with its carefully carved and polished flat surface, did not appear to have been worn on the body, for there was no hole for its suspension and the back had been left rough and uncut. Clearly, it was the front that had been intended for display.

The object lay in his palm, rough side uppermost. He turned it over. Was that something scratched onto the face? The light in the room was poor. Darkness was descending fast to deepen the gloom of the rainy evening.

Anthony switched on the bedside lamp and reached for his glasses. Yes, he could see it now, a figure etched into the jet. It was faint, but it was clear, particularly if he turned it to the lamp so that the light played across it. He saw a human figure outlined in the jet, a figure which seemed to be wearing a great cloak with a hood over the head and a face staring out below, small and oval-shaped, with a short dash for a mouth and two pinpricks for eyes.

Straightaway, a fear of the figure, outlined so lightly in the black jet, entered him, so that his stomach tightened and a sweat broke out on his palms and on his brow. He told himself this was irrational, but it did not help. He carried the object to the bed and placed it face down on the white counterpane, wiping his tingling fingers with his handkerchief, while he tried to assemble his racing thoughts.

He knew what this figure represented. He had read about them, but he also seemed to know instinctively, as if the knowledge came from some other place, one filled with more than book learning. This was a *Genius Cucullatus*, a 'hooded spirit of the place – a Celtic deity, often perceived as an importunate sprite. The *Genii* were frightening, for they seemed to bear an aura of evil about them. Sometimes also they were depicted in groups, side by side.

He held out the object at arm's length. It was probably the most important find he had ever made, and he felt such fear of it. Was that not the same fear as he had felt from the shadowed figure at Wandlebury? He knew how absurd he was being. Yet, despite all reason, he could not suppress the sense of terror, its coldness playing over his body as if he was wriggling naked upon a block of ice.

What chance it was that he had found this thing at the very bottom of the well? – and so nearly discarded it, but something had held him back, something very strange. It was unsettling, unnerving, threatening his world once more with chaos. Mad or not, he knew he did not want to keep it. It was clear what he must do, and the revelation came with a further fear, for he realised it would demand an action beyond his reason.

He picked up the black object, holding it not now against his palm but by his fingertips, while he unlatched the door and strode down the corridor. He pushed open the front door and went out into the darkness and the rain. A path led from the farmyard into the fields beyond, partly in stubble and partly newly ploughed, the furrows running away in straight lines until they disappeared into the darkness over a swell of the land. He walked along one of the furrows for twenty paces or so, the mud clinging to his shoes, and with one clean movement swung back his arm and launched the object with all his strength into the air. He saw it hang there for a moment in the mist and rain, and then plummet steeply to the ground. The *Genius Cucullatus* was returned to earth.

23

Anthony slept well that night. Given the new turmoil in his mind, he had not expected to, and had lain on his bed full of fear and despondency, going over and over what he had done, and seeing again the wedge of black jet flying like a dart against the sky, as far from sleep as it would seem possible to be. Yet something within him must have taken pity, or simply grown weary of the long self-analysis, for it switched off his consciousness as suddenly as an electric light, plunging him into a deep, dreamless sleep that lasted until the first grey light of the new dawn.

He woke greatly refreshed, but hardly had he made out the shape of the room and remembered where he was then the impact of what he had done last night struck against him like a wave crashing on a shore. He wrapped his head with his arms and slid down beneath the bedclothes. Oh, how could he have been so foolish! There was not even the blurring stimulus of alcohol to blame. Indeed…indeed, he must have been out of his mind!

When he calmed a little and he realised he was not mad – not yet anyhow! – but just overburdened by too many stimuli that had affected his judgements, he rose, washed, and dressed as quickly as he could and, before breakfast, went out into the rain-washed morning. He walked to the spot where he had thrown the *Genius Cucullatus* into the field, and realised he could not walk there now in the daylight for he would stand out from the farmhouse like an ambulant scarecrow plodding the furrows. He doubted if he would find the small black object anyhow for he had thrown it a long way into the darkness and he was not even sure of the direction of his throw.

Despite his worry at his action, if the truth be told he was not sorry he had cast it away, for its import still worried him: the fear it had engendered last night still lingered within him. No, it had never existed. That is what he told himself. No one knew about it, only he. It had never existed and never would. Yet, as he looked across the plough furrows, he could almost see the *Genius Cucullatus* picking itself up from its earth bed, brushing itself down, and looking about, restored and strengthened by the light of the new day. Anthony went inside to clean his shoes, determined to banish once and for all such neurotic reflections on the pagan powers of the past.

They completed the well that day. Even Olaf took a turn down the shaft. Something in Anthony had made him insist he do this, although Olaf had not been very keen. If there are risks, Anthony had thought, why should it be me that takes them all? Let Olaf take his share. If he's so good at putting up Giuditta's tent, he can do this as well.

He had seen her tent, blue with white edging, looking taut and trim in the row facing the car park, so close to Olaf's that its guy ropes crossed with his. There was no sign of her, and he had not wanted to ask after her. Olaf had looked a little moody, quieter than normal, when he joined the rest of the team by the well. Perhaps he had not slept well, lying there so close to her body.

So, in this edgy, irritated mood – a mood verging on anger, yet he was not certain what about – it was a pleasure for Anthony to gaze down at Olaf working far below, operating the pump, then scooping out the last of the muddy soil and water. As he had anticipated, the well bottomed out in a broad bowl of rock, with a narrow ledge around its circumference on which the base of the limestone walling neatly sat. There was even a last niche here to complete the sequence of eight footholds from the top of the shaft.

Anthony helped haul up the last buckets of liquid mud, and was disappointed that there were no finds other than for a scattering of oyster shells. So – if he chose to recognise its brief existence yesterday – the jet object had lain by itself at the very bottom of the well, covered by a drift of dirt and perhaps decaying vegetable matter that had gradually settled upon it. It seemed likely, therefore, that it had been deliberately deposited, or perhaps, Anthony thought, thrown in by someone wishing to rid themselves of it, much as he had done. Very strange. But not a subject now for further reflection, for it had never existed.

When the well was finished, the four members of the team – Brian also – held a ceremony at its top, opening a bottle of wine and pouring a libation into the shaft, with much mumbo-jumbo and pseudo prayers to Roman gods. Anthony even descended the well to place a bunch of wilting poppies in one of the niches near the bottom.

'To propitiate the virgin sacrifices', he said, which made Stan, of course, prick up his ears and repeat the idea to future female visitors. One of these a little later, was Giuditta, who had appeared at last, looking fresh, neat and tidy, with her hair tied back, as Anthony remembered it on the day of their Stonea visit.

She spoke to Anthony. She was digging on the main site, she told him, but it was all weeds and dust, not very exciting at all. She looked wistfully at the well, and, he thought, at him too, giving him a fresh stirring of hope that was soon extinguished when he saw Olaf come up to talk to her, and they walked away together.

Brian now split up the well team. Stan and Miles were sent away to the main site to work with Giuditta on an extension to the section she was digging – it was mainly trowelling work – while Anthony, disconsolate, and wishing he could join them as well, was allotted the task of working with Olaf in the trench next to the well to try and find evidence of any structure that might have been built covering the shaft. Brian worked on the well, himself, for a time, recording it and drawing some of the stonework. Finishing this, he told Anthony to remove the ladder and board it over. No one must be allowed access to the shaft without Brian's permission.

'What are you going to do with it?' Anthony asked.

'It'll have to be filled in. It's too dangerous to leave as it is.'

'What straightaway?'

'No, get the work around it completed, then, after the main dig's over, I'll think about getting some labour in to do the backfilling.'

'It's a shame. It's such a wonderful structure.'

'Well, at least we won't be destroying it, just covering it up again.'

That was a point, thought Anthony. Much of archaeology was about destruction, removing floors and walls and surfaces to get at what was underneath. That is why it was important to keep a meticulous record, as you could never put back what you had dug away. The well, however, would remain set deep in the earth, and could always be re-excavated by future generations, although all its original contents had now gone. These included, of course, the jet object flung into a field three miles away by a madman. Despite his earlier attempt to justify his action, Anthony still could not get the matter out of his mind.

His labours in the well shaft over, Anthony was content now to allow Olaf to do much of the digging, while he idled time away, even occasionally sitting on the side of the trench scenting the sunlit air, something he would not normally dream of doing. Although Giuditta's presence on the site remained a constant misery to him, he did begin to relax a little and start to enjoy the dig, chatting and bantering with his fellow diggers at the lunch and tea breaks. He resumed acquaintances with several people he knew, who asked about the well and what was going to happen to it. When he said, 'it'll be filled in soon', they all expressed suitable horror and declared they would be along soon to take a proper look.

'The shaft's boarded over now,' Anthony said. 'Perhaps we can organise a viewing at some point. I'll mention it to Brian.'

And so the digging day slid slowly to its close. Anthony's area proved inconclusive. Olaf had revealed various stony features, but nothing that looked like a wall line or a post hole. After the excavation of the well, it was all pretty dull stuff, and Anthony wandered away to the main site to watch Stan and Miles working with Giuditta.

She was wearing shorts and a tee-shirt, her bare legs a wonderful honey colour as she bent and lifted, and occasionally took up a mattock to tap at the surface. Miles's patch was next to hers, but he was standing staring into the sky, watching a light aircraft that was doing aerobatics overhead.

Back at his trench, Anthony found that Olaf was still hard at work, apparently oblivious to the free show in the sky, which was now taking the attention of most of the site. He attempted to engage him in conversation, concerned that he was developing an unfair dislike of him based on the familiarity he seemed to be gaining with Giuditta. It would never do to misinterpret that and be jealous of it. That would really degrade him and bring him down to a level he must avoid at all costs. Olaf was a pleasant young man. He had enjoyed his company.

'What did you do last night, Olaf?' he asked innocently enough. 'Where do you go in the evening?'

Olaf was trowelling up a surface of beaten earth. He paused to look up at Anthony, perhaps puzzled by this sudden interest. 'We go to the pub.'

'We? A group of you on the site?'

'Giuditta and me. I take her for a ride on my bike, and then the pub. She likes to drink the beer.'

Anthony had walked straight into this and it was like hitting an oak door with his head. He looked at Olaf's face to see if he might be deliberately taunting him, but, no, Olaf seemed unaware of any special interest by Anthony.

'Oh, Giuditta,' Anthony said, pretending innocence too. 'She's the one in the tent next to you, isn't she?'

'Yes. I make it there for her. She not sleep well.'

'What do you mean?'

'She wake me in the night. She want to talk.'

'How come?' Anthony's blood was beginning to freeze.

'She says she is frightened of the dark. I comfort her.'

He grinned at Anthony, all knowing, men together, a nod and a wink, 'you know what I mean, mate?', and Anthony did – or thought he did – and he was horrified beyond belief. Giuditta would never behave like that, not the Giuditta he had known – never, never. She was so much older than Olaf, anyhow. No, Olaf must have comforted her with words. Anything else was unthinkable.

'We do more comforting tonight. Perhaps,' Olaf said with a smirk. 'Miles go away and leave caravan. He say we can use it.'

Anthony's world had fallen away once more. Suddenly, by his jealousy, expecting his suspicions to be shown as nothing, instead he had descended into a new hell, a hell where his beautiful Giuditta had changed incredibly – and so suddenly, in the speaking of a few casual words – into a promiscuous tart, lying with any man on the shake of a dice or the roar of a motor bike exhaust, for the promise of young virility, to bring comfort in loneliness and distress. Why had she not wanted him then? – but had chosen a complete stranger instead, any available meat, Olaf with his bronzed legs and chest, and his blonde hair, and his thick member rising between her legs. Oh God! It was unbearable.

He did not know what to say or do. He could not stay any longer with Olaf, whom he could see was looking at him curiously.

'Was that the tea bell?' Anthony mumbled, and lurched away across the site to be on his own, to think, to try to get order back to his disintegrating world. He met Miles on the way, appearing from behind a spoil heap where he had been relieving himself. His hands were still zipping his fly and Anthony felt an overpowering urge to kick his boot up into his groin and smash those hanging bits that had become one with Olaf's, bringing him so such anguish.

He felt it hard to speak. 'Olaf tells me you're going off site for a while. You've got it all arranged with him, your caravan and….' He couldn't bring himself to say it.

Miles placed a hand consolingly on his arm. 'That's right. I'm away for a couple of nights. Got to attend to some business back in Bristol. I told Olaf he could have the run of the caravan.'

'Do you know about him and Giuditta?' The question hurt him to ask, as if he'd plunged a knife into his own chest.

'No, not really.'

Miles's eyes were darting away from Anthony, and he looked shifty. So, you *do* know, you bastard. And you didn't say a thing to me. Miles's hand slid to Anthony's elbow and tightened there. 'I've noted they seem to be getting on. But nothing more. Come on, Anthony, mate, it'll be for the best.'

Anthony didn't say anything but turned abruptly away. After all he'd done for them, for his team digging that fucking well, and that was how they treated him. He saw Stan in the distance looking across at him, and he thought: I bet that silly little sod knows too. God! I must get away from here.

He went to his Land Rover and climbed in, aware now of the eyes of several others on him, including Brian. Oh how they would be talking about him and laughing. And Giuditta would be telling them so many things – about his nastiness, his gloominess, his insensitivity, and his preposterous hopes of seducing her, and all his ridiculous ideas – what he called his union with the past – and his bad dreams and his high-wired inability to sleep, and his absurd hopes of writing a novel, when all he had in his head really was a heap of crap, of bits and pieces, ill-formed and inconsequential and going nowhere, as he himself was – nowhere but slow old age and lonely death.

Hell! It was the most awful drive back to the farm. He would have liked to have gone on driving, on and on, to anywhere, to new horizons without fear, where hope and happiness could blossom again. If he simply kept on driving, surely he would find such a place – somewhere perhaps by the sea where the long waves rolled into the bay and broke into a million, million spumes of white against the rocks, there he could wash himself clean and breathe again. And surely he could find someone to love – and who would love him too – in simple truth without lust or pretence, just the peace of being together and sharing and feeling, meeting other eyes without flinching away. But, no, here was the farm, and here was a gaggle of other guests about their cars, and he must pass them with a snarl and bury himself in his room, head down in the bed with the horror of this day beating in his brain.

He stayed like that for a full two hours, and then straightened himself and rose. What horror? he thought. What horror have I imagined? It cannot be anything like that. Why should I allow that girl to destroy my life? I am stronger than her, than all of them. I can bear whatever is thrown at me. I shall never give up. I shall go back to the site again and face them all, and smile and laugh and pretend…..pretend like the rest of the world does. I shall not let them think – least of all, her – that anything is wrong. If they ask why I left the site so early and so suddenly, I shall say I had things to do. Simply that. Why should I bother about their questions, anyhow?

It was six o'clock when he arrived back. A number of people were standing around, but no one looked at him as he arrived. He walked across the grass, noting that Miles's car no longer stood by his caravan. So he had left already. Were Olaf and Giuditta even now ensconced inside? Surely it was too early for them to be rolling about on the benches, with the light still very strong and with so many others passing by.

Someone called across to him. He saw it was Brian's wife, who came to the site each day to organise the food that was served at lunchtime and generally help with the administration of the camp. She was a pretty-faced woman, of rotund build like her husband. She seemed to complement him perfectly.

'Have you come for the barbecue, Anthony?'

He felt himself shrinking inside, then thought: Why not?

'Yes, if I'm not too late.'

'No, we're just starting.'

Brian was bending over a hearth constructed out of Roman tile pieces, fanning the flames that were beginning to spurt upward beneath a heavy, black cooking grill. People were gathered about in groups, mainly the older diggers and their friends from the village, but with some youngsters as well. Soon Anthony was buried deep in conversation. The talk at least was about his subjects – the Romans and the well. He began almost to enjoy himself, as he was able to hold centre stage. Food was brought to him, charred burgers and sausages in rolls, washed down with ginger beer and lemonade.

Somewhere in the whirl of people and amongst the smoke from the fire he came up against Brian, who greeted him heartily enough.

'You must be pleased to get the well finished.'

'Oh, yes. Easy work from now on.'

'Some most excellent finds too. Well done.' Praise from Brian was rare. Anthony lapped it up like a dog at its water bowl on a hot day.

'People would like to see it. Perhaps even go down it,' Anthony said.

'I'm thinking of having an open day at the end of the dig. Possibly on the last Saturday afternoon. We'll open the well up then and let everyone see it properly. But not to descend it. That's impossible for safety reasons. You're still due to be here then, aren't you?'

'Oh yes, I'm doing the whole stretch. I'd be leaving that evening, though.'

'Good. So it should work out fine. Until then, no private viewings. Keep them away from the area. I don't want any accidents.'

'Of course, Brian. You can rely on me.'

Anthony swung his head around the congregation. Brian had begun to dampen down the fire. The light was fading from the sky; the talking heads, the hands holding paper plates, were being shrouded by swirls of smoke. Beyond them, a spoil heap rose like a misshapen pyramid against the red-stained sky.

He walked away from the people for a moment or two, and gazed out into the sunset across a flat field of yellow stubble. In the mid-distance was a hedgerow, and beyond that the fire in the sky seemed to reach down to the earth. Something caught his eye. He looked away and blinked, thinking some smut from the smoke had come before his view. Then he turned back to the hedgerow, and he saw clearly a black figure in a hood looking at him over the hedge.

A voice called out to him. 'Anthony, do you want any more?', and his mind jerked abruptly back to the present. When he had a chance to look again the figure had gone.

Blackness was spreading over the site as the barbecue finished. Cars were being started. Rubbish was being borne off to the bins. Anthony walked amongst the caravans and the tents looking for Giuditta. There was no sign of her, or of Olaf either. Olaf's motorbike was absent. He had little doubt that they had gone off somewhere together – probably up to the Red Cow. Without helmets, Olaf would not travel much further. Should he drive there to find them? No, he would wait. He would like to watch them when they came back. He would like to see how much comfort Olaf was giving her. But if he left his Land Rover on site they would know he was here. So he drove it a way up the track until he came to a side turning, only a footpath really, very narrow and overhung by trees. He forced the Land Rover in until it was screened by the trees, and he waited.

It was a long time to sit in silence and to suppress thought. Night fell fast until the space beneath the trees became like a black tunnel through which a strong breeze swirled. Branches thumped against the roof of the vehicle, leaves rustled against the windows. To Anthony, watching through the windscreen, it was as if he was sitting at the centre of a vortex moving through night. He refused to think. There was nothing now he wanted to think about. He just wished the action of waiting. The waiting held a purpose. It would produce an outcome, perhaps for the worst, but at least it would be an outcome. Thinking alone, in some distant place separated from the consequences of those thoughts, would be too much to bear. He was finished with thinking.

Even the hooded figure seen against the dying light of the day, he refused to contemplate. His blood froze cold upon it, but he would not wonder or fear any more. He wanted substance now, the release of action, the doing of something tangible so that he would *know*, one way or the other. He was not frightened of the positive, the definite. What he feared most was not knowing and not having any way of finding out.

At last – he glanced at his watch: it was nearly 10.30 – he saw a shaft of light flickering through the leaves around him, sending shadows and swirls of brightness chasing across the windscreen and over his hands held out before him, and then he heard the roar of an engine, growling and snarling, from a machine picking its way along the track beyond the wooded screen where the Land Rover sat. The sound came closer and closer and the light stabbed more and more brightly until Anthony feared they must see the naked outline of the vehicle amongst the bushes, but perhaps the headlamp was blinded to all but its stabbing pool of yellow light directly ahead; the machine did not stop but passed on with a great roar of its engine, now dwindling down the track towards the camp.

Anthony left the Land Rover and blundered over the grass, pushing back the fronds of the trees, until he stood on the open track. A black, moonless sky studded with stars swung above him. He began stumbling up the track, as fast as he could go, towards the site of the villa lying on the crest of the rise ahead. As he passed the first of the spoil heaps, he slowed down and looked around him, seeing some moving lights, probably the torches of people going to their tents. He did not want to be seen. Coming closer, he crossed the grassy area of the car park and now could make out the first line of the tents. Yes, he could see the shape of Olaf's bike too, rising blacker than the blackness behind, like a great black spider poised beside his tent and that of Giuditta on the further side.

He was right up to the tents now, trying to walk without sliding his boots through the grass so as to make less noise. He could smell the hot oil of the bike, feel the heat of its cooling exhaust on the air. To one side rose Miles's caravan, with the long, dark shape of the main spoil heap behind it. A light was on in the caravan window, a dull orange light powered by Miles's dwindling battery. The curtains were drawn and the caravan door was closed. Were they both inside?

He went to the rear of the caravan where it stood against the spoil heap. Miles had placed some plastic jerry cans here and Anthony stumbled against them, holding his breath in case the noise had been heard. All was quiet. He could hear nothing from within. In the rear end of the caravan there was one wide window where the curtains were imperfectly drawn. At the centre there was a gap through which Anthony could peer. He pressed one eye up close to the glass.

He was looking along the length of the caravan. Closest to his point of vision was Miles's bedroom, with his shower cubicle to one side, and beyond that the kitchen. Furthest away from him was the sitting area, with its table for eating, and it was there – on the bench seats where Anthony himself had often sat – that he now saw Olaf and Giuditta. They were seated, drinking. A green bottle stood on the table before them, and Anthony could see it was gin. A bottle of tonic water stood beside it.

Olaf looked very relaxed and confident, Anthony thought, sprawled back on one of the seats, his glass of gin in his hand. He was talking and smiling. Giuditta sat to one side of him, facing directly towards Anthony as he peered from the far end of the caravan. She was wearing a white tee-shirt and dark trousers, and she had clearly just released her hair from the band at the back, for even as he watched she was shaking out the long dark hair and smoothing it down with her hand. Her glass stood on the table before her. Was she drinking just tonic? He hoped she was. She had never drunk much alcohol with him. But, as he watched, she reached for the gin bottle and tipped a little into her glass, reaching across to pour into Olaf's glass as well. Then she poured from the tonic bottle too. So that was their second drink, and they had only just arrived.

Anthony saw the window misting before his eye, and he looked away. He could not bear this and wanted to run away. But he was drawn back as a moth flies into a flame. Olaf was still talking. What he said was making her laugh. He could just hear her laughter, in fact – oh, that lovely laugh of hers! – rippling through the caravan's metal walls. Now Olaf was reaching a hand out towards her and running it through her hair, resting it on the side of her neck just below the ear, and she smiled upon him.

It was impossible to watch. He hated himself for what he was doing, for this snooping and prying and peeping, and in truth he would rather be a million miles from here – yet something forced him to go on looking. He must find out for sure. There was a terrible compulsion within him that he should know.

The light was dim within the caravan. Anthony's viewpoint was narrow. The two had risen to their feet and moved away from the table, and he could not see them clearly now within the shadows of the room, half out of sight behind a projecting cupboard. He could see arms and legs, though, that moved frantically, hands raised high holding clothing that trailed from clutched fists, and he knew with horror that – as in the long nightmare he had foreseen – they were undressing themselves, or each other; he did not know which, for most of their bodies were out of his line of sight, just the arms he could see, or half a shoulder, and the clothes falling on the table behind, spread over the gin bottle and the glasses, teeshirts and belts, and her bra, and the heavier bulk of trousers flung suddenly onto the seat beside.

His heart raced and the misery swelled within him, bursting out of his eyes so that he began sobbing, his forehead against the window glass, and still he could not look away. She had come into view, in the centre of the small lounge where the kitchen began, bare breasted with just the flimsiest white band across her hips and over her dark mound, her buttocks turning to him naked, and she was dancing, swaying her hips to music; or perhaps it was she who was singing for he could see her lips moving, and he watched her place her hands over her small, sharp breasts and gyrate her hips, and he knew that Olaf would be standing there somewhere just out of sight, taking all this in with his quiet eyes.

It was enough! At all costs, he must not see Olaf. He did not want to watch him move to take her, to touch that flesh that should be only his to smooth and cherish. He who had lost everything, even the dream of her innocence: she was revealed now as brazen, lascivious and enticing – a prancing whore like…like…and he remembered the wall painting of the Bacchanalia dance they had viewed together, and how she had giggled then, and he knew that things had come full circle and he cursed himself for his stupidity and his naivety.

He fell away from the caravan, literally, for he caught a leg on some rope and tumbled to the ground hurting his knee on a sharp object, and he did not care and blundered away, oblivious now of any noise he might be making. The camp was black, and no one seemed to be stirring; just the one light showed in the caravan he had left, shining out through the curtains in a blur of orange – that place of fornication where Anthony's dreams had ended. Were they all lying here in their tents, sleeping the sleep of innocence, or were they too coupling and writhing and fucking, so that he passed here beneath the black sky and the milky stars, while all around him stained depravity was oozing into the earth?

He came to the edge of the camp where the field of stubble began, and he sank to his feet and he cried, for he knew if he did not cry he would go mad, and he did not wish madness upon himself, although he could hope that death in a hooded cloak might come and take him.

When he felt relieved of his misery and was able to stand again, his brain quiet now and not dwelling on anything but the earth before his feet and the wheeling sky above, he walked out into the field a way until he stood at the top of a low ridge and looked back at the camp. The tents and the caravans lay submerged in the blackness, although in the faint light of the stars, as his eyes grew accustomed, he could see the darker shapes of the spoil heaps and the hedgerow bordering the track running up to the site.

He was thinking of the past now – as he so often did to rid himself of the present that he did not wish to meet or understand – and he imagined the Roman villa as it had stood there in its shallow valley before him. It was daylight, and the red roofs of the white-plastered buildings shone in sunlight, with birds rising and swooping amongst the bright-painted eaves. To one side in a courtyard, a fire was burning, white smoke drifting upwards, and beyond were square fields, divided by thin hedges, set like a green grid against the turned earth. Through them ran a broad road metalled with brown gravel: it crossed the fields towards a high gateway in the wall of the outer court before the villa house. On a far slope, a small, square building had a dome which flashed golden in the sunlight: smoke was rising here too, and beyond stood a dark wood, at the edge of which a hunting party moved, horses and riders and men on foot with spears, and a thin line of bearers struggling up the slope behind.

All these things Anthony saw in a flash, but he could not see the well he had dug, for even then it had been filled in, a hundred years or more earlier, but he knew where it had stood, for a garden of flowers covered it now and a lady in a dark blue robe walked there – and she looked up at him and smiled.

Anthony came back into the camp knowing something was changing, and it might be for the better and not the worse, and that, despite all that had happened, and all that he had seen and heard, the story might not yet be over. That smile – that vision, for a moment shining through the enclosing blackness of his mind – had afforded him the briefest glimpse of hope. Was there yet a way out? Would that he could keep up the strength of belief to outshine night, to keep at bay those powers from the past that sought yet to destroy.

Did he have such strength? For this one night he felt he did, and that was perhaps all he sought – for a short period to suspend his own judgement, his jealousy and complaint, and to have compassion and understanding. For it is love that will last through the longest darkness. Without love, there is nothing. And so, in these thoughts, miraculously, the prophecy of his waking dream was fulfilled.

As he approached the camp again, he heard cries, and one high shriek, then angry voices in German shouting. They came from Miles's caravan, and a small knot of campers, dragging themselves from the nearest tents, were gathered outside, listening, not knowing what to do. Into these Anthony strode, just as the caravan door burst open and a naked Giuditta tumbled out.

'*Weg won mir!* Get away from me!' she screamed as an equally naked Olaf appeared at the door. Anthony had a brief glimpse of his angry, engorged penis before he covered it with his hands and stepped back.

Anthony raised her from the grass. 'Get a blanket, a coat, anything,' he snapped at the nearest camper.

He wrapped his arms around her, shielding her nakedness, and her white face rolled around, her eyes wide and uncomprehending. 'Are you a ghost?' she said.

When a blanket was thrust at him, he went to wrap it around her, but she was recovering a little and took it from him and attended to this herself. One of the girl campers now helped her for she was crying, and Anthony tugged at the caravan door but found it locked.

'Olaf! Open up!' he shouted.

'What you want?'

'Not you. Her clothes.'

After a few moments, the door was opened and Olaf appeared, still bare chested but thankfully now in shorts, and he thrust out a bundle of clothing.

'Not my fault,' he said. 'She want it.' He was frightened. It was not rape, he was saying. And Anthony knew he spoke the truth.

'Keep inside,' he said. 'I'll look after her.'

He had to get her back from the other helpers now, reassert his right to her, to be able to help her himself, if only she would not scream at him too as her comprehension began to come back.

He went to where she was standing and held out her clothes and said, 'Put these on. In your tent *now*.'

She heard the strength in his voice and did as he asked, and then he turned to the others and told them to go away. With side looks and some muttering, they obeyed, merging back into the darkness, and he stood there in the night by Giuditta's tent, waiting for her to come out again, but she didn't. He paced the grass outside for a while, and saw the light in the caravan suddenly flick out. Olaf must want his own darkness to hide within: his eyes might probe the night but there would be no rest for him.

The rustlings in the tent had ceased, and, impatient, he pulled back the flap and looked inside. She sat, clothed now, her knees raised, and her face was very white and her eyes huge as she stared out at him. He saw she was trembling, and he crawled into the tent and took her in his arms.

'Poor baby. Poor baby. You trust me, don't you?'

Her body was shaking all over, and her cheek felt cold to his lips when he kissed her. 'I love you, you silly girl. I love you so much.'

She nodded and looked down at the ground. 'I'm sorry,' she said.

'What are you sorry for?'

'For being so nasty to you. For trying to make you jealous.'

It was what he had wanted to hear. Some pressure in her mind – in his too – had burst with this shock, and he knew she saw him now as a friend – no longer the enemy that her twisted reasoning, whatever its cause, had made him – and he must help her, for the shock was still heavy upon her.

'Come with me,' he said.

'Where are we going?'

'To the farm. You need to be where it's warm and comfortable and you need to rest.'

She began to protest, but he cut in. 'You can't stay here now. You can have the bed. I'll sleep on the floor. We'll sort it out with Mrs. Reynolds in the morning.'

She leant against him as, carrying her rucksack, they stumbled along the track to his car. She was utterly exhausted.

Once in the Land Rover, and she in her seat beside him, as he remembered her sitting there before, her head fell against his chest, and he let it lie there for a time while he smoothed her hair, until at last – reluctantly – he gunned the engine. She raised her head, startled. 'Close your eyes again. We'll soon be there.'

In the car park at the farm, the security lights came on, flooding them with white light as they climbed down from the Land Rover. It was the latest he had ever returned there at night, but he had a key to the outer door and he doubted if anyone would be looking out. He did not care, anyhow. He would explain in the morning.

She was tired, but she was perhaps less in shock now, for she was aware of her surroundings, and a little awkward as they came into the room and saw the large bed with its white counterpane and the small area of the floor around.

She did not know, of course – would never know – that he had watched her naked through the caravan window, but she must be aware that he had raised her unclothed body from the grass, and that others would have seen her too. Her world was in sudden turmoil and it was important for her now to cling to normality as far as possible under these disordered circumstances. She might be sharing a room with a man – an older man, a friend – but modesty was paramount. She went to the bathroom and closed the door, then made him turn his back on her return, rummaging in her rucksack until at last he heard the bed creaking as she got in.

She lay with her back to him, perfectly still, her hair spread on the pillow as he had always imagined it. Was she asleep? He undressed quickly, pulling on his sleeping things and taking from the wardrobe a thick coat he had brought in case of cold, which he had intended to place over himself on the floor.

'What are you doing?'

'I thought you were sleeping. I'm nearly ready. I'll turn off the light just now.'

'Where are you?'

'I said I'd sleep on the floor.'

'You can't do that. It'll be too uncomfortable. Get into bed.'

He was too tired to argue, or to feel anything or to think about anything other than the need for sleep, and he switched off the light and slid between the sheets, sensing her there so close to him, hearing her breathing. Then she stirred and he felt her fingers on his arm. Anthony lay as if frozen, hardly daring to move.

'Yes?'

Her body moved across him and he felt the brush of her breasts against his chest. Her lips found his cheek. 'Thank you. You're my hero.'

'Sleep well.'

'You too.'

But he couldn't sleep. Not for some time. He would have found it easier if he were not lying alongside her, but curled up on the floor, as he had planned, or outside in his car. For what man can sleep when the object of his desire lies like a nun beside him? – a nun indeed whom he has just seen behave like a whore. It was all unreal and quite wrong, and could not go on.

He had saved her and shown compassion to her and kept his jealousy at bay. He had told her again he loved her, and that was very true. And now he was her hero and his cheek still tingled with her kiss. He must not think, for he did not know what it was he should be thinking. This was the last – the most extreme – torment he would put himself through. If she did not go home tomorrow, he would be the one to leave. He could decide that at least. Tomorrow it must end.

That is what he told himself during the night. Yet Anthony was never master of his own fate. His power to control events did not outlast the dawn.

24

He awoke in the grey light between night and dawn, suspended between sleeping and waking, so that for a few moments the material earth seemed without form and his mind free to range without the usual constraints of place and time – then abruptly full consciousness, with its consort, reality, came tumbling back.

Where was she? She was sleeping still, her face turned on the pillow towards him, her lips apart, the air breathing in through nostrils and mouth, then out again so that the corner of the pillow case trembled the smallest fraction with the air she expelled. Did he dare touch her? He reached across and held his hand above her hair, letting his finger tips flick against some loose strands lying like a tangle of black lace against the white linen, and then he moved his foot beneath the sheets, inch by careful inch, until it was just resting against the smoothness of her leg.

She stirred and opened her eyes, and seeing his gaze upon her, looked confused for a moment, but then she smiled – and that waking smile, of all thoughts and sights and memories of this last day, was to haunt Anthony during the terrible darkness to come.

'What time is it?'

He looked at his watch. 'Just past eight. Sleep on. You don't need to get up.'

She closed her eyes. 'What am I doing in bed with you, Mr. Winters?' she said, lightly and with humour, for her lips were smiling, and then she drifted back into sleep. He watched her for a while, and then slid quietly from the bed, taking his clothes to the bathroom where he washed and dressed. When he had finished, she was still sleeping, so he switched on the kettle in the room and made tea.

She awoke at the sounds of these preparations, and sat up in bed with a start, looking a little embarrassed – which was hardly surprising given the circumstances.

'Would the *signorina* like her tea here or on the terrace. The air is lovely this morning. The sun has risen and the sea is a translucent blue.'

She took her tea cup and looked at him wonderingly.

'I was just imagining how nice it would be to be on holiday with you in your own country, by the sea, with the pine forests coming down to the water and the mountains behind. Breakfast on the terrace and days with no worries.'

'Find me the place, Anthony, and I will come.'

He felt a glow of pleasure at that – even of hope – despite the realities, knowing it must end. She was so lovely, as he had felt when he had first seen her – her hair, her face, her accent – a fusion and perfection of form, and of sound and movement about her, so that in his eyes she seemed at the centre of an aura of bright light: she was resting her shoulders against the bed-head, wearing a grey tee-shirt with some Italian word across its front which he could not read.

'I'm going to see Mrs. Reynolds now and sort things out with her. She'll probably keep breakfast for us.'

'I don't want to see her, Anthony.' She looked distressed now. The horror of yesterday was returning.

'No, of course not. We must talk about what you wish to do.'

'I want to go home.'

'Of course.' He was pleased by that. He didn't want her to stay on now. 'I'll take you back.'

'Oh, no. I couldn't ask you to do that. This is your place. Your holiday.'

'I think I've had enough for this year. The well's finished. The rest would be an anti-climax. I'd be much happier helping you.'

She didn't argue any more, for he knew that really she wanted him to help her, although she wouldn't say so directly yet. He had to tread as carefully as ever with her – perhaps even more so now. There was still much he wanted to learn about what had happened last night. If he could be alone with her, he would have the chance to find out. Otherwise, he might never know or understand, and he felt he could not live with that. He was prepared to accept that their relationship must end – for her own good as much as his – but he did not wish to live with memories that were shrouded with mystery, with 'whys?' and 'hows' or what might have been if he had only said or done something else.

'I'll tell Mrs. Reynolds we're both leaving then, and pay her. Don't worry, I'll think up a good story.'

'I'm not worried. I just want to go without any fuss.'

'We'll have to go to the site though and pick up your gear.'

She hung her head. 'Could you do that for me? I don't want to see *him* again, or any of them. I'm ashamed.'

He looked at her, and decided this was not the time to hold her and reassure her.

'I'm going to see Mrs. Reynolds,' he said briskly. 'You get up and dressed while I'm away, if that's okay?' She nodded, still looking down. 'I'll be fifteen minutes or so.'

As he had anticipated, Mrs. Reynolds gave little reaction when he told her about the second guest in his room. She was a practical woman of solid sensibilities who had known Anthony for many years; certainly not a person to make any moral judgements on him or the girl who had arrived with him in the middle of the night. It was unnecessary even for Anthony to refer to Giuditta as the same person who had stayed here back at Easter. Mrs. Reynolds was busy with her breakfasts and with a table load of middle-aged singletons from Hampshire on a walking tour, some of whom might have been getting up to worse things than Anthony in the night. She was perhaps a little less sanguine when Anthony told her he had to cut short his booking with her.

'Oh well, a change of plan might not come amiss. I wonder at you doing all that digging each year. One day you'll wear yourself right out.' She had laughed out loud at her own humour, and Anthony knew there would be no lingering ill feeling.

When he had paid what he owed, he had had a quick cup of coffee and a bowl of cereal, happily by himself on a table distant from the ramblers, who were all jolly in shorts, until he thought enough time had passed to return to Giuditta.

He knocked on the bedroom door. 'Come in,' she called after a pause when he thought she had not heard him. She was fully dressed and brushing out her hair, using Anthony's brush.

'I must put some clean things on to travel,' she said, 'as soon as I can get back to my tent. I'd unpacked most of my clothes, you see, and left them there.

Anthony was encouraged. She had dropped her reluctance to return to the site and seemed to be developing a more pragmatic approach to her problems. He didn't want her to come face to face with Olaf again, but he thought she could at least pack up her tent and perhaps say goodbye to Brian. He hoped no one had said anything to him yet about what had happened, but feared they might.

Then something he had forgotten about suddenly occurred to him. It was Thursday today – the mid point to a full digging week which would include the weekend. Thursday was usually the day off, when you might dig if you wished and your supervisor agreed, but when otherwise you went off site for a break and a change of scenery, or simply caught up on personal affairs. Therefore, far fewer people would be on the site than was normally the case. Brian, for one, was unlikely to be there. Perhaps they should call at his house instead to say goodbye.

If Giuditta was agreeable, it might be a sensible thing to do that, to give Brian some sort of quick account of what had happened, one that would not necessarily accuse Olaf of anything, but would set out Giuditta's innocence – and his own for that matter – just in case of any complaint. He still needed to discuss this with her, but he wasn't sure at the moment how to approach her. Would she be prepared to talk about such personal things? He knew what he had seen, but he didn't yet understand why or what had gone wrong.

'How beautiful your hair is,' he said. Sunlight was spilling through the half-drawn curtains shining upon Giuditta's hair as she brushed it, bringing out those reddish colours that had first tantalised him months ago.

'I should have it cut it short.'

'Why?'

'I have been bad. I should be punished.'

Sometimes, even now, he was not sure of her. Was she being serious, or was she pulling his leg, making fun of his uncertainty as he wrestled with the complex of thoughts and desires that she aroused in him?

'You need some breakfast,' he said.

'Oh, no, not here.'

'I'll buy you some. There's a café I know by the A303. It's called the Happy Sausage.' She giggled at that. It was good to see her spirits returning. He hoped that, after some food, she might be better fortified to re-face Glastington.

They left not long afterwards. Anthony carried her rucksack to the Land Rover with his own bags. Giuditta, with her head down, scurried to the vehicle. Anthony could sympathise with her desire not to be seen. Not only would she feel demoralised by what had happened, but unclean as well in yesterday's clothes – those very ones which he had seen her shedding in Miles's caravan under the spell of her own music. What on earth had been in her head then? Would he ever be able to understand?

The Happy Sausage was a cheery place, with red-check tablecloths and squeezy bottles of brown sauce, its walls covered with foreign licence plates and flags of St. George: it was peopled largely by truck drivers. Anthony noted how Giuditta earned several glances as they weaved their way between the tables. She was hungry, as he had thought she would be. He ordered her a 'full English' and had a bacon sandwich himself. He was glad she could eat. It proved she possessed the resilience to recover. Despite everything that had happened, he felt more confident with her now, more able to assert himself without worrying about her reaction.

Once back in the Land Rover, she laid her fingers on his hand and squeezed it gently. 'Thank you.'

'You don't need to thank me for anything. I've wanted to go to that place every time I've passed.'

'You could be a lorry driver and go there often.'

He laughed. 'I'd rather cut my balls off.' He didn't know why he had to make a comment as crude as that, but he was pleased to see it made her smile.

'We'll drive towards Glastington now,' he said, 'and see if Brian's home.'

As they entered a tangle of lanes bordered by high hedgerows amongst which he struggled to pick his way, he was aware of how quiet she had become.

'A penny for your thoughts.'

'What? Oh. I was just thinking…'

'Anything in particular?'

'About my father.'

'Of course! You saw him recently. How did it go?' Before last night's events, this had been the one thing Anthony had most wanted to ask her about.

She didn't answer. 'Look, could we stop a moment. I feel a little sick.'

He pulled into the opening to a field. Ahead lay a sweep of long grass bordered by a thick wood. At the edge of the shadow cast by the wood, the tips of the grass blades caught the sun in a line of gold so that it looked as if a magic sword had been laid upon the field, its rays spreading outward in shining stripes as the grass moved in the breeze. Is that Excalibur? breathed Anthony, entranced by the sight – King Arthur's sword rising out of the earth.

She got down from the car and stood in the grass, gazing out across the field towards the wood. At first he did not join her, thinking she might want to be by herself, but he saw she turned to look for him, so he hastened to her side.

'How are you feeling?'

'A little nauseous' – she found it hard to pronounce that word – 'but not too bad.'

She sat, creating a small, round nest in the thick grass, and he sat too, pulling a blade of grass to suck at its soft, juicy core.

'What happened last night?' he asked. He needed to know.

He had banished the image of her in the caravan, but it was burning back into his brain. He wanted it to go away.

'I'm not sure.' She was sitting upright. Her head just topped the grass, and her hair blew amongst its grey-green feathers as if she too was growing from the earth. 'Sometimes I think I go a little mad.'

'In what way?'

'In many ways. You know, Anthony. You have seen my moods.'

He did not deny what she said. It was important that she understood herself.

'You hurt me – back then, in Ely, Cambridge, wherever it was. You were so poo poo, so bloody right. It angered me when I was telling you my sad, lonely secrets.'

'I didn't mean to be poo poo,' he said smiling, hoping to make her smile too.

'I am not laughing, Anthony. It is too serious. I do not want to go mad.'

Now she was one with his own fears, expressed so often of late, and he reached across and took her shoulders, and eased her into his arms. 'You will not go mad. Not while you're with me. Because I love you, my girl. More than I can say.'

She looked up at him. 'No one has ever told me that before. Only you.'

'You deserve to be loved. You have suffered too much.'

'Oh, Anthony. If you were only younger. I cannot get from my mind that you could be my father.'

'I don't feel like your father.' And he kissed her forehead, and wonderfully her mouth turned up to him and for the first time he kissed her properly, fully, tasting her lips – moments of sheer bliss – until she suddenly bent her face down.

'No, it cannot be. You are even like my father. Your face, your manner – at times – your gruffness.'

He knew it was best not to argue or plead his case. 'How was your father when you saw him in Cambridge?'

'I didn't.'

'You didn't!'

She met his eyes. He could see the shadows in her own eyes that seemed to come like a black rash when she was under stress. 'He died in America, the day before he was due to leave for Europe. A heart attack. His tart found him. I was right, all his money went to her.'

'Oh, I'm so sorry.' Anthony did not know what to say. He held her shoulders again and tried to touch her face with his lips. 'Did you go to the funeral?'

'I was not asked. I was not even told the date. I could not have afforded it, anyhow.' – Anthony thought, if she had only been with me and asked me I would have paid – 'My brother's arranged for his ashes to be brought back to Italy – to the farm. They will be interred at our church. One day I shall go again and pay my respects. He *was* my father.'

There was silence while she continued to stare down at the tangle of crushed grass beneath them. Anthony plucked stem after stem, then flung them away. The breeze would reach down to them occasionally into the grass and stir their hair and their clothes. Anthony's mind was quiet. All he wished was to sit here beside her, and for the long silence to go on and on without the need for questioning or for any worry now about what had been, for only this present mattered.

'My old man,' she said at last, touching Anthony's arm. 'What a dance I have led you.'

'I'm happy to have danced.'

'I would not make you happy.'

'You might try.'

'Perhaps. But not today.'

She was rising to her feet. Anthony was alive with excitement. So there was still a chance. 'Let me kiss you again.'

302

They kissed, standing in the sunlight in the field of grass, and her head lay in his arms and her hair flowed over his hands, and he loved her. God! How he loved her! His body and his soul ached for her. One day she would be his. Had she not said that? The dream would not be ending – neither by his will or hers – but would become true.

Back inside the Land Rover, he placed his hand on her thigh, almost casually now for he knew she would allow it; the barriers between them were broken down. The old man and the young woman, father and daughter, had ceased to exist. They were man and woman now, of one flesh, one desire.

'What do you hope for?' he asked.

'Not much really. Just simple things. They may sound trite, the words overused. But what I seek most is contentment; above all, peace. How I want simply to be still again and happy, and look at the sky, and know I have a place where I belong.'

'It will come. There is hope, I feel certain.'

She kissed him, and wrapped her arms around him, pulling him close to her.

'What happened?' he asked again. 'With Olaf, I mean. Did he hurt you?'

She pulled away, embarrassed now, but he knew she would answer and not be angry, as she might once have been. 'No. He's a nice boy. Quiet. Very shy. Too young for me. I was a fool. I egged him on. I think he just wanted to be a friend, not a lover.' She would not look at Anthony. 'I'm ashamed of my lusts. I desired him. I gave myself to him. He didn't know what to do.'

'I find that hard to believe.' Anthony remembered Olaf's own smug words about comforting her. And he knew what he had seen through the caravan window. Yet what *had* he seen?

'It is the truth, although I don't wish to say it for it is very private. But you have a right to know. He couldn't – how do I say? – rise to me. It was too sudden. Perhaps I frightened him.

I shocked him certainly – the older woman with the boy, only a big boy really. He had his girls in the village, he told me. I was jealous, I suppose. I also wanted to hurt you – I'm sorry, I admit that. Why could I have not left him alone? I know I am bad. I am sick. I want sex, lots of sex – but there is no feeling. I don't mean orgasm, I mean emotion. I am dead inside. It is all….bang, bang' – she thumped Anthony's leg with her fist – 'let's get it over and done with. I repulse myself like that. He tried….he tried….'

She broke off and began sobbing, and Anthony was alarmed. He did not want to hear any more. He pulled her close to him. 'It's alright, you don't need to tell me. I think I understand.'

'No, you don't, you can't. The terror I am left with. Oh, Anthony, if I ever let you make love to me, just do it quickly, fuck me properly – not that other stuff, that fiddling about. I hate it!' – she held up a finger – 'It will not go away. *It will not go away*! Can you possibly understand!?'

'Shhh, my love. Giuditta. I do understand. I tell you I do.' He wanted to wriggle away from this horror, this embarrassment – as he had in the Cathedral – but at least he knew now.

It was ironic, wasn't it? – the young and the old, how it all worked, body and soul. With her, there was perfection. The past, the years between, the age that bore down on flesh were all irrelevant to this moment.

25

They found Brian Radleigh at his house, hard at work in the shed he used for an office. His wife had shown them there and offered coffee. She looked harassed and care-worn, thought Anthony. It must be tiring being the wife to an archaeologist, who thought more of his site – his sections, his trenches, his layers, his contexts and, above all his finds – than he did of his own home. Evidence of this lay all around in the garden they trod to reach the shed – a riot of weeds and overgrown lawn, with a jungle of ivy climbing up the sagging fences. What a contrast it made with the ordered earth of the site, where everything was made perfect with spade and trowel, trench sides vertical, surfaces cleaned, walls brushed, unruly grass trimmed, weeds uprooted or burnt out with poison.

Brian would be oblivious of any such contrast. The site was his work, and that was where he concentrated his effort. His home was his wife's domain, and he scarcely noted its condition, unless a pile of books tumbled across the lounge floor or a tray of pottery sherds overflowed into the cooking – and then he would grunt and say a few cross words until enough order was restored for the archaeological work to continue.

So now he was deep into the problem of 3rd century wall plaster appearing in what was assumed to be a 1st century context, and really did not take much account of Giuditta and Anthony at all when they appeared at the shed door. His head however, did raise itself sharply from a close contemplation of the plaster fragments when Anthony announced he was taking Giuditta to the site to collect her belongings, and then would be heading home with her.

'I'll try to get back for that open day at the end of the month,' Anthony declared, feeling suddenly rather guilty at letting Brian down.

'Oh, fine. I'm sure we'll manage without you, if you can't return. But I hope you can make it. Other things to do, eh?'

It was for personal reasons that she had to leave early, Giuditta told Brian. She did not expand. He gave her a shrewd look, but did not ask any questions.

Anthony, however, had felt suddenly self-conscious and awkward, hoping Brian would make no comment about their relationship, as he had done before. It was unlikely he would say anything in front of Giuditta, but perhaps he might if he could get Anthony by himself.

The chance seemed to come when Giuditta excused herself to go to the toilet. There was a confusion of movement at this time as Mrs. Radleigh arrived with the coffee just as Giuditta was going out through the shed door. As soon as order was restored, Anthony forestalled any immediate remark by Brian by telling him there had been a little contretemps involving Giuditta on the site last night.

'It was nothing much. A misunderstanding really. But I happened to be there to help her. I thought you should know in case anyone says anything. There was a little bit of noise for a while.'

Brian looked displeased. He was having to abandon his wall plaster and come to a consideration of things he did not really want to hear about.

'Well, it's best she's going then. I don't know about you, though. I think you're very foolish to get involved.'

There it was! – Brian's critical comment. It was bad, but not as bad as he had feared. He didn't reply, but sipped his coffee and soon Giuditta returned.

As they got up to leave, Brian said, 'Just check the well before you leave the site. Make sure no one's playing silly buggers there. Some of those new youngsters, I'm still not too sure about.'

'Of course,' Anthony replied, a little disconcerted. Did he really want to leave his well when it might be interfered with by others?

'Stan should be up there. I've asked him to keep an eye out also.'

Anthony's heart sank at this news. He'd assumed Stan would be at home today. Now he'd probably have to run a gauntlet of questions and 'nudge, nudge, wink, wink' comments before they could escape. He looked at his watch. It was approaching 12.00. They should be away by one, and could get some food on the journey.

They said farewell to Brian at his front door. It was a hot day. The sun was beating down on the strip of faded grass that made up Brian's front garden. There was no sign of his wife: she must be busy with some chore deep in the house. Anthony noted that Brian went back inside before he had even opened the doors of the Land Rover.

A plume of dust followed them as they ploughed the track to the site, the engine of the Land Rover snarling reassuringly as the wheels gripped the ruts and brought them into the paddock of grass that served as the car park. Here, Anthony saw two things straightaway – the first that Olaf's bike was not in its usual place amongst the first row of tents, which filled him with much relief – but, second, that something unusual seemed to be going on. There were only a few cars in the car park, but amongst them, on the side nearest the camp, was a large, blue Mercedes, against which a uniformed chauffeur lounged, his jacket unbuttoned and his peaked cap pushed back from his sweating brow. Even as Anthony looked on amazed by this sight, a small, white dog bounded across the grass, jumped against the chauffeur's legs, then, yapping, raced back towards a lady and a man just coming into view around the site caravan. The man was Stan – ridiculous in a red and green rugby shirt and calf-length shorts – and, as he saw Anthony, he called out, 'There he is now'. The lady – it took Anthony's fuddled brain a moment or two to recognise her – was Juliana, whom he had met at the Italian Institute.

How slim and elegant she is, was Anthony's first impression, and so immaculately clothed, in a loose, pale blue dress trimmed with white, her honey-coloured hair perfectly arranged and held in place by a silver clasp at the back, and with dangling earrings shaped like the crescent moon. In clothes like that, she was, of course, out of place on the site, yet at the same time, not so, for she matched the role of the distinguished visitor perfectly, the type of visitor before whom all obstacles fell away.

'Now, Bruno,' she said to the barking dog, raising her finger. 'Stop that noise at once', and the dog sat at her feet and was quiet.

'Ah, what a lovely dog.' Giuditta was on her knees before it, stroking its head and its little upright ears, while it jabbed its wet nose against her arms.

Juliana smiled at Anthony, and he found himself smiling automatically back, although he was perplexed as to what she was doing here when she had told him she would phone him to give a date to visit at the end of the month.

Juliana's greeting, embracing Giuditta as well, was relaxed, without any suggestion of awkwardness, as might have been expected from such a sudden, unannounced visit complete with liveried attendant.

'What a wonderful place,' she said. 'How exciting it is to see all those Roman walls. And the well, the one you told me about. Stan here says it's finished – you've got to the bottom, I understand. I wish I could see it, but it's covered over.'

'Yes, indeed,' Anthony replied, feeling suddenly very formal with her, but finding he wanted to tell her about what they had found. She seemed to have that effect on him – a desire, a compulsion almost, to explain things to her, to describe the organisation, the difficulties, the danger of the work, the objects they had found; all in truth – he admitted this – to try and impress her. It had been like that at the Institute, he remembered, when he had rambled on about himself to her, a complete stranger.

'But I was expecting you to come later,' he said. 'I'm about to leave the site for a few days.'

'My plans had to alter.' She was looking at him a little plaintively, as if appealing to him. 'The friend I'm staying with hasn't been too well, so I'm having to go home much earlier than intended. Today was the only opportunity I had to get out and about as I had hoped, so I hired a car – and a man to drive it – and here I am, early in the day and ready for everything! I didn't phone you. I thought, if you're here, you're here, and, if not, you're not. But here, indeed, you are! Do you have time to show me the well? I'd so like to see it.'

She was cajoling now, her body leaning forward, her face looking up into his, her lips apart, a hint of a smile. What a beautiful woman she's been, he thought. I shouldn't think there's much that's ever been denied her.

He turned to Giuditta. 'Can you manage to get your tent down while I show Juliana the well?'

'Yes. Don't worry. I can do that.'

There was something in Giuditta's eye, however, that told him she was uncomfortable about this development. He could not think what it was. He only needed to leave her for a few minutes, while he slid back the boards over the shaft and pointed out to Juliana the features of the well. Stan would help him. Brian had told him not to show anyone the well until 'open day', but Brian had not expected the wife of a senior official at the Italian Institute in London to be visiting his site. If Brian were here, Anthony was sure he would agree – indeed there was little doubt Brian would have shown Juliana the well himself.

'Come this way.' Anthony smiled ingratiatingly at Juliana, waving her in the direction of the site caravan.

'Mike. Would you be kind enough to hold my dog?' Juliana was speaking to the chauffeur, who straightened himself reluctantly and took – equally reluctantly – the lead Juliana had been clasping in one hand and had now attached to Bruno's collar. 'And let him have some water from the bottle in the boot.'

'I'll look after him,' Giuditta said eagerly. 'As soon as I've got my tent down. I'll come and get him from you.'

She looked at Mike, who nodded. Anthony could see the chauffeur was a little bit bemused by all these goings-on in a Somerset field. He was probably more used to fast motorway runs that ended in long gravelled drives and the porticos of Queen Anne-style mansions.

'Well that's fine,' said Juliana, extending her smile in all directions. 'Bruno will be well entertained. He's such a little darling.'

Anthony, in his eagerness to entertain not Bruno but Juliana, remembered in time to turn to Giudutta and to kiss his fingers, waving them in her direction, so that she looked down demurely, aware perhaps of the gaze of others on her. Oh dear, thought Anthony, perhaps I should not have done that, not with Stan standing there taking everything in. But Stan was already leading Juliana forward, even taking her by the arm at one point as he warned her to avoid a guy rope by the canteen tent.

'I won't be long,' Anthony called behind him to Giuditta. 'I'll give you a hand when I've finished. Then we'll be away.'

He saw her smile back at him over the long width of grass, standing there with the yellow sunlight in her hair, and then she turned and approached her tent, her half-empty rucksack dangling from one shoulder. For some reason, he thought how alone she looks now, how very vulnerable.

At the well, Anthony saw the hazard tape had already been removed from across the opening to the trench containing the well shaft. He did not query this, assuming Stan had brought Juliana here earlier. He was pleased, in fact, Stan had not sought to uncover the well itself; some at least of his instructions – Brian's instructions too – seemed to have stuck in his head.

He asked Juliana to stand clear to one side while he worked with Stan to raise one of the heavy boards across the top of the shaft. When they had been digging, both boards had been lifted and placed on the ground close by, but now it was enough to slide one back so that Juliana could peer into the shaft and see the stone walling and the vertical line of niches going down. If she were careful and leant out over the well – Anthony determined that he, and not Stan, would support her while she did this – she might be able to glimpse the water eighteen feet below. Anthony checked this himself. The sun was high in the sky and shining directly into the well. Once the board had been moved and his eyes had adjusted to the difference in light levels, he could clearly see the glint of the water. He thought: I'll drop a stone in, so she can hear the splash.

He called Juliana over to the limestone edge of the shaft. 'If you don't mind, I'll hold your hand. Just in case of a stumble.'

'Yes. Please. I'm a little nervous.'

She approached carefully, placing her feet in their sensible shoes – at least in that regard she has come prepared, he thought – on the stones that formed the upper layer of the well lining, at the point between the Acrow bars where the ladder had rested when it had been placed in the shaft. He took her left arm in one hand. Her skin was thin and he could feel the bone through it. He had not noticed before that her arms were like sticks. With his other hand, he flicked in the stone he had got ready. It ricocheted from the side of the shaft so its splash into the water was not as clear as he had hoped. She seemed impressed, however.

'You see how carefully made the shaft is,' he said, 'with the bands of stone laid concentrically for most of the depth.'

He pointed out the area where the lining had fallen away and the niches where Roman feet had been placed climbing in and out. She wanted to see the water at the bottom but needed to bend further forward.

'Hold me round the waist. I'll feel safer.'

He put his arms around her, his fingers pressing through the silky material of her dress into her soft stomach. Out of the corner of his eye, he could see Stan standing half-behind them with a grin on his face.

'Oh for a photograph,' he said loud enough for Juliana to hear.

Juliana, straightening up, laughed. 'Yes, my husband might wonder what was going on.'

She was a good sport, Anthony thought. Interested and enthusiastic, with a sense of humour. She must be wealthy too to be able to hire Mercedes cars and chauffeurs at the drop of a hat. He wondered what that cost per day.

They stepped back from the well while Anthony told her some of the details of the digging, and who had done what, while all the time Stan competed for his say. Anthony in fact let him take over when it came to describing the finds, in particular the Venus figurine which had been Stan's own discovery in his wheel barrow.

'It was well moulded, very detailed,' said Stan with a leer, 'if you know what I mean.'

'Goodness,' said Juliana with mock shock. 'I think I do. Where are the finds now?'

'Oh, Brian – the director – has them,' Anthony said. 'He'll be here later. If you're still around then, I'm sure he'll show you. It's the jewellery you need to see. It's magnificent.' He had already told her about the discovery of the necklace and the earrings, and of how one of the latter had turned up later in the discharge from the pump. She had been horrified by that, thinking how nearly it had been lost.

'It's a pity,' she said. 'I'd have liked to talk to Brian , but I'll need to be leaving before too long because I'm due to meet a friend in Yeovil for lunch and to do some shopping.'

Anthony at this point was aware of a sound on the air, a distant grumble at first, gradually growing into the growl, then the roar of a powerful motorbike coming up the track, and he knew it would be Olaf. Blast it! And Giuditta would be out there with her tent just where he would come face to face with her. He was suddenly anxious for her.

But, wonderfully, here was Giuditta now, with Bruno on the lead, pulling ahead of her as they came up the path to the well, the dog having scented its mistress, his mouth wide open and gasping with these exertions in the heat.

'Hi there.' Anthony was very pleased to see her looking so happy with the dog.

'Hello, my little Bruno,' called out Juliana across the well.

'Bones! Bones!' shouted Stan idiotically, seeking to be funny. 'Bones for the doggie from the well.'

Bruno jumped up barking, tugging frantically against the lead. The clasp broke – perhaps it had not been fastened to the collar properly – and Bruno was free. He jumped through the hazard tape, into the trench and onto the remaining board still in place across the shaft. Here he halted his momentum for a moment, confused by his mistress's sudden scream, saw the gaping hole ahead and tried to jump it, his claws scrabbling on the smooth wood. He hit the topmost stones on the far side with his front paws, and disappeared with a yelp into the depths below. This time there was no doubting the sickening splash that followed.

'You fucking idiot, Stan!' Anthony yelled.

Giuditta was on her knees on the board, peering over the edge.

'Careful! Careful!' They were all shouting the warning. The board was moving under her weight.

'I can hear him. He's alive.'

Anthony leant over. He too could hear the sound of whimpering and see a white shape on the water. The dog must be swimming, as the water would be much deeper than he could stand up in.

'Get this board off,' Giuditta said, stepping back from it and tugging at one end. 'Where's the ladder?'

Anthony and Stan came round to her side of the well to help her. It was dangerous here as the trench wall came close to the shaft and there was not much room to move. Juliana, Anthony saw, remained rooted to the ground, her hands over her face.

'Where's the ladder?' Giuditta repeated. 'Where's the bloody ladder?' The swear word sounded almost comical with her accent.

'It's underneath the site caravan.'

'Go and get it. Ah, Olaf' – incredibly the disgraced Olaf had appeared, with one or two others from the camp, attracted by the shouting – '*Olaf, Hilfe holen die Leiter!*' she screamed at him, frantic for some action. Olaf disappeared at a run, taking the other new arrivals with him.

By now Anthony and Stan had raised the board and stood it against the side of the trench. Its removal revealed the full circumference of the shaft and the Acrow bars that crossed over at its top.

'There he is. Don't give up, little dog.' Giuditta was jumping up and down in her anxiety close to the edge of the shaft.

'Careful! Careful you don't fall.' Anthony could see she was getting out of control. At all costs, there mustn't be another accident.

Giuditta crouched on the ground, peering into the shaft. 'He's not crying any more. And he's hardly moving. He must have been injured falling.'

Juliana was beginning to sob. She came up to the shaft trying to look in, but Anthony pushed her firmly away.

'I'm going down,' Giuditta said.

'What do you mean? You can't!'

'The... what do you call them?' – she pointed – 'The holes in the stone. I'll use them.' She did not know the word niche. She was referring to the Roman ladder in the stone.

'You can't. You'll fall. It's too dangerous!' Anthony and Stan shouted different parts of that warning.

'Well, what do you propose? He's going to drown if we wait.'

She was not going to listen to any objection. She was already on her knees at the edge of the shaft, reaching down with one leg for the uppermost niche.

'Hold my hand, Anthony.'

Reluctantly, he took her hand, then as she went lower moved his grip to her upper arm. 'Be careful. Be careful', he kept on calling out, knowing this was madness. The dog's life was not worth this danger.

She was scrabbling with her fingers now, seeking a purchase amongst the stones with one hand, clutching at one of the Acrow bars with the other. Anthony thought he saw the bar move a fraction. 'Be careful. Don't rely on that bar,' he shouted at her. But her foot was now in a niche, and she was feeling with her other leg for the one below – and found it, dropping down against the wall like a spider, her body bent outwards, shifting her handholds to the upper niche, her head lower already than Anthony's arms could reach.

He watched her open-mouthed. What to do if she fell? She must not fall. Where was that fucking ladder? They would need the ladder to get her out. She couldn't climb up the wall again holding the dog. A bucket, perhaps. Could she put the dog in a bucket, and they haul him up that way? It didn't matter about the dog, anyway. What mattered was getting Giuditta out of the well without injury.

'Stan! Run and get a bucket; one with a rope attached.'

Stan, who had been standing helplessly, obeyed immediately. He was pleased to have something to do.

Giuditta had reached the water. He saw her skim its surface with the toe of one foot, the disturbed water bubbling in a ray of light. The dog's head bobbed near her foot. A whimper, a little yap. Now she was trying to position herself lower against the wall so as to be able to reach down with one hand to seize him by the collar.

As if in slow motion, he saw her hand on the stone slip, and with a scream she tumbled sideways into the water, landing on her back, her arms and head bent against the far wall of the shaft, her trunk and her legs beneath the water. Even like that she pulled the dog to herself, lifting him onto her submerged chest and holding him there, the greater part of his body out of the water.

'Are you alright?' Horrified, he saw her try to move, only to collapse back.

'I've hurt myself.' Her voice was high with fear and pain.

Her head had dropped back against the stone lining. She could not get any purchase with her legs – perhaps she could not use them – and her body was sinking ever further into the bowl beneath her carved out of the smooth, living rock. He saw her struggling once more to raise herself, flailing her arms against the stone, but her face was only just above the level of the water now. She had released her hold on the dog but he still sat there crying on her breast, submerged to his neck.

There was no one around the well now, only Juliana who still stood frozen with shock. Anthony could not ask her to help him. He crawled to the edge of the shaft and dangled his feet over at the point where Giuditta had descended. 'Tell them when they come we're both down there,' he called to Juliana. 'Get someone to dial 999.'

She reacted to that, and clambered up the side of the trench, falling on her knees and tearing her dress. She made for the path, just as two others – student diggers – came into sight. 'The ladder's on the way,' Anthony heard them shouting.

'Dial 999!' Her voice was shrill but under control. 'I haven't got my mobile on me. Do you have a mobile on you?...Oh, do you have one....? Someone's been hurt. Please phone for an ambulance.'

Anthony was descending the wall of the shaft now, finding the hand and foot holds, as Giuditta had done. The worst bit had been at the top for there had been no one to support him, but somehow he had managed by pressing himself as close as he could to the curving wall, seeking holds amongst the stones

317

for his fingers while he kicked down with his legs, knowing that if necessary he could grab the Acrow bar above him – that's if it were not too loose to take his weight. One or two stones came away as he probed at them with his hands and fell down the wall into the water at Giuditta's feet.

'I'm nearly there,' he called to her, gasping for breath, for he knew she would not be able to see him, only hear him. His voice echoed hollowly against the stone. 'I'll soon have you safe.'

'Watch that last bit,' he heard her say weakly. 'Don't fall on top of me.'

It was easier once he could get his feet and hands into the niches. Soon he had reached the position she had been in when she fell. Now he heard the noise of the others above arriving with the ladder, and Stan calling down.

'We're going to put the ladder in.'

'Wait until I get to her. She's hurt. I've got to get her head out of the water.'

He located the last niche below the water, and placed a foot in it, so he was able to twist his body and kneel on the sloping side of the well bottom with a hand against the slippery rock. He touched her face. The water was almost up to her chin. Bruno's head was close to hers. He could see the wretched animal's tail wagging beneath the water.

'I'm going to hold your head. Can you move at all?'

'No. I don't think so.'

'Is it just the position you're in or…?'

'My legs don't seem to want to work.' Her voice was shrill.

He called up. 'Is the ambulance on the way?'

'Ja. I phoned.' That was Olaf. He could see his face now looking down and Stan beside him.

'She's hurt her back. Tell them they'll probably need a special stretcher. We can't do anything until they come.' He heard his instructions being passed on in a babble of voices.

'Oh God,' groaned Giuditta. 'All for a dog. How crazy am I!'

Her face was very white and her hair plastered to her cheeks, the ends floating in the water. He tried to pull Bruno away from her, but the dog did not want to move. He could feel it trembling.

'Stan. Have you got that bucket? We'll get the dog up while we're waiting.'

After a few moments, the bucket came bumping down the shaft, and Anthony had to let go of Giuditta's head for a moment to seize hold of it. The water was high against her face now and she began to panic. 'Hold me up! Hold me up!'

Anthony had to abandon the bucket idea: he did not think Bruno would have allowed himself to be placed in it, anyhow. He held Giuditta's head as high as he could out of the water.

'Not long now, my love. Not long. Help's on the way.'

A thought occurred to him. Had anyone phoned to tell Brian what had happened? He could not face that, knowing how Brian would blame him. No, don't worry about that now. Let's deal with the immediate danger first and get Giuditta safe. Then would be the time for any reckoning.

'Shall we lower the ladder now?' It was Stan's voice again. 'So it's in place when the ambulance arrives.'

'Yes, but do it very slowly. There's not much room down here.'

Anthony, looking up, ran his eyes around the circle of the shaft, seeing the grey bands of encircling stone and the deep black niches, which had come back into use again, and the broken area where the stone lining had fallen, and, over all, the bright orb of light at the top crossed by the black Acrow bars, with the faces that came and went, looking down at them. Their voices, muffled and distant, penetrated to him – with the occasional louder shout when a new arrival learnt what had happened.

He was aware of numbers of people now at the top of the shaft. He could see many shifting legs and feet, and the air around him seemed to thud with their movement. Then, sharp and clear, he heard the sudden clang of the aluminium ladder as it was raised vertically to be inserted in the shaft. The first rungs appeared, shining silver in the sunlight, and holding them many bare hands and arms, with splashes of colour behind from shirts and shorts, then legs again and boots stamping the earth.

From Olaf, 'Easy. Easy.' And from Stan. 'Take the weight at the back. Take the weight now.'

Slowly the ladder was coming into the shaft, clanging against an Acrow bar, grinding against the upper layers of stone walling. The stairway to heaven, Anthony thought ridiculously. For Giuditta and him, the stairway to the stars. She would get better. One day – soon, very soon – they would be together and this nightmare ended.

At first it was just a flicker of movement, to one side of the shaft as he gazed upwards, seeing the silver ladder coming down. Then, in the stone, it was like a ripple, like the quick whip of the wind across a field of grass or the lash of a wave on a sandy shore. The stone was moving a fraction; it had shifted and settled, and was now on the move again, bulging outwards in a ring around the top of the shaft, beneath the place where the many feet stood, and the ladder was coming, coming down to them into the depths of the well.

A moment of sheer terror, with Anthony starting upwards out of the water, abandoning Giuditta for the moment, his arms spread outwards, seeing one of the Acrow bars falling first like a broken javelin, then a wall of stone and earth behind it cascading upon them, crashing through the ladder, peeling around the walls in strips from the top of the shaft, like dominoes in a circle falling outwards, a sudden avalanche smashing down upon them at the bottom of the well.

Giuditta, seeing the black cloud falling into her trapped eyes, shrieked terribly, and Anthony, with his arms spread out over his head to protect himself could not reach her, knowing it was vital he did not fall; then the crash of the stones hit him and hit Giuditta below him and smashed them back against the rock beneath, all mixed with the churned and frothing water. The roar seemed to go on and on, blending with a sharper crash as the bottom section of the ladder broke free, twisted and fell – and then suddenly it was over.

Unutterably shocked, like people petrified in chaos, they looked down from the top. The bottom half of the well was filled with stone, like an inverted cone with the lowest point at its centre, the upper walls now bare earth still bearing the imprint of the stone, amongst which was bent a glittering length of metal ladder and a dangling Acrow bar.

Olaf was first in the shaft, scrambling down the sides, and flinging out the upper stones lying at the middle, just chucking them out of the shaft, throwing them high over his shoulder, until someone got the buckets working, which were filled and hauled up with frenzied haste. Olaf found Anthony almost immediately, uncovering his face and allowing him to breathe, although he was sliding in and out of unconsciousness. He had managed to straighten himself against the first cascade of stone and met it, standing, with his arms raised to protect himself, only to be knocked senseless by blocks that struck through his cushioning arms, his body held upright by the tide of stone and soil rising around him which in seconds covered his head, but by good fortune only thinly. The fallen ladder had also protected one side of his body. Below him – Anthony tried to yell this out as soon as his face and head were clear and consciousness flickering back, but he could only splutter and cough – was Giuditta. She was alive, he knew, for she was holding his leg, and he could feel the pressure of her hands opening and closing.

Above all this tumult by the well came the sudden howl of sirens approaching.

Anthony must have blacked out again, for he had heard the helicopter landing, and then nothing until they were lifting him from the shaft, bound tight to a board, then placing him on a stretcher; and he had yelled out again, this time clearly and surely, that Giuditta had been below him and alive for he had felt her hands moving on his leg. He did not want to leave her! They must not take him away! – not until she had been brought out and he could see she was alive.

He remembered being carried to the helicopter, and passing through lines of silent, watching faces, some in tears, and seeing Brian there too, his face shrunken and white, and then little more other than for the roar of the engines, which made him cry out and try to cover his head once more, only he could not move his arms, until – an age later, or so it seemed to him – he awoke in a hospital bed.

For a few days, faces would come and go, and he did not know what was going on, although he knew they had operated on him and his arms were in plaster and there were bandages around his middle which they came and changed. He accepted that he was here, and they were looking after him, and soon they would tell him about Giuditta – but he should not trouble them yet with too many questions. Then, when he felt a little better and they still had told him nothing, he began to ask, and became angry when they didn't answer him, telling him instead to rest and not to worry about anything, only getting better.

The trouble was he was in such a murk of drugs that the day was just the misty panel of light set in the ceiling above him, upon which his mind and his soul crawled like some insect beneath the sun, and for a while he did not know for sure if he had even asked them what he most wanted to know.

He knew about himself, however – that, but for Olaf's quick actions in clearing his face, he would have suffocated and died. He had been concussed, his nose and jaw were broken, his front teeth were knocked out – they were implants anyhow – and he had some broken ribs, and both arms were fractured – oh, and they had taken out his spleen as well; that, he knew, he didn't need – but really he had been so very lucky. Any one of those stones, hundreds of them, falling free, might have split open his skull. It had been a miracle he had been able to protect his head as he had.

But what had happened to Giuditta? How badly was she hurt? He knew she had lived still when they had rescued him. Had they reached her in time? He had to know now! He would not be put off with half truths anymore. So, when they felt he was strong enough, they told him.

It was Brian they used to give him the news. He sat very sombrely and uncomfortably in a chair at his bedside. Anthony did not want Brian to see him, and he did not want to hear what he said: 'Of all people, dear Lord, not him, telling me about what is most precious in the world to me.' But who else? Not Pamela, whom he could recall visiting once, sounding and looking impatient, in a tight blue dress. Or Juliana, who came early on, when all he could make out of her was her necklace shimmering against a blaze of light. Both had held his fingers – where the plaster ended – and told him to get well.

Well! It was that word again. Well. Ding dong bell. Ding dong bell. We're all smashed up in the well. Christ! What an awful mess it was. And his fault. His fault alone. If only, if only….His beautiful Giuditta, whom he had loved and killed, who had died holding his leg in that hellish, fucking well.

For Brian, looking and sounding very nervous, hands intertwined, wriggling his fingers, had given him the terrible information. Giuditta was dead. Olaf and Stan and others –

students, paramedics, policemen, firemen – had flung out the fallen stone and shovelled out the earth, working like madmen, long after hope of life had faded, and reached her at last lying in the bowl at the very bottom of the well, where she had first fallen, her body deep in sludge and water, curled up holding the dog, which was dead too, against her breast.

'But I felt her hand like a pulse on my leg,' Anthony said. 'I could feel her hand opening and closing, holding me, telling me she was alive.' He cried for her now. His grief was never going to end.

Later, when the police came to take a statement – not long before they discharged him – and he told the police sergeant this story, the sergeant, speaking softly and with appropriate consideration for his feelings, said that that would have been impossible, for the post mortem showed she had died almost at once from a crushed skull. In any event, she could never have extended her arm through the debris from the point where she lay to where Anthony had been found.

Anthony wept at that for now he realised he had not even been with her when she died. He had saved himself but not her. He had promised to protect her – to the very end – and he had failed.

He tortured himself with how she had reached out for him in her agony. Even now he could feel the pressure of her hand on his leg. And, although the pain from his broken ribs made it difficult, he managed to stick his right leg out from under the sheet and look down at his right calf, and he saw red blotches there on the white skin spread out in a fan, like the finger and thumb marks of a hand.

26

As soon as his injuries were healed sufficiently for him to travel, he flew out to Italy and stayed for a week in Venice. It was late December and the weather was wet and cold. He spent days treading the rain-swept *calli*, seeking the place that Giuditta had described to him – the café bar in the Dorsoduro where she had loved to sit at the window watching the people coming up the long, stone-paved *calle*, knocking their noses against the glass. She had told him she would always be there, sitting within, waiting. Had she felt the place too as a fulcrum upon which her life swung, he wondered? – the present and the past, and perhaps the future as well, meeting here in a fusion of light.

When he found the café at last, he had no doubt it was the one Giuditta had known for he could sense her everywhere within its dark interior, and he sat and looked out through the front window, as she would have done, seeking her amongst the few people scurrying by in the rain, thinking she might appear to him there, just a quick glimpse of her, perhaps wrapped in a dark coat, her body bent as she used to when she laughed, her face turned to him – so white it would be and her eyes large, framed by her tumbling hair. And when she did not come – not even the flicker of a shadow of her – he left and walked by the canals she had known, lined by tenements with carved balconies and plastered walls, over the little hump-backed bridges, seeing the blank eyes of the shuttered windows through the rain, from any one of which she might once have looked out.

The dark water flowed beside him, and in one of the small boats tied up to door posts and window sills, she might have laid herself down and been borne away, his dark Lady of Shalott, whose lovely face had been crushed by rock and pressed down into mud – she whom he had loved so very much. And he had been the cause of her dying. Knowing this, how could he breathe now himself? How could he live, having done this in his vanity, his stupidity, and have feeling, sense, and being ever again?

He could not cry for her now, as he had grieved when he had first been told of her death, and later, during the long black hours of his own recovery, when only a nurse, coming to help him wash himself and change his dressings, had been there to see him. Now his tears were dried up, and his soul did not seem to be within him any more – that old vainglorious, hating and doubting soul. The warped, barbed, lusting personality that had once been Anthony Winters was a nobody who had destroyed what he loved most – a girl of such beauty and feeling – and the greatest part of the tragedy was that she had trusted in him.

Beyond what he had done, he had no cares now. All his worries about life – his anxieties about money and growing old and having to live and do things by himself – had disappeared. He flew to Venice and checked in and out of hotels, moving often when the hotel did not provide the seclusion he craved, borrowed money on credit cards, and hired a car, and – although he had never driven overseas before – he drove away from the airport at Venice into the wide countryside of the Veneto to find some of the other places Giuditta had known.

He went first to Aquileia, where Giuditta had taken part in an archaeological excavation, and he loved this small town – more like an extended village – with its Roman ruins rising out of the flat, green fields and, in the far distance, the long line of the high Alps shining white against the sky. He booked into a hotel at its centre – the Hotel Patriarchi – and wondered if it was here that Giuditta had drunk with the other diggers, as she had described to him.

The hotel staff were most friendly, and he managed with the language with a confidence he would never have had before. He saw the great medieval basilica, a stone's throw from the hotel, with the wonderful Byzantine-period mosaics beneath it. Then he walked to the Roman forum, whose re-erected columns rose like stumps of fingers against the sky, and found, close by, the site of the public baths; here Giuditta had dug and uncovered her mosaic. He weaved his way down side roads, passing houses with beautiful, elaborate cribs set up in their front gardens – for it was nearly Christmas and the people were preparing to celebrate Christ's birth – and found at last the street of tombs that Giuditta had described seeing by moonlight. He shivered here, and came away quickly, for it spoke to him too sharply of the dead.

In the evening he visited the museum – everything was open here at hours when in England they would have been long closed – and was lost in such a wonderland of Roman objects that for a few minutes he quite forgot himself and the great unhappiness he bore, until coming upon a case of jewellery he saw a necklace that looked very similar to the one they had found in the well, and then all the horror returned.

At the hotel, he learnt that a coach party of English tourists had arrived, a cultural tour spending the Christmas holiday away from home, and he found the people so friendly and charming when he met them in the bar that he ate with them later in the restaurant, and – despite his earlier desire to be left alone in his misery – enjoyed their company greatly. They found him, he thought, a curiosity – an Englishman by himself in this out of the way place, and he cultivated the air of eccentricity this gave him to cover the real reason he was here, which he had no desire to talk about.

He extended his stay at the Patriarchi so as to spend Christmas Day there, and eat a vast meal with his new friends – a banquet of many courses served in an enormous room, with many locals present at tables around the English guests, so the place hummed like a hive of the very busiest bees – faces animated, eating and drinking, joking and laughing, so that for a short while he felt life was coming back to him and might still be worth the living.

That evening he took a taxi into the nearby town of Grado, lying on the coast amongst a series of great, open lagoons, and saw heron standing like pale ghosts between the mud flats and the darkening sky. He walked in the streets of the old town, and went into churches where white candle light flared and where further superb cribs, many automated with moving figures, stood against the ancient walls. Later he drank in a tunnel of marquees set up by the harbour where a jazz band played, and he got so drunk he could hardly find a taxi to take him back to Aquileia. The next day he left, heading south towards the valley of the Po.

He drove first to Padua, where Giuditta had gone to university, and then, the following day, to Ferrara, in the vicinity of which, somewhere to the east, lay the family farm on which she had been brought up. He did not know where this was exactly because Giuditta had never told him, and Lika and Robin – Giuditta's particular friend and her employer – both of whom he had spoken to on the phone some weeks after the tragedy, had not said either, although they had attended her funeral, which had taken place at a church nearby. Lika *had* told him that. She had clearly decided he had a right to know where her friend had been buried.

She lay in the graveyard of the little church of Santa Maria del Carmine, which stood by itself amongst the marshes close to the River Po. Once there had been a monastery there, but it had long since crumbled into dust. The nearest place of any size was called Viconovo. Lika and Robin, who had travelled out together, had stayed at the hotel there. The farm, he assumed, must be somewhere nearby, but he was not concerned to find it: he felt it would be a place of bad memories, of a time long before he had known Giuditta, but with an influence that had come to taint what should have been their present. All he wished to see was where they had laid her to rest.

No one had informed him directly about the funeral. It had taken place while he was still in hospital. It had been he who had had to hunt out Lika and Robin's numbers when he got home and make contact with them. This had been a most difficult thing for him to do, but it had been the only way he had been able to obtain any information. They had been polite to him, but not friendly. He wondered what stories they had been told. Probably they blamed him, as he imagined everyone did.

He had had to make a further statement to the police, this time in writing. And he had received some papers from an inspector from the Health and Safety Executive, which he had left unanswered before going out to Italy. He had been informed – he could not remember now exactly by whom – that the local coroner would be holding an inquest into the accident and he would probably have to appear as a witness. All these things would have to be faced on his return.

He had already told them all the fault was his, so it was hardly surprising that Lika and Robin blamed him for

Giuditta's death. He had not heard again from Brian either. Brian would be furious with him for disobeying his specific instructions – that was for sure. Someone had told him – who had it been? Ah, yes, Miles, phoning him when he was first back from hospital to see how he was bearing up – that the Glastington site had been closed down, and it was unlikely any more digging would ever take place. Yes, how Brian would blame him for the curtailment of what had been his life's work.

It was a cold afternoon of drizzling rain when he came to Viconovo, and drove out into the flat fields beyond. He asked a man with a bicycle at the roadside, *'Dove si trova la chiesa di Santa Maria?'*, but the man shrugged his shoulders: he either did not know or did not understand.

Anthony continued along the narrow, straight roads. On either side, flat fields stretched away, and there were drainage ditches intersecting the fields, just like the Cambridgeshire Fens. A mist hung over everything, preventing him from seeing too far. Occasionally, he would pass a white-plastered farm, or a huddle of barns. Somewhere to his left flowed the river, so he looked for a track that would lead him there, for he knew the church stood on its bank.

He saw a driveway that ran off to the right, passing under a wooden gateway and leading to a farm. He could see that the land rose a little in the distance, but the buildings were shrouded in the mist. It seemed a large estate. He wondered if it had been Giuditta's home. A short distance further on, the cultivated land became more marsh-like, with rough, swampy grass and beds of reeds on either side, crossed by the road on an embankment. At a line of tall trees, whose topmost branches hung like wraiths in the mist, he found the turning he sought. A leaning, wooden sign bore the one word, 'Chiesa'.

He came to the church along a narrow track made with cinders laid onto the earth. The church was tiny – as Lika had said. The grey stone nave rose ahead of him, its tiled roof running with rain. There were many red bricks in its walls. It seemed to have once been part of a much larger church, for broken stumps of other walls ran from it, and he could see these continuing as lines of stones amongst the grass. The mullioned windows were set high up, and the one wooden door, beyond a small, decorated porch, was locked.

The church seemed to be hanging in the mist, as if borne up a little into thin air. Anthony walked into the graveyard, his shoes wet in the long grass. He found what he was seeking straightaway, for there were only a handful of recent graves ringed by cypress bushes close to a tumbled wall. The cold, wet air beaded on Anthony's face, and he felt he had to expand his lungs against the dampness, taking extra breaths just to stand here by Giuditta's grave. Everywhere there was the smell of the earth, of the winter season, of the dying grass, of the long, grey mounds of the many dead interred here over the centuries. Was this how he wished to think of Giuditta, amongst the wetness and the decay? In the spring and the summer, it would be different. The earth would be dry then and the sun hot, and the coloured petals of the flowers would blow across this place where his Giuditta lay.

He started crying when he saw her stone – 'Giuditta Marietta Ponti' and the dates of her life, ending so cruelly on that day that was burnt into him and would never fade. In the foreign fashion, a photograph of her was inserted in the white stone – a picture taken when she was much younger, perhaps even in her teens, with her hair piled on her head and her eyes innocently wide, an uncertain, wistful smile on her lips. It was not the Giuditta he had known. He blinked the image away.

'Hello, my love,' he whispered. 'I came. I said I would. Just to tell you how much I love you. How I will always love you. And of how sorry I am. I told you to hope – how certain I was of that hope – but it was not to be. I cannot say any more, for you will know as surely as myself what is in my thoughts.'

And he stood in the rain, which soaked his hair and flowed onto his face, joining his own tears, and he wished the water would wash the earth away, and he with it, for he did not wish to live now without Giuditta.

A spray of white lilies lay upon her grave and across another dug beside it. Anthony could see that the low mound of earth here had been turned recently. Was this where Giuditta father's ashes had been interred, he wondered? Was the stone in his memory still to be raised? Father and daughter reconciled in death. That was right. Such physical symbols did not matter, anyhow. What mattered lay in the mind, in the memory, lingering still, of those who had known. Anthony could make no judgements now. But he knew her family would judge *him*.

'*Bellissima*' – the one word was whispered to him as he stepped back from the grave. He looked around him. There was no one there, only the dripping air and the white mist, and the old, dark stones of the church. *Bellissima*. That was how she had always been to him, body and soul. The word was in his head.

He drove away and the next evening he flew home. *Bellissima*. My lovely girl. He had done what he came for, but she did not yet rest. There was no peace there beneath that sky.

27

As soon as he was back home, his headaches began again. All night he felt his brain was going to burst and he found it very difficult to sleep. His dreams returned too in the short hours of fitful sleeping. He saw the man in the tower once more, watching him from the window where the wooden shutters were flung wide open, and, behind him, sometimes a woman wearing rich jewellery on her neck and head stared down at him as well.

He thought much of the camp at Stonea, for that is where he knew the tower stood, as he had looked upon its site with Giuditta those long months back. The tower was high and built of stone, and its red tiled roof seemed to touch the clouds. The land beneath was crossed by roads of orange gravel beside which ran canals of silvered water. Here sailed boats with swans' heads for prows; they came to the tower from over the rim of the world, far beyond the sunlit horizon. In his dreams he saw Giuditta borne on one of these boats. She was clothed in white and lay on cushions in the bottom of the boat, and, although her eyes were wide open, he thought at first that she was dead. Then he saw her raise her head and look about her, but, even though he stood before her, she did not appear to notice him, and the boat passed on to a great lake beyond the tower where it disappeared from his sight.

He awoke bathed in sweat from these dreams, and one day made an appointment with his doctor who prescribed him some sleeping tablets and told him to see him again in a month or so. The tablets, however, only brought on darker dreams, in one of which he saw the man in the hood again, who reached out for him with hands that had long nails like claws – and he knew then there was no way he could escape from the nightmare he dwelt within.

He had received a pile of forms from the Health and Safety people, and a request that he attend an interview, and a further notification from the Coroner's Court came one morning that he opened but did not read. He did not want Giuditta to be killed over and over again at the hands of these people, and for her crushed body to be exposed for all to goggle upon as part of their entertainment – for one day of sensation, no more. But that was long enough in his anticipation for him to make up his mind what he had to do.

A letter from Brian arrived a few days later. It was a typed letter with a copy to a firm of solicitors in Yeovil, and he read the first few lines which spoke of Anthony's 'irresponsible behaviour despite all my instruction and advice', and indicated that some sort of legal action might follow – but Anthony did not read any further to find out what that might be. Instead he put the letter, with a covering note, in the post to his own solicitor – the one who long ago had made out his will: he did not even know if she was still in business.

Juliana had sent him a number of emails, each increasingly chatty, although he answered none of them. She wondered how he was getting on, and asked if he would like to meet her in London: they could have a meal together or go to the theatre. She had a new dog now – son of Bruno, or Bruno2, she joked: what a dear little dog he was…. What a tragedy it had been – 'best to try and put these things behind you and move on, however difficult…..'

She added, almost as an afterthought, that her husband had left her. There had been problems for a long time. He had found a much younger woman back in Italy….. And so on, and so on……Anthony wasn't interested. He was angry with Juliana. It was she, by her visit, who had been the cause of the accident. It may have been his fault, but it had been her who had caused him to act as he did. He remembered how he had held her bony arm and felt her soft stomach, and he shuddered. He could not get out of his mind that she might be the woman in his dream who wore the fine jewellery on her neck and in her hair – like Giuditta's hair hung with stars. He deleted her three emails and no more came.

It was a raw day in late January when he knew he had to go back to Stonea. He put the Yaris away carefully in his garage, and filled the Land Rover with the things he would need – not a great deal for it would only be for a day. He shut up his flat, and arranged his unread books, his unanswered correspondence, and the notes for the novel he was going to write in neat piles on his desk. Then he left. It was early one midweek morning.

He drove steadily on the motorways, never at much more than 50mph, all that long way again as he had travelled with such pleasure and anticipation eight months ago. North of Cambridge, he took the A10 and came into the level Fens – once more into the land of swamp and reed where flights of birds wheeled across the mist-veiled sun. He stopped at Ely, and had a bacon and egg toasted sandwich for his late breakfast. He would not need to eat again. He bought a half-bottle of expensive malt whisky in an off-licence and placed it in the pocket of his padded coat. The air was very cold.

In the Cathedral, he stood for a while in the Lady Chapel and looked at the statue of Mary, with her arms raised, staring down at him, trying to see the blessing here but feeling only a threat that pierced him with fear. His determination began to waver. He was such a long time standing before the statue that a man in a black cassock came up to him and asked him if he was alright.

'Not really. Can I talk to you?'

'Yes, of course. Let me just get rid of these first,' – he was carrying a tray of candle lights – 'and I'll come back to you.' 'Give me five minutes,' he said over his shoulder.

Anthony waited for three of those minutes, and then left. He paced steadily down the long nave and went out through the great west door.

He came down the long track to Stonea and parked the Land Rover neatly in the little car park, locking the doors and placing the key in his pocket. His journey had ended. He was all alone. Even the sheep had vanished from the pasture.

For an hour or so, he paced the ramparts of the Iron Age camp, and saw them blaze again as Giuditta had seen them, and the Romans coming with their men of war, and the screaming and the death, all happening here again and again, beneath these wide, watching skies. And he saw the tower in the fields beyond the camp growing stone by stone out of the earth until it hung over him with its shuttered windows. But no one was looking out at him now.

He sat in the shelter of one of the ramparts, and he took the whisky bottle from his pocket and had a couple of sips, and then a bigger gulp. The whisky burnt down his throat. It warmed his body, and quietened his racing mind, allowing him to think of his purpose again.

The sky was becoming greyer from the east. Perhaps it would rain soon, or even snow for it was cold enough. He rose and walked to the bank where they had sat and eaten their picnic on that day of sun. The grass on the bank lay flat and grey. It did not seem possible – that what had happened, had been and would not come again, not in its colours and its beauty ever more; it had gone and had passed into night as everything must pass and end.

He stood and took a deep breath of the cold air, filling his lungs and flapping his arms at his sides as if he were some great bird that could not fly away. He gulped down another slug of the whisky, replaced the screw cap, and left the bottle on the bank. He walked slowly to the pond behind.

It lay there as still as black glass. At the edges there was a thin crust of ice. He picked up a stick fallen from the tree above and poked at the ice, which split into jagged fragments.

He took another great breath. He could feel the whisky pounding in his brain. Then he saw her – at first a shifting, misty shadow on the water, then her body, white and beautiful, floating towards him, her face upturned. He stepped into the water. Really it was not cold at all, just a pleasurable tingling in his legs. And he waded through the water to meet her. When he came up to her face, he knelt down to kiss her, and he spread out his body on the water beside her.

The mirrored surface burst and he fell through to the darkness beneath.

FINIS

AFTERWORD

The impetus to write this novel arose out of my involvement with the digging of a well at Piddington Roman villa in Northamptonshire in the 1990s. However, although it would be untrue to say that the Piddington experience did not help add colour to my story, it would be quite wrong to identify anyone, or any event, presented here as anything but fictional.

The Piddington dig was run most expertly by the Upper Nene Archaeological Society under their splendid director, Roy Friendship-Taylor. I am grateful to him for very many happy days of digging. A particular stalwart of the site was Len Johnson, to whom I dedicate this book. I know he would have loved to have read it, and would probably have been critical of at least some of its detail.

Rest in peace, my Leonard.

William Foot (writing as John Aubin)
February 2025